THE MARLOWE CONSPIRACY

A NOVEL

M. G. SCARSBROOK

AUTHOR OF

POISON IN THE BLOOD: THE MEMOIRS OF LUCREZIA BORGIA

Selected type was set using the free font Priory by www.1001freefonts.com. The free software package GNU Image Manipulation Program (GIMP) was used in the graphical design process.

Scarsbrook, M. G.
The Marlowe Conspiracy / M. G. Scarsbrook
ISBN-13: 978-1456310967
ISBN-10: 1456310968
BISAC: Fiction / Mystery & Detective / Historical

Printed in the United States of America

For my parents, Graham and Sandra

SCOTLAND

RENAISSANCE ENGLAND

NORTH SEA

IRISH SEA

LEASOWE CASTLE

STRATFORD-upon-AVON

WALES

LONDON

SCADBURY MANOR DOVER
CANTERBURY

CALAIS

PORTSMOUTH

ENGLISH CHANNEL

FRANCE

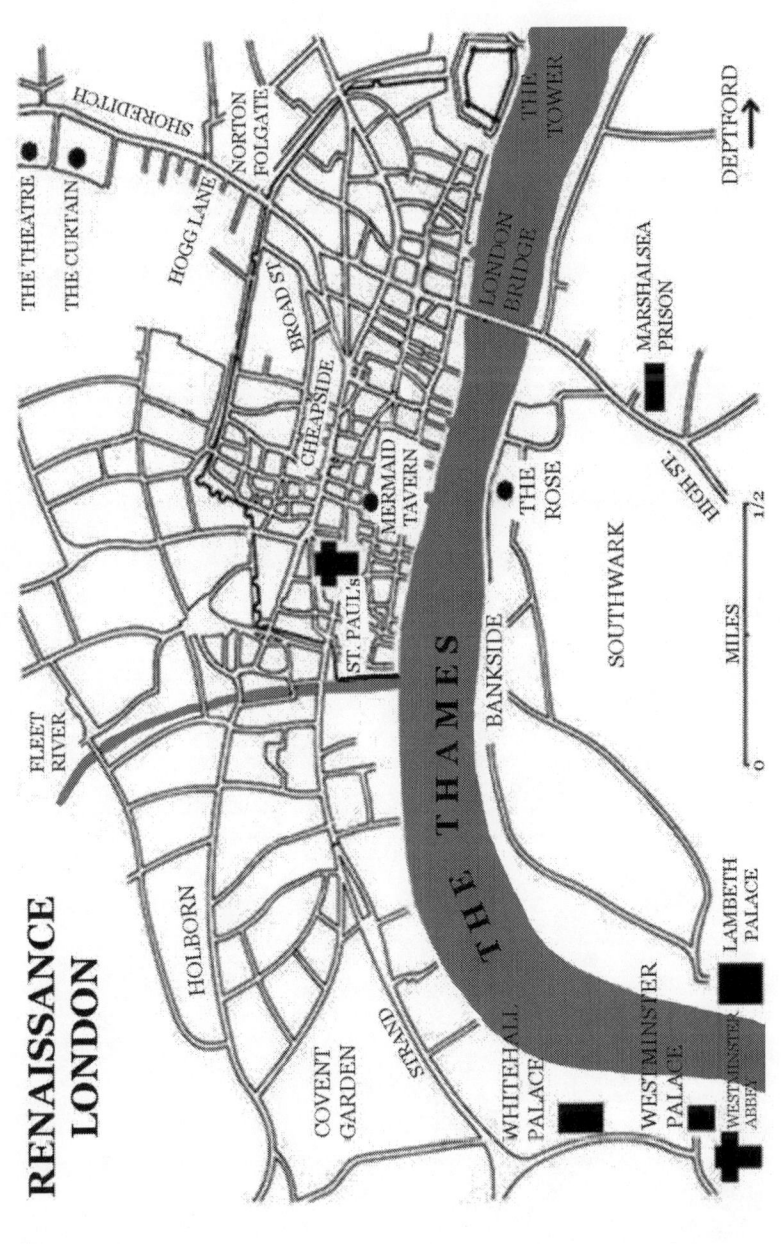

RENAISSANCE LONDON

THE THEATRE
THE CURTAIN
SHOREDITCH
NORTON FOLGATE
HOGG LANE
BROAD ST.
CHEAPSIDE
MERMAID TAVERN
ST. PAUL's
FLEET RIVER
HOLBORN
COVENT GARDEN
STRAND
WHITEHALL PALACE
WESTMINSTER PALACE
WESTMINSTER ABBEY
LAMBETH PALACE
BANKSIDE
THE ROSE
SOUTHWARK
HIGH ST.
MARSHALSEA PRISON
LONDON BRIDGE
THE TOWER
DEPTFORD

THE THAMES

0   MILES   1/2

PROLOGUE

May, 1593: Elizabethan England.

Plague, famine, and religious persecution blast the land and rouse the people to rebel. Enemies at home and abroad loosen the Queen's grip on her country. Now is a time of poison, plots, and spies.

ACT I

SCENE ONE

Northern France. The Port of Calais.

The moon looked flat and pale and ready for a kill. Below, in the blue haziness of dusk, Calais had never been more dangerous for an English spy. Fort Risban trained its cannons across the mouth of the city harbor. Sentries with spears prowled up and down the ramparts. City guards fanned out through the streets, watched at street corners, and made random checks on anyone passing through the shadows.

Along one street, a pair of guards strolled past an old inn known as 'Auberge du Passeur'. Above, at a second floor room, the shadow of a man moved past the window...

Inside that room, motes of dust flickered through the light of a single candle. At the far wall, before a small mirror hung askew, Christopher 'Kit' Marlowe stood and dressed himself quickly.

Kit was tall, with lithe arms and compact shoulders. Oval of face, he wore his long brown hair pulled back from his brow, and he grew a faint moustache over his lip and a thin beard on his chin. Dark, sun-strained eyes stared back at him from the looking glass. Between his slanted eyebrows lay a small crease worn into the skin through frowning. In his late twenties, he was a man fully in his prime. He was also a man of hidden tension: focused yet undisciplined; alert but frustrated; confident yet racked by anxiety.

Hastily, Kit grabbed a long black gown from the stool and slipped it over his simple doublet. Next he donned a red, triple-peaked hat that signified the profession of medical doctor.

Lastly, and most carefully of all, he leaned over to the desk and lifted a thick fake beard and applied it to his face. The hair of the beard smelt musty. The glue felt warm and pinched a little as it dried hard on the skin. Now fully dressed, he stepped back in front of the mirror to inspect his disguise. Moonlight from the window cast a bone-white shade in the looking glass. He stared at his reflection – stared almost through it. The back of his neck tightened. He took a shallow breath. His eyes narrowed slightly. He shook his head and grimaced.

At a nearby desk, he laid his fingers on a document, rolled it tightly, and slid it inside a small pewter tube. He secured the tube inside a leather-sided medical bag full of instruments, pots, and vials.

Pigeon wings suddenly battered at the window.

Kit flinched and turned.

After a second, he calmed himself, drew open the window, and discovered a messenger pigeon clinging to the windowsill. A tiny note was attached to the bird's left foot. Gently, he unclipped the note and read the following words:

> 'Ship to England on schedule.
> May God be with you.'

The pigeon flapped off into the dusk sky. Kit poked his head outside and surveyed the streets of Calais.

Below, a man drove a cart down the road. From the shadows, two guards jumped out in front, waved him down, and proceeded to search both him and the wooden crates aboard the cart-bed. Stress began to twist its way through Kit's limbs. The French were unusually nervous tonight.

For centuries, Calais had been ruled by England, but thirty-five years ago the Duke of Guise had mounted a dramatic invasion and reclaimed the port for France. Calais was valuable since its proximity to England meant the harbor bustled daily with English galleons laden with cloth, tin, lead, and wool. At the docks, these were readily traded for steel rapiers, hand-woven rugs, sumptuous rolls of silk, and expensive bottles of claret. Calais was one of the most lucrative towns in France, and the French were anxious of losing it again – especially as Spain had amassed troops close by in the Netherlands. Now was not the time to be in Calais.

Kit's eyes lifted. In the distance, the masts of galleons in the harbor peeked over the rooftops and chimney stacks. For the span of a heartbeat he remained still and noiseless and tranquil.

He shut the window and turned back into the room. With hardly another glance in the mirror, he burst into a whirl of activity, whisked over the floorboards, collected his belongings, closed the medical bag, heaved it up from the floor, and blew out the candle. Teeth clenched, heart swelling up into his throat, he left the relative safety of his room, tramped down a creaking staircase, found the inn keeper and returned the room key. He paused briefly, tilted his hat down, and approached the door to the street.

Scene Two

Calais. High Street.

Light sea-fog drifted in from the harbor and brushed along crooked alleyways and streets. Kit paced quickly down the high street and headed for the Place d'Armes, the town square. By foot, the docks were ten minutes away. His eyes flicked left and right searching for danger but the street seemed clear. Clamped in his hand, the straps of the medical bag already felt sweaty. He checked the street again. No one. Yet just as he reached the marketplace, his skin prickled with the sensation he was not alone. The scuff of a heel sounded behind him.

"Stand fast!" a voice called in French. "Halt!"

The pit of Kit's stomach tightened. He resisted the urge to spin around sharply. He took a breath, waited, and slowly turned to face two guards.

The first guard was tall and young. The second guard looked older, and when he opened his mouth to speak his front tooth was missing.

"Papers," said the toothless guard, thrusting out his hand.

Kit opened his medical bag and pulled out his papers. While the toothless guard checked every word, the young guard rifled through the bag. Kit tried his best to suppress any movements that might betray his nerves. The toothless guard looked up from the papers and glared at him skeptically.

"What business have you in Calais, monsieur?"

"I'm a doctor," Kit replied in French.

"You are?"

"Yes."

"Pray tell me why isn't it written in your papers?"

"It should... it should be there." He frowned and leaned forward and pointed to the second paragraph in his papers.

The guard eyed the paragraph with a grunt.

"Very well. But I've never heard of you."

"Oh no, you wouldn't. My practice isn't of this town."

"Is that so?"

"Yes. I'm just stopping here overnight before I travel on to Rouen."

The guard shook his head.

"Why didn't you halt when we signaled you?"

"I didn't see any signal. It must have been the mist."

"The mist, ay? Or perhaps there's something in your bag you don't wish us to find?"

"No."

"We'll see..."

They stood in silence. The toothless guard locked eyes with Kit. At long last, the young guard finished with the medical bag and stood upright.

"Everything's in order," said the young guard flatly.

The toothless guard nodded and passed the papers back to Kit.

"Forgive me," said Kit, "but is there some hazard in town tonight?"

"There's report of an English spy," said the toothless guard. "We're searching everyone. Good morrow to you." He gave Kit a last look, then both the guards turned and prowled off down the street.

Kit watched them go and put his papers away.

The mist seemed to gather in the shadows and blur the eaves and gables of homes. Most people were now indoors and only the odd horseman or carriage drifted past. Kit stepped swiftly down the street. As he strode through the deserted marketplace, a church bell tolled out crisply into the night. From here it was only five minutes to the docks.

He left the square and entered a side-street. His feet instantly slowed. Ahead, near the steps of a home, a worried knot of men and women had formed around someone lying on the ground. Kit frowned and walked cautiously towards the opposite side of the road.

Too late. A short, plump woman perked up as he moved past. With one hand, she hiked up the front of her skirt and rushed toward him, waving.

"I pray you, Doctor, help me!" she said, panting from the short burst of energy. "Something ails my husband. Will you look?"

Kit fixed his gaze in front and didn't stop.

"I'm sorry, I can't do anything now. I have another appointment." He forged onwards and left her behind.

She hustled back to his side.

"Wait!" she said loudly and lurched toward him. "If it's the money, we have enough. You must help us."

He stopped reluctantly and glanced back toward the market square. The two guards now patrolled by a church – their helmets caught the occasional luster of moonlight. He sighed and nodded reluctantly to the woman. Her face lit up.

"God save you, Doctor!" She grabbed his hand and beckoned him over to the group of people.

At his presence, the bodies by the house parted to reveal the woman's husband sat on the ground, his back slumped against the wall. He was a portly man with ruddy cheeks. His eyes were shut and his head lay tipped to one side. Kit paused and gulped. He felt the stares of the crowd drill into him. His mouth turned dry.

For lack of anything else to do, he set his bag down and touched the husband's wrist to take the pulse. He pretended to learn a great deal from the pulse beats. While he considered what to do next, he drew close, sniffed the man's chest, and the mellow smell of ale tickled his nostrils. A sense of relief washed over him. He turned back to the plump woman.

"Madame, I know this man's ailment."

"You do? Is it awful? Oh lord, I know it's bad. Tell me, I must know."

"No need to worry – this man is drunk, that's all. He's had too much ale."

6

She jerked her head back and recoiled.

"What?"

"He's drunk."

Her cheeks suddenly turned crimson and she looked at the others.

"No, no, no – not my husband. He's given all that up. It must be his heart. Don't you think I know what drunk is, young man? It's his heart, I tell you, his heart."

"I'm afraid not."

"Yes, it is."

"No."

"Yes, it, is," she said through clenched teeth. "It's his heart. Now do something about it."

Absolute silence. Everyone waited for Kit to act.

He stood still in defiance, but his eyes floated nervously back to the market square. While scowling, he gave in and bent down to rummage through his medical bag, combing through pots of treacle, vials of scorpion lotion, and jars of saffron powder. His hand brushed against a pot of leeches. With a grand gesture, he brandished the pot before the faces of the group. They drew closer, interested. Even the plump woman seemed impressed.

Kit unscrewed the lid, pinched one of the leeches, and looked at the husband's face, neck, hands, and belly. Anywhere seemed appropriate. With as much artfulness as he could feign, he placed the leach in the center of the man's forehead. Pleased with his work, he stepped back to let the crowd see. The leech stretched its black, fat, sucking bulk almost clear across the husband's forehead. The others peered down at it and shook their heads.

"There," said Kit authoritatively, "he should be fine now. There's nothing like a good leech to mend the heart." He turned and packed the bag fast.

The plump woman put her hands on her hips.

"I've never seen a doctor do that... On his forehead, like that... He looks ridiculous."

7

Grumbles and mutters arose within the crowd. The plump woman sensed the others were on her side. Angrily, she tapped Kit on the shoulder and pointed a stubby finger at her husband.

"You're not finished yet, Doctor."

Kit ignored her and finished packing his bag. She curled her lip at him.

"I'll wager you're not even a doctor at all, are you?"

Kit froze momentarily and stared at her. She sneered and pushed her face toward him.

"I knew it! You're no doctor!"

He snapped his bag shut and shoved his way through the crowd. She started after him.

"Come back here! Who are you?" She grabbed his arm excitedly and half-shouted. "Who are you?"

"A doctor," he snapped.

"No you're not!"

"Alright, then I'm no one. Whoever you say I am." He wrenched his arm from her tight-fingered grasp and sped away without looking back.

She threw her hands in the air.

"A devil! That's who you are! A devil! A devil! A devil!" Her words echoed through the air behind him.

In the marketplace, the guards had already turned their heads suspiciously at the scene. They stalked their way into the street with hands near their sword hilts. They paced in Kit's direction. On the verge of running, he quickened his steps, pressed forward into the mist, and veered hard around the nearest corner.

His heart thumping in his ears, Kit swept briskly down the next street. Sweat trickled down his spine. The beard began to itch.

The two guards dashed around the corner after him. The young guard tightened his grip on his spear shaft and the toothless guard drew his sword. Without breaking his stride, Kit reached into his bag, took out the dark vial, removed the pewter tube, and hid it up his sleeve. Moments later, the guards caught up to him.

Before they could act, Kit spun around. Crashed the medical bag into the toothless guard's face. The blow flung the guard heavily to the ground.

The young guard looked startled, then lunged at Kit, stabbed the spear-tip at his head. Kit ducked, but the guard paced forward, agile on his feet. Again and again, the spear jabbed at Kit's shoulder, his chest, his gut. Kit peddled back on his heels and smacked his legs into something hard – the wall of a street well.

The young guard took his chance, made a strong thrust at Kit's torso. Kit shifted left. The spear cut past him. He snatched hold of the shaft, pulled the guard forward, and threw him over the side of the well. The guard's yell echoed in the darkness and turned deep as he plummeted down and splashed into the water.

For a moment, Kit peered down after the guard, then pivoted at the sound of movement behind him. Half-dazed, the toothless guard was back on his feet, sword in hand. Kit leaned over and grabbed the well's rope and bucket.

"I'll have you now!" growled the toothless guard. He rushed toward Kit and slashed down at his neck.

Kit parried with the bucket. Darted across the guard. Tangled him in the rope. The guard struggled, but couldn't free himself. Kit clutched the bucket tightly, drew it back, and slugged the guard on the head. The guard tumbled to the cobblestones, knocked-out cold.

The spectacle of the fight had drawn the attention of men stood outside a tavern. Shouts sounded down the street. Hands pointed in alarm. Within moments, four more guards dashed around the corner.

Still panting from the fight, Kit swiped up the toothless guard's sword from the ground. Frantically, he turned and found a cooper's shop across the road, now closed-up for the night. He flew towards the door, launched his shoulder at the center and crashed through easily into the shop.

Inside, the hazy scent of sawdust filled his nose. He crept toward the right side of the shop where a line of barrels lay sideways, resting on their middle bulge. As best he could, he

9

crouched behind the tallest ones in the corner. He kept still and waited.

Slow and silent, the four guards tracked him into the shop. They fanned out, checked the shadows, explored behind a wood-pile, and cautiously moved their way down the line of barrels.

Kit huddled low and rocked forward onto the balls of his feet and prepared to strike. At that very moment, he noticed the shelf above him bore some of the largest barrels in the shop. Big, heavy barrels that could squash a man. His eyes widened and he watched as one... two... three... four guards came to stand in front of the shelf, still searching the recesses of the shop.

He took his chance. Pounced up. Hacked his sword into the shelf. Dived out of the way as it collapsed.

Barrels thundered down.

Bowled the guards to the floor.

Before they could recover, Kit streaked toward the back of the shop, found the rear door, and burst outside.

The door opened out onto a small courtyard where he found a waiting cart. A tall shire horse stood harnessed at the front. At the back of the cart, a short sturdy man unloaded crates from the cart bed. Kit darted forward, leapt up to the driver's seat, and whipped the reins against the horse's rump. As the cart jerked into motion, the sturdy man pushed back his sleeves and hustled around the side.

"Hey!" shouted the man. "What are you doing there?" He started to jog after the cart.

Kit whipped the reins again. The horse lurched into a canter, leaving the man behind.

The hard wheels of the cart roared against the cobblestones as Kit drove out of the courtyard. From the height of the cart he still couldn't see above the moon-dazzled mist. Unsure of the route to the docks, he chanced left, quickly found the main road, and made a wide cumbersome turn.

He rumbled along unimpeded at first, but when he glanced behind he discovered six guards on horseback, all armed with crossbows, galloping after him. He bellowed at the horse and cracked the reins. Behind him, the guard's boots spurred their stallions onwards. Within seconds they closed the distance between themselves and Kit. In comparison, Kit's horse gave deep breaths and the harness strained at his shoulders and the cart's weight slowed him immeasurably. Kit peered down into the cart bed – it lay full with heavy flour sacks. He rolled his eyes.

"God's death!" he cried.

The guards drew within shouting distance.

"Halt!" yelled the nearest guard. "Halt, in the name of the Duke!"

Kit leaned forward and he spotted the entrance to a narrow alleyway ahead. His face hardened with an idea. He yelled at the horse again, swerved the cart to the left, and bore straight toward the alley.

Thunk! Thunk! Thunk!

A hail of short arrows sliced through the air and spiked into the wooden frame of the cart. The guards were almost level with him. They tried to reach out and drag him from his seat. He scowled, bit his lip, and strengthened his hold on the reins. The alley sped closer. It seemed impossibly small... but he didn't stop.

He leaned out of his seat, picked a spot on the horse's back, sprang forward from the cart, and landed onto the horse. Under the violent momentum, he nearly slipped clear off the horse's back and fell under the crushing wheels of the cart. He grappled desperately onto the horse's mane and neck, pulled himself upright, and reached back for the link between the harness and the brackets of the cart. His greasy fingers fumbled at the middle pin. The alleyway loomed over him. The guards bellowed at him to stop. He scratched feverishly at the pin. Just as he reached the alley's entrance, his finger hooked it, ripped it out.

The cart detached from the horse.

Sheered right.

Smashed into the alley wall.

Karoomph! On impact it exploded into a cloud – a white, booming rush of flour and splinters that swept up and swirled outwards. The guards behind lacked the time to stop and collided with the twisted wreckage of the cart. Their horses reared and

11

hurled them from the saddle. They landed headfirst into the torn bags, broken wheels, and ruptured wood.

In the alleyway beyond, Kit pressed his knees against the warm flesh of his horse and rode it bareback. He held the reins close to his chest and galloped away as fast as he could.

Over at the docks, dense moonlit fog shrouded the moored galleons and fishing boats. Waves swayed and lapped against hulls. Still on horseback, Kit rushed over to a galleon just as a group of sailors started to remove the gangplank. He slid down from the horse, produced a strip of paper, and handed it to the nearest sailor. The sailor gave a small nod. Kit scrambled up the gangplank, listening carefully to hear if he had been followed. Apart from the creak and knock of ropes, the docks lay silent in the mist. He took a deep breath, tore away the fake beard, slipped off the gown, and stepped up onto the ship.

SCENE THREE

England. Canterbury Cathedral.

Next morning, in the heart of Kent, lavish royal carriages and idle footmen waited outside the entrance to the Cathedral.

Inside, carved marble pillars soared high above the nave and fanned into the vaults of the ceiling. The vaults crisscrossed the roof and shadows bided there throughout the day. Below, sun cascaded through stained glass windows, washed gold across the pillars, and sprinkled onto the shaded floor, dappling the flagstones. From the altar, a plush red carpet stretched down the central aisle, and upon the carpet Archbishop Whitgift and Queen Elizabeth strolled side by side toward the exit. The Queen's servants trailed behind at a polite distance.

Whitgift wore a simple cap and a white and black cassock. He stood at middle height, but his posture was as straight and stiff as a figure in a stained glass window. A gold chain hung around his potent, blocky shoulders. Like his eyes, his complexion was brown and this served to darken the wrinkles imprinted on his brow and the grooves cut into his fleshy cheeks. A span of gray beard, neither too long nor too thick, dropped sharply from his chin and pointed against the ruff at his jaw. Beneath the folds of his gown moved an aged but virile body and his hands pushed through the air with robust assurance.

Beside him, Elizabeth looked more like a picture of herself than a real person. Dressed in black velvet and a white lace ruff, she had painted herself in pearls: pearls hung in teardrops from her ears; pearls rode in the gold embroidery of her sleeves; and pearl hairpins studded her dark red tresses. Her face, with its wide-set eyes and delicate bone structure, was heavily applied with white lead foundation and brushed with red at the cheeks and lips. In all, she had enough pigment to paint a portrait of a woman. Her fifty-nine years did not show – yet neither did the charisma of her youth filter its way through her guise.

Whitgift sauntered down the aisle and made sure his pace did not exceed Elizabeth's. As they strolled, she looked ahead, her eyes clouded with distraction. He noticed and gave a pained smile.

"The service was pleasing to your majesty?"

"Very much so," replied Elizabeth.

"And I trust your majesty's stay was also agreeable?"

"You have spoiled me, as ever."

"In truth?"

"Yes, of course. You've pampered me as a parent indulges a child."

"Ah..." His face darkened slightly and he raised his chin.

"You don't have one, do you, John?"

"What is that, your majesty?"

"A child."

"No, I fear not. I have the will but... my position allows no time for marriage."

She nodded her head with gentle understanding, yet her focus was clearly elsewhere. As they left the pews behind them she turned to him sadly.

"Without the troubles in London I should've stayed longer."

"Is it the riots?"

"Yes."

"I cannot tell you how they sicken me," he said solemnly.

"Indeed."

"To see the violence of neighbor on neighbor..." He trailed off and sighed deeply.

She raised her eyebrows, impressed by his emotion.

"If only all my ministers felt so strongly as you, John. Perhaps then we'd be rid of all plagues and famines."

He drew himself up.

14

"But the people's unrest is far deeper than mere disease or lack of food."

"I beg your pardon?"

"Doubt is the plague that blights their souls. Atheism is the people's famine."

She shook her head.

"I have no time for church issues now."

"But–"

"Talk to me on this at a calmer date."

"There will be no calmer date."

She narrowed her eyes.

"What?"

"The people will never obey their earthly ruler till they heed the commands of their master in heaven."

They reached the entrance and Elizabeth stopped under a silver chandelier.

"Mark this," she said firmly, "if you wish to cut open my policies, at least do so with a point."

"Your grace, Catholics and Puritans have torn this country apart with their violent heresies. Catholics never tire of plotting to return England to the Pope. And Puritans are ceaseless in thrusting our church toward the extremes of Protestantism. Ever since–"

"I have no need of history lectures."

"Of course not," he continued breathlessly. "I was merely recounting the fact that each group is so powerful that we cannot hope to defeat them entirely. We can only contain them and deter their future rebellions."

"At this moment, the only thing that begs containment is your speech."

"But another group now rises to threaten the people – atheists and freethinkers who doubt the very existence of our church. Such a group will unleash a terror and bloodshed greater than this nation has ever seen." He tipped his head closer and caught her eye. "My point is this: unlike Catholics and Puritans, atheists are still mercifully few in number. We may still destroy them before they grow too powerful. We need only to target the heart of their inspiration and cut it out."

"Such as?"

He paused and carefully picked his next words.

"Stop the mouths of playwrights."

Her lips tightened into a smile.

"Brilliant! If life isn't already hard enough already, I can always ban our entertainment."

"Not ban. Just control. Every play that opens seems more sinful than the last, and more popular too."

"I disagree."

His fingers played nervously with the edge of his cassock.

"Of all playwrights, no name is more profane or worshipped than Christopher Marlowe. Execute him for atheism and you'll silence the rest."

She drew her mouth small and spoke in a testy manner.

"You obviously haven't heard – I'm to see Marlowe's new play at court tomorrow."

His eyes widened in dismay and he glanced away toward the north-east transept, the place where Thomas Becket lay murdered four centuries ago. Bitterness writhed around in his stomach.

"Whatever your majesty thinks is wise…"

She gave him a piercing look.

"Marlowe may be controversial, but his work purges the people of rebellion by releasing all their thoughts of dissent harmlessly on the stage."

"Harmlessly?"

"Yes, *harmlessly.*" She stared at him, watchful for any further sign of disagreement.

His fingers pinched his cassock hard, but he bowed his head.

She didn't take her eyes off him for a moment.

"Providing Marlowe's plays continue to stay inside the theater and no one acts them out in the streets, I have no quarrel with him." She waited a moment more, then took a step back and offered him her hand.

He pecked it with due correctness. The bitterness still gnawed away inside him.

16

"Farewell, your majesty."

"Farewell."

She beckoned her servants to the door, then turned and departed for the carriage.

As Whitgift watched the footmen help her up to the carriage seat, deeper lines cut into his brow. With greater authority to censor, torture, and execute heretics, he could still rip atheism up by the roots before it spread to the general population. But time was fast expiring. Something had to be done soon. Very soon.

The royal carriage rolled into motion and departed. Whitgift watched it leave, stuck his angular beard forward, spun sharply, and walked back into the cathedral, his cassock spreading out behind his agitated steps.

SCENE FOUR

England. Dover.

Good weather on the channel meant Kit made the crossing in half a day. On Wednesday morning, he arrived at Dover just in time to see the colors of the sunrise change upon the chalk cliffs, as if the sun had peeled off the white and exposed the raw pinks, yellows, and golds hidden underneath the stone. He rented a horse and headed straight for London. By riding steadily, and changing tired horses at inns, he journeyed to the outskirts of the capital in only a day and half – the document carried safely in the pouch at his belt. His time on the galleon had given him the chance to write peacefully and also within the pouch lay his most recent work: the last scene of his play *'Doctor Faustus'*. Though he had made the crossing in good time, somehow he had still fallen behind schedule. Many people had expected him at Whitehall Palace on Thursday morning, not the afternoon.

At the palace, gate guards checked Kit over as usual and let him past. He paced swiftly over the main courtyard and aimed for the ballroom.

The interior of the palace ballroom was long and rectangular and graced with chandeliers, sweet beeswax candles, and great tapestries of forest scenes. At the back of the room, Kit stood and gazed over the heads of seated nobles watching the stage. The play had already begun. In a large, cushioned chair, Elizabeth sat at the far end just a few feet away from the actors. She leant slightly forward, enthralled.

At the very center of the stage, Edward Alleyn planted his feet apart and swept his eyes across the audience. He played the starring role of Doctor Faustus: a scholar who sells his soul to the devil in return for great knowledge and power. Also on stage with Alleyn stood an actor dressed in a red cape, taking the part of Mephistopheles; and two more actors played the Angel of Good and the Angel of Evil. Maliciously, the angel's began to circle Alleyn's Faustus.

"Faustus, repent," said the Good Angel, "yet God will pity thee."

"Thou art a spirit," said the Evil Angel, "God cannot pity thee."

Faustus raised his head and looked at them both with despair.

"Who buzzeth in mine ears I am a spirit?

Be I a devil, yet God may pity me;

Ay, God will pity me, if I repent."

The Evil Angel swept up to his side.

"Ay, but Faustus never shall repent."

Faustus turned away slowly and his shoulders sagged.

Kit smiled in admiration, but his face soon turned serious as he spotted two figures seated by the aisle: Thomas Walsingham and his wife Audrey. With hushed steps, Kit tiptoed down the aisle and came to stand beside Thomas.

Thomas was both a patron of Kit's writing and also his employer for espionage work in service of the government. Thomas's cousin had been the famous and powerful Sir Francis Walsingham, the Queen's ex-spymaster. Hence, even though Sir Francis was now dead, Thomas still had many influential connections at court.

As usual, Thomas wore a conservative blue doublet and breeches. Though only a few years senior to Kit, his hairline had receded, leaving a pointed forelock in the center of his forehead. He was narrow of face, with a short neck and shoulders, and simple, quick hands. His wide, intelligent eyes seemed to study all they beheld and he pressed his lips together thin and straight as if brooding on some injustice. When Kit arrived, he perked up immediately.

Kit crouched to Thomas's level. As discreetly as possible, he pulled out a set of papers from his pouch and handed them over.

Without inspecting them, Thomas pushed the papers inside his doublet and tilted his head close to whisper.

"You made good time," he said precisely.

"Later than I planned," Kit replied.

"Trouble?"

"Some."

"Nothing was compromised, I trust?"

"No."

While they whispered, Audrey frowned and strained to watch the play. Her eyes constantly wandered over to rest upon Kit. In reaction, Kit looked firmly at Thomas, though he saw her gaze from the corner of his eye.

"How's business with our 'supplier'?" said Thomas.

Kit didn't reply. Despite his best efforts, Audrey stirred his thoughts and distracted him. She and Thomas had been married less than a year. They both seemed miserable together. Even so, she had not become wildly discontent or flirtatious: she never turned her eye to the many attractive men in Elizabeth's court. She only noticed Kit. Every time she looked at him, he found her gaze was soft yet strangely penetrating, as if it drifted right through him.

Thomas bit the inside of his lip. Annoyed, he bent his head closer to repeat the question.

"I said: how is business with—"

"Not well," said Kit regaining focus. "Our 'supplier' thinks his services are undervalued."

"Is that so?"

"Yes... considering the rarity of his product."

Thomas smiled icily.

"Really? I highly doubt that. He's not as rare as he thinks..."

Again, Audrey looked toward Kit. To Thomas's displeasure, she suddenly gave up trying to watch the play and leaned across to speak with him.

"Your play's wonderful, Christopher."

Kit nodded pleasantly.

"Thank you, my lady."

"In faith, it's probably your best yet."

"Hopefully the Queen agrees with you."

"She will."

Thomas gave a small huff. She ignored him and leaned across further.

"Tell me something..."

"Yes?"

"Will he go to Hell at the end?"

Kit jerked his head back, suddenly troubled.

"Hell?"

"Yes, Hell." She looked at him quizzically. "What's wrong?"

He sprang upright, raising his voice a little.

"Oh *Hell*! The last scene!"

The noblemen and ladies nearby muttered at him to be quiet. He pulled a deep breath into his lungs and felt little coils of stress wind around his heart. As silently as he could, he took his leave of Thomas and Audrey, turned away, and scampered off down the aisle toward the exit.

When the play reached intermission, Kit re-entered the ballroom through a door behind the stage and wended his way into the chaos of actors, costumes, and stagehands. Around them all hustled the small, round figure of Philip Henslowe, the play company's manager. As soon as he saw Kit, he rushed forward, cheeks flustered, eyes rolling, hands waving.

"Three hours late!" Henslowe whined.

Kit hung his head.

"I know."

"Three! Not one or two... Three!"

"I'm sorry, but if you only knew–"

"Oh, I'll tell you what I know." He poked Kit in the chest. "I know that you've never, ever, been this late before."

"I'm here now."

"Yes, and where's my end?"

A tiny smirk crept onto Kit's lips.

"It's behind you, I think."

Henslowe shook his head, not amused. His face dropped with worry, like an anxious school boy, and he held his palms up.

21

"My ending, Kit. Don't fool around. You *do* have it, don't you?"

Kit nodded and reached down to his pouch. As he undid the drawstring, the actors and stagehands stopped their business and huddled close to see the last scene. When he drew out the pages, Henslowe snatched them away instantly. He tried to read them but was too hyper to concentrate for long. Instead, he grabbed at the tufts of hair on the side of his head and continued to rant.

"Do you realize the position you've put the Admiral's Men into?"

Kit nodded slowly and fixed his eyes elsewhere. Henslowe swept his hand towards the faces of those standing near.

"Fie me! We're performing a play that's not even finished. Have you ever heard of such a thing? No, I'll bet you haven't." He turned and stabbed his finger toward an opening in the stage screen. "That's the Queen out there, you know. The Queen. She'll ask for more than her money back." He rubbed a worried hand at the base of his neck. Finally, he calmed himself enough to scan the pages over. Everyone waited for his reaction. After a few seconds, he frowned and showed them to Alleyn.

"That's a strange last scene if ever I've seen one," said Henslowe.

Alleyn stuck out his lower lip and peered down. He began to read slowly in his deep voice.

"A catalogue of recent words between Henry IV of France and the Duke of–"

Kit snapped to attention. A look of horror formed upon his face. He lunged forward and seized back the secret document before they could read any more.

Everyone froze in surprise. Without stopping to explain, he pivoted on his heel and sped away, nearly tripping on some wooden tree props. Henslowe paced after him.

"Where's my scene, Kit?" he cried. "I want my scene!"

Kit left him behind and didn't turn back. Urgently, he dived out the exit and stalked off to the reception room. He paused and peeked through the doorframe.

Inside, noblemen and ladies sipped at their goblets and murmured about the play. Relaxed flights of laughter drifted among the conversations. Trying his best not to attract attention, Kit nipped into the room and searched for Thomas. He rolled the document in his hand and held it down at his side. The skin around his neck began to prickle with heat. Tiny beads of sweat gathered at the top of his brow. At last, around the middle of the room, he finally spied Thomas's blue doublet next to Audrey's black dress. Quickly but carefully, he threaded towards them and forced a nonchalant look upon his face. He tapped Thomas on the shoulder. Thomas turned around immediately and Audrey raised her eyebrows at his presence.

"Have you come to steal my husband from me?" she said merrily.

Thomas's neck stiffened in surprise. Kit gave an awkward laugh.

"Not so, my lady. Merely to borrow him."

"Oh..." Her eyes sparkled.

"You may have him back anon."

"Is that a threat?" she snickered and drew a few stares from the surrounding lords and ladies.

Kit smiled. Thomas watched them both and glowered jealously.

"Really, Audrey!" he said under his breath. "This is court, not a brothel. I think you've had enough wine this evening." He reached over, took her goblet, and gave it to a passing servant.

Audrey bridled and gave a wry, unrepentant smile. She turned away to speak with a passing woman.

Afterwards, Kit led Thomas off to the side of the room. He straightened the document and pushed it into Thomas's hand.

"This is the document."

"What is?" said Thomas.

"This. What I gave you earlier was..."

"Go on."

"...it was something else."

Thomas regarded him a moment, then retrieved the pages of the play from inside his doublet and ran his eyes over them. Before he swapped them with Kit, he shook his head.

"Very sloppy, Christopher. This isn't like you."

"It won't happen again."

Thomas lowered his voice, but his tone lost none of its cold precision.

"Remember, your work for her majesty is paramount."

"I'm well aware of that."

"You're not a spy and a playwright in equal measure."

Kit raised his eyebrows sarcastically.

"Thanks for telling me."

Thomas snarled. His hands worked on the document and his lips pressed tight.

"I'll tell you something else, too: foul up like this again and you'll be neither a spy nor a playwright. At least not on my payroll." He glared and waited for a response but Kit had no reply. Satisfied that the point had been made, he paced back through the room and rejoined Audrey.

Once Thomas had gone, Kit closed his eyes as the pressure in his head spiked into a full-blown headache. The room's temperature seemed to rise. His shirt cuffs pinched around his wrists like manacles. The ceiling felt low and trapping. He tried to loosen his collar as he barreled for the door.

SCENE FIVE

Whitehall Palace. Ballroom.

Later, after Kit had finally given Henslowe the last scene and
tendered many apologies, he lingered behind the stage to watch
the remainder of *'Doctor Faustus'*. Through a flap in the screen
where actors entered and exited the stage, he peeked out and eagerly surveyed the faces of the audience.

Throughout the room a peculiar quietness had descended.
Were people on the edge of their seats? Bored? Even outraged?
Only the applause – or lack of one – at the end of the performance would fully answer that question. Kit peeped toward Elizabeth. Her onyx-black eyes still followed the actors keenly, but
her face showed no sign of her reaction. As *'Doctor Faustus'*
reached its climax, Henslowe shifted silently over to Kit's side
and they both peered out into the ballroom.

On the stage, Alleyn's Faustus stood before a group of devils.
Each devil was dressed fantastically in red, with gold horns and
long black talons. The audience sweltered at the room's rising
heat. Candles on the chandeliers above winked in the turbulent
air. Faustus's voice thundered against the walls.

"My God, my God, look not so fierce on me!
Adders and serpents, let me breathe a while!
Ugly hell, gape not! Come not, Lucifer!
I'll burn my books! -Ah, Mephistopheles!"

The devils fell upon Faustus and dragged him slowly, miserably, through the screen parting to the backstage area. Every actor and stagehand behind the screen pushed forward and
crammed together to see out into the ballroom.

On stage, the chorus – a single, plainly clad actor – now addressed the audience to conclude the play.

"...regard his hellish fall," said the chorus solemnly,

"Whose fiendish fortunes may exhort the wise,

Only to wonder at unlawful things,

Whose deepness doth entice such wits

To practice more than heavenly power permits."

The chorus exited and the play ended.

Silence. A room of tense faces. Eyes stared toward the stage. Lips parted and mouths hung open. No one knew how to react. Slowly, Elizabeth wrenched herself from the chair, stood up straight, and her jewels glinted in the candlelight. With a quizzical look in her eyes, she paused, then raised both her hands and... started clapping. The gentle *tip-tip-tip* of her palms resounded in the room. Immediately, all the lords and ladies stood up and joined her in the ovation. Within moments, the clapping grew to a frenzy of applause.

Backstage, Kit felt a tide of relief momentarily dissolve the stress in his chest and shoulders. The clapping noise swam in dizzy circles around his head. Energy rippled through his veins and vivified his bones. Before anyone else, he leapt out through the screen parting and strode onto stage. As the applause continued, he stood and basked in glory. A look of mirth sparkled on his face and he waved and urged the audience for more. Almost everyone in the room joined in with the ovation. Only one man kept silent...

At the side of the room, Archbishop Whitgift remained firmly in his seat, his hands clamped to the arms of his chair, knuckles white. His jaw flexed with agitation. As the clapping continued, he grew rigid with anger.

When the ovation gradually dispelled, Elizabeth paraded forward and stepped up onto the stage. Kit, and all the other actors, bowed deeply before her.

"Congratulations, Master Marlowe," she said jovially.

"My humble thanks, your majesty." He stood up straight and did his best to look modest.

She pointed to the audience.

26

"Your play is a resounding success, I believe."

"Your kindness overwhelms me."

"No, it is your due." She gave him a reserved smile.

Whitgift could bear no more. Suddenly, he lunged to his feet and worked his way toward the stage. Elizabeth turned, startled at the commotion. Kit watched him with concern. Whitgift approached fast, his face stained red.

"My Queen! Surely you don't plan to release this play upon the people?" He stopped near Elizabeth's feet, the chest of his cassock almost pressed against the stage.

Elizabeth peered down at him critically.

"What is your complaint?"

"If I only knew where to start! It is atheism as entertainment. It's atheism as I have never seen it before. The hero fakes his religion, he desires god-like power, and he spends his time conversing with the devil!"

"At the end of which he is damned."

"A poor substitute for two hours of sin."

Elizabeth stamped her heel onto the stage.

"Do you doubt my judgment, Archbishop?"

Whitgift stood back and his gaze fell. Elizabeth pinched her mouth tight.

"Do you?"

"Not at all, your majesty. I only doubt the judgment of the people. They have not the learning of their lords. They are as children to the wisdom of their rulers. This play cannot but harm their faith and cause more riots."

Kit's heart fluttered as Elizabeth turned toward him frankly. Her broad forehead shone white and hard below the light of the chandeliers. She had never looked more austere.

"What say you to this?" she said. "The Archbishop thinks this is a terrible play."

"I quite agree," Kit replied archly.

"You do?"

"Of course... but who am I to stand against the opinion of my Queen and so many of her noblemen?"

Laughter trickled throughout the audience. Whitgift grimaced and clasped the edge of the stage. He looked visibly nauseated.

"But this play will only drag the people further from their faith, as all his other plays have done before it." He looked up at Elizabeth with imploring eyes. "Again, I ask your majesty to ban this man's work."

Elizabeth refused to answer. Whitgift sighed and let go of the stage. His anger fully subsided into anguish. He looked Kit straight in the eye and spoke in a lower, more reasonable voice.

"My son, will you not write more conservative plays now England is in turmoil?"

"Conservative?"

"You must write more conservatively."

"But I thought this play *was* conservative." Kit glanced toward Elizabeth sarcastically and put his hand on his hip. "I always aim to be conservative."

Elizabeth smirked. Whitgift stared up at her. The next moment, he gave a shallow bow.

"It was hasty of me to make such a scene," he said curtly. "I beg leave of your majesty." He pivoted and marched off toward the door. His broad, blocky shoulders charged past rows of concerned noblemen and ladies.

As he approached the exit, the doormen stepped across his path and looked at the Queen for instruction. Her gaze lingered upon them briefly, but she nodded and the doormen stepped back. Whitgift stormed out of the room, his chin raised, his beard pointed forward...

Outside, the afternoon air chilled at the onset of night. The sunset poured a milky afterglow through the sky and the clouds drunk from it till they were fat with red and orange. The colors then faded in the twilight and the moon poked above the horizon, tough and white, like a dry teat. With the moon's appearance, a deep shade drifted over the Thames, draped across the masts of galleons, and covered the rooftops of London till all was unified in white. Clouds shriveled and turned hard and brittle. Winds from the eastern hills braced the palace buildings for a storm, and inside the ballroom at Whitehall, the nobles could hear a scraping from the roof as the winds picked underneath the slate roof-tiles.

After the play, most of the audience had gathered in the reception room for more spiced wine and little marzipan biscuits baked into the shape of roses. Kit spent much of the time shaking hands and accepting compliments on the play. By now, the stress of recent days began to set-in and fray his nerves. Red veins traced over the whites of his eyes. His head throbbed.

As the crowd gradually thinned, he found himself in the company of Thomas and Audrey. Each displayed great interest in speaking with him: indeed, he felt they almost competed against each other to hold his sole attention.

"...anyway, I must get myself home," he said and rubbed the side of his eyes, trying to relieve the pressure. "I have need for the softness of a good bed."

"Where is it you keep rooms now?" asked Thomas. "Not London, I trust?"

"Well... up in Norton Folgate."

"That's almost London."

Kit nodded. In reaction, Audrey almost dropped the cake in her hand.

"But, oh, but you can't!" she chirped. "The plague, Christopher!"

Kit shrugged.

"I'll survive it somehow."

"No, no. You must come home with us. I insist. I insist upon it most strongly. At least till the worst has passed."

"You're very kind, my lady... but I can manage on my own."

"Nonsense," said Thomas. "Besides, it looks well for a playwright to live with his patron. I'm surprised you haven't been our guest more often."

Kit didn't answer. His gaze drifted past Audrey. Thomas pretended not to notice and gave him a friendly pat on the arm.

"Then it's settled."

Audrey slipped the last of her cake in her mouth and waved her hand as if she had something more to say. Thomas reacted before she could get a word out.

"Doesn't the Queen have need of you now, Audrey?"

She quickly finished eating her cake.

"Not yet," she replied defiantly. She motioned to a tall, white-haired man at the end of the room. "Oh, look, that's Burghley, isn't it? I thought you had to speak with him tonight?"

Thomas's face tightened.

"I'll just be a moment," he said to Kit, "then we'll leave." He followed Burghley out of the room and into the corridor.

Once alone, an awkward silence fell between Kit and Audrey.

Young and slender, Audrey's eyes were gray-blue, the color of twilight, and a fleck in the left eye enhanced the iris and grew bright when she laughed. She'd tied her hair back in a taut bun, but privately she let it fall to her shoulders in smooth brown curls. Her skin bore the complexion of apple blossom, though in some lights it turned stark and white like an alabaster statue. Her composure was also statue-like: angular, graceful, alive and dead in the same moment.

Only a few nobles remained in the room. Nearby, a solemn-faced serving man cleaned away dirty goblets left on a walnut table. He used the cuff of his sleeve to wipe and shine the table. Kit cleared his throat.

"Palace servants have a sad lot... They touch the image of royalty, but not the substance."

Audrey nodded candidly.

"Yes, you're right, we're miserable most of the time."

"Oh... I didn't mean you," he said with embarrassment. "You're not a servant."

"No?"

"Ladies-in-waiting aren't officially servants."

"I'll remember that."

He coughed a little, his throat dry with nerves.

"How fares it as Gentlewoman to the Privy Chamber?"

"Fine."

"You must know the Queen's mind more than all her ministers put together."

"I know her mind," she said breaking his gaze, "at the expense of my own, of course."

"I always thought..." He trailed off, not knowing what to say. Suddenly, he became aware of someone at his left shoulder.

He turned and discovered a young maiden beaming at him. She tipped up onto the front of her toes excitedly. She had long, blonde hair streaming down to the middle of her back. A diamond tiara sparkled on a head that was too large for her shoulders. She gaped at Kit and moved so close she almost stood on his feet.

"Sorry to interrupt," she said breathlessly, "but I just had to talk to you."

"Yes?"

"It's your plays! They're so beautiful, and so exciting, and I know them all by heart. You've touched my life like no other writer."

"I'm glad you enjoyed them."

"I don't enjoy them. I love them – love them, love them, love them!"

"Which one did you-"

Without waiting for him to finish, she thrust her hand out.

"Would you do me the honor of kissing my hand?"

He paused in surprise, then rolled his eyes at Audrey.

"Of course." He reached out politely, took her hand, and pecked it. "A pleasure to have met you."

The maiden gave a big smile. He turned away from her and tried to resume his conversation with Audrey.

"Anyway," he said rubbing his brow, "will you be traveling home with Thomas and myself tonight?"

"Afraid not," Audrey replied. "The Queen always delays me a few hours. I'll journey back to Scadbury later this evening."

The maiden hadn't moved from Kit's side. She frowned at Audrey, grew impatient, and tapped Kit on the shoulder. He jerked his shoulders in surprise.

"Yes? Was there something else?"

She tilted her head down coyly.

"I wonder... No... I shouldn't ask."

"What?"

"Could I have something, some memento, so that I might always cherish our meeting?"

Kit sighed and scratched his cheek. The silver buttons on his doublet caught his eye. He ripped one off and dropped it into her hand. She tipped up onto the front of her toes again.

"Thank you, so much," she said in a cooing voice. "You don't know how I'll–"

"I trust that contents you?" he said a little gruffly. Without letting her answer, he turned his back and refocused his attention on Audrey. Audrey arched her eyebrows.

"Looks like you have quite the admirer," she said.

"Yes, and it's because of those admirers that I have to write the same play over and over. They never want anything new."

"Oh, but I'm sure they might if you..." Audrey grew quiet and flicked her eyes pointedly over Kit's shoulder to indicate that they were still not alone.

Before Kit could move, the maiden nipped around his side and stood in front of Audrey, blocking her from view. He scowled, but she seemed undeterred. She pushed a bound copy of his play *'Tamburlaine the Great'* in front of his nose: a tragedy about an invincible warlord who conquers nation after nation.

"I have your first play," she gushed. "No one can match your artistry."

"What now?"

"Could I ask you to make your mark upon it?"

Kit took a deep breath. He gave her a severe look. *'Tamburlaine'* had made him famous beyond his dreams: not only for its rich array of characters, plot, and theme but also for its revolutionary new style . From *'Tamburlaine'*s first performance, all other playwrights had sought to emulate its vivid, refreshing use of blank verse. Kit himself had never been able to escape its influence since. *'Tamburlaine'*s ghost still haunted all his work.

The maiden tapped her foot impatiently at him.

"No," Kit muttered. "I've given you enough. I must ask you to leave me alone."

Her body straightened and her face turned hard.

32

"Do you know who my father is?" she said haughtily.

"Who?"

"He's Lord Rochester."

"Oh, he's Lord Rochester, is he?" Kit replied through clenched teeth. "Why didn't you say so before? What was it you wanted again?"

"Your mark on this."

He took the play from her. Drew his dagger in a flash. Stabbed it into the center of the book. The blade pierced straight through and came out the back.

The maiden fixed her eyes on him, utterly shocked. He handed the play back to her with the dagger still impaled. She regarded the book, half-unsure what to think, then her face slowly lit into a grin, clearly impressed.

"My thanks!" she said and skipped away, still regarding the impaled book.

Kit scowled after her. This time, he watched to make sure she left the ballroom. When he finally turned back to Audrey, his mood lifted, and the corners of his mouth crept into a smile. Audrey stood still, almost poised, her head cocked to the side. One hand rested on the farthingale of her skirt, and her nails tapped lightly on the fine gold chain decorating her hips. Her eyes had a look of fertile and tender emotion. He smiled at her and she smiled back.

SCENE SIX

The Thames. Walsingham Barge.

Rain lashed the Walsingham barge from all sides as it glided across the river's black expanse. Six liveried men sat at the oars and sliced the paddle blades into the river, pulling the barge rhythmically forward. At the end of the barge stood an enclosed wooden cab. Raindrops clattered on the roof. Wind whistled at the doorframe.

Inside the cab, Kit and Thomas lounged on velvet, embroidered cushions. Warm, balming scents wafted down on them from a pomander above as they sat quietly. The softness of the cushions felt good on Kit's weary back, but no matter how much he tried to relax, he found himself assailed by troubling thoughts. A blast of wind shook fiercely at the door. Thomas flinched.

"Ungodly weather tonight, isn't it?"

Kit didn't answer. His arms were crossed. Thomas paused a moment, then raised his eyebrows and coughed a little, seemingly nervous that he had Kit's undivided attention.

"How was the weather on your trip?"

"Bearable," Kit muttered faintly, his mind distracted.

"Do you ever long for home when you travel abroad?"

"Yes... Sometimes..."

"I always miss your company when you're gone." He corrected himself rapidly. "I mean Audrey and myself always miss you."

Kit didn't reply and the cab resounded with the muffled clatter of rain outside. Thomas leaned slightly closer, his face apologetic.

"I hope you're not stung by what I said earlier. Forgive me if I was a little prickly."

Kit twitched his head as if he hadn't paid attention.

"It's not that," he replied gravely. "I was just thinking..."

"About?"

"My future as a playwright is shorter than a hangman's rope."

Thomas sat up straighter in surprise. He broke into a small chuckle.

"You're worried about Whitgift?"

"You saw him..."

"Don't let that performance get to you. For a man who dislike's the stage, he's certainly full of his own theatrics."

"He'll have his way sooner or later."

"Don't be absurd! After all, Whitgift's been after you forever."

"Since university."

"Tried to ban your master's degree or something, didn't he?" Thomas frowned and smiled simultaneously. "He couldn't touch you then and he won't touch you now."

"I don't know..."

"I do. Mark this, Burghley's taken you under his wing – the head of the intelligence service, no less! And even the Queen favors you at the moment. That's protection enough for any man."

Kit declined to answer. His hands felt fidgety. He reached over, drew back the drapes at the window, and peeked outside. Gusts of rain drove over the length of the barge. His breath gradually misted against the glass and he turned back slowly to Thomas.

"I want no more assignments for a while."

Thomas frowned and looked at him askew.

"That's a little extreme, isn't it?"

"My efforts should be focused on my plays... Just until Whitgift settles down."

"Don't be so hasty about this. Let's consider what you're saying."

"I'm not your only spy."

"You're important to my operations."

"No, you have others you can use."

"But you're my best. To people like Burghley, your efficiency becomes my efficiency." He tripped his fingers over his pointed forelock. "You just need a break, that's all."

"A break from service to her majesty."

Thomas sat upright and crossed his legs. He put his hands together on his lap and spliced his fingers.

"You know," said Thomas precisely, "I'll take you with me as my position advances."

Kit gave him a look of utter contempt.

"You're also patron of my plays, aren't you? Don't you care about my writing?"

"My interest in you is solely as your employer for the government. I've supported your writing this past year on behalf of my wife, not myself."

Kit shook his head firmly.

"No more assignments."

Thomas's chest expanded as he breathed in through his nose. The buttons on his doublet bristled.

"I see. You must be richer than I thought to throw away employment so easily."

"You know I'm not... I have debts all over the place."

"I think you are. When we get home I'll have to rethink how much I'm willing to indulge my wife's fancies. You obviously don't need my cash."

Kit glared back. A thousand insults rattled inside his head, mingling with the clatter of rain upon the cab's roof. He clenched his jaw and looked away dejectedly. They sat the rest of the journey in silence.

Shortly, the barge drifted to a dock on the south bank of the Thames. From there, Kit and Thomas caught a waiting carriage and traveled out of London and deep into the countryside of Cray Valley, Kent.

At the eastern boundary of Chislehurst parish, Scadbury Manor stood atop a wooded hill that overlooked the valley. Scadbury was the primary estate of the Walsingham family. The only approach to the manor was by a winding gravel drive that twisted through the grounds, through circles of forest, through rings of lawns and gardens. At the last corner, the fort-like mansion suddenly appeared and loomed above the visitor. Reddish brick armored every stocky wall, shielded the semi-hexagonal bays, protected deep-sunk windows, and extended up all three stories to a roof of jarring gables and high chimneys pots.

That night, the rain-soaked bricks of Scadbury were brown and water streamed in tiny rivulets off the gables. The Walsingham carriage trundled up to the main entrance and a servant opened the front door, making a square of light upon the gravel drive. Kit fetched a bag of his belongings and followed Thomas inside the house.

A strained quietness still lingered as Thomas led Kit up the grand strapwork staircase to a guest bedchamber. Inside the guest chamber, a single window punctured the dark and a fireplace scooped out a wall on the left. The air smelt of old lavender. His face grim, Kit dragged his feet across the floorboards. He lugged the satchel of his belongings up onto the bed. Thomas remained at the door and watched Kit, as if mesmerized by his every movement.

"This is one of our finest bedchambers," he said across the room.

Kit nodded. He had nothing to say and waited for Thomas to leave. They exchanged a tense look. Thomas pressed his lips together and his neck seemed to retreat into his collar.

"I hope I don't need to remind you how much influence I have with Lord Burghley and the Queen. Their favor can be swayed if I chose to do so."

Kit looked away.

"Yes, you've made your position very clear." He slumped down on the bed. Fatigue made his head feel heavy, like a block of stone. He waited for Thomas to go.

Instead of leaving, Thomas wandered over to the bed and came to lean on the bedpost. His hands crawled down the pole to the surface of the quilt. His fingers extended and fiddled idly with

Kit's satchel. As he spoke, he started to unpack Kit's clothes and lay them on the bed.

"I hate to fight with you," he complained. His voice softened its timbre and he let down his guard slightly. "Friends shouldn't fight. I am your friend, aren't I?"

Kit's eyes grew small under his eyelids. He was too absent-minded to pay much attention to Thomas's ramblings. His body itched all over with tiredness and frustration. He sighed, got up from the bed, and strolled over to the window. Outside, the moon left an ashen mantle over the lawn.

Thomas studied Kit, desperately trying to judge his mood. While standing at the bedside, he pulled out one of Kit's shirts and laid it on the quilt and neatly smoothed out the creases.

"I've taken a passion to archery, at the moment. Perhaps I'll erect some targets in the gardens this week? We could shoot together?"

Kit remained silent. He glanced at Thomas's image in the window.

"Of course," Thomas continued, "I'm not very good yet. No matter how I set my sights, my arrow drifts away from its target."

Kit let his head droop, making no attempt to show any interest. Thomas continued in a voice soft and tenuous.

"Do you think that makes me a naturally bad archer, just because I miss from time to time?"

Kit shrugged and turned back toward the bed. As he approached, he suddenly noticed Thomas unpacking his clothes. Thomas never took his eyes away and continued speaking slowly.

"I can always improve my skills. I can always learn accuracy... with discipline." He gently extended an amorous hand towards Kit's cheek.

Tired and sluggish of mind, Kit stood there spellbound and only half-comprehended how to react. He'd always known this would happen. Ever since they first met, he had understood that Thomas held a very strong affection for him. He understood that his patron loved men more than women.

All ideas fled from his mind and his limbs froze at their joints. He stood passively as Thomas's fingertips came closer, even closer, nearly brushing his skin. For an instant, his body seemed to trap him, seemed to fix him on the spot, as if it belonged to Thomas rather than himself.

Just before Thomas touched him, Kit's instincts snapped into activity. He jerked his head backwards and out of reach.

Thomas was unprepared for the action. His posture shriveled as if he'd been shot through with embarrassment. He dropped his eyes to the floor and snatched back his hand.

"Anyway, it's late," he said curtly and stepped back from the bed. "You should get these clothes in chests. Good-night." His shoulders hunched up to his neck. Without another word, he paced out of the room.

Kit stayed very still as Thomas's footsteps echoed heavily down the corridor outside, grew fainter, fainter still, and died away. Emotions tore through his heart like wild dogs. He was nauseous; strangely flattered; angry and indignant; almost guilty he couldn't return the same feelings. Most of all, he felt frightened at what refusing Thomas could mean for the future.

To make sure Thomas had gone, he listened and remained still a moment longer, then shuffled toward the door and shut it noiselessly against the frame. He turned around and leant against the wall. His face paled.

Scene Seven

Scadbury Manor. Guest Bedchamber.

Kit collapsed into bed and tried his best to sleep. He couldn't unwind. When he finally banished Thomas from his thoughts, his mind still proved restless and wandered back onto the topic of Whitgift and all his accusations.

Tonight wasn't the first time Kit had been called an atheist – such claims were often whispered behind his back or written in pamphlets that criticized the stage. But no one as influential as Whitgift had ever accused him so forcefully. The charge wasn't even true: he had no love for the gods that civilizations fabricated and discarded like the cloth backdrop of a play; yet nor did he feel atheists offered a solid answer to the mystery of existence. Instead, he sensed that the soul of the universe lay somewhere far beyond his grasp, somewhere hidden, as if behind the motion of the sun or moon. It was somewhere everyone sought for and few ever found.

Frustrated, he got up from bed, fetched parchment from his satchel, and sat down at the desk with a quill and ink pot. Almost immediately he wrote a full page: the furious soliloquy of an Italian king. He gave no title at the top and his letters scrawled long and messy over the parchment. When he reached the end of the page, he stopped and read it, tapping a finger on his lips. Gradually, his face hardened. He slammed his hand into the page, crumpled it, and lobbed it across the room. It skidded over to the far corner. Soon, hour drifted into hour and the corner filled with crumpled page after crumpled page.

A deep knock thudded at the door.

He flinched and turned.

The knock sounded again a little harder. He scowled at the door and shrunk back in his chair. Hushed and perturbed, he waited for what seemed like a minute. The knock thudded again. Kit closed his eyes.

"Thomas, is that you?" he said nervously.

"No," came the whisper from the door. "Audrey."

His eyes popped back open. Suddenly relieved, he dragged himself up, combed his fingers through his hair, flattened his shirt neatly on his chest, and opened the door as calmly as possible. Audrey stood outside in the corridor with a candle. She had just arrived home from the palace and still wore her fur coat. She jutted her head forward and whispered.

"I hope I'm not disturbing you?"

"No," Kit replied.

"Are you certain? I know it's late. I'm not disturbing you, am I?"

"Not in the least, my lady."

"I noticed you were still up, that's all. I saw the flicker of your light."

"I'm starting a new play."

"Oh, really?"

"Trying to start one, anyway..."

"So soon after the last? In truth, that *is* impressive. You have such a generous mind."

"And such a beggarly purse," he added with resentment seeping into his voice.

She looked past him into the room and spied the crumpled paper on the floor.

"Are your words blocked?"

"Precisely the opposite. The words march out easily onto the page, like they've been written for me already."

"I'm sorry to hear it."

"Sometimes..." he sighed and wondered if he should finish the sentence. "Sometimes... I think I hate Christopher Marlowe."

She peered into his eyes and gave a comforting smile.

"There's an easy answer for that. Would you like to know?"

He nodded with intrigue. She put a finger to her lips.

"Ah, but it's a closely guarded secret. It's been passed down in my family for centuries. You can't tell a living soul."

"What?"

Her eyes twinkled. She checked over her shoulder in mock secrecy, then leant nearer and lowered her voice to a whisper.

"Be someone else."

He looked at her seriously. A tiny smile cut through his grave expression and he shook his head at her.

"I didn't think of that. Your wisdom overwhelms me, my lady."

"Yes, I know, I'm truly wonderful, aren't I?"

For a fleeting moment, they both laughed gently under their breath. Kit felt the muscles in his shoulders loosen. He was grateful for her presence, but he reminded himself that she was only a friend. She was only a friend and could never be anything more.

Audrey stopped laughing first. An unmistakable restraint descended upon her, and her face acquired a carved stillness. She shifted her feet as if tired of standing. Kit stood back from the doorframe.

"Would you like to come in?"

"Oh, no, that's fine." She peeked into the room. "How are you settling in? Is your room to your satisfaction? I trust Thomas gave you a hand in finding everything?"

Kit's eyes floated above her.

"Yes, he gave me a... My room is well, thank you."

Silence followed and seemed to stretch the space between them. He watched the candlelight trace over the line of her supple lips. She glanced down. The toe of her shoe pointed beyond the fringe of her dress. She pulled it back under the hem and out of view.

"I wonder if you'd go with me to town on the morrow?" she said softly.

"To town?"

"Yes. There's a royal banquet approaching and I need to see a tailor about final adjustments on my dress. I'd value your opinion on it."

42

He considered the offer.

"You flatter me," he said politely.

"But?"

"But... I don't think I can make it."

"Oh."

Another silence passed and threatened to end the conversation. Kit searched quickly for something to say.

"Where will the banquet be held?"

"At Nonsuch Palace. The Queen has one every year in honor of summer. The entire nobility have to attend."

"It sound's magnificent."

"You know, if you came to town, it wouldn't take long." She held her hands together. "Thomas will be with us, too."

"I'm sorry, my lady. I'll have to decline."

She tilted her head back a little and looked away down the corridor.

"I understand. It's just a silly dress, anyway. I don't know why I thought you'd be interested." She started to tread off down the corridor.

A lump swelled up in his throat as he watched her go. He pursed his lips in thought and leant further out of the door.

"Wait," he said, straining to subdue his voice. "What time are you going?"

She made a half-turn back towards him.

"Nine."

He nodded.

"I'll be there."

"You're sure?"

"I can take care of my business afterwards."

A moment passed and each waited for the other to speak.

"Good-night," she said with a faint, sad smile.

"Good-night." He lingered and watched her shuffle off towards her bedchamber. He quietly disappeared back into his room and shut the door.

SCENE EIGHT

Scadbury Manor. Upstairs Corridor.

Audrey tiptoed along toward her bedchamber. The ends of her coat dragged lightly on the floor behind her. A sudden coolness in the night air caressed the nape of her neck and she pulled the coat close around her angular shoulders. She snuggled her chin into the fur collar. Just as she reached her room, she turned to see across the corridor. Light spilled out from under the door of Thomas's bedchamber. She gave a long, regretful look at it.

Their families had pushed them into a marriage that should have worked: Thomas had the wealth and she had the respectability through her relation to Anne Boleyn, the Queen's mother. Of course, love was never the object of their union. Even so, she had soon learnt the true reason why he wasn't interest in her or in any other woman.

Reluctantly, she glided across to his bedchamber and cracked the door open.

Inside the vast room, Thomas laid in bed staring up at the ceiling. A single candle burnt next to him. He made no sign that he acknowledged her presence. She remained in the corridor but pushed her head forward into the room.

"I've invited Christopher to town with us on the morrow," she said weakly and her voice trailed away into the silence.

Thomas stared upwards, his face blank.

"Did you hear me?" she asked more forcibly.

He coughed as if clearing his throat.

"I just received a note a few hours ago," he replied coldly. "There's something I must attend to. I won't be able to go with you."

She expelled a small groan and wondered if he was lying.

"But we can't cancel the trip! The banquet's only a few days hence, it's unfair, I won't have time to see the tailor otherwise."

He reached over and his quick fingers snuffed the candle out.

"I only said I couldn't go. You can still see the tailor with Christopher." In the darkness, he turned on his side away from her, clasping the sheets tightly. He lay there stiff, his mind relentlessly brooding.

She frowned at him. Her gaze fell and she drew her head back out of the room.

"As you wish," she muttered and closed the door.

Exasperated by his attitude, she walked away from his chamber and thought about it more and more. How could she feel guilty about thoughts of Kit when she was married to such a husband? Thomas made it easy for her. She was glad he wouldn't be there tomorrow.

SCENE NINE

London.

Kit and Audrey traveled by carriage into the city. To enter London, they crossed the Thames at London Bridge, the only bridge constructed over the river, and gaped up at a set of spikes thrusting severed heads into the air. The heads belonged to Catholic traitors. The elements had wrinkled and rotted the skin.

Once over the bridge, the carriage launched into shaded, serpentine streets. Houses, shops, and taverns jostled together along the roadsides, their tall buildings darkening the cobblestones and furtive alleyways. Most buildings started at the base with herringbone brick then, as if someone had cut the floors in two, changed to a second story of black half-timbers and white-plastered nogging. The second story often bulged over the foundations and overhung the first floor, while the doorways and roof lines sagged to one side or the other. Beneath leaded window-panes, the odd flower box added a pinch of green, yellow, and pink to the shadows and dirt.

Apart from the starvation of light, one most noticed the noise of the streets. Horses' hooves and heavy cartwheels droned over the cobblestones and the din amplified off the close walls. Rowdy washerwomen chatted on doorsteps and scrubbed rags in tubs, apprentices stood under shop awnings and shouted to friends across the road, dogs barked and roamed loose, and children screamed and ran wild among the gutters.

The Walsingham carriage rattled speedily through East Cheapside, for this area had the worst of the plague. Though they skirted the most pestilent districts, the roads here were emptier and some buildings had boards nailed over their windows and doorways. A peculiar stench of rotten cabbage suffocated the air.

As if some formal division had been made, the carriage suddenly ventured away from the slums and into broader roads and stronger, prestigious buildings. In the warmth of the morning sun, the timbers of the buildings expanded with squeaks and groans, as if the sunlight played upon their beams like the strings of a musical instrument. At the convergence of Cornhill and Threadneedle Street, Kit and Audrey passed the Royal Exchange – the center of London commerce and home of banks, money-lenders, and wholesale traders of wool, lead, cloth, and tin. Everyday, rich lords and ladies jammed into the courtyard with their servants to shop the stalls. Feather-plumed hats bobbed in front of striped awnings as the nobles browsed and lingered at displays of perfumes, imported wines, Persian silks, and expensive wigs.

Beyond the Exchange, Kit and Audrey entered the busiest streets of London and their carriage slowed to walking pace among the crowds and traffic. Cries of hawkers assaulted Kit's ears. Maids with baskets hooked over their forearms haggled with the traders. Kit's mouth watered as the carriage passed the a bakery fragrant with loaves, rolls, and biscuits; yet the air soon fell heavy with the wet fumes of haddock at a fishmonger's stall and the sweaty, bitter smell of iron from a blacksmith's workshop. Among the crowd of shoppers, cut-purses darted through with concealed daggers. Their ears twitched at the clink of purses dangling from the belts. Stealthily, they swept-up behind a fat purse, slit the fabric, and caught the flow of coins that tumbled out. Above it all, along the rooftops, pigeons sat in neat rows and eyed the kites circling in the warm drafts overhead.

After the Walsingham carriage had slogged its way past St Paul's churchyard, it turned into the streets of West Cheapside and found a refined row of haberdashers and tailors. Kit and Audrey exited the carriage outside a shop nestled between two large homes. The symbol on the shop sign indicated it was 'Golding & Co. Tailors.'

Half an hour later, Kit stood inside the shop and watched Audrey flaunt her new gown. It swished on the floor as she strut-

47

ted past, and the fabric twisted at the rear as she turned and walked back. He nodded appreciatively.

"Lovely."

She scrutinized his face.

"You really think so? I want your honest opinion. I can still make changes."

"Quite befitting of a lady."

"Yes, but to your eye, is there anything misjudged? Anything at all? Feel at liberty to say."

"I'm no expert... but I see nothing wrong."

"The sleeve's aren't too full?"

"No. They're lovely."

"The gown?"

He gave a small chuckle.

"It's lovely too!"

She glanced at him, slightly mistrustfully. Today, there was an odd seriousness about her manner. In the light from the window, her face and hands seemed imbued with a marble-like sheen. As soon as she stopped walking, a stubby tailor with thin brown hair and horsy teeth set about making measurements at her waist. With glasses perched low on his nose, he hung the tape measure around his neck, bent down, clamped a pin between his teeth, and stuck another pin into the fabric at her hip.

Like the wives of noblemen at court, Audrey dressed sedately and wore a gown of black and white. A Spanish, cone-shaped farthingale puffed out her skirt and gave her an overall 'A' shape that was now fashionable. Her taffeta bodice squeezed tight around the incline of her midriff. Above, on her chest, she wore a sheer white partlet with lace trim – a decoration that matched the blackwork silk of her gown, her drooping sleeves, and the fleur-de-lis embroidery of her forepart.

With a pretend, carefree air, she turned toward Kit and tapped her finger just above the slope of her bosom.

"Mark this: the gold stitch-work, I had it added specially. The fashion at court is for plainness at the moment, but I don't care."

He raised his eyebrows. In reaction, her face turned grim.

"You don't think it's too much, do you?"

"Not at all," he replied quickly. "I'm sure if I attended the banquet I should see all the other ladies look enviously at you."

"In all honesty?"

"Yes... if I attended..."

The tailor scowled and battled with a pin at her waist.

"Stand straight for me, my lady," he said in a clipped manner.

She arched her back more and straightened her shoulders. Eventually, the tailor wedged the pin into the fabric. Kit took a deep breath and stared off to the side of the shop. He walked ponderously by the shelves.

"I'd love to know more of courtly life," he said almost to himself.

"I thought like that, once," Audrey replied. "All that finery and ceremony, all the spectacle and sound..."

"You're very fortunate to have the position you do."

Her expression saddened but she concealed it with a half-smile.

"Yes. I'm certainly fortunate. You might even say I'm fortune's wife."

The tailor rolled his eyes in annoyance.

"Straight, please, my lady. *Straight.*"

She ignored him and kept her body twisted toward Kit. She continued slowly.

"Of course, I doubt if I should please such a husband... I'm sure... I'm sure... I'd disappoint him."

"My *lady*," said the tailor, "I need–"

She slapped his hand away.

"I'll stand straight when I want to and not a moment before! Remember your place, good sir!" Her chin trembled as she glared at him. Her composure began to crack. A tear slipped down her cheek.

Kit reacted immediately and strode toward her. He waved the tailor away.

"Give us a few minutes alone."

The tailor huffed, made a short bow, and left the corner of the shop.

Audrey recovered almost instantly, but her cheeks turned blotchy as she dabbed the tears away with her fingers. Kit stood at her side, concerned.

"Is there anything wrong?"

"No," she replied with mock confusion. "Why would you think that?"

They both smiled a little. Kit offered her his handkerchief and she finished drying her eyes. A small silence followed. He searched for a way to lighten her mood.

"Thomas tells me he funds my work because of you."

"I'm afraid that's right."

"So... I only think it fitting that you should decide the subject of my next play."

She paused and cocked her head to the side in thought.

"Make it about love."

"Agreed."

"Yes, love. Though I'm not sure if it should be a comedy or a tragedy."

Kit's eyes suddenly widened.

"How about neither? Why not just a story about the union of two people, and how they overcome the obstacles between them?"

"It's good. Yes, I like that."

"There's hasn't been such a play before."

"Oh, but what would the heroine look like?" She plucked her thumb and forefinger at the sides of her gown. "Would she have a dress like this?"

"No, much more colorful. Perhaps green."

"Or purple."

"And her kirtle could be blue."

They began to laugh at the bizarre design. Audrey fluttered her fingers over her head.

"I see her in a big myrtle wreath."

"How about a necklace made out of pebbles?"

"Pebbles?"

He nodded, and they both continued to laugh. She dabbed at the corner of her eye, then stepped forward lightly and embraced him.

"My thanks, Christopher. You always manage to cheer me."

The action surprised him with its boldness, yet he put his hands on her arms and held her briefly. She was only a friend. He told himself that truth over and over. There was no reason to feel threatened. There was no reason to be thrilled at her embrace. She was only a friend and in need of his support.

They stayed together only a moment. However, when she tried to step back, her body suddenly jerked to a halt. A brooch on the breast of his doublet had snagged the front of her gown, threatening to rip the fabric. She gave a look of dread.

"Oh dear! Careful, don't let it tear."

They stood locked together. Kit worked his hands up to the front of her bodice and felt for the top of the brooch to untangle it. While his fingers carefully picked away at the brooch, his attention wandered. He noticed how the incline of her shoulders pressed against his chest. He could feel the pillowy rise and fall of her bosom. She was close. Very, very close. Her lips lay just a short gap, a tantalizing gap, from his own. Her breath tickled his neck. Her hair brought lemon fragrances to his nose. She noted the direction of his eyes and her cheeks bloomed pink with embarrassment.

At last, he managed to unclip the brooch. Their bodies parted and they stepped back slowly, almost reluctantly.

"I don't think it harmed the fabric," he said quietly.

She shook her head in agreement, not daring to speak yet. They looked at each other. He raised his hand and gave her the brooch. It was made of dark gold and fashioned in the circular shape of an ouroboros: a snake swallowing its own tail.

"Perhaps you should have it," he said. "It seems to like you."

They stood in silence as she took the brooch, glanced down, and smiled gratefully. She turned the brooch so it glowed in the sunlight from the window as if it were alive. His face darkened. Without looking up, she whispered to him.

"Kit..."

51

He drew himself together.

"I should go now, my lady," he said abruptly. "I need to see Henslowe about an advance."

She shifted her weight uneasily.

"Yes, well, don't let me keep you."

His eyes drifted over her one last time. He gave a small bow and paced away toward the door.

She stared after him despondently. Once he was gone she raised her hand and gestured for the tailor to rejoin her.

SCENE TEN

London. Outside Tailor Shop.

Thomas pressed up to the edge of the tailor's window, his face against the glass and looking in. Beside him stood Ingram Frizer, his red-haired, weasel-faced secretary.

"We should move back, sir," Frizer pleaded in his nasal voice.

Thomas ignored him. Frizer waited and looked at him aslant.

"Sir... Sir... come, let's away."

"Fie upon it!" Thomas hissed. "Will you button your mouth!" He kept his head pressed against the glass and continued to look inside.

Thomas's claim that he couldn't go town had simply been a ruse to make Audrey and Kit go alone. He wanted to observe in secret the true extent of their relationship. As soon as Audrey's carriage had left Scadbury, he and Frizer had set out in pursuit and followed them to the shop. For the last half an hour, they stood outside the window with a clear view inside. Thomas's eyes had witnessed everything that occurred.

Suddenly, they watched as Kit approached the door to leave. They pulled back from the window. Their images ghosted over the surface of the glass and flitted away. Hastily, they searched for a hiding place. Frizer pointed to a spot ahead – a tavern doorstep. It was deep enough to conceal both their bodies. Within moments, they rushed over to it and crammed into its depths.

Kit exited the shop, strode along a few paces and passed directly in front of the tavern doorway. His mind was occupied. He didn't see anyone lurking in the shadows. Seconds later, he crossed over the road and hurried off down the street.

When Kit was far enough gone, Thomas lurched out of the doorway. He quickly took control of himself. A riot of feelings battered away inside him but he gave them no expression in his face. His eyes followed Kit with a dry, unblinking stare. His jaw was loose. Only the faintest lines traveled across his brow. How could he have misjudged Kit so badly?

Frizer wandered out of the doorway and watched Kit move away further down the street.

"If you wish, I could follow him, sir."

Thomas pressed his lips thin.

"No need for that," he replied in a collected, exact voice. "I have something else in mind."

"If I may ask... what do you think it means?"

"Isn't it clear?"

Frizer shrugged. Thomas scowled at him.

"It's an affair," he gulped. "I've known it for some time."

"Are you sure?"

"What? Didn't you see the embrace with your own two eyes? In broad daylight, no less."

Frizer nodded and kept a wary distance.

Meanwhile, Thomas gazed emptily down the street, watching as Kit finally turned the corner and disappeared from view. Kit already knew too much about his feelings. But this indiscreet relationship with Audrey promised to reveal his marriage as a sham. It threatened his place at court. That could never be allowed to happen. Never.

His eyes found the tailor shop again. He shook his head coldly.

"I expected this from her. Not him." He sneered and looked at the window as if still seeing the embrace. He muttered under his breath. "The mountebank and the harlot..."

"Sound's like a play," said Frizer.

Thomas turned on him coldly. Frizer hung his head and shut his mouth.

SCENE ELEVEN

Bankside. The Rose Theatre.

In the late afternoon bustle of London, Kit strolled down to the river and caught a wherry for the Rose Theatre at Bankside.

The Rose Theater stood on an open patch of dirt once used as a rose garden. Roughly circular in design, like an open flower, the theater blossomed three stories high and outmatched all surrounding buildings with its height and girth. From roots of brick, its frame grew upwards into stalks of black oak timber and white lime plaster. The roof opened to the sky in the style of roman amphitheaters, but a slender thatch of reeds rimmed the very top. Though Henslowe had constructed the theater some time ago, the years had initially been barren for The Rose until Alleyn and The Admiral's Men had pollinated it with their skill and fame. Now the theater was truly full-blown: shows regularly filled the building to capacity – two thousand seats. The Rose may have been London's fifth theater, but it was the first in Bankside, and the very best of its kind anywhere in the kingdom.

With a determined gait, Kit strode up to the front door and barged inside the theater. Right now there should have been a play in progress, but the theater was mostly empty since the plague outbreak had shut all playhouses for the foreseeable future. This meant the Admiral's Men had to tour the provinces when they weren't performing at court. Kit whisked inside to the center of the yard. Sawdust puffed at his feet. The surrounding tiers and balconies reached up and seemed to slant over him. Afternoon sun penetrated the shade of the stands and made a slow-creeping toward the stage.

Though most members of the play company were now in the provinces, some actors had stayed behind to rehearse. Currently on stage stood the figure of Tom Kyd, a lanky, blonde, long-fingered playwright. Next to him were a group of players performing his new work. One player, a young boy, was dressed as a girl while several others posed as a gaggle of monsters. With a horrified expression, the girl knelt before the monsters and begged for her life. An armored man bounded onto stage, metal clunking around his armpits, and stood bravely in between the monsters and the girl.

"By all the powers in heaven," bellowed the armored man to the monsters, "thou shalt not take this girl."

Tom peered up from the script in his hand and shook his head.

"No, not like that," he moaned in his nasal voice.

"Then how?" replied the armored man.

"More conviction."

"I *am* trying, you know."

"Yes, but let the audience truly feel your rebellion. Let them feel it."

"Alright, alright..."

Kit watched the scene briefly, then passed by the stage and frowned.

"Devil's on stage!" he said caustically. "Good idea – wish I'd thought of it. Oh, wait, I did."

As if ready for his comment, the players turned and grimaced. The actor dressed as a girl stuck his tongue out. Tom took a moment to register Kit's remark, but soon paced downstage toward him.

"Actually," said Tom, nostrils flaring, "they're not devils – they're goblins."

"Goblin's? Is that so?"

"You didn't have that idea, did you?"

"No, you're right, I didn't."

"Thank you."

"You're genius is staggering." Kit gave a short, dismissive laugh and continued on his way.

56

At the back of the stage stood a roofed structure called the tiring house: during a performance, props and painted cloths transformed the house into anything from a soldier's garrison, to a prison, to a royal palace, and actors used its doorways to make their way on and off stage. Kit strode around into a back passage and entered the house.

Immediately, he chanced upon an argument between Henslowe and William Shakespeare. He halted at the side among the props and costumes, and observed both Will and Henslowe with interest.

Will was the same age as Kit. He wore brown breeches and a linen shirt open at the neck in a showy, gallant style common to many actors. In fact, nothing really set Will apart from the others: not his hazel eyes, not his auburn-brown hair, nor his slim waist. His skinny arms hung loose from the shoulder. He spoke with a country accent which he tried to conceal. He was a husband, a father of three, and a mediocre player. Recently, he'd even tried his hand at playwriting and received a half-decent success, though ultimately most people could still meet and forget him while in the same room. However, as soon as one got him involved in a meaningful conversation, he could change startlingly. An odd light began to show within – some furnace of vivifying power that had the misfortune to be housed inside his dull form. It lit the corner of his sun-bright eyes with mirth, simmered in the enthusiasm of his voice, and flared in the ideas he left hanging about the air like glowing embers. At the moment, he seemed locked in some vehement disagreement, and Henslowe flapped his mouth and hands in the air fervidly.

"No, no, no – how many times do I have to say it!" Henslowe wailed.

"Think it through, I beg you," Will replied.

"No. The public currently has a taste for tragedy. That is the only type of play I'll bankroll."

"Their taste could change, couldn't it?"

"When it does, I'll let you know."

"But what if my play itself changed the public's desire?"

"What if? Hmm..." Henslowe put his hands on his rotund stomach and pretended to think. "If you want your pig to fly it'll need stronger wings than that."

"I'll take it elsewhere, then."

"Do as you like."

"You're not the only playhouse in town."

Henslowe chuckled derisively.

"No, I've heard Burbage up at The Theatre is fond of bacon."

Will continued to glare, but Henslowe spotted Kit waiting at the back and began to strut away.

"If you go," said Henslowe over his shoulder, "I'll just drag in another playwright off the street. There's plenty more of your ilk around here, master Shakespeare." He turned towards Kit and stuck out his hand. "But there's only one Marlowe. How are you Kit?"

Kit shook his hand, but glanced sympathetically over to Will.

Later, Henslowe and Kit wandered into the stands and took a seat in the second tier. The rehearsals still continued on the stage below – the girl still knelt before the monsters. As succinctly as he could, Kit tried to tell Henslowe about his new idea for a play, yet under Henslowe's candid gaze he began to falter and rush the explanation.

Once he was done, Henslowe put his foot up on the balcony in front and squirmed a little in his seat.

"A what?" he said with a frown.

"A story about love," Kit replied.

"I don't know..."

"It can be comic and tragic, but escape the bounds of either style." He coughed a little and tried to clear his throat. "It'll be a new type of drama."

Henslowe raised his eyebrows and played with the tufts of hair on the side of his head.

"New?"

"Yes, new."

"You know I don't like that word. Haven't you got any other ideas?"

"None."

"Another sequel to *'Tamburlaine'*, perchance?"

"He died in the last play."

"Oh, well, you could do a prequel instead. Or how about another *'Doctor Faustus'*? Yes, that's a splendid idea. Let's see what happens when Doctor Faustus is taken to Hell. How about that?"

Kit shook his head and waited for a decision. Henslowe paused and tapped his chin thoughtfully.

"You see," he explained, "when people come to watch a Marlowe play they expect certain things." He counted them out using his fingers: "poetry, violence, tragedy, a hero fighting the world..."

"Don't remind me."

"What you're proposing isn't really a Marlowe play at all."

"Yet I would be the author, nonetheless. I would still create it."

"But it wouldn't be you."

"You're insane!"

"It would be like I'd bought the work of someone else."

"Who?"

"An untested playwright."

Kit threw his hands in the air.

"So you don't want it?"

"Now wait a minute. Just wait. I didn't say that, exactly."

"Then what *are* you saying?"

"I'll need to see it first." Henslowe stood up slowly and patted the dust from the back of his breeches. "Bring me half and we'll discuss an advance then."

"No," Kit said through clenched teeth. "I need the money now."

Henslowe shrugged and smacked his lips frankly. There was nothing more to be said.

Kit sat still for a moment. Only his leg shook, tapping his heel on the floor. Everything around him, the seats, the stage, even Henslowe, seemed so perfectly hard and defined, unmovable from its place. Anger spiked through his body. Suddenly enraged, he gripped hold of the banister rail, sprang to his feet, and thundered down the stairs to the yard. He curled his hands into fists as he marched toward the exit. In doing so, he passed near the front of the stage where the armored man lunged once more before the monsters.

"By all the powers..." said the armored man. "By all the powers... By all the powers in heaven..."

"How could anyone write such a god-awful scene?" growled Kit, finishing the sentence. He gave Tom and all the players a scathing glance. "You're just a bunch of hacks, I hope you know that!"

The girl player tore off his wig and threw it to the floor. The other players barked a host of dirty epithets in Kit's direction: cries of "Pignut!", "Wagtail!", "Clot-pole!", and "Maggot-pie!" were flung roughly through the air. In particular, Tom turned pale with deep offense. He lowered his eyes condescendingly towards Kit and stepped forward.

"I'm just about tired of your mouth, Kit," he said acidly. "Why don't you go to hell along with your last hero?" He turned back to the players for support. "That is, if Satan would have you!"

The players wheezed and snickered. Kit smiled bitterly and waited for them to finish.

"Tom," he said, "I've seen turds in the gutter that frighten me more than you." He raised his voice to the stands. "Come to think of it, they could write a better play, as well. I'm surprised Henslowe doesn't get some in here. Or perhaps we already have enough refuse lying about the place!"

Tom and the players stood speechless. Henslowe retreated back into the shade of the stands. Kit waved his hands as if to dismiss them all, slapped the theater door open, and stormed out of the building.

SCENE TWELVE

Outside The Rose Theater.

Kit paced through Bankside and soon began to cool down. In the western hills, the afternoon sun poured into the horizon and ran through the fields in gushes of purple light. Damp grass smells lurked around the town. Gradually, he worked back toward the wherries at the riverbank.

Up ahead, ambling along in the same direction, he sighted Will. Intrigued, Kit increased his pace and caught up to him.

"Mind if I walk with you a moment?" he asked.

"Not at all," said Will, relishing Kit's attention. "Please do."

"Where are you going?"

"Nowhere, really – at least that's what Henslowe thinks."

"Quite a piece of work, isn't he?"

"Yes, and it's a shame he won't let us work in peace."

"Nicely worded."

"Ah, if only my words could impress everyone. Still, maybe he'll mend his opinions in time."

"I doubt it."

"You don't think so?"

"No. Time wounds all heals, as they say... and Henslowe can certainly be a heel at times."

Will smiled, still partially awe-struck by Kit's unexpected company. They strolled onwards a little slower and Kit relaxed more and felt increasingly comfortable in Will's presence. Behind them, darkness bled through the streets and homes and windows of Bankside. Everywhere, the dens and brothels stirred into life. Mutters seeped outside from shaded doorways. Casement windows opened and leaked groans into the air.

Kit glanced at Will curiously.

"Anyway, what did you try to push on Henslowe?"

"A comedy."

"Really?"

Will nodded his head.

"The body of it comes from a novel by Thomas Lodge, but I've added the soul. I think the title was *'Rosalynde: Euphues Golden Legacie'*. Ever heard of it?"

"No. Why did you choose comedy?"

Will's eyes twinkled.

"No offense," he said earnestly, "but I don't want to write another tragedy. I like your work – who doesn't? At bottom, anyone would be pleased to have written such plays as *'Tamburlaine the Great'*, *'The Jew of Malta'*, *'Edward the Second'*, and *'Doctor Faustus'*. Yet I always tend towards humor."

Kit hung his head slightly.

"Don't you think comedy is out of place in a world like ours?" He tried to restrain the sourness tainting his voice. "What's funny about poverty, injustice, and brutality?"

"Nothing..."

"But?"

"There's more to the world than that." Will huddled closer to him. "There are forces that transcend our suffering – that exist beyond our limitations. Life becomes a tragedy when we miss them, but a comedy when we find them."

Kit scratched his head and narrowed his eyes skeptically. As they walked, their shadows glided smoothly over the cobblestones at their side.

"Forces like what, exactly? God?"

"No. Love." Will glanced over at Kit, anxious for his reaction.

Kit paused a moment, then patted him on the back, knocking him forward half a pace.

"I don't know about you," said Kit, "but I'm thirsty. Want a drink somewhere?"

Will gave an eager nod.

Partly to avoid the risks of town, partly to avoid another confrontation with Tom Kyd and the players, Kit and Will traveled back across the Thames into London and found a tavern to the east of St. Paul's Cathedral. The tavern sign was painted with the image of a comely mermaid.

Within the tavern, pipe-smoke clouded the air. Customers sat on low-slung benches and stools with uneven legs. At the back wall, a hearth yawned wide and a boar turned on a spit in the fire. Kit and Will sauntered over to the bar. The floor rushes squelched with every step. Behind the bar, the taps of the casks gleamed and reflected the lazy hands of the ostler as he poured drinks. The tavern served ale flat and flavored with pepper or rosemary. Rhenish or claret were the most popular, and each wine was spiced with ginger, cinnamon, or nutmeg. After slight deliberation, Kit leant forward to order.

"What price for rhenish?" asked Kit.

"Twopence by tankard, a groat by pitcher," slurred the ostler in reply.

"A groat, sirrah!"

"Tankard or pitcher?" repeated the ostler blandly.

"That's a steep price for a drink steeped in Thames water, no?"

The ostler waited and regarded both Will and Kit with bored, half-open eyelids.

"A tankard of cinnamon rhenish," said Kit looking away.

"Same for me, good sir," Will chirped up.

Once loaded with tankards brim-full of wine, they started towards the benches to find a seat.

Tonight, a mute gloominess consumed the tavern. Musicians with pipes and fiddles normally strutted around the tables, but now the room was so quiet that one could hear the boar's fat hiss in the fireplace. The low conversation of the customers – all men – was dour and filled with morose grumbles. Their jerkins were well-worn and patched. The dye on their tights had faded. Hard eyes shined in their faces, like two pieces of flint, and their jowls were slack and tired. Hatred seemed part of the brew they gulped down.

Kit and Will wove through the stools and found an empty bench by the fire.

"This place isn't usually so dead," said Kit in a low voice.

Will gave an uneasy look and perched on the edge of the bench.

"Perhaps we should go somewhere else?" he replied.

Kit scanned the room, shook his head, then sipped his wine. The liquid wrapped his tongue in a dense blanket of sweetness and fell warmly into his stomach.

Will set his tankard on the table without drinking.

"What was it like speaking with the Queen the other day?" he said in a bemused manner.

"Frightening," Kit replied, "but exhilarating in the same breath."

"I imagine so."

"How about your new comedy? Is it to be set in courtly circles?"

"No," said Will shrugging his shoulders. "I don't really know much about that side of life."

"Why not?"

"I don't have the connections you do."

"Well, I don't see nearly enough of that life myself." Kit sighed and peered down. "God, the day is too short to eke it out in hovels like this!"

"It's not so bad... It's just today."

"No, it's everyday." He leaned his elbow on the table, shaking the grease lamp. "But not for everyone, of course. Not for people like Thomas Walsingham who have a nice cushion of wealth, rather than a hard bench, to sit on." He raised his tankard and took a deep draught of wine. He drank on an empty stomach and felt the effects of the wine quickly.

Will lifted his tankard in both hands and filled his mouth with rhenish. Afterwards, he picked off a lump of spice that had stuck to his front tooth.

"Tell me something..." said Will.

"Yes."

64

"Do you think it possible for a man to write himself?" He waited keenly for Kit's answer.

"In words and plays, perhaps." Kit waved his hand around the room. "But not in reality. Out here, we don't decide who we are."

"You've lost me. What d'you mean?"

"I mean that in our plays we hold lives, continents, even the whole universe at the point of a quill. In this place, though, we're paupers in debt up to our lugholes. We're just servants to the whims of the public and the fancies of the Queen."

"I only ask because my plays have trouble getting the same strength of voice that speaks in your work."

"That's because you try to slip inside other characters."

"What do you do?"

"I only put myself in one." Kit smiled wisely. "The hero."

"Don't you feel that confines you?"

Kit's face dropped. He glanced toward the fire and the boar's fat hissed in the flames.

"Well, yes, but–"

Before he could finish his reply, his eyes floated towards the tavern door. He sat up sharply.

Henslowe barged into the room with a harried expression. Within seconds, he spotted Kit and Will and dashed over to their table, his gut jiggling all the way. He arrived panting and out of breath. Kit jabbed Will with his elbow.

"Look," said Kit with a malicious smile. "He's come to beg an apology."

Henslowe rolled his eyes and regained his breath.

"Kit," Henslowe said faintly, "there's something you must, you have to–"

"Save it, Henslowe. You're tongue's wagged enough today."

"No. You don't understand." Henslowe pointed toward the window. "Outside. In the street-"

Kit slammed his tankard on the table.

"Unless you've some cash for me right now, I'm not interest-ed."

Henslowe glowered at him.

65

"Listen to me!" he shouted.

Kit and Will exchanged a startled look. Henslowe was deadly serious.

"What?" said Kit suspiciously.

"Let me show you," replied Henslowe with a pained expression. He started away and beckoned them to follow. "Quickly!"

Kit remained seated. Fat dripped from the boar and hissed in the fire. He shrugged his shoulders at Will, totally mystified. Henslowe beckoned again. Kit and Will shot to their feet and followed Henslowe out of the tavern.

Scene Thirteen

London. Broad Street.

Led by Henslowe, Kit and Will hurried along silently. Henslowe strode ahead with such vigor his lips parted for air. His purse swayed and chinked rhythmically against his hip. Next to Will, Kit lagged a few paces behind, his head buzzing with rhenish. He kept his hand near his dagger and his eyes probed the dark alleys and doorways.

They walked for minutes without seeing another person. Kit shook his drunken head, trying to keep his focus. Fear warmed his blood to an uncomfortable degree.

Suddenly, his eyes widened and strained at the sight ahead: a horde of people gathered around the front door of a quaint church. All were faced inwards and staring at something on the door. His mouth turned stale with remnants of wine and he followed as Henslowe led him straight for the church door.

As they gradually drew closer, Kit realized that most of the people around the church were Puritans. They were crowded together so densely it was hard to see the cause of their distress. Kit and Will reached the edge of the crowd and pushed in after Henslowe. They tried not to stand on anyone's toes as they moved toward the door. Eventually, Kit moved in close enough to see the cause of the disturbance.

Nailed high above, a large poster glared down at the anxious faces. Henslowe turned to Kit, eyes large and troubled.

"One of these appears on nearly every street," said Henslowe.

Kit frowned in confusion, stepped forward, and peered over the brims of hats and the tops of smooth linen caps. In large black letters the poster read:

'MARCH AGAINST THE POWERS OF HEAVEN!'

The bottom of the poster lay obscured by the backs of the people in front.

He shrugged and gave Henslowe a cautious look. Similar posters – known as libels – had appeared anonymously around London since mid-April. Provoked by a failing economy, rising disease, and unending war in the Low Countries, the libels always threatened violence against the church and state. No one knew the person or group responsible, but the rebellious nature of the libels unnerved the government.

"Terrible," said Kit. "But what has this to do with me?"

Henslowe barged through to the very front of the crowd and pointed to the name of the author signed at the bottom of the poster. Kit craned his head closer and blinked. In big bold letters it read:

'CHRISTOPHER MARLOWE.'

His lithe body remained still and balanced. His heart jumped and pounded in his chest. He gave a short, shuddering laugh and ran a hand nervously across the tip of his chin.

"They've taken my words," he said desperately. "It's from one of my plays."

"They'll have you on treason for this," said Henslowe. "You know the punishment for treason, don't you?"

Kit froze in terror. A series of images flurried through his mind…. himself on the gallows, hanging by the neck before the eyes of a cheering crowd…. executioners cutting him down, splashing water on his face to revive him… his torso lying on a table as sharp instruments severed his bowls, his genitals… an axe whistling through the air, thudding down into his neck… his mutilated limbs on display around the city….

He rubbed his sweaty fingertips on the front of his doublet and shook his head. "You know I didn't do this," he pleaded.

Henslowe and Will regarded him a little suspiciously.

"I don't know what to say," muttered Henslowe.

Kit hesitated. The voices of the crowd seemed to thicken and form pillows around his ears. This was all that Whitgift needed to turn the Queen against him.

With a shudder, he bowed his head and tried to take it all in. The hairs on his arm tingled. Scared but furious, he spun around.

"I didn't write this damn thing!"

"Then who?" said Will.

Kit lunged for the poster and dug his nails into the parchment. He ripped it from the door.

"Let's find out!"

Instantly, two men at his right stood back in shock. A woman with a mole on her chin gazed at him and pointed.

"It's him," she called to the others. "Marlowe! He's the one! He's Marlowe!"

Commotion rippled through the crowd. Men grumbled. Women scowled. Kit didn't give them a chance to act and rampaged off down the street. Seconds later, Will forced his way through the crowd and hastened after him.

As Kit marched along with a half-mad gleam in his eye, the torn poster fluttered in his hand. Will jogged up alongside him.

"Where are you going?" asked Will.

Kit shook the poster.

"To find the charlatan who printed this venomned thing."

Kit rounded the corner and soon discovered yet another poster on the wall of a home. A shop over the road then took his interest. Above, in fancy paintwork, the sign bore the symbol of Edward Blount, the printmaker.

He hurtled toward the shop. Launched his shoulder into the black oak door. The frame shook, but he rebounded, making no effect.

Will stopped and gave him a sidelong glance.

"How d'you know it's this one?"

"I don't," said Kit with breath laced by the sugared fumes of wine. "But if it's not him, he probably knows who." He braced himself and rammed into the door again. It didn't budge. He staggered back, winded and reeling from the impact.

Will stood in front of him and tried to guide him away.

"Don't be such a fool," Will reasoned. "Anyone in England – nay, anyone in all of Europe – could have printed it."

Kit nodded. A moment passed and his temper seemed to ease. However, as soon as Will stepped out of the way, he rushed forward and crashed into the door again. His body thudded desperately into the wood, recoiled, and he slumped onto the doorstep gripping his sore shoulder.

Will knelt beside him.

"You know what this means, don't you?" Kit groaned.

"That you need a stronger shoulder?" replied Will.

"It means I have no protection."

"How so?"

"These libels have posted a fence between myself and the Queen. She only protected me while my plays did no harm."

Will looked at him, surprised. Neither of them spoke. It was true: even if she didn't believe he authored the libels, Elizabeth would still distance herself from Kit. This disturbance had made him into an embarrassment, a weakness, a sign that her judgment was not always to be trusted. He would never be allowed to approach her again.

Will took the poster from Kit's hand and scanned the parchment.

"These weren't cheap, you know. Think about it." He gave Kit a friendly shove. "It took power and organization to post so many. Are there any lords who wish you dead?"

Kit shrugged and heaved himself to his feet. Somewhere in the distance, a man's voice called out. Other voices answered it. For a moment, he cocked his head and listened till he was satisfied the noise was sufficiently distant. He turned to Will with a foreboding look.

"You have a horse I can borrow?"

"No," said Will. His face suddenly brightened. "But Henslowe has some at The Rose."

Kit closed his eyes and nodded. Without a moment to waste, he thanked Will and raced away down the street. The slap of his leather-sole shoes echoed off the cobblestones. His lungs felt constricted with air and he puffed, and fought, for every, breath. He veered left to turn the corner into the next street.

At the printer's shop, Will waited and expected to see Kit disappear around the corner. Then something strange happened. Kit stopped dead. Slowly, he took a tentative step backwards. Then another step. And another. Will watched half-amused, half-concerned. Finally, a sense of terror seized him and he understood what was happening.

Torchlight hunted its way around the corner accompanied by the crackle and hiss of many voices. The fire, the voices, grew sharply brighter and louder. A mob of Puritans blazed around the corner and into the street after Kit. Many faces were familiar from the church, but the crowd had greatly expanded and spread out wide, completely dwarfing Kit's silhouetted image. Their eyes burnt into him. Torchlight flashed off their hot, incensed cheeks.

"Heretic!" shouted a man at the front of the mob.

"Hang the scoundrel!" yelled the woman with a mole on her chin.

Kit pivoted. On the balls of his feet he sprinted back towards Will. His sudden movement fanned the instincts of the crowd. They hollered, screamed, and broke into a chase.

A small way down the street, Will stumbled and pressed back against the wall in fright. He didn't dare to wait and darted away down an alley.

Kit continued to sprint as fast as possible, but his body soon began to slow down from the stress, and from the wine, and from the shock. His feet tired and his legs slacked their speed and his lungs burnt with the cool night air.

The mob descended fast and fell upon him...

Scene Fourteen

London. City Park.

Kit fought with every ounce of energy he possessed yet was powerless to escape: the mob hit him in one solid blast and caught him helpless in their flow. He thrashed around, used his full body weight against them, but had no defense against their elemental pull. Limbs bombarded him from all sides. Shoulders squeezed, hands battered, arms jostled, elbows pummeled into his ribs and back, and nails scratched the flesh on his hands. At first, they seemed to toss him about aimlessly, round and round, almost trampling him down, but soon he realized they had swept him into a nearby park nestled among the houses.

As the mob pushed him along he tripped over their feet. Someone behind kept smacking his head. Calls, whistles, whoops, and yells combusted about his ears. He felt the wetness of grass under his feet and peered ahead, his vision jogged, to the leaf-shrouded boughs of a giant oak. Suddenly, he smelt the dirty odor of hemp as someone slung a noose over his head. The rope pulled tight around his throat, stifling his breath. He tried hard to reach up and tear it away, but they held his arms down. The rope rubbed coarse against the back of his head and cut the skin underneath his ears. Already beginning to choke, he bridled against the rope, but they dragged him onwards to the tree.

At the oak, ivy twined around the mighty bulk of the trunk and trailed upwards to wreathe around knotted, corrugated branches. The bark was tough and had weathered centuries. Like raindrops upon waxy leaves, the lives of numerous men had come and gone, and the tree had survived them all. Three men cast the rope up and looped it over one of the highest boughs. The rest of the mob stepped back as the men hoisted Kit into the air. With unbearable force the rope gnawed into his throat. His neck ached under the weight of his body.

His feet left the ground sharply.

He clawed at the noose but couldn't undo it.

Higher and higher, in little tugs, he rose up and up and over the jeers of the crowd, kicking his feet wildly. He caught sight of the faces below, watched them change from fierceness to awe as the life began to trickle out of him. Some chose to look away...

Suddenly, at the edge of the park, Henslowe appeared with a large crowd of men behind him, many of them from the tavern. Their sleeves were rolled up and their posture was stooped forward in readiness, spoiling for a fight.

Henslowe whipped his fingers into the air.

"Here we are lads!" he cried. "Let's send them to their maker!"

The men unleashed a thunderous roar and swelled into the park towards the oak. Frightened at the noise, the Puritans spun around to face the new threat. The tavern-goers surged into the mob, punching both men and women alike, pounding them with heels and knuckles. The Puritans soon recovered and the groups clashed at even force.

In the distraction, few were still concerned about the hanging. Kit summoned the last of his strength and gripped the rope above him and worked at rocking his legs to and fro till a momentum built and sent him swinging near the trunk of the oak. He swung closer with each arc, his toes just inches away, just a fraction away, then reaching the tree. With all the force left inside him he pushed his feet off the trunk and careened out towards the men holding the rope and kicked at their hands and their heads. He freed the rope. Plummeted downwards. Slammed his back into the earth. Within moments, he sprang to his feet, tore away the noose, struck out at his captors, and fought to escape the turmoil of fists and elbows.

Meanwhile, Will rode into the park on horseback, drawing another horse along behind him. At the edge of the mob he halted and waved frantically to get Kit's attention.

"Kit!" he bawled. "Over here!"

Through the mass of bodies, flailing arms, bleeding faces, thumps and moans, Kit spotted him. He filled with aching gratitude. Will hadn't abandoned him after all. Fighting all the way, Kit rived through the crowd, dived toward Will and the horses, and leapt up into the saddle.

"Where to?" said Will.

"Scadbury Manor," replied Kit.

They spurred their horses hard and started into a gallop. As they disappeared, the rioters behind continued the ruckus unaware of Kit's departure.

Kit and Will galloped almost non-stop the entire way to Scadbury Manor. Their horses began to foam at the mouth, pant, and toss their sweaty manes with exhaustion. Nevertheless, they made it to the manor grounds in almost record time. Horses' hooves rasped in the gravel drive as they approached the blank, staunch walls of Scadbury. They dismounted at the entrance, but before they could climb the steps, Thomas opened the front door and looked at them grimly.

Kit stopped in his tracks.

"You've heard already?"

Thomas nodded and stepped back to let them enter.

A short time later, Kit stood at the fireplace in the living room, thrusting the poker into the glowing orange coals of the fire. Behind him, Thomas leant forward in an armchair, clasping a goblet of brandy. He swirled the brandy around till it almost reached the brim. At the back of the room, Will lingered by a table of ornaments, pretending to show interest in a set of carved wooden doves. In fact, he was really observing Thomas.

"When?" said Kit miserably.

"Two hours past," replied Thomas, with a slight gleam in his eye.

"That soon?"

"The Privy Council doesn't delay on such matters. They met for an emergency meeting."

"Well, isn't Westminster efficient?" Kit thrust the poker viciously into the coals. "And what kind of mandate did they grant Whitgift?"

Thomas leaned on the arm of his chair, as if pained.

"A fairly extensive one."

"Wonderful."

"I know. It surprised me, too. There'll be a proclamation about all this on the morrow at Guildhall."

"Exactly what powers did they bestow upon him?"

"He has full authority to seek and arrest any and all persons responsible for the posting of the libel."

"Meaning myself."

"Some counselors doubt that you would be so bold as to sign the libel with your own name, but..."

"They still think it's me."

"Obviously you're a prime suspect."

Kit turned his head slightly toward them.

"Well, gentlemen, if you're not too busy, I cordially invite you to my execution." He gave a dry smile. "It should only be a few days hence."

Silence fell. Thomas leant back in his chair and the seat creaked. He took a sip of brandy and noted Will watching him from the corner. Will rapped his nails on the shiny veneer of a table at his side.

"Exactly how long are you going to hang around?" said Will with annoyance.

"The executioner decides that, I think," Kit replied.

Will stepped a little closer.

"You need to get on this tonight. If you find out who's helping Whitgift, there's still time."

"Yes," said Thomas with a magnanimous wave of his hand, "and if there's anything I can do to help, you only have to ask. Perhaps you could take some of my men to aid–"

"No, I'll do this alone," said Kit sharply.

"Nonsense!"

"I can't trust anyone else."

"My thanks for your confidence, Christopher."

"I meant no offense... but I have to be careful now."

"Look, there must be someone. Surely there is at least one person who can be of service to you?"

A second passed. They both turned slowly and glanced at Will. Flecks of red flushed into Will's cheeks. He looked down awkwardly.

"I don't know," he said in a quiet voice. "I don't know."

Still grasping the hot poker in his hand, Kit padded across the room towards him.

"It's up to you, of course," said Kit pointing at him distractedly with the poker. "I don't wish to force anything on you... but I'll have to investigate lords, so you'll get the chance to see life in noble circles."

Will flinched slightly at the poker waving back and forth. Kit suddenly noted the poker was close to Will's face and lowered it.

"You might even see more of life inside court. That could help your writing."

Will didn't respond. Thomas arose slowly from his chair.

"Master Shakespeare," said Thomas grandly, "if your efforts are successful you may also count me as a future patron."

Will hung his head and thought. Kit waited tensely and put the poker down and sighed.

"I guess life has more limits than you think, Will," he said and turned away.

Will finally raised his head and glared at Kit as if scandalized.

"That's a cheap trick!" Will complained.

"What?"

"Playing my words against me like that."

"I'm a playwright. What do you expect?"

They exchanged a quick smile.

"Then you'll help?" said Kit hopefully.

Will paused a moment longer, looked Kit in the eye, and gave a gentle nod.

ACT II

Scene One

London. Lambeth Palace.

On the south bank of the Thames, far removed from the anarchy of Bankside, stood Lambeth Palace. Just minutes upstream from Westminster, Lambeth was the official residence of the Archbishop of Canterbury while he visited London.

The same night that the mob attacked Kit, the moon concealed the stones, turrets, and four towers of the palace in uniform whiteness. Inside the main building, heels rapped down corridors and mingled with the echoes of agitated voices. Bodies rushed past. Candles flickered. Of all areas in the palace, the third floor was the busiest: here lay the offices of administration for the Anglican Church, rooms committed to the censorship of publications, and staff devoted to the location and arrest of Catholic agitators, radical Puritans, and nonconforming church ministers. Not since April, when Whitgift had successfully executed John Greenwood and Henry Barrow for the heretical Marprelate Tracts, had the halls and offices bustled with so much action.

In the largest office, row on row of desks sliced across the room, each one heaped tall with files and parchment. Behind the desks sat clerks on stools trying their best to make sense of the rising mounds of work presented to them.

Past their jaded faces, Whitgift buzzed through the room, his cassock belling out behind him, his sleeves fluttering as he barked orders left and right. The dim light smoothed the wrinkles of his skin, imparting him with a look of youth. Suddenly, he slowed, trod back a few paces, and paused at the desk of a clerk with shaggy hair.

"Sykes," said Whitgift, his voice loud and excited.

"Yes, your worship?" the clerk replied meekly.

"Where's that list I requested?"

"It's–"

"You've had long enough, haven't you?"

"It nears completion as we speak."

"Forsooth! Must I chide everyone in this room to get what I want?"

"I crave forgiveness, your worship."

"Get it to me within the hour."

The clerk nodded, then resumed his work and tried to sweep the hair out of his eyes.

Briefly, Whitgift panned his gaze across the hive of rushing feet, strained eyes, and worn-out faces. His strong fingers twiddled. With a glorious verve, he straightened his shoulders, took a full breath, and propelled his way to the end of the room. He clapped his hands. The noise boomed and rattled the ears of the sleepy clerks.

"You're attention please, everyone," he announced.

The clerks at desks swiveled on their stools to face him. Priests and constables jolted to a stop as they entered the room. Silently, they found a place at the side to listen.

Whitgift ran his eyes over his audience.

"Tonight, we begin to lance out the canker infecting the body and soul of this realm. The morrow's sunrise will light the greatest investigation our kingdom has ever seen." He paraded between the desks waving his hands through the air. "We will hunt down all witnesses of these libels; search and seize property of all suspects; arrest, convict, and execute all who are guilty." Silence passed as he allowed tension to rise within his listeners. He continued, but raised his voice and pulled at the air with his fingers: "We must be equal to our era. If the times are brutal, we must be ever brutal in response. Mercy is for the heart, not for the hand."

Heads nodded in agreement and people swapped comments with their neighbor. A gangly priest shuffled up to Whitgift's side and whispered in his ear. It took only a second, but Whitgift's shoulders drooped a little, his head tilted down, and his posture lessened. The priest stepped back and Whitgift dismissed the room with a jerk of his hand.

"Go! Get yourselves to work."

The clerks turned loathingly back to their files. The doors again jammed with people passing in and out. The hubbub quickly mounted to its previous pitch. Whitgift stuck out his chin and paced toward the exit.

The Archbishop's personal office lay at the end of a twisting corridor, slightly apart from the tumult of the administration room. Inside the office, Thomas now sat across from a grand desk and waited. He yawned nervously and shifted in his seat.

In front of him, Whitgift's desk was fashioned from dark oak and felt sticky to the touch. Surprisingly, the broad, white-walled room contained very little furniture: apart from the desk, there was only a bookcase in one corner, a brown cross on the wall, and a tall cupboard that smelt of incense and damp paper. A draft iced its way around his feet and he shivered inside his coat.

At the back of the room, the door handle shook and Whitgift entered abruptly. Thomas bowed his head.

"A drink, master Walsingham?" Whitgift offered as he sidled around the desk.

"No, thank you," Thomas replied.

"Are you sure? I have some excellent Brandywine."

"I'm fine, your worship." He tried to seem at ease in the hard chair. "How goes the work, so far?"

"Excellent..."

"No trouble?"

"Not yet. Indeed, I believe it was a stroke of genius to post the libel."

Thomas tipped his head graciously.

A small silence followed the comment. Each man seemed to scrutinize the other. Slowly, Whitgift took to his throne-like seat, the back of which stretched high over his head.

"Have you waited long?"

"I entered while you were speaking, actually." A slightly abrasive tone crept into Thomas's voice. "What you said back there sounded very noble."

"I hope so..."

"Do you really believe it all?"

Whitgift smiled wisely.

"To you, the people are just an abstraction, aren't they?"

"Perhaps..."

"Not for myself, master Walsingham. I'm glad to say that I see each and every face. Were they my own children, I couldn't love them more."

"Are you not a little harsh to be their father?"

"No, not at all. I'm simply clear in what I desire and I don't believe there's anything harsh about that. Never underestimate the potency of doubt, or the violence it might cause, if one allowed it to worm into the minds of the people. Ambiguity is the only harshness in life." Whitgift turned his head towards the wall. His eyes lingered on the wooden cross and the thick shadow it cast over the white paint. "There are worse fathers than I."

Thomas frowned curiously and shifted in his seat. Gradually, Whitgift regained his focus. He rapped his fingers on the desk.

"Are you sure the espionage services at your disposal will suffice to stop the spread of atheism?"

"I can give you access to intelligence reports from every major European city," Thomas replied. "Confidential delivery of sensitive documents. Weapons. A legion of men skilled in sabotage, entrapment, manipulation, and assassination. You would want for nothing."

"Good. If the Queen won't do it, I must have my own secret means to censor, torture, and execute heretics."

Thomas nods.

"And Christopher Marlowe," said Whitgift. "Where is he now?"

"Gone to press the Earl of Derby."

"The Earl? Was that wise?"

"He won't find anything. I sent him there with Will Shakespeare, another playwright."

"As long as he's distracted..."

The draft around Thomas's legs returned. He drew his feet under the chair and inched forward.

"From now on," said Thomas precisely, "our actions need to be more discreet."

"Agreed."

"If we turn this into a simple witch-hunt for Marlowe, certain members of the government will get suspicious."

"Yes, I fully agree, but neither can we relax our pace. What do you suggest as our next action?"

"I'll tell you when it's fully arranged." Thomas leaned forward a little more. "At the moment, I just need you to pay half for printing and posting the libel." He pointed to the top of the desk. "I put the bond to the printmaker there."

Whitgift peered down. A scroll of parchment lay unrolled before him. He surveyed the words, grew disinterested, took a quill, stabbed it into the ink pot and scrawled his signature at the bottom of the bond.

Thomas stood eagerly and reached over. Yet before he could touch the bond, Whitgift pulled it back and out of grasp.

"By the way," said Whitgift archly, "I don't believe you've ever really explained your complaint with Marlowe."

"Yes, you must have forgotten it, your worship. May I have the bond?"

"Would you remind me, then?"

"We'll speak on this later."

"No, we will not. For me to venture into the spy world and have dealings with you is a risky affair, to say the least. It will draw censure and attack against from more than one lord. I must know that I can wholly rely upon you. After all, you know *my* reasons why I wish for Marlowe's public execution – that's why you approached me – but I know only a trifle about what you hope to gain."

"Let's just say he's an obstacle to my advancement," Thomas said reluctantly. "He's a reckless hinde who betrayed the wrong person. I have the strongest reasons to seek his death." He tugged the bond from Whitgift's grip and nervously pushed it inside his coat. "Good enough?"

Whitgift gave him a gratified nod.

"Indeed…. Fare safely and may God be with you, my son."

Thomas bowed swiftly and turned to leave.

Through the maze of corridors, Thomas strode away from the administration offices and met with Frizer, his personal secretary, who stood hunched and waiting at the stairwell. Frizer's red cheeks made him look mawkish. Thomas gave a short huff as he passed down the stairs. They walked light and quick, speaking in hushed tones.

"You got it, sir?" said Frizer, close on Thomas's heels.

Thomas delved inside his coat and teased the bond out of his pocket: a standard note to pay a printmaker with Whitgift's signature on the bottom.

"On one side we have a signed bond..." said Thomas. He turned the bond over "...and on the other, we have the first draft of the libel."

On the reverse side was the original draft of the libel posted throughout London. Thomas and Whitgift had dictated the wording to a clerk who had copied it onto the draft. A trusted printmaker had then printed the draft thirty times onto much larger parchment. Even in the dim light of the stairwell, the signature 'CHRISTOPHER MARLOWE' stood out easily to the eye. Through connecting the draft to Whitgift's bond to pay the printer, Thomas had enough evidence to prove that the Archbishop was unquestionably involved with the libels. In contrast, Thomas had made sure nothing linked himself with the crime.

Frizer's cheeks reddened in admiration.

"Wasn't it dangerous?"

"It'd be far more dangerous not to have it." Thomas slowed and cocked his head. "Remember, the first rule of espionage: never let your guard down."

Frizer nodded wisely as they turned down the last flight of stairs.

"Should thing's go wrong," Thomas continued, "good old Whitgift's the Archbishop of Canterbury, Primate of all England, second only to the royal family. Where's my protection against that?"

Frizer shrugged. Thomas looked at him searchingly, gave a deep sigh, and waved the parchment below his nose.

"This!"

"Oh..."

"This is my protection, you tickle-brained lout!"

Frizer quickly nodded his head.

Thomas burst forward in annoyance, slipped the bond back into his coat, and walked across the hall of the main building. Frizer quickened his pace to keep up. They pushed out of the exit and into the night.

SCENE TWO

London. Coaching Inn.

In order to question the Earl of Derby, Kit and Will had to travel the immense distance from London to the county of Cheshire in the northwest of England. Such a journey took the best part of a week and was taxing even for the young and healthy, therefore they decided to take a coach rather than suffer the saddle-sores and weather exposure involved in riding horses.

Surrounded by the clatter, shouts, and passengers of the inn, Kit and Will waited for their carriage to arrive at the inn's courtyard and pick them up.

"It's strange," said Kit wistfully, "I was just thinking… I may never see my next birthday."

"When is it?" Will replied.

"February."

"Really? What year?"

"Every year," Kit said with a tiny smile.

Will rolled his eyes.

"I love sarcasm first thing in the morning." He crossed his arms. "Anyway, why must our investigation start with Derby? There must be plenty of other people who wish you harm. Indeed, I can't say I really blame them…"

"It has to be a lord. You said it yourself, remember? No one else is likely to command the power and organization needed to post so many libels. Derby's not just my suspect. Thomas suggested him, too. And we both know the Earl no longer favors me."

"So, what's your plan?"

"Plan?" Kit replied dryly.

"The Earl of Derby is an heir to the throne. When we arrive at his castle, you can't just barge in, accusing him of conspiracy."

"No. I'll knock first."

"He's always been very cordial to me."

"That doesn't change anything."

"Just because he canceled your patronage, I don't think—"

"It's one thing to cancel patronage, and quite another to give no reason for it."

Will shook his head, unconvinced. Kit stood up straighter and turned to him.

"He's up to something. The Earl was a fixture at court. Now he's a recluse. Virtually no one's heard of him for the last five months." He arched an eyebrow. "That's worth a few questions, don't you think?"

Will gave a dubious nod. They yanked their bags up from the floor as a carriage finally wheeled into the yard towards them.

During the journey, the rocking of the cab often coaxed Will to sleep, but Kit remained awake and tried to write.

On the first day, he laid a few leaves of parchment over his lap and wrote the title *'Hero and Leander'* at the top of the page. This small amount was almost his total output for the day. Every time he concentrated and slowed his heartbeat and moved the quill nearer to the page, the coach seemed to lurch, jerk to a halt, and collect more passengers. Body after body crammed into the cab and squeezed him tight into the corner. Moreover, the carriage wheels constantly tripped over rocks and bumps, jogging his hand, spitting ink spots everywhere. Five messy, crossed-out pages later, he had written the opening of a poem, not a play. The struggle to create made him irritable for the rest of the night and he rarely answered more than "yes" or "no" to Will as they ate and slept at an inn.

The next day, Will joined Kit in writing as they trundled through the countryside. Now the carriage was empty of passengers they both put their heels up on the seat in front. Kit laid a new sheet of parchment on his knees and stared at its clear open form. The blankness unnerved him. He rolled the quill's nib between his thumb and forefinger. The blankness was still there. He glanced over to Will and watched him fluidly scribble words. Somehow he needed to write a description of Hero. As he sat there in a quiet torture of thought, his eyelids slowly sagged and he lapsed into a doze.

A laugh rang in his ear. His eyes popped open and he frowned, wide awake. It had sounded like a woman's laugh: joyful and lilting but with an undercurrent of plight, reminiscent of the way Audrey had laughed in the tailor's shop. He'd seen many of Elizabeth's handmaids and gentlewomen before, most of them doll-like replicas of the Queen, but Audrey had wit and charm and beauty. It wasn't long since he had seen her in London, yet he hungered for her presence, her embrace more than ever. He bent over his parchment and began to write about Hero:

> 'The outside of her garments were of lawn,
> The lining purple silk, with gilt stars drawn;
> Her wide sleeves green, and bordered with a grove,
> Where Venus in her naked glory strove
> To please the careless and disdainful eyes
> Of proud Adonis, that before her lies.
> Her kirtle blue, whereon was many a stain,
> Made with the blood of wretched lovers slain.
> Upon her head she ware a myrtle wreath,
> From whence her veil reached to the ground beneath.
> Her veil was artificial flowers and leaves
> Whose workmanship both man and beast deceives.
> Many would praise the sweet smell as she passed,
> When 'twas the odor which her breath forth cast;
> And there for honey bees have sought in vain,
> And, beat from thence, have lighted there again.
> About her neck hung chains of pebblestone,
> Which, lightened by her neck, like diamonds shone.
> She ware no gloves; for neither sun nor wind
> Would burn or parch her hands, but to her mind,
> Or warm or cool them, for they took delight
> To play upon those hands, they were so white.

Buskins of shells, all silvered used she,
And branched with blushing coral to the knee;
Where sparrows perched of hollow pearl and gold,
Such as the world would wonder to behold.
Those with sweet water oft her handmaid fills,
Which, as she went, would chirrup through the bills.
Some say for her the fairest Cupid pined
And looking in her face was strooken blind.
But this is true: so like was one the other,
As he imagined Hero was his mother.
And oftentimes into her bosom flew,
About her naked neck his bare arms threw,
And laid his childish head upon her breast,
And, with still panting rocked, there took his rest.
So lovely fair was Hero, Venus' nun,
As Nature wept, thinking she was undone,
Because she took more from her than she left,
And of such wondrous beauty her bereft.
Therefore, in sign her treasure suffered wrack,
Since Hero's time...'

Kit's hand paused. He tried to think how to end the passage –
how to complete the rhyming couplet. Minutes later he still had
nothing.

By contrast, after filling over ten pages, Will had finished his
writing for the day and now turned his interest toward Kit. The
two rarely discussed their work in progress. Nevertheless, Will
ventured a peek.

"May I see?" said Will hopefully.

"If you must." Kit replied. He kept his hand on the page but
tilted it so Will could read.

As Will sped through the final lines, he hummed to himself
and put a finger on his lip.

"How about: Since Hero's time hath half the world been
black."

Kit nodded gently as if running the words over in his mind.

"Half the world... been black... I don't know..."

With a reluctant smile, he turned and gave Will a sardonic look.

"Bob Green was right," said Kit.

"What about?"

"You *are* an upstart crow."

Will grinned back at him.

"Well, this crow's famished right about now."

"You're always hungry."

"No, I'm not. When are we stopping?"

Before Kit could answer, the carriage wheels found the smooth dirt road of a village and churned to a stop by the village well. Just a few yards up the road was an alehouse. Will gave a cry of joy, quickly packed his work away, leapt out of the carriage, and made straight for the alehouse door. Kit stayed behind briefly. Once he was sure that he was alone he wrote Will's suggestion down to finish the description.

"Upstart crow," he mumbled to himself with a smile.

The journey up to Cheshire took Kit and Will through the counties of Buckingham, Northampton, and Stafford. Luckily, they rode through Warwickshire and Will suggested they spend a night in Stratford-upon-Avon with his wife Anne and his three children. Kit was tired of the poor quality inns they had seen so far and readily obliged.

Will's home in Stratford consisted of two rooms over a grain merchant's shop on the main street: one room served as the master chamber, the other served as the kitchen, living room, and children's bedchamber. Since Will had been unable to send word in advance, their visit surprised Anne.

Anne had lank, mouse-brown hair, a matronly frame and strong wrists. Older than the two men, she exuded a demure confidence and moved about languorously. She was quickly overjoyed to see Will after so many months away in London and scolded him gently for not replying promptly enough to her letters. Towards Kit, she played the generous hostess and took every care to make him feel at home. Though her kitchen was mean, she prepared them all a delicious pea soup, and rapidly cooked some parsnips to go with a smoked ham she'd been saving. For desert, they shared half an apple tart – the crust brittle and golden, yet creamy to the palate. Kit said it was the best meal he'd ever tasted.

As for the children, little Judith took a liking to Kit immediately: he couldn't sit down without her climbing up onto his knee, and before bed she'd enticed him in to telling her a story. Hamnet, her twin brother, was poorly with stomach cramps and lay confined to his bed in the corner. In contrast, Susana, though only ten years old, was the eldest child and had already acquired a degree of maturity. She followed her mother everywhere. When asked a question, she stood on the spot with her hands precociously clasped behind her back and answered in an articulate, serious manner.

In the late evening hours, once the children were asleep, Anne, Will, and Kit sat around the fire and chatted over pewter cups brimful with Brandywine. Will and Anne snuggled together, and hardly a moment passed when Will didn't dote on her in some way – refilling her cup, picking off the crumbs from the coarse fabric of her dress, or stroking her hand. Kit watched them with a smile. The next day, when he and Will started back on the road, he told Anne he was sorry to leave and he meant it deeply.

During the second half of the journey, the countryside became full of heaths and windswept pastures, and the roads pressed through the dips and rises of wide, bare-back hills. Fields now lay vast and open, studded with soft black molehills and pale, twisting long grasses. Horsechestnuts grew near the roadside and bared their pointed white blooms to the sky like teeth.

Finally, at the journey's end, the coach rolled into Cheshire and the driver dropped them at the large town of Wallasey on the Wirral Peninsula. From there, Kit and Will rented horses and rode out into the lands of Leasowe Castle, home of the Earl of Derby.

About ten miles of land surrounded the Earl's castle. Kit couldn't believe the grounds that Derby possessed: to him, it seemed like a country within a country. Exhausted from the hectic days of travel, they cantered along a cliff edge and gazed across to the castle on the horizon – a single, octagonal tower.

From a distance, Leasowe struck up from the earth as a proud, white column.

Up close, however, the castle looked less as a shining pillar, and more as a block of brown stone locked into place by a flat roof. Kit had only been there once in the past and he now frowned at the sight before him. The sides were broad and blank. Windows squinted at the sun and were mullioned with thick lead bars.

Will and Kit called at the front door and were received by a Porter with a beakish nose and tiny eyes. He led them through the hall with his head tilted up, like a bird displaying its plumage.

"You should've announced your visit in writing... sir," said the Porter with mild annoyance.

"We lacked the time," Kit grumbled back.

"Even so, I cannot guarantee his lordship will be delighted at the prospect of guests. I fear you may have wasted your trip. I doubt very much he will see either of you."

"Just tell him our names: Christopher Marlowe and –"

"Yes, you've told me already, sir." He jabbed his finger toward a bench. "Wait there, if you will, while I inform his lordship of your company." He strutted away and climbed a grand staircase, the floorboards squeaking beneath his feet.

Will gaped at the splendor of his surroundings. Kit rubbed his sore neck. Black, interlocking oak beams ran across the hall ceiling and pillars stood at the sides of the room. Everything was oversized and grand, but there was nothing elaborate or imaginative in the design – no wood inlays, no carving, and little paint. To the right a deer's head was mounted high up the wall and the deer's glazed eyes gave a dull gleam in the light. Both the men took a seat on the bench and waited.

Nearly half an hour later, the Porter still hadn't returned. Will took the chance to lay back and nap against the wall. Meanwhile, Kit pulled out a leaf of parchment and a pencil and tried to write. Despite his attempts, he progressed no further with *'Hero and Leander'*. Slowly, Will's body slid across and leaned into him, so that Will's sleepy head rested on his shoulder. He sighed.

92

The Porter tramped down the stairs and approached the two men. Kit shook Will and they both rose to their feet.

"His lordship cannot see anyone, today," said the Porter dryly.

"You told him our names?"

"Yes."

"You're sure?"

"Very."

Kit scratched the side of his cheek. His eyes roamed around his surroundings.

"But... I don't understand... Why would he..."

The Porter ignored him and gestured to the door. A barrel-chested Doorman opened it.

"My apologies," said the Porter, again pointing to the door. "If you'll be so good as to leave now."

"No," said Kit through clenched teeth. "Do you know how long we've traveled to get here? Do you have any idea?"

"And what is it you want from me?"

"I demand a reason."

"Demand what you like, sir, but do it elsewhere."

Kit took a step forward.

"Where? Upstairs, for instance?"

The Porter furrowed his brow and glanced nervously to the Doorman for support.

Suddenly, Kit burst into a run. Charged past the Porter. Dashed across the hall, flew up the staircase, clearing two, three steps at a time.

Will, the Porter, and the Doorman hesitated with surprise, then chased after him.

"You can't go up there!" yelled the Porter.

Kit rushed up the first flight of stairs in seconds. Fingers grasping the banister rail, he swung his body around the corner and bounded up the next staircase to the third floor. Feet trammeled the steps just behind him.

At the top, he spied two giant oak doors at the end of the corridor – the doors to a master bedchamber. He veered left toward them. Heels and toes stampeded around the corridor just behind him. The sound lashed at his growing sense of panic. He sprinted harder. The doors loomed quickly before him. Without breaking stride, he dived for the handles, tore the doors open, and barged inside to find the Earl.

SCENE THREE

Leasowe Castle. Master Bedchamber.

The room was airless. Dark. It appeared to cramp around Kit like a cavern. Musty, half-drawn curtains oppressed the windows. An odor of sweat percolated throughout the room. As soon as Kit entered he halted in shock. Upon a bed, mired in swathes of quilted covers, lay the weak, sickly frame of the Earl of Derby.

Derby's ashen skin aged his looks beyond his thirty-four years. Diluted blue irises swam around the center of his eyes. Fair but faded hair drooped from his head. He had suffered a tremendous weight-loss since Kit had last seen him in London: his nose and cheeks protruded from his face, and his jaw looked as brittle as the rim of a glass goblet. His bed-shirt seemed baggy around his neck, and he gripped his sheets with skeletal fingers. There was little left of the princely socialite and patron of the arts that Kit had once known.

On Kit's entry, Derby sat up and leant back on supportive pillows. The two men regarded one another in silence till the thunder of feet arrived at the room's entrance. The Porter and the Doorman instantly lunged for Kit and grabbed him by the arms. Will stood anxiously to the side.

"Leave them be a minute," croaked Derby.

"But, my lord, they're not–"

"Enough! I said let them alone."

Both the Porter and the Doorman gave Derby a surprised look. They released Kit and retreated from the room. Once they were gone, Kit padded closer to the bed.

"Pray pardon, your lordship."

"For what?"

"I didn't know you were so unwell."

"Would it have made a difference if you *had* known?"

"I'd never have–"

"Spare me the pleasantries. You haven't come here to be polite."

"I didn't mean to upset you, my lord."

"You're not upsetting me. You're disturbing me at my meal." Derby glanced down at the tray of food on his lap: a kipper, orange segments, a bowl of walnuts, and slices of wheat bread. Gold leaf edgework rimmed the tray and glistered with small specks of light. He glared up at Kit bitterly. "I take it you're here about the libels in London."

Kit raised his eyebrows.

"Word certainly travels fast to this corner of the country."

"Faster than the crow flies."

"I didn't think you'd know about it so soon."

"Oh, I think you'd be surprised at what I know." Derby looked hesitantly at a slice of bread. His hand shook a little as he raised it to his mouth and nibbled at the crust.

Will observed him with interest but remained quiet at the side of the room. Kit straightened his posture and suddenly looked awkward.

"My lord, there's something I'm compelled to ask you."

"You think I had something to do with it?" Derby's bloodless lips twisted into a smile. "The libels? That's what you want to ask, isn't it?"

"Did you?"

"Why do you question me, I wonder? Because I canceled your patronage?"

Kit wiped his brow and didn't answer.

"I canceled your patronage," continued Derby, "because I support only art, not artfulness."

"So, then... it's in the open." He sighed and locked eyes with Derby. "You found out?"

Each man watched the other with a wary expression. Neither knew what to say next.

96

Will frowned at them both. He crossed over the room and moved nearer the bed, touching the glossy bedpost with his fingertips.

"Am I missing something? Found out about what?" he asked innocently.

Derby craned his head toward him.

"Oh, didn't you know? He hasn't told you yet?"

Will shrugged. Kit froze on the spot and turned strangely expressionless and held the breath in his lungs. After a moment, Derby grew impatient and answered for him.

"Your friend's a spy in the service of Lord Burghley."

Will's face dropped in surprise. He glanced at Kit from the corner of his eye.

"It's not true, is it?"

Kit nodded slowly.

"They recruited me at Cambridge," he explained with difficulty. "It was just a way to escape the monotony of classes... see the world... put a little money in my purse..."

"I can't believe this."

"Well, it's true," said Derby. "And I have the sources to prove it." He shifted his position in bed, as if suddenly tiring, and turned back to face Kit. "So, I believe your questions is answered. Now if you don't mind, gentlemen, I'd like to eat in privacy."

Silence. Kit watched the dust fall in little semi-circles through the air. The front of his shirt clung to his chest, slightly damp from sweat. His back ached all over. Both he and Will bowed solemnly and moved towards the door. Derby picked up another slice of bread with his bony hands, tore it in two, and put the smallest piece to his lips. As Kit and Will reached the door, Will shook his head slightly, as if recovering from Kit's revelation, and pivoted back towards Derby.

"May I ask one thing, my lord?" said Will.

Derby held a piece of bread and waited for Will to continue.

"How long have they been poisoning you?"

Derby closed his eyes.

"Nearly half a year," he replied under his breath.

Kit's eyes shot back and forth between Will and Derby, unsure what to make of it.

"I don't understand," said Kit. "Who's poisoning you?" He strode back into the room. "Why would anyone–"

"Enough!" croaked Derby. He released a small, guttural moan which hinted at the corrosion inside of him. He continued speaking in a fainter voice. "I'm being poisoned because there are forces abroad that see me as a powerful Catholic figurehead. They want me on the throne – not our Protestant Queen. Such forces use men like yourself, master Marlowe, to coerce me. They think they can poison me into betrayal."

Kit felt dizzy from the shock. He knelt at the bed.

"But... you don't have to live like this."

"I've tried everything."

"No. There must be something more you can do. You can't live like this."

"I doubt I'll have that problem much longer."

"Oh god... there must be something you haven't tried?"

Derby shook his faded blond hair.

"I replace my cooks, my entire staff every week. Nothing works. And I have no wish to endanger friends with my situation."

"But you're *Derby*. You have so much wealth."

"Wealth doesn't break limits, it merely changes them. This castle is a cell. My servants are my wardens."

Both Kit and Will watched in horror as Derby ate his slice of bread.

"*Quod me nutrit me destruit*, gentlemen: what nourishes me destroys me. In future, I suggest you probe the spy network for conspiracy, not sickly lords."

Kit stood motionless. Pity descended upon him like a dark blanket, but it couldn't smother the rising fear in his belly. A thick sheen of sweat coated the Earl's forehead. Kit raised the back of his hand and wiped the sweat now beading on his own brow.

Outside, clouds drove across the sky in furrows, each seeded with pink and blue. The sun ploughed below the horizon and the

promise of rain hung about the air. After the stuffiness of the castle, the coolness of the twilight sky felt refreshing to the skin.

With a strained silence between them, Kit and Will exited
the castle, found where they had tethered their horses, and
climbed back up into the saddle. Apart from the distant whisper
of waves, the only sound on the drive was the champ of horses'
teeth and the rattle of halter chains. Kit uttered a deep sigh and
looked pleadingly at Will.

"Look, it's not something I can go around telling everyone."

Will narrowed his eyes.

"I didn't want you to tell everyone," he replied sharply.

"Will–"

"Maybe you don't believe in yourself, but I *do* expect you to
trust in me."

Kit bowed his head.

"I'm sorry. I should've told you sooner. It's just that I'm not
accustomed to working with others. That's how I've survived as a
spy." After a moment, he leaned closer to Will and changed the
subject. "Anyway, for what we have to do next, I should explain
the ways of espionage in our country."

"If you're sure you can trust me…"

Kit lowered his voice and did his best to describe the confusing labyrinth of the intelligence world. He explained that all spies
served the Queen officially, but in reality they worked for any
lord who offered them advancement and money. Since most lords
were rivals for the Queen's favor, their private spies spent more
time sabotaging each other than engaged in any useful work. Sir
Francis Walsingham had briefly centralized the intelligence service under his sole command and eliminated the in-fighting and
rivalries of noblemen. However, after Sir Francis died, Lord
Burghley had assumed control of the network. Burghley was now
old and his immense power was gradually slipping. Hence, the
espionage system had begun to crumble once again.

Stunned and slightly repulsed, Will listened to it all quietly.

"Who do you work for, then?" he asked.

"Lord Burghley," Kit replied. "He might be aged, but he still
controls the most powerful spy circle in the land. Thomas works

as one of his section chiefs in charge of an entire group of men. One of those men… is me."

"So what now? How do we learn which other lords are set against you?"

"We need to get our hands on some intelligence reports. On the morrow we'll head back toward London, stop overnight, then go on to Portsmouth – there's a man there who intercepts messages from the continent. Maybe he has some answers?"

Will hunched his back a little and gave a slight nod. He had nothing more to say.

"Just be careful from now on," Kit warned. "The spy world is thick with knives and shadows." He spurred his horse into a canter and rode off down the drive.

SCENE FOUR

Scadbury Manor.

Rays of morning sun fell slanted around the gardens and speared into the leaves of rose bushes. Flourishes of redness burst from the blooms – deep and rich like freshly struck blood. Thorns dripped with dew. Roots suckled at the warming soil.

Inside the manor, despite the early hour, Audrey had already awoken and dressed for the day. Since the Queen arose at six thirty, Audrey herself had to be washed and dressed by five thirty so as to make the journey into London in good time. As Gentlewoman of the Privy Chamber, Audrey was considered a companion to the Queen and had a clearly defined set of duties that Elizabeth expected her to perform every morning and every evening.

Her most important morning task was to help Elizabeth select garments for the day, and give advice on make-up, jewelry, and styling of hair. Once Elizabeth had dressed and eaten her morning sustenance, Audrey and the gentlewomen then accompanied her to Morning Prayer. Thereafter, the Queen's day formally began and the gentlewomen could retire from her presence to administer their own affairs until the evening.

At midmorning, Audrey left the palace and would return at five o'clock in the afternoon. Her evening duties mainly involved providing musical entertainment for the Queen. Indeed, her skills with the harp originally helped sway the Queen to appoint her to the prestigious title of gentlewoman over the many other ladies who were suitable for the position.

Throughout the middle of the day, Audrey spent her own time overseeing the household staff at Scadbury. On Monday, during the third week of May, Kit sent word on his return trip that he would arrive at Scadbury that evening. As soon as Audrey received the note, she went into a frenzy of preparations: she had the guest chamber made-up again, ordered more supplies for the buttery and beer cellar, had the silverware polished, and visited the kitchen to give requests for supper that evening. Once all was done, she tried to relax a little. The news of Kit's arrival had half-elated her; half filled her with despair and guilt. Strange scenarios and fantasies drifted through her thoughts – words that should never be spoken, meetings that should never exist, embraces that should never last. It was wrong to break her marriage vows, but she could think of nothing else. Part of her spirit withered away every time she curtsied to the Queen or pretended to smile and laugh with her husband at a ball. She visualized her soul wasted and crinkled, like a dried autumn leaf. Kit was the only one who made her feel fresh and lush with youth. He was worth caring about.

To clear her head before Kit arrived, Audrey decided she needed some time outside and elected to take a ride through the manor grounds. With a riding crop in hand, she stood just inside the entrance to the stables and waited while the stable groom limped around and saddled her sleek, white-and-gray stallion. She turned idly and caught an odd flashing movement in the corner of her vision.

She twisted her head fully to the right and stared out of the stables. Across the back lawns, from a set of brushwood bordering the forest, a man emerged: the distance blurred his features, but his clothes and hair were brown. He strode swiftly over the lawn toward the back of the house. Audrey lowered the crop. She squinted at his figure.

"Is that Peter?" she murmured into the stables.

The stable groom glanced over the saddled horse, then shrugged and returned to fiddling with the saddle straps.

Audrey took a lazy step out of the stable door.

"I need to speak with him about the roses. They're diseased again."

The stable groom didn't reply. She left the stables behind and ambled after the man.

"Peter!" she called in a lilting voice. "Peter, I must speak with you!"

The man didn't turn, nor slow, nor react in any way. He kept up his pace and seemed not to hear. Audrey filled her lungs and called again.

"Peter! Stay a minute!"

This time, the man definitely heard her voice. He quickened his gait. Turned the corner to the back of the house and disappeared.

Audrey took a few more paces and paused. She tapped the riding crop suspiciously against the side of her leg, then shot forward and marched across the drive. Her feet crunched on the gravel. Her dress whished about her legs.

When she turned the corner the man had vanished. She twitched her nose and prowled ahead slowly, uneasily, her eyes and ears keen to catch the smallest movement or noise. A blackbird tore a brown worm out of the grass. A windowpane creaked.

At the back of the house, there were two doors, but she always kept them locked. She approached each one and checked the handle. It wouldn't turn. Flummoxed, she scanned the forest, the lawn, and the rose gardens. She stopped, her brow crossed. She inspected the border of shrubs along the rear wall of the house and drew her breath sharply. A large laurel hedge showed a broken twig.

She stepped closer and examined it. The break was white and fresh. Carefully, using one hand and the riding crop, she pushed back the leaves and branches.

Nestled just behind in the wall lay a small door.

Her eyes widened with surprise.

She took a small look over her shoulder and squeezed around the bush to the wall. Laurel leaves rustled loudly. Branches picked at her waist. The hidden door stood at half the normal size and she had to stoop to grip the handle. It turned stiffly, as if rusted, but soon clicked and the door opened. She craned her head down to see. It was dark inside.

She hesitated and considered what to do next. The handle had left a burgundy stain on her palm, like dried blood, and she wiped it off. Her heart pumped sharply. As she bent down further, the sides of her bodice pinched her breath. With another look over her shoulder, she made certain no one was around, then peeled the door back enough to enter...

SCENE FIVE

Secret Passage.

Audrey ventured a step through the door. Darkness increased rapidly. She stopped and crouched, ready for anything. She listened but heard only her own breathing. The space felt narrow and strangely warm, but the hairs on her arm turned brittle as if frozen, and the surface of her skin bobbled into goose bumps. She bumped her toe against a hard object in front. Just enough light came from the open door behind her to define the edge of a step – the start of a winding staircase. She went to move up the staircase, then turned back and shut the door behind her so that no one outside would discover the passage.

She now stood in total darkness. Coal-black shadows sooted the air. Walls pinched her shoulders. The ceiling scraped her head. She crept forward, feeling her way, pointing her toes, placing each foot lightly, noiselessly down as she climbed the tight, winding staircase all the way to the top. All the while, the silk sleeves of her dress whispered as she crept, hissing an alarm at her presence. As she climbed higher and higher, round and round, step by step, a steady glow projected onto the stones from somewhere ahead.

After she had climbed enough steps to be on the second floor, the staircase ended abruptly at another door. It was closed. Light fringed it on all sides. Muffled voices leaked away from it into the passageway. She moved closer to hear, reached out gently, slowly extending her hand. Her fingertips alighted the door's flatness. Softly, she pressed close to the door, turned her head, and laid her ear flat to the wood to listen...

...On the other side of the door lay Thomas's study. Wood paneling covered the walls from floor to ceiling and the joins seamlessly hid the secret door in the left wall. Thomas's long desk stood in the very center of the room. On the left chair, now reading through a document in his hands, sat the man that Audrey had followed. Thomas stood at his side and crossed his arms. Meanwhile, at the back of the room, Whitgift stood by a window and gazed outside into the gardens.

The man in the chair went by the name of Richard Cholmeley: a spy employed by Thomas. Cholmeley's face was gray and he wore a brown tunic – the sleeves tied on at the shoulder with crude black rope. At his waist, a black-hilted dagger jutted from a scabbard and the awkward way in which he sat suggested that other weapons were hidden about his person. While reading, Cholmeley's mouth opened, but before he could ask a question, Thomas cut him off.

"Just read it through to the end," Thomas snapped.

Cholmeley's face darkened with misgiving, but he returned to his reading.

Minutes passed and Thomas glanced disinterestedly around his study. At the far end, a portrait of his cousin Sir Francis Walsingham hung in a position of honor over the mantelpiece. Sir Francis was dressed in a black gown and cap set against a black background. A cropped beard almost hid his lips. His eyes were blank and interrogating. Thomas looked on the portrait enviously: he longed for its effortless power. Sir Francis had known the unorthodox views, the scandalous vices, and guilty passions of everyone at court but had never once fallen victim to his own desires. He was the very icon of control. He was sublime. Quietly, Thomas turned back to Cholmeley and continued to supervise him.

Meanwhile, over at the window, Whitgift seemed entranced by the view outside. The study overlooked the rose gardens at the side of the house: in the middle of the gardens a shiny-faced maid now sat on a bench with a small boy on her lap. Another boy played with a wooden toy in the dirt at her feet.

"Are those your boys, Thomas?" said Whitgift, his breath turning to small, clear droplets on the window glass.

Thomas looked up from Cholmeley, annoyed at the distraction.

"What?" Thomas replied.

"Are you the father of those children out in the rose garden?"

"What children?"

"Out there."

"No."

"Your marriage is childless, then?"

"Evidently."

"Ah... Pity about that..." Whitgift pulled on the wisps of his beard as he mused. "There's no love like the affection shared between parent and child."

"If you say so."

"I had such wonderful parents, God rest their souls. Perhaps in heaven–"

"Actually, Archbishop, we have some earthly matters in need of attention."

Whitgift raised his eyebrows and parted from his reverie. With a last look at the rose gardens and the children, he shuffled around over to the desk and came to stand on the other side of Cholmeley.

Cholmeley set the document down uneasily. He rested back a little on the cushion, his face pensive.

"Well?" said Thomas, growing impatient.

"Let me understand this," Cholmeley replied. "Someone's gonna make these charges against me to get at Marlowe?"

Thomas unfolded his arms and stood up straight.

"Yes, the various accusations in this document aren't important."

"Then why are they–"

"Only one charge matters."

"What one?"

"The charge that states you've heard Marlowe deliver atheist lectures to prominent government ministers."

At this, Cholmeley lowered his eyes thoughtfully but said nothing. Whitgift laid a fatherly hand on his shoulder.

"My dear fellow," said Whitgift, "we just need to log the charges on record. Once they're filed, my people will try to hunt you down – but just for appearances. They won't really catch you."

Cholmeley nodded.

"And what's in it for me?"

Thomas cleared his throat.

"When the Archbishop and I consolidate our fledgling spy network, we'll promote you."

"To what?"

"Case Officer on the continent."

"Why me, anyway? Why do I have to do this?"

"Must I recount your debts?"

Cholmeley grunted and turned his head away. Thomas leant nearer to him.

"If you do this, I'll absolve you of all monies owed to me."

"Hmm..."

"Do we have an agreement?"

"I don't know. I want a written note that the charges are false, in case I'm caught." Cholmeley watched Thomas for any sign of disagreement.

Thomas shrugged.

"Anything else?"

"Wait a minute... Yeah, I want a guarantee of promotion, too."

Thomas glanced over at Whitgift.

"Done," he said resolutely.

A moment passed as Cholmeley watched Thomas and Whitgift. Finally, he eased himself up from the chair and shook hands with both men to seal the agreement...

...Back inside the secret passageway, Audrey stood away from the door. She had to stop herself from tripping backwards. Her mouth gaped open in shock.

SCENE SIX

Scadbury Manor.

The grounds of Scadbury mellowed in the late afternoon sunlight. Bees murmured between rose petals. Birdsong echoed beneath the limbs of cool oaks and shaded maples. On a rented horse, Kit trotted up the long gravel drive, rounded the last corner, and came into view of the manor. He sat back in the saddle and relaxed. He slued his horse left towards the stables. At the stable entrance he dismounted, called for the stable groom, but no voice replied. With a shrug of his shoulders, he led the horse into the stables himself and found a vacant stall.

Much of the stalls were shadowed and sunlight raked through the cracks in the wall, stippling the straw. As he drew his horse into the stall, it jerked its head in refusal. He stroked its nose to calm it and spoke soothingly. Eventually, he reached to undo the saddle straps, but the horse stamped loudly, thudding the straw.

Kit suddenly halted all his movements. He felt strangely exposed. His back tingled with nerves. He detected the scent of someone else in the stall with him.

While keeping both hands on the saddle, he turned his head slowly and peered into the shadows of the corner. Audrey stared back at him.

"In faith! Audrey!" he said, smiling and recovering quickly from the shock. "You scared the life out of me!"

She didn't reply. He looked closer at her and his face soon became serious.

"What in god's name are you doing here?"

With clasped hands, she trod slightly nearer, her face taut and grave. She looked queasy.

"What's wrong?" he asked, growing more and more concerned with every moment.

"I heard him..." she replied, her voice faint.

"Who?"

"They were scheming together."

"Who was?"

"In the study."

"You're not making any sense. Who did you hear in the study?"

"Thomas, I heard Thomas."

Kit stood away from the horse and waited for her to finish. She gulped.

"With Whitgift."

His eyes dropped to the ground. Nervously, he scuffed his foot against the straw.

"Nothing's unseemly about that," he said, unconvinced by his own words. "I'm sure there are many reasons that could press them to meet."

"No, you must believe me, you must."

"Perchance you're mistaken?"

She shook her head.

"They were plotting against you."

He grimaced. Nausea shivered through him. In truth, the news wasn't really so unexpected. He muttered to himself pensively.

"This is worse than I thought.... if Thomas works for Lord Burghley, it must mean Whitgift... Whitgift and Burghley have formed a union against me..."

For a few moments, neither he nor Audrey spoke. The stables sounded only with the rattle of halter chains and the scrape of horses in stalls. Ever since that night in the guest chamber, Kit had worried that his patron would seek some form of devious retribution. Thomas had probably leapt at the chance to help Whitgift and even talked Lord Burghley into a permanent alliance. Now it seemed the two most powerful men the realm –

the Archbishop of Canterbury and the Lord High Treasurer –
were both set on achieving his public execution.

Outside, someone's footsteps crunched along the gravel and
moved closer to the stables. Kit and Audrey flinched. The steps
were heavy and plodding.

"Who's that?" Kit whispered.

"Probably the maid," Audrey whispered back.

At the stable door, a short, plump shadow blocked out the
light.

"My lady, supper is served," the maid called through the stable doors.

Audrey paced out of the stall and up to the entrance.

"I'll be there anon," she replied firmly.

The maid sauntered off to the house. Once she had gone,
Audrey circled back around to the stall. Kit strode toward her.
The muscles in his back drew taut.

"What did you hear?" he said urgently. "I must know every
word they said."

Audrey gave a nervous glance out of the stables and was
slow to respond.

"Tell me," he pleaded.

She put her hand lightly on his chest.

"Not now," she replied.

"When?"

"Meet me at midnight in the hall. I'll show you how to get into the study undetected. You can search it yourself."

Still in shock, the tension in Kit's posture subsided. He nodded his head. Audrey's eyes lingered on him sympathetically,
then she stepped out of the stables and headed for the house.

Kit tucked a lock of hair behind his ear and his finger trembled. He watched Audrey disappear and tipped his head up and
looked out of the stables, down the drive, over the tree tops, and
beyond into the Cray Valley. On the farthest ridge, the chalky
white tip of the moon arose and marked the sky.

SCENE SEVEN

Scadbury Manor. Guest Bedchamber.

The moon cast a shade over Kit's face as he sat on his bed. After an awkward supper with Audrey and Thomas, Audrey had departed for the royal palace at Greenwich and Kit had retired for the night. Despite Thomas's protests, Kit had managed to slink away while apologizing and explaining that he was tired from his journey.

As soon as he was alone in the bedchamber, his face drained of expression and he fell into a deep maelstrom of thought. After hours of contemplation, he flopped onto the bed exhausted. A drippy candle on his side table displayed roman numerals down its length to mark the hours: eleven o'clock.

He rolled onto his side and collected a wad of parchment from the side table. With a small moan, he lifted the quill, dipped it in the ink and paused. His mind returned to *'Hero and Leander'*. Now that he had made a physical description of both Hero and Leander, he needed to write the first meeting of the two lovers. Pensively, he nibbled the feathers of his quill and tried to think of all that he wanted to show. His lips were dry. His mouth tasted sour. He looked over to the candle again. It still wasn't twelve o'clock. He dipped the quill with ink once more, then lowered his hand to the page. Almost through a sheer act of will he put the nib of his quill to the parchment and scratched several pages. He ended the scene with the following words:

> *'It lies not in our power to love or hate,*
> *For will in us is overruled by fate.*

When two are stripped, long ere the course begin
We wish that one should lose, the other win.
And one especially do we affect
Of two gold ingots like in each respect.
The reason no man knows; let it suffice
What we behold is censured by our eyes.
Where both deliberate, the love is slight:
Who ever loved, that loved not at first sight?'

Contentedly, he scanned over the passage and wafted the page through the air to dry the ink.

Sprightly footsteps tapped down the corridor outside. He sat up and listened as they breezed past his room. He stayed motionless but heard no other sounds.

Immediately, his hands turned greasy. He collected the sheets of writing on his bed into a pile, got up, slipped shoes on his feet, and went for the door. He opened it smoothly, but not wide, and poked his head out into the corridor. No one around. No lights shone from any bedchamber.

Silently, he left his room and tiptoed along the corridor to the stairs, barely drawing a breath. Once down the staircase, he stepped out warily across the hall tiles, his long shadow following him in the moonlight. His eyes searched but found no one. Stoked by fear, an odd warmth trickled through his chest and stomach.

"Audrey," he whispered out into the hall.

Silence. His nerves felt raw. He crept forward, his desperation growing with every step. He rubbed his eyes, prowled near the wall, and whispered out again.

"Audrey!"

No answer.

"Audrey, are you there!"

Still waiting for a reply he passed by a shadowed corner.

A hand snatched out at his shoulder.

He spun around, drew his dagger instantly, almost struck...

He looked closer. The hand was pale and delicate, without marks or calluses. Long, elegant fingers extended with almond-shaped nails. Kit pressed into the shadows, his eyes adjusted, and he found Audrey now stood before him. She waved for him to follow and together they whisked away over the tiles to leave the hall.

Suddenly, Audrey lurched to a stop. Kit nearly toppled into her. Crouched together, they both listened carefully: from ahead came a steady footfall – the clomping steps of a nightwatchman. She pulled Kit back. They flatted their shoulder blades against the side of the staircase. In front, the nightwatchman's dim figure emerged as he passed by the hall. A ring of keys dangled from his belt. Once he was gone, Kit and Audrey scurried off.

Audrey led Kit deep into the manor, down corridors and passages he had never seen before, to the back staircase. From there, they descended to the servant quarters, passed the servant bedchambers, the meal room, and left the house through the kitchen's rear door.

Outside, they ventured warily onto the path behind the house. The half moon glinted in the night sky like a shard of broken glass. Audrey held a candlestick and lighted it on a wall torch. Her breath misted through the cold.

"Over here," she whispered, leading him to the laurel bush.

Gently, he helped her push back the waxy leaves and crackling twigs. She stooped forward and threw candlelight upon the secret door. Kit bent his head nearer and looked back at her in disbelief. Within moments, they ducked underneath the door and entered the passageway.

Audrey lit the way along the passage with her candle. The light reflected off the narrow walls, almost blinding them as they mounted the staircase. Kit noticed that whenever Audrey glanced downwards her eyelashes made tiny shadows on the tops of her cheeks. Without makeup her skin looked fresh and clear. He checked himself: this wasn't the time to stop and admire her. He kept his head down and concentrated on climbing the steps in front. One step. Two step. He couldn't help it – he looked up again. Her hips swayed in front of him. Raven tresses of hair bounced against her shoulders. Her bodice defined the crisp arch of her back. To climb easier, she hitched her shirt up just above her shoes and he glimpsed the shapely outline of her anklebone beneath her white silk stocking. It couldn't have been more erotic if he'd seen her own flesh.

At the top of the staircase, she reached out, found the latch, tugged the bolt over, and teased open the secret door. With silent, tiny steps, she showed Kit into Thomas's study.

Near the window they stood together and surveyed the gloom. To prevent the candlelight from being noticed by anyone outside the study, Audrey shielded it with a cupped hand, making the light glow red through her fingers. In front, the glister of varnished wood, the shadowy lines of furniture, and the eyes of Francis Walsingham's portrait peered back at them through the dark. Audrey tilted her head close to Kit and whispered.

"I don't understand the secret service," she said innocently.

"Neither do I," Kit whispered back. "No one does."

"But why would they turn on you? You've never betrayed them, have you?"

"No."

"I thought not. You'd never do that. So, why are they against you now?"

"Because there isn't just one secret service – there's many."

"Many?"

"Yes. Lord Burghley heads the official intelligence network, but there are rival spy circles controlled by individual lords. For instance, the Earl of Essex is collecting his own forces to challenge Burghley."

"How strange!"

"It wasn't always so. Sir Francis Walsingham used to dominate all forms of espionage in this country. Ever since he died there's been a power vacuum that Burghley's struggled to fill. Maybe that's why he's made a union with Whitgift?" He shook his head. "It's all becoming a dangerous muddle."

"And which circle do you work in?"

"Thomas and I work in Burghley's..." He picked distractedly at a button on his doublet. "You see, just like the rest of the country, we're at war with ourselves. One circle tries to eliminate the other. Perhaps Burghley's union with Whitgift has provoked him to clean house? Get rid of people he can't trust?"

Audrey glanced down at the candle.

"I'll do my best to help. You know that, don't you?"

"We haven't much time," Kit warned.

"What should I look for?"

"Something that ties Whitgift or Burghley to the libels."

She nodded resolutely.

A moment later, they crept over to the desk, pulled back the drawers at either side, and set to work.

SCENE EIGHT

The Study.

The files held everything from bound reports, to loose sheets, to oddly sized notes of paper that tried to flutter away. Kit and Audrey laid the removed files in neat piles atop the desk, paying special attention to the stacking order so they could replace everything exactly as found. For over half an hour they searched without finding anything of use.

Just as Kit slid a file out from a large desk drawer, he stood up sharply and grabbed Audrey's shoulder. She halted on the spot. From the corridor outside the study came the nightwatchman's footsteps. Slow and dawdling, the footsteps clomped up to the door and moved past and the noise died away again.

Kit and Audrey returned to searching the files. He noticed a glimmer on her shoulder and peered down: the ouroboros brooch he had given her was pinned to the top of her bodice. Candlelight flickered on the scales of the golden serpent. He gazed at it with fascination, as if he had never seen it before: the snake's flat head and straight-lipped mouth devouring its own slender tail. He pointed to it. Audrey smiled and blushed in the gentle candlelight.

"Just wanted to look nice," she said. "It's not everyday I break into my husband's study."

He nodded and smiled. She glanced away and studied the file in her hand.

"Found something?" he said hopefully.

"Yes, I think so."

"Something important?"

"Something important?"

"Maybe. Maybe not."

"Let me look."

"It's a conspiracy." She touched a paragraph in the middle of the page and traced her finger along one of the lines. "It says here the Queen is really a man – that's why she wears so much make-up!"

He smiled, gave a quiet chuckle, and shook his head.

"Come, my lady, let's stay focused."

She closed the file and stacked it carefully on the desk. Afterwards, Kit tried to read the parchment in his own hands but strained to concentrate. He peeked over at her and watched the way she pointed with her little left finger. Her fingertips made graceful, darting movements and her knuckles rose and fell as she curled her petite hand. She had such a nimbleness of touch.

As he watched her, tiny pinches of anger tightened in his neck and shoulders. It was dangerous to feel this way. It only made him vulnerable and did nothing to help his predicament.

Audrey's eyes lit up. She almost jumped as she ran her finger over some words in a file.

"Christopher!"

"What now?"

"Mark this!"

"Another conspiracy, I'll wager."

"No, not this time, I'm in all seriousness, I promise you. It links Thomas with Cholmeley. A certificate of promotion in one year."

He rolled his eyes.

"Can't you do better than that?"

She shoved the file at him. He regarded her quizzically, then realized she was serious and took it from her. Their fingers brushed. Inside the cover of the file he scanned through a note scrawled in Thomas's handwriting. Quite clearly it linked Thomas with Cholmeley. While he read the note a second time, she stood nearer to him and peered down at the note, proud of her work.

"It's a start," he said with a hint of pleasure. He turned his head toward her, noticing she was close.

Their eyes locked together. Her face was so near that her eyes looked unusually large. His tiny image reflected in her iris. Without the slightest effort, their mouths drifted closer, her supple lips so near he could almost taste them, almost feel their full, smooth warmth upon his skin...

Just a mere fraction from kissing her, he pulled back.

"What's wrong?" she asked.

He paused, unable to answer. She waited and fixed herself to the spot with a static posture and an unwavering gaze: the utter stillness of a sculpture.

"Don't worry for Thomas," she muttered under her breath. "We both know he loves men more than women."

"It's not that…"

She stepped back sadly.

"Oh, I see..."

"What?"

"...you're still being Christopher Marlowe."

He frowned, surprised at the harshness of her tone.

"And who else should I be?"

She shrugged and looked away.

He turned quickly back to the files, sorting through them with trembling hands. She shook her head at him. Her mind elsewhere, she swiveled toward the desk to continue working. Then it happened.

Her sleeve snagged accidentally on a stack of files.

Sent them walloping down.

Paper whooshed out from the files, twirled in the air, scattered, slapped onto the wood floor, and spilt far across the room. Both of them stood and stared at the mess. Instinctively, she bent down to clear the files up.

"My apologies, Christopher! Oh, dear, my deepest apologies."

Kit hooked her by the arm to stop her from moving. Footsteps clattered down the corridor outside. In mere seconds, the nightwatchman's knuckles banged on the door. He shook the handle violently.

"Who's in there?"

Keys jangled, scraped at the lock.

"Who's there?"

A crash of metal sounded as the nightwatchman dropped them to the floor.

"Oh, you fobbing jolt-head!" he cursed at himself. He filled his lungs and yelled at the top of his voice. "Thieves! Thieves! Thieves in the house!"

Kit took a jarring breath. Clenched his teeth so hard a vein pulsed in his jaw. He burst into action. With Cholmeley's note clamped in his hand, he ushered Audrey back towards the secret passage.

BAM! BAM! BAM! BAM! The nightwatchman beat his fists against the door, too excited to untangle his keys.

Kit and Audrey rushed across the office, files slipping under their feet. Audrey's face contorted with panic. Her hair flailed out behind her as she ran. Half tripping on the corner of a chest, they reached for the secret door. Flung it open. Dived into the passageway.

As they shut the door and raced back down the winding staircase, they failed to notice they had dropped behind one tiny, delicate, but important object. Back in the office, lying atop a mess of paper near the wall, the ouroboros brooch shimmered in the moonlight...

Scene Nine

Secret Passage.

Kit and Audrey flew back down the passage steps and fought their way back through the laurel bush. Along the crunching path at the back of the house, they hastened toward the kitchen door and stole back through the corridors of the manor.

At one corner, they pressed close to the wall and looked down to the end of the far corridor: Thomas and a gaggle of servants, all in their linen bed-shirts and nightcaps, stood around the entrance to the study. The door was now wide open, and everyone prattled with shock and agitation while gawking at the chaos inside. Kit heard someone say that the nightwatchman had alerted the courtyard guards and was now stalking the manor grounds.

Unseen by the others, Kit and Audrey darted away. With light toes and softly tapping heels, they swept across the hall, ascended the stairs, and scampered back to their bedchambers. Before he entered his room, Kit glanced down the corridor to Audrey. She paused at her door, looked at him with scared, candid, loving eyes, and vanished into her room.

The next morning, Scadbury buzzed with the events of the previous night. Every servant invented theories, named suspects, and criticized the slackness of the guards and the nightwatchman.

In the living room, servants had opened the tall windows to expel the stale air that had collected during the night. A morning gust now blew inside, fragrant with the freshness of the lawns and dew-laden shrubs. The air flapped in the white curtains, made them pull at their brass rings, and swept them back into the room to tussle and snap over the woven surface of a fine blue rug. In an armchair by the wall, Thomas crossed his legs and reclined quietly. His brown hair and pointed forelock were neatly combed. With a small, sharp knife, he sliced an apple into segments and crushed the flesh between his teeth. His face looked dark with brooding. Behind him, Frizer slunk about by the hearth.

Kit appeared cautiously in the doorway and both Thomas and Frizer turned and stared at him. A red spot blotched Kit's chin from where he'd cut himself while shaving. Bags puffed beneath his eyes. His hair looked mussed and direct from the pillow.

"Sleep well, Christopher?" said Thomas.

"No," Kit replied awkwardly. "Not after the break-in."

"Ah..."

"They didn't take anything, I hope?"

Thomas and Frizer exchanged a knowing glance.

"It's hard to pin down what's missing," Thomas replied. He bit into a segment of apple.

Kit paused a moment. He felt Cholmeley's note inside his shirt, tucked under his belt.

"Anyway, I've packed my possessions," he mumbled. "I just came to say farewell."

Thomas raised his eyebrows and sat forward.

"Where are you off today? London, perchance?"

"Yes... to London..."

"Is that a safe choice?"

"Probably not, but it's a necessary one."

"I believe you can't stay away from that city."

"The Earl of Derby gave me a few leads I need to explore there."

Silence followed. Curtains snapped at the window. Kit shifted his weight and looked down. He felt a tiny sense of regret that their friendship had come to this.

Thomas pressed his lips tight.

"Fare thee well, Christopher."

Kit gave a curt bow, then turned away sadly and dipped out of the room.

122

When Kit's footsteps had faded away, Thomas raised his hand and beckoned Frizer to his side. Frizer craned his long neck down to listen.

"He's not to London," said Thomas in a low voice.

"I knew he was lying, sir," Frizer replied, trying not to appear too surprised. "You can see it in the face. Never fools me."

"Who do we have who needs work?"

"Baines."

"No one else?"

"Not that I know of, sir. Of course, you could get me to follow him..."

"I need you here."

"Oh, thank you, sir."

"Have Baines follow him from now on. But he reports only to me. Remember that."

Frizer nodded, then took his leave and paced for the door. Thomas watched him go and sliced again into his apple.

SCENE TEN

Portsmouth.

Two days later, Kit and Will rode horses near the south coast of England and finally reached the walled town of Portsmouth. A long line of people waited at the city gates to be admitted by guards. Nervously, Kit and Will joined the queue and readied their travel papers for inspection.

After inspection, Kit and Will trotted down into the labyrinth of streets. They soon found their way to the market at the harbor front, tethered their horses, and walked off into a square now crammed with stalls of red, white, and black awnings, and loud merchants desperately touting their wares.

Through the throng of shoppers, seamen heaved sea-chests on their back ready for loading onto the ships. Naval officers outside a tavern cavorted with women on their laps and pointed to their warships in the harbor. At one corner, the symbol of sign above indicated it was moneylender's shop. Next door, gaudy dresses hung outside a draper's stand, and mothers and daughters surrounded it to paw at taffeta folds or run fine lace trimmings through their fingers. Above the shops, washing poles stuck out from the windows of homes, drying dull-colored shirts, sleeves, tights, and breeches. Sometimes a flurry of wind sailed inside a pair of breeches and puffed-out the legs. In another window, a man in a red gown and white cap leant out, watched the scenes of the market below, and the smoke from his pipe spiraled up and drifted into the washing poles.

Within minutes, Kit and Will crossed the square to the far side. Down a nearby alleyway, prostitutes with died blonde hair and loose bodices waggled their chests, waved, and called out raunchy solicitations. Kit, however, was more concerned about a man he noticed standing over at a butcher's stall: beside a pig's head on a crate stood a man Kit instantly recognized as Baines – one of Walsingham's spies.

At almost forty years old, Baines looked haggard by an uncertain life yet still seemed oddly inexperienced and gormless. Spiked black hair accentuated the flatness of his broad, moon-shaped forehead. Dense stubble roughened his chin. His stiff, over-muscled body wore a murky brown tunic and black breeches. Gloves stretched tight over his hands, his shirt collar pinched into his neck, and a hole in his shoe revealed bare toes.

Kit hustled along and pretended not to see him. In return, Baines made no sign he had identified Kit – he just continued browsing past the meat.

As Kit and Will left the butcher's stall behind, Will suddenly began chatting and worked his way onto recent events.

"So you're still on good terms with Thomas?" said Will searchingly.

"Yes," Kit replied.

"Nothing happened at Scadbury?"

Kit hesitated and looked away with guilt. He felt Cholmeley's note touch his skin inside his shirt.

"No. Nothing really." His throat dried up. He hated lying to Will, but the instinct to hide information was too strong to resist. He would explain it all later. Some other time.

After a moment, he slowed his gait and turned his head for a second look at Baines.

Will took a glance in the same direction and frowned.

"What? Are you lost?"

"No," replied Kit. He resumed his pace and quickly changed the subject. "Whenever I have business on the continent I leave from here. That's how I know Poley – the man we're going to see."

"What exactly does Poley do for the government?"

"He intercepts and decodes messages coming through the port."

"I see..."

"If anything's happening, he usually knows about it first."

Will nodded and they left the market square.

A few streets away, Kit led Will up to the front of a book shop known as 'Chaucer's Books': a narrow window with a jumbled shelf of books, and a tiny, stooped doorway to the side. The sign above was faded with dirt. Will paused and gazed inquisitively through the window. Kit waved him onwards and they entered the shop.

Scene Eleven

Chaucer's Books.

Dampness lingered inside. On every side of the store, fusty bookshelves hid the walls. From the window came the hot fumes of book leather in sunlight. Kit led Will deep into the shop and padded over to a clerk stood behind a semicircular counter at the back. The clerk leant one hand on the counter, as if he might topple over without support.

"I've come for some *new editions*," said Kit brusquely.

"Have you?" the clerk replied. He pointed a finger at Will. "And who's this?"

Kit gritted his teeth.

"No one."

"I need to know who he is first."

"Just let us through. You know who I am, don't you?"

"Who is he?"

"No one... Henry the Eighth... Now, are you going to let me in this century or the next?" He put his hands flat on the counter. His eyes knifed into the clerk. "I won't ask you again."

The clerk scowled and made no rush to let Kit and Will around the counter. He turned, unlocked the door behind, and threw it open: a straight, dark staircase descending to a basement below the shop. Without hesitation, Kit ventured forward and tramped down the stairs. Will crouched slightly and followed close behind. The clerk stayed in the shop above, and Will jumped as he slammed the door after them.

The staircase led down into a dark basement room choked with dusty chests, shelves, and wooden boxes full of paperwork and files. To the right, a shaky stack of boxes reached from the floor to the ceiling. A letter poked out from one of the files. Will bent his neck closer and frowned: it was written in a strange, symbolic language he didn't recognize. The only light in the room came from a candle behind a far shelf. It stretched the shadow of a lone man across the back wall. Kit and Will picked their feet carefully through the clutter of sharp-cornered chests and walked toward the light.

Behind the shelf sat Poley: a fat, blonde, spectacled man and the best decoder working for the government. From the hours he spent inside away from the sun, his skin had acquired a decayed, ashen tone. By the time Kit approached, Poley was already standing beside his desk. He smiled harmlessly and feigned a pathetic manner, but a deadly seriousness lay close to the skin. One could almost see a set of cogs and levers working inside him, making calculation upon calculation.

"Kit!" said Poley, smiling as if greeting an old associate. "I hadn't reckoned on seeing you today."

"I'll wager you didn't," Kit leered at him.

"How is everything?"

"Poley, you're a weedy, fly-bitten codpiece. You know why I'm here."

"Now, now, let's be nice, Kit. We can all be friends, can't we?"

"Don't tell me you haven't heard about the libels in London."

"Ah, yes."

"Well?"

"Terrible business..."

"But whose business is it, I wonder?" Kit tilted his head and looked him firmly in the eye.

"I don't know what you mean."

"Like hell, you don't. I want all correspondence that concerns Lord Burghley or Whitgift over the last three months."

Poley adjusted his glasses nervously. He put a hand on his desk and smiled.

"Certainly. As soon as I see your authorization."

Kit nodded at Will.

"Show him."

Immediately, Will grabbed a pouch hanging from his belt, drew open the string, and started rummaging. Poley's glasses slipped lower on his nose skeptically.

"You don't really have authorization, do you?"

"It's here somewhere," said Will in a thin, apologetic voice. He continued rummaging and moved closer to the candlelight. Suddenly, he knocked his elbow into a pile of letters collated together on the desk. Poley watched in despair as they tipped to the floor.

"The devil take you!" he cried. "D'you know how long they took me to organize?" He shot to his knees and started picking them up.

Without answering, Will bent down to help him.

Swiftly, Kit unsheathed his dagger and crept behind Poley. He drew his arm back. Swung forward. Slugged Poley on the temple with the butt of his dagger. Poley staggered two steps, then flopped to the floor over the letters and fell unconscious. Kit loomed over him, ready to strike again if necessary, but Poley didn't move. The papers on the floor by his mouth rustled slightly as he breathed. Will stood up and twisted his lips, mildly shocked.

"You didn't have to hit him!"

"I didn't mean to," Kit replied. "It was an accident. Get his legs, will you?"

They carried his body to a corner hidden from view of the basement door and sat Poley down carefully, his back leaning on the wall. Will looked at the body and shook his head.

"You accidentally, brutally, smacked him over the head with your dagger?" said Will dryly.

Kit shrugged.

"What else was I to do? Tie him up with parchment? Gag him with a file?"

Will gave a reluctant smile.

"What happens when he wakes up?"

Kit stopped in consideration and put a finger to his lips.

129

"Another accident, probably. I'm feeling very unlucky today."

Soon after, they set to work and searched through the boxes for any evidence that Burghley and Whitgift were involved with the libels. They found orders sent from the continent to Catholic radicals in England. Arrangements sent to priests in hiding. Surveillance work. Troop movements. Fleet locations. Mostly, however, they encountered simple intelligence reports of news and notable events happening in European cities like Paris, Hamburg, Vienna, Brussels, and Rome. Kit knew some of the codes and deciphered many documents easily; but for other documents he still needed to refer to one of Poley's code books or cipher sheets. He also had to check suspicious documents for signs of invisible ink. If deep quill scratches were found, if the parchment's surface was unusually rough, or if odd words were sighted within the context of the document, he had to uncork a bottle of ammonia and wave the fumes over the document till the hidden writing appeared.

Time wore away slowly. They had no windows or clocks in the basement to chart the passage of hours, but they knew the day must nearly be over. Occasionally, the clerk from upstairs came down and nosed about and they had to find ways to see him off. Nevertheless, Kit knew they couldn't stay there much longer.

At Poley's desk, he bent down, gripped hold of a small chest, and heaved it up to the desktop. His fingers and eyes tired from searching, he riffled through the files and rubbed his brow. Will sat on the floor nearby and climbed eagerly through a mountain of paperwork.

"I need the other code book," said Will without looking up.

"Here," said Kit, grabbing a red book on the desk. He slung it over to Will.

Kit straightened his spine until he heard the bones gently crack. Something was wrong. It would take days to go through everything, but he should have been able to find at least some documents regarding Burghley and Whitgift or the libels. He stooped back over the desk and sighed before poking listlessly at yet another file...

In the early evening, when Kit and Will finally exited 'Chaucer's Books', the air had cooled and the stink of waste from the ditches mingled with coarse salt odors drifting from the harbor. The sunset overflowed with redness: red gushed through the sky in all directions, rained from the tattered clouds, dripped faintly from the rooftops, made veins about the cracked stone walls, and sprung up from the tops of cobblestones in the street. Their faces tired and perturbed, Kit and Will strolled away from the shop.

"You know," said Kit in vacant tone, "I think nature is at her cruelest when she forges an artist."

"Things could be a lot worse," Will replied with a surprised frown.

"I doubt it. How can we have so much power when we write and so little when we live?"

Will didn't answer. Kit looked behind and twitched his eyes about the darkening shadows of the street.

"They knew we were coming," he said abruptly.

"Oh..."

"Someone cleared out anything of use."

"But how could anyone have known where you were going?"

Kit shrugged and glanced into a passing alleyway. Will waited a moment, then looked askance at Kit.

"Was it something to do with the man in the market?"

Kit turned to him with surprise.

"You noticed him?"

"Yes, and I noticed you noticing him."

"Bloody hell, Will! You'd make a good spy."

"Is he dangerous?"

"Baines?" said Kit slowing his pace. He rubbed the tip of his chin pensively and gave a small nod.

Will gulped. Kit took him aside and spoke in a quieter voice.

"Once, we sent him over to spy on the seminary at Rheims. He tried to poison the water supply. Wanted to wipe-out all enemies."

"My god..."

"They caught him, though. Lashed him a hundred times. I didn't know he was still active."

Will listened closely, his face lined with concern. Kit gave him a friendly slap on the shoulder.

"Anyway, don't worry about him for now."

"What should I worry about if not a dangerous criminal stalking us?"

Kit glanced at the evening sky.

"How much cash have you?"

Will shook the purse hanging from his belt. No coins jangled.

"Almost a penny," he replied.

"I'm broke, too. Fie upon it! We need enough for rooms at least." Kit pushed a strand of hair behind his ear, paused as if deciding something, then expelled a small huff. "Find the cheapest rooms you can and meet me back here."

"Where are you going?"

"I'll go and see someone who can lend us a few bob."

"But... What about Baines? I don't think we should split up. Can't I come with you?"

Deaf to Will's objections, Kit strode away up the street. Will raised his palms to the sky, shook his head, and ambled off in the opposite direction.

With powerful, agitated strides, Kit barreled along Portsmouth's high street. He almost knocked shoulders with people walking in the opposite direction. His eyes inspected every face, watched every movement for danger.

He walked on in silence and glimpsed a slender flag flying over the rooftops from a ship in the harbor. The flag tapered away from the mast and became thin and fine and dark at the end, like a strand of Audrey's hair. Memories of their last meeting in the study fluttered back through his mind.

In the sky, the colors of the sunset trickled away into night. He passed an alley and flinched as a rat scampered away through the litter. As he continued down the street, he took an almost casual, instinctive glance behind...

This time, the sight deeply unnerved him. His face turned severe. Down the street behind him, about fifteen paces back, Baines followed at a distance.

Scene Twelve

Portsmouth High Street.

Baines plunged his heavy hands into the pockets of his overcoat, straining the seams. He plodded close to the wall, letting others pass in front of him, believing himself hidden.

Kit immediately increased his speed, veered left, shot between the traffic, and hotfooted it across the road. Seconds later, Baines meandered out and crossed the road after him.

Kit hurried towards a cross street ahead. He'd left Baines slightly in his tracks, yet in a few seconds the advantage would be lost. Breathing fast, his eyes strained in all directions. A myriad of streets, alleys, and doors led away from the road, but none seemed useful. Suddenly, the grating wheels of a carriage trundled near: two horses, a driver, and a little green cab. Kit leapt out in the road to cross before it. For the briefest, tiniest moment, the carriage completely blocked him from view. When it rumbled onwards, he didn't reappear on the other side of the road or in any of the side alleys or in the doorways. He seemed to have vanished.

Panic-struck, Baines pushed his way up to the cross street. With a clueless frown, he panned his gaze from one end of the street to the other, almost turning a complete circle. Kit was nowhere to be seen...

...The green carriage moved onwards and followed a bend in the road. On the other side of the carriage, Kit held on desperately, nearly pitched to the ground with every bump and jolt. His left hand clamped onto the cab's roof; his right hand clasped the window frame; and his feet lay tucked into the loading step. Nervously, he watched the broad wheels turning beneath him.

The carriage itself was well-constructed and ornate. Gold leaf decoration lined the side panels. He lowered his head and peered through the glassless window and found a shocked middle-aged husband and wife staring back at him. He smiled politely.

"Nice weather we're having, no?"

At first, the husband was too scared to answer. His wife nervously jabbed him in the ribs with her elbow.

"Er... yes..." replied the husband. "Not too cloudy."

The carriage turned into another street and Kit readied himself to jump. He sprang away from the carriage side. His feet hit the cobblestones lightly. Momentum swept him forwards but he didn't stumble. Seconds later, the carriage rumbled onwards out of sight, and he started away down the road to find his destination.

The streets of Portsmouth fell dark. Constables with large yellow clubs patrolled the lit areas of the city. Chimney smoke dirtied the night air. Curtains drew across windows. Music and song spilled out from the ale houses and stews.

Kit arrived at a side alley and recognized some of the slouching buildings. The alleyway was deserted and strewn with smashed crates and broken barrels. He approached a small shop and noted a small light glowing inside. The ratty sign held the symbol of 'Goldsmith'. He stole over to the door, rapped on it hard, then stood back and waited.

A shuffling of feet sounded inside the shop. The door bolt clicked undone and a stout, ruddy-cheeked goldsmith named Gifford Gilbert appeared and stared at him.

"Working late, I see," said Kit.

Gilbert grinned.

"Come in, Master Marlowe, come in..."

Within the shop, tables and trays occupied the front area but were now empty – their jeweled bracelets, brooches, rings, and necklaces were stashed away for the evening. Amid the low light and the grimy floors and walls, Kit waited patiently and watched as Gilbert rushed around whipping the curtains shut.

"They're our best batch yet!" said Gilbert excitedly. "No defects."

Kit put a hand on his hip.

"That would be a first."

"No defects. Honest. Liz's portrait is exact this time."

"What about the color?"

"The color's good. The color's very good – very, very good, if I may say so, in fact."

Kit licked his lips. He started to echo Gilbert's enthusiasm.

"Where are they? Have you tested them yet?"

"Tested them?"

"You have, haven't you?"

Gilbert gave a sly grin then beckoned Kit to follow. They moved to the back of the shop and passed Gilbert's workbench scattered with delicate files resting next to soldering irons, mixing bowls, and a large cast.

Gilbert fiddled with a lock and they entered a back room crowded with three iron safes. At the nearest safe, Gilbert stuck a key in the door and a large clunk sounded. He clutched the handle with both hands, gave a small moan, and heaved open a door three inches thick. Kit bent down and peeped inside: nothing lay on the shelves – nothing, save for a polishing rag in the middle. It seemed to cover a small bump.

With gusto, Gilbert whisked away the rag and revealed a stack of gold coins. They looked harmless and dainty surrounded by the walls of the giant safe.

"I used one yesterday to settle a bond," said Gilbert.

"And?"

"They mistook it for genuine. No doubt at all."

Slowly, Kit reached inside, plucked one of the coins from the pile and held it up to the candlelight. He studied Queen Elizabeth's image and turned it to admire the shape and tone.

"You're a genius, Gilbert, a bloody genius!"

Gilbert clasped his hands together.

"Beauty, ain't it?"

Kit nodded. Reverently, he made the coin glint in the candlelight.

A short time later, Kit stepped out into the back alley and left the goldsmith's shop behind. He now held a small leather bag in his hand. As he turned out into the main street, he wedged the leather bag tight under his arm for safety.

Unseen by Kit, another figure stood and watched at the opposite end of the alleyway: lurking by the corner, his blank face just visible in the dark, Baines observed Kit leave and walk up the street.

SCENE THIRTEEN

Tavern.

Once Kit had collected Will from the meeting place, they went straight to a boarding house that Will had discovered, and Kit used the counterfeit money to pay for two rooms. Since neither of them had filled their bellies with much sustenance over the last two days, their thoughts soon turned to food and they went for supper at a tavern on the harbor front.

Inside the tavern, light gray walls and a high ceiling bounded the single, large room. A whitish glow hung over the many tables like a harbor mist and seemed to soften the faces and shapes of customers sitting in the haze. People everywhere leant over the backs of stools, tilting on two legs, and talked to their neighbor, while men and women linked arms and danced together in circles at the center of the room, the straps of their biggins and muffin caps bouncing and flying as they swung into the steps and danced in time to the tunes of the piper, fiddler, and drummer working the tables of men seated at nearby stools, stomping their feet, thumping the tabletops, trying hard to keep in rhythm to the music, their drunken moves soon falling out of time and reducing them to fits of giggles. Above, dangling from the ceiling, bushels of rosemary and sage perfumed the air and kept the room from stinking of the fish bones stamped into the sawdust covering the floorboards.

A ravenous Kit and Will moved through the tavern towards a meal counter. A swarthy, plump-breasted wench served them bread flavored with nodules of cheese, onion, and lashings of ale, then ladled some fish soup into deep bowls. Once Kit and Will had their bowls, their bread, and a tankard of 'Dragon's Milk' ale, they sauntered over to a window table in the corner and settled down to eat.

Their hunger sharpened all their taste buds, heightening the sweet aroma of the soup, adding to creaminess of its texture as it slipped over their tongues and down their gullets. Kit couldn't eat fast enough.

"It's so hot it burnt my mouth!" he laughed.

While they continued to swish their spoons into their bowls, Will sat back a little in his chair and glanced over at Kit suspiciously.

"You're friend is certainly very generous."

Kit strained to hear over the noise.

"What's that?"

"I said your friend must be very generous to lend us so many coins."

"Yes... yes he is."

"You should give me his address."

"Why?"

"So I can repay him for my room and meal."

Kit paused slightly between mouthfuls of soup and ale.

"Oh..."

"Something wrong?"

"No need to worry about repaying him."

"Maybe not," Will muttered under his breath.

Nervy with stress and guilt, Kit wiped his mouth and looked around. He eyed the wenches threading through the room, slapping away the roaming hands, wiping up messes, and stooping to fill tankards. His eyes widened and he turned to peer out of the window behind.

"Anyway, as we're on the subject of acquaintances, I wonder how our *other* friend's doing tonight?"

Will swiveled in his chair and pressed his face close to the window to see.

Outside, across the street, Baines stood inside a darkened doorway. His entire figure was almost hidden, save for two feet that poked out beyond the shadows into the bare moonlight. They could see the hole in his shoe.

Kit turned thoughtfully to Will.

"It's about time I introduced you to him, isn't it?"

Will looked back and shrugged.

Half an hour later, Kit exited the tavern alone. His hand close to the dagger at his waist, he ambled up the street with a languid gait and crooked path, as if terribly drunk. He turned the next corner and passed out of sight.

Once he was gone, Baines left the shadowed doorstep and flitted up the street. He swiftly rounded the corner.

He stopped. He came face to face with Kit who already had a dagger drawn. In a dull state of panic, Baines pivoted around and tried to run the other way, but found himself now blocked by Will who had secretly left the tavern and crept up behind him.

Before Baines's hand could snap down towards the knife on his own hip, Kit disarmed him, shoved him to the wall, and pointed the dagger tip under his chin. With clenched teeth, Baines stared hard over Kit's head.

"I wonder what's in your future, Baines?" said Kit. "Can you see it? It's a little murky. I see a dead body floating in the harbor, or a signed statement that you know Whitgift and Burghley are conspiring against me."

Baines continued his blank stare. Kit frowned incredulously.

"Did I just speak to myself?"

Baines kept still and quiet. Up close, his face seemed round and tough. Kit tapped him lightly on the head.

"Is there anyone in there?"

Still no response.

"Anyone at all?"

He glanced over to Will and shook his head.

"He's a complete nonperson!" Kit took a grasp of Baines's tunic, yanked him forward, and slammed him harder into the wall. He pressed the dagger blade firmer into Baines's throat so that it almost broke the skin. "The statement," he demanded.

Baines finally curled his lip.

"You'll have to cut my throat before I tell you anything," said Baines in his stentorian voice.

"But if I cut your throat you won't be able to tell me anything, will you?"

"I went to a goldsmith today."

"Did you? How nice?"

"Perhaps you know him. His name is—"

"Do what you like with your own time, Baines, but don't waste mine. Now will you or will you not write a statement?"

"I'll do it..."

"For what?"

"...a piece of the action."

As Will looked on with interest, Kit hesitated and glowered. Suddenly, Baines stuck his head forward threateningly, his nostrils flaring.

Kit scoffed.

"The only action you'll get is my knife in your forehead."

"I could report you to the authorities, I could. Would you prefer that instead?"

Will inched closer. He looked back and forth between Kit and Baines, then tilted his head in surprise.

"What the hell's he talking about, Kit?" said Will, his voice wavering. "Report what?"

With a reluctant, guilt-laced expression, Kit turned fully towards Will. He opened his mouth to explain... but never got the chance.

Baines acted instantly.

Head-butted Kit square above the eye, twisted Kit's arm and whacked it into the wall, making him drop the dagger. Kit flailed out with his fists – a jab, an uppercut – but missed both times. Baines struck him in the face and landed a knee deep into his stomach, flooring him.

Will's face contorted in terror. He curled his hand into a fist and started forward to help, not knowing how best to start. Almost by sheer instinct Baines saw him coming, whirled around, lunged and kicked him in the chest – Will flew back, cracked his shoulder into the wall and fell to his knees.

Afterwards, Baines lurched into a sprint and bolted off down the street. Within moments, he was far away and into the shadows.

By the time Kit recovered and heaved himself to his feet, there was no point in attempting a pursuit. He stared down the road after Baines, then huffed and kicked the wall in frustration. The head-butt had dazed him and he touched the swelling over his left eyebrow with his fingertips. Already the skin was tight and tender.

From his knees, Will looked up, panting for air, his lips wrinkled as if he were queasy. Kit wandered over to him.

"I think that went quite well, don't you?"

Will didn't laugh. Kit hung his head shamefully.

"He was talking about the money I showed you."

"I knew you were lying..."

"It's from a counterfeit scheme I have with a goldsmith."

Will put a hand on the wall to steady himself.

"You're a playwright, spy, and a criminal," he replied. "Anything else?"

Kit stooped down to Will and put a hand under his arm to help him up.

"I'm no criminal."

"Really?"

"No, but I'll tell you what *is* criminal."

"Oh, please do."

"Criminal is working yourself to the grave for a penny or two, hoping for the day when you can live as you want." He forced a smile and pulled Will gently upright. "Anyway, what does the Queen do when she needs some cash? She mints it. I'm only following the example of dear old gloriana."

Will glared at him.

"Why didn't you tell me earlier?"

"I'm sorry..."

"No, you're not."

"I should've told you... I wanted to... I don't know why I didn't. I pray forgiveness, Will."

Will stood up on his own two feet and pushed Kit away.

"God I feel sick!"

"It'll wear off in a minute."

"No, it won't – it's you I'm sick with!"

The words jarred Kit to a halt. He averted his eyes nervously. This was the first time he had witnessed Will in a true state of anger. It was impressive to see him fired by so much emotion. His anger seemed pure, almost physical and tangible.

From the distant tavern the lively strains of a fiddle danced into the street. A new song began and rowdy voices chanted the verses. Kit's whole body appeared to wither. He extended a hand, pleadingly.

"It won't happen again. Believe me, I'm sorry."

Will rubbed his sore back and didn't reply. Kit groaned at him. His face fell into an expression of anguish.

"Look, Will, it's just that I'm used to operating alone. Forsooth! I can't change overnight."

"Yes you can!" Will replied savagely. He started off down the road. He turned his head to call back. "You're the one who makes the limits, Kit. No one else. No one. Lie to me again and you can suffer the rest of the way on your own."

"Will..."

"I mean it!"

Kit nodded and looked away darkly.

Later in the evening, Kit returned alone to his room at the boarding house – just a simple second-floor room overlooking the street. His bruised forehead throbbed. His head swam with agony, with the events of the day, with agony. Rampant energy ran purling through his blood. His heart lightened till it almost felt nonexistent.

He lit some candles and tossed his bag onto the bed and sat down next to it. From the bag he unfurled rolls of parchment, plucked out a quill, and filled his ink pot. He read back quickly through his poem and reminded himself how Hero had attended a great banquet and then left it to visit the temple of Venus. At the temple, Leander had first laid eyes on her and fallen instantly in love.

Kit seized the quill and scribbled so many notes on a leaf of parchment that the paper gradually appeared more black than yellow-brown. Again, he touched his forehead lightly and ran his fingertips over the smooth, tight, hard bump. His eyelids began to droop and his head bent down a little. On the floor, he noticed his shadowed outline: a rounded back, stooped shoulders, and a bent neck. He straightened his posture. Afterwards, his eyes still lingered on the shadow, peering deep into the blackness with ardent attention, as if something were behind it, beyond all range of color and sound, something that defied taste, resisted smell, and receded from touch. Furiously, he set his quill nib to the page and wrote lines, passages, and whole pages in close succession. Mistakes and poor words choices abounded on every leaf, but he let the words escape from him without interruption.

He wrote of how the lovers touched, how Hero played coy, and how Leander implored her against her chastity. All the while, as Leander argued, Hero denied him and tried to smother her own inclinations, her own self. Yet no matter how she tried, her nature resisted and she couldn't help but give Leander cause to hope. At the end of a long argument, Leander prepared to make his move:

> 'With that Leander stooped to have embraced her
> But from his spreading arms away she cast her,
> And thus bespake him: "Gentle youth, forbear
> To touch the sacred garments which I wear.
> Upon a rock and underneath a hill
> Far from the town (where all is whist and still,
> Save that the sea, playing on yellow sand,
> Sends forth a rattling murmur to the land,
> Whose sound allures the golden Morpheus
> In silence of the night to visit us)
> My turret stands and there, God knows, I play.
> With Venus' swans and sparrows all the day.
> A dwarfish beldam bears me company,
> That hops about the chamber where I lie,
> And spends the night (that might be better spent)
> In vain discourse and apish merriment.

Come thither." As she spake this, her tongue tripped,
For unawares "come thither" from her slipped.
And suddenly her former colour changed,
And here and there her eyes through anger ranged.
And like a planet, moving several ways,
At one self instant she, poor soul, assays,
Loving, not to love at all, and every part
Strove to resist the motions of her heart.
And hands so pure, so innocent, nay, such
As might have made heaven stoop to have a touch,
Did she uphold to Venus, and again
Vowed spotless chastity, but all in vain.'

Kit barely stopped to read the lines before he pressed onwards and finished the encounter. He wrote well into the early
morning hours and even added a small story about the silliness of
the gods. With the quill and parchment still on his lap, he fell asleep sitting up in bed.

The next dawn, Portsmouth awoke slowly to the first sun-
beams of day. In the harbor, ship bells clanged softly and flags
slept at their poles without any wind. Carts rumbled and donkeys
clopped down the roads. A shepherd urged a small flock of sheep
down a street toward the harbor.

In Kit's room at the boarding house, a gentle light sifted
through his shut curtains. His lower lip protruded as he slept and
the bump on his forehead had shrunk a little, though it had now
turned a shade of deep blue and purple. The parchment from the
night before still lay upon his lap, with sheet placed across sheet
and his loose-fingered hand relaxed upon them all. Noise from
the road seemed to dwindle at his bedside, and the dead air hardly
stirred with his peaceful snores...

At first, he didn't wake at the thudding in the hall of the
boarding house. Nor did his eyelids flutter at the rush of feet
trammeling upstairs. As the noise continued and heels thundered
down the corridor, approaching his room, he was just beginning
to flicker his eyelids.

Suddenly, his door flung open.

Slammed back on its hinges.

A squad of city guards crashed into his room.

He barely had time to raise his head, force his eyes open, or defend himself, before the guards ripped him out of bed.

Scene Fourteen

Boarding House. Kit's Room.

In total, seven city guards filled the room, their limbs gleaming with armor. Snug helmets exposed their faces. Cuirasses plated their chests and back – some with large dents and battered edges. The fingers of the steel gloves creaked and squealed as they clasped their hands around a pike: a long wooden shaft tipped with steel, reminiscent of a tribal spear. At the center of all the guards stood the captain. A stocky man, he stood shorter than the rest – all head and square shoulders. He grasped a document in his hands, smartly unrolled it, and wetted his lips.

"Christopher Marlowe," said the captain in a curt manner, "I hereby place you under arrest on charge of counterfeiting."

Two guards stepped forward and pinched Kit's arms with their gauntlets. Kit threw his head back.

"What?" he replied, struggling to understand. "Who made such a charge?"

The captain's eyes dropped back to the document and he read aloud.

"Richard Baines lodged the charges. You're to be escorted to see Lord Burghley at Westminster."

The guards yanked him across the room to the door. Everything was going too quickly: the last thing he wanted was to be delivered up to Burghley. Although he was still in his clothes from the night before, he had removed his shoes and his belt for comfort and laid them on the back of the chair. He stuck his heels into the floorboards and twisted toward the captain.

"At least let me garb myself properly."

The captain tipped his head at the request and the guards released Kit so he could dress.

Kit's request had saved only a few seconds in order to think. He padded over to his chair, slowly lifted his belt, wrapped it around his waist and closed the buckle. He slid his feet inside his shoes. The parchment he had written on was now scattered all over on the floor and the guards trampled it under their boots as they moved about. He scanned the room for some way of escape. The guards had stationed themselves to cover both the window and the door. One of them held his dagger. Another guard rummaged through his bag of belongings. Before long, the captain gestured to the guards and they grabbed him again and thrust him toward the door.

In the corridor, the door of the room opposite opened wide and Will leant out anxiously. Next to the impenetrable armor filling the corridor, Will's skinny arms and frail neck seemed laughable.

"In faith!" Will gasped. "What's this!"

A guard immediately rounded on him and cross-checked him with a pike.

"Go to, sir!" the guard grunted.

Color rushed into Will's cheeks and he pushed back, ready to fight. Kit looked him in the eye and shook his head. Will understood and backed down.

As the guards dragged him through the doorframe, Kit prepared himself to act. His mouth turned dry. His tongue withered at the root. His ears became sensitive to every grating movement of armor, every footfall.

He broke their hold. Thrashed left and right, banging his captors into the wall. The guards behind reacted, tried to catch him in their arms, but he dived through them and dashed back into the empty room.

His feet pattered lightly over the floor. He rushed straight for the window and threw it open.

The casements swung back and hit the outside of the house. He glanced down below: more shiny helmets and cuirasses and pikes waited on the road.

148

Thooomph!

He wheeled around back into the room and saw a pike-tip stabbed into the wall next to him. Guards flooded into the room again. One guard raised his arm to the throw another pike.

Kit panicked. Grabbed onto the windowsill, raised his knee, jumped up and clambered out the window onto the ledge outside. The drop to the street seemed to increase sharply. The pointed pikes below glinted up at him.

Fingers pressed white onto any handhold he could find, he shuffled his feet along the narrow ledge. Cool morning air tickled around his knees. He balanced as best he could and looked back toward the window.

Two of the bravest guards followed him out onto the ledge.

Kit inched toward a beam supporting the roof. From pressing so close to the side of the house, white plaster smeared across the front of his doublet and breeches. He extended an arm and struggled to touch the beam overhead. The guards were nearly on him now. He had no choice.

He jumped. Caught both hands around the beam and dug his nails into the wood. His feet swung helpless beneath him. The beam pricked his hands with splinters as he scrabbled up, hand over hand, till he gripped onto the edge of the roof and heaved himself up carefully onto the rooftop.

Now two stories high, with a sweeping view of the city, he crouched low, checking he could balance on the tiles. Fortunately, the rooftop slanted gently, making it easy to run across. From the street below, voices yelled and cajoled, urging the guards on the ledge to hurry.

To Kit's surprise, a hand suddenly appeared on the rooftop. Then another. Within moments, both the guards chasing him had hoisted themselves successfully onto the roof.

He streaked over the rooftop. The guards followed soon after.

A peak rose before him. He sprang forward, vaulted it, slid down the other side. He thundered along so hard his feet dislodged tiles – they slid out in all directions, slicing left, right, and off the roof, smashing to bits on the cobblestones below.

149

The roof of the boardinghouse ended rapidly. A small gap spanned the distance between the next rooftop.

He rushed onwards, gaining in speed. His lungs burnt with air. His hands dampened with sweat. The gap in the rooftops moved closer and closer, yet with every stride it broadened, exposing a great wide breach between the buildings. At the last moment, he slid to a halt. It was far too big to jump.

His eyes scouted around for another way down. No other rooftops stood nearby. No beams to climb down. Nothing lay below to break his fall.

The guards in the street caught up, their pikes bobbing up and down as they ran to stand beneath the gap. He pivoted. On the rooftop, the guards chasing behind him slowed their pace gingerly as they came nearer. Long-bladed daggers stuck out from their hands. Kit had nothing: no armor or weapons to fight with.

He glanced at the belt around his waist. Long, and made of thick leather, the belt was well-cut with clean edges that had yet to crack or split. Instantly, he whipped it undone from his hips and locked it into a large loop.

The guards stepped even closer and prepared to fight. A tile cracked. They crouched, ready for anything.

Kit didn't waste another second. Both guards watched in surprise as he turned sharply, sprinted over the tiles, and hurtled toward the edge. It seemed suicidal! Legs pumping, arms swinging, Kit accelerated his pace, faster and faster. At the very last point, he did the unthinkable – hurled himself into the air as high as he could.

For a moment, there was complete silence. On the ground below no one moved. On the rooftop behind, the guards stood awestruck and watched Kit in the air.

The far roof sped toward Kit in the space of a long, majestic second. He felt he would make it, but his stomach turned and he knew he would fall short.

He flung his arms out desperately.

Whirled the belt through the air.

A fraction before the rest of his body, his chest slammed into the wall of the building. His knees, hands, feet smashed into the bricks. Yet he didn't fall. Somehow he'd snagged the belt onto the building's cornice above.

He dangled there by one hand, his feet free and kicking beneath him. The belt strained to hold him. Little by little it slipped and worked itself off the cornice.

The rooftop guards chuckled to themselves.

"Nice one, mate!" one of them yelled across the gap.

Kit didn't hear. Blood rushed to his head and air sat in his lungs and his ears felt muffled. His arm twisted, ready to tear from its socket. The belt slipped to the very lip of the cornice. He pawed at the wall for something, anything, to grip on to but his nails scratched away uselessly.

He refused to give up and grabbed onto the belt with his other hand. Stomach muscles tensed, he pulled hard on the leather and raised himself up an inch, then a little more, two inches, even more – it was enough to reach out quick and grab hold of the cornice. Gradually, his arms heaved his body level with the roof and he climbed up fully to the top.

Exhausted, he managed to stand only by planting his feet wide apart. To his dismay this rooftop pitched steeper than the others. The tiles beneath him shuddered with his weight. Before he started off, he peered over to the guards on the far rooftop and gave a cheeky wave.

"Tell you what, gentlemen – if you jump it I'll try and catch you. How about that?"

They scowled back at him. Kit laughed and started away.

"You'll have to go to Westminster without me, I'm afraid."

He shimmied along the tall peak of the roof. Yet no sooner had he moved his foot, than the tiles pulled loose and completely slipped out underneath.

In one tiny avalanche, tile after tile gushed out of place. Kit tried to scrabble out of it. He fell onto his back. With a long yell, he slid down the roof feet-first and skidded over the edge...

Scaffolding on the other side of the building caught him in mid-fall. His back pounded into planks supported by a frame of oak poles. On impact, the entire scaffolding swayed and groaned at the joints. Before he could recover, it broke apart and clattered with him to the ground.

Half-covered by poles and planks, Kit lay prostrate amid the debris and waited for the dust to clear. It drifted away and revealed a set of street guards surrounding him. They pointed their pikes down in a ring around his head.

Act III

Scene One

Prison Cart.

Drizzle. Clouds pulled gray, glaring sheets over the sky in all directions. Thin raindrops fell upon the roads and dripped onto the roof of the prison cart as it trundled into the grounds of Westminster Palace and jerked to a halt.

Once the cart's back door was unlocked, a guard with hooded, wrinkled eyes reached inside and pulled Kit out.

"I don't want to hear nothing from you, savvy?"

Kit stood still and didn't respond. He rubbed the sores on his back. The bruises on his arms throbbed where he had injured himself in the fall from the roof. The guard shook him.

"Answer when I ask you something, sirrah!"

"I thought you told me–"

"Shut it you dog! I told you not to speak!" The guard spluttered into laughter and pulled him along.

Though the journey had seemed exhausting, they made the distance from Portsmouth in under a day and a half, arriving at Westminster by noon.

Westminster Palace sat proudly on the north bank of the Thames, within easy sight of London, Bankside, and Lambeth Palace. Once used as the main residence of the monarchy, a fire sixty years ago had damaged parts of the palace and the royal family had vacated it ever since. Thus, while the palace officially remained a royal establishment, its main function now lay in the housing of parliament and the law courts.

The guards escorted Kit towards a back entrance. The palace's gothic stonework, high towers, and long pointed windows rose above him. A small river wind gusted off the nearby Thames, breezed along the limestone walls, and tickled past his cheeks.

"Enjoying the sights, are we?" snarled the guard with hooded eyes. "Get in with you!"

The guards shoved him up the entrance steps and through an archway and back into gloom.

The corridors inside the palace ran long and broad, with high ceilings. Lanterns with dirty glass panels lit the way. As Kit walked along with bare feet and shackled hands, guards escorted him at both shoulders. The guard with hooded eyes unnecessarily placed a palm on his back to guide him around the many corners. They moved past the palace staff – little men who dressed in correct, plain attire and who spoke in modest tones. At the sides of the corridors, large oak doors held plaques with names of lords, lobbies, galleries, and committee chambers in thick red letters. Some doors led to unknown rooms, as if some great treasure or wealth of secrets lay behind them, yet just as likely they led to more corridors and more oak doors.

Kit's eyes widened as the guards escorted him to a doorway he knew: the office of Lord Burghley, the Queen's highest minister of government. The guards opened the door and pushed him forward through the frame.

"Stay in there and keep that puking mouth shut," said the guard with hooded eyes. "And don't even think of any foolery. Me and Bullcalf will be waiting out here to skin your toad-spotted hide, understood?"

The door slammed shut. Afterwards, as promised, both guards shuffled to either side of the door and manned it in case he should attempt another escape.

Inside Burghley's office, a line of arched windows looped along the back wall. Before the windows sat a polished teak desk with tapering legs and leaf designs at the bottom. On top of the desk, pots, seal-stamps and letters were set in neat, exact places. On two walls, bookshelves held tightly wedged books in clean, flush rows. The last wall bustled with giant maps and charts of Arabia, India, European states, and the Americas. Names of cities, border-lines, rivers, and mountain ranges cluttered each continent, and drawings of little galleons contended with sea monsters upon the oceans.

When Kit entered, however, his eyes looked past the charts and speared into the figure of Baines sitting on one of the chairs in front of Burghley's desk.

"You!" Kit hissed.

Baines glared back. He said nothing but he looked ready to brawl. His eyes were puffy, his spiked hair had flattened a little, and he shared the same musty odor as Kit. With his jaw clenched, Kit paced silently across the room and took a seat at the desk. He kept his head tilted toward the window but never lost sight of Baines out of the corner of his eye.

For ten minutes, the only sound between them came from the air wheezing in Baines's nose as he inhaled and exhaled. At last, the door-handle turned and Burghley entered the office.

Scene Two

Westminster Palace. Lord Burghley's Office.

As soon as Lord Burghley entered the room, Kit rose to his feet. In contrast, Baines remained seated, but turned his head around nervously.

"My lord," said Kit.

"My lord," said Baines.

They both watched as the most powerful man in the kingdom limped around the desk to his chair.

A velvet doublet with black and gold sleeves clothed Lord Burghley's elderly frame, and a silk, wafer-thin ruff encircled his neck. From his shoulders hung links of a treasury chain that rubbed against the center of his stomach. In his right hand he leant upon a thin cane, and as he walked its regular taps interspersed his steps. Long of face, his hoary beard made his chin still longer. Tiny pink lips protruded through the beard and he had a thick nose, wispy eyebrows, and watery, hesitant eyes. Once, his tall erect carriage had conveyed a steadfast strength, but time and the stress of his position had now worn it away. For over twenty years, the majority of Elizabeth's reign, Lord Burghley had acted as both the Queen's main advisor and as Lord High Treasurer – the most important official in government. Last year, however, he'd suffered a heart attack and a stroke. His hands now shook. Deafness almost entirely claimed his hearing. Nevertheless, despite his age and frailty, he still retained an aura of trustfulness: his eyes never strayed, his voice never shouted, and his hands were never raised in anger. His reserved nature instilled you with confidence, assuring you that your problems were little trifles soon to be dispensed with. He moved slowly but with dignity, and he wore his raiment well – perhaps too well, as if it were grafted to his skin.

He approached the desk via the right-hand side. One got the sense he always took the same path. At his chair, he stopped and settled his eyes on Baines who still remained seated.

"Is that chair comfortable enough for you?" said Burghley in a flat tone.

Baines squirmed a little.

"Yes," Baines replied seriously.

"What was that you said?"

"I said yes. Thank you for asking, my lord."

"Stand up, Baines!"

Baines's mouth dropped open. He stood up quickly. Lord Burghley scoured both Kit and Baines with tired eyes, then splayed his fingers, huffed, and placed his hands on his desk.

"It's a disgrace to have you both here under such circumstances." His eyes shifted toward Kit. "Particularly you."

Kit hung his head.

"Forgive me, your lordship."

"Counterfeiting undermines the economic security of this country."

"I didn't intend–"

"In some quarters it is even considered treason."

Kit shuffled his feet, uncomfortable under Burghley's gaze. His shackles clinked.

"Tell me," said Lord Burghley, "how many goldsmiths does your conspiracy encompass?"

"Only one," Kit replied.

"One?"

"There was little method to it – I just wanted to see if it was possible." He sighed and looked away bitterly. "I don't have the same powers of conspiracy as you do, my lord."

Lord Burghley raised his eyebrows and observed Kit closely. A long pause followed. When he next spoke his voice sounded gravelly.

"Ordinarily I wouldn't advocate leniency in such a case... but considering this poster business, and the loyal service you've rendered the Queen in the past, I'm prepared to waive punishment so you may endeavor to clear your name."

With a clink of his shackles, Kit jerked his head and looked at Lord Burghley with a mixture of surprise and gratitude.

In the chair next to him, Baines's eyes bulged. His face turned sour.

"My lord – I must protest!"

Lord Burghley took his hands from the desk and slowly prowled towards Baines.

"Ah, and now for Baines..." He raised hand. "Let me tell you a story, Baines. It's about a spy who went to Portsmouth without permission and reported another spy to the authorities, making a public spectacle of hitherto secret operations." He paused and his knuckles tightened around his cane. "Do you know what happened to this spy?"

Baines shook his head. After a moment, Lord Burghley sighed and looked searchingly at him.

"You're sure?" said Lord Burghley.

Baines screwed his face up and strained to think of an answer.

"He got a reward?" Baines finally answered.

"No, he got fired."

"Oh..."

"Would you like to leave now?"

"No, thank you, my lord, I'm fine here."

Lord Burghley turned livid and got close to shouting.

"Get you out of this palace this minute. If I ever find you've interfered with my operations again you may consider yourself a permanent resident of Marshalsea prison." He pointed a shaking finger at the door. "Go!" he commanded.

Baines traipsed over to the door, dragging his feet. Suddenly, he turned and sent a venomous glance at Kit.

"You'll hang before I'm finished," said Baines.

Kit smiled back.

"I love you, too," he replied.

Not wanting to provoke Lord Burghley further, Baines yanked open the door and exited. Afterwards, Kit's eyes dropped thoughtfully. When he raised them again he looked up at Burghley.

"God reward you, my lord," he said quietly. "I can't offer enough thanks."

Burghley's lips peeled into a gentle smile. He ambled back towards the desk.

"No, I don't think you can."

Soon after, Burghley ordered the guards into the room and had them unshackle Kit. Kit and Burghley then took to their chairs and Kit explained all he had gleaned from his investigations into the posters and the conspiracy. Burghley listened intently, but made few comments – he just nodded and let Kit speak all he wished. For about half an hour they remained in the office, until Burghley remembered an appointment he had to keep.

With a file in his hand, Burghley tapped his cane out of the office and strolled down the corridor alongside Kit.

"Dear, dear... you can't honestly have thought it was me?" said Burghley.

Kit's cheeks blushed with embarrassment.

"I'm at a dead end," he replied miserably.

"I wouldn't go that far."

"If Walsingham isn't acting under your orders, then who else does he serve?" He shook his head and sighed deeply.

Burghley gave him a wise look.

"I've seen your plays, Master Marlowe. I know you're a creative man – think it through."

"What have plays to do with reality?"

"Judging from their popularity, I should think they have quite a lot to do with reality."

"No... In this world I command nothing. I command nothing, least of all my thoughts."

"If that was true, then why should Whitgift have any concern for you at all?"

Kit frowned and slowed his pace. Burghley halted outside one of the nameless doors leading away from the corridor. Kit stopped beside him, his face grave and thoughtful.

"Lord Essex..." said Kit gradually. "I suppose he could have poached Walsingham from your spy network."

Burghley stood up a little straighter.

"As Lord high Treasurer to the Queen, I cannot advise you to investigate another lord."

"Understood," said Kit demoralized.

"Nor can I tell you that Essex has recently become the Queen's new favorite, and that his power in court advances daily."

Kit's face slowly brightened. Burghley leant closer and continued.

"In fact, it would be sheer villainy to suggest that the posters are a stunt by Essex to create trouble and thereby challenge my position as the Queen's chief advisor."

Kit smiled in agreement.

"Yes, that *would* be villainous."

Burghley nodded to him curtly and opened the oak door and passed inside. The door closed and knocked back into its frame, sending a small boom down the corridor.

Kit stood there motionless. His thoughts raced and his mind struggled to keep abreast with the sudden turn of events. Slowly, an unusual sense of hope warmed his heart. Elation crept through his veins. He set his jaw, turned, and paced away from the door. Alongside him, palace staff proceeded down the corridor and regarded him curiously. His stride became faster and faster, fueled with new determination.

SCENE THREE

London. City Street.

Kit strode along with Will and informed him of all he'd learnt from Burghley. The street around them lay virtually deserted in the afternoon heat – a reminder that the plague-infested end of Cheapside wasn't far away. Kit clicked his fingers as he paced along. He swung his arms easily. A bright energy seemed to ripple through him. He could still taste the clean sweetness of an apple he'd just eaten.

Next to him, Will looked oddly serious. He spoke very little. The lining of his collar irritated the back of his neck and he scratched the skin with annoyance. In the road ahead, a raven hopped around the carcass of a dead animal and rived through the flesh with its beak. Will averted his eyes.

As they moved onwards up the road, Kit explained his next plan.

"...yes," said Kit enthusiastically, "but the Queen's giving a banquet at Nonsuch, tonight."

"What good will that possibly do us?" said Will.

"We'll question him then."

"You honestly think you can go there? You won't get within a mile of that palace without getting caught. I doubt we have any chance of getting inside."

"Don't worry. I'll see to that."

"Hmm..."

"Interrogating Essex is the thing to mind."

"How so?"

"There isn't a lord more savvy or dangerous."

"Wonderful."

"That's why we need some chemical assistance."

Will didn't respond. Kit frowned and looked at him askance.

"Will, I don't mean to pry, but..."

"Yes?"

"...is there... anything wrong?"

"Why do you ask?"

"You just seem a little gloomier today."

Will scratched the back of his neck again. His eyes looked dark.

"Don't mind me. It's nothing that lies within your power to mend, anyway."

"Are you certain?"

"Yes."

"What is it?"

"Just a little trouble writing, that's all," Will said with some testiness. "When I sat down yesterday the words weren't there."

Kit nodded sympathetically. He felt a slight pang of guilt. He walked on and they continued down the street in silence.

Soon, they found the apothecary shop Kit had been searching for and stopped. Two large bay windows bulged either side of the door. Behind the window lay a display of glass jars – blue, red, green, and yellow, each one filled with strange granules, liquids, or sticks.

"By the way, I should warn you," said Kit under his breath. "This fellow's sampled one too many potions..."

"What does that mean?"

"...but don't stare. He hates it when people stare."

Will raised his eyebrows.

"Stare?" He looked again into the window, concerned. "What shouldn't I stare at?"

Without answering, Kit pulled back the door and they entered the shop.

Inside, swept wooden floors led to a jumble of objects: a full medical skeleton; a candle in a glass dome; books with drawings of curved knifes, needles, and other instruments; and in the corner, dust and fingerprints covered a large celestial globe. Around the walls, wainscoting added interest to the green paint and from the ceiling hung the silhouette of a stuffed crocodile.

Lazell, the apothecary, stood by a shelf near the door, fiddling with a collection of pots. Tall, with a grim countenance, he had intense staring eyes, long fingers, and a pointed hat that looked like the beak of a vulture. As soon as they entered, Lazell turned in his flowing black gown and bowed politely.

"How now, my good man?" said Kit in a loud, jovial voice.

Lazell clasped his hands together, pleasantly.

"Sir, it's most delightful to make your acquaintance once again. It's been too long since you've graced my shop."

Kit gestured toward Will at his side.

"Lazell, meet Will Shakespeare."

Lazell extended a long hand.

"Nice to meet you, master Shakespeare."

Will reached forth and shook hands politely. As he did so, Lazell's head gave a violent twitch to the left. The action came suddenly, dramatically, without any kind of warning. Will stood there stunned. His lips parted in shock.

"Nice to... nice to..." said Will distractedly. He trailed off for a moment, as if seeing the twitch again in his mind. His cheeks grew flushed.

"Is there something the matter with you?" Lazell asked.

"No... I'm sorry... what was I saying?"

Lazell's head twitched again. Will's eyes grew large, completely mesmerized. In contrast, neither Kit nor Lazell seemed to care about the twitch. Kit gave Will a small look, then stood forward and patted Lazell on the shoulder.

"We're in search of a truth potion," he said quickly.

"Ah," replied Lazell. "A rare concoction, indeed."

"You have one?"

"Perhaps. I'm not sure. But I'll do my very best to find out."

His head twitching randomly, Lazell ushered them both towards a long counter at the back of the store. Along the entire wall behind hung lines of shelves laden with porcelain vials, urns, and little pots with labels wrapped around the sides. Kit and Will waited patiently while Lazell surveyed the shelves for the potion.

165

"Love ointments, poisons, lotions for the skin, sleeping powders, fertility balsams," muttered Lazell as he searched through a group of pots. He turned back to them gravely. "No. I'm afraid to say it, gentlemen, but it seems I possess no truth potion today."

As Kit and Lazell discussed alternatives, Will's eyes leapt up to a top shelf. There, behind a two dark urns, lay a bottle marked 'Truth Serum'. Will pointed to it.

"There's some at the top, I think," he said.

Lazell stood on his tiptoes to see.

"Where?" Lazell asked. His head gave another sudden twitch.

For fear of laughing, Will bit his lip and looked away. He still pointed to the top shelf.

"In the middle..."

Lazell strained to find it.

"The blue or the green one?"

"...it's there somewhere."

With mock disapproval, Kit rolled his eyes at Will. He leant over the counter to help.

"The green one," he told Lazell.

Lazell reached up and tugged the bottle toward the edge of the shelf with his fingertips. When he had it safely in hand, he took it down and scanned the label. He handed it over to Kit with a small, vanishing smile.

"This one's very strong," said Lazell, his face serious again.

"How strong, exactly?"

"A single drop can loosen any man's tongue."

"And what will such a miracle cost us?"

"For others I would charge a shilling or even more. But for you fine gentlemen, it is yours for merely sixpence."

"I'll give you a groat."

"Ah, regretfully, I can go no lower than sixpence. Perchance there is something else you would like to buy, instead? I have many other potions for a groat."

Kit ignored him and took the cork stopper off the bottle. He sniffed the contents: it had a sticky, over-ripe smell.

Meanwhile, Will eventually worked up enough self-control to look back in Lazell's direction.

"Does it have any side effects?" he asked.

Lazell eyed him sternly. His head twitched, nearly knocking his hat off. Will mistook it for an answer.

"Oh, that's good," said Will.

"No," Lazell corrected him. "Not completely free... Of course, you won't have any potion without some side effects."

"What effects does this one have?"

Lazell fidgeted on the spot.

"It creates a little mirth in whoever takes it." He waved his hand nonchalantly. "Nothing really, gentlemen. Nothing you would notice."

Kit turned the bottle in the smooth of his palm. He considered the smell once more and studied Lazell suspiciously. Both Will and Lazell waited for his decision. Finally, he set the bottle on the countertop.

"We'll take it," he said resolutely.

SCENE FOUR

Scadbury Manor. Audrey's Bedchamber.

Audrey took hours to dress for the Nonsuch banquet that evening.

Once she had tied herself into a bodice, untangled the willow strips and ropes of her Spanish farthingale, applied a satin kirtle, forepart, and a partlet over her chest, she finally put on her black and white gown with its matching sleeves. She played with the gold tassels on the cuffs while her maid worked on her hair.

To complete her final appearance, Audrey adorned herself with various items of jewelry. She pushed diamond rings down her gloved fingers. Squeezed her wrists into hoped ivory bracelets that rubbed the bone. However, she saved the space on the center of her bodice, just over her heart, for her most prized brooch of all...

She sat at her dressing table, an oval mirror in front, and rummaged through her jewelry box for Kit's brooch. Her maid stood behind, watching.

"It's here somewhere, in know it, I'm certain," Audrey mumbled, steadily growing flustered. "I don't understand. Why is so hard to find one simple piece of jewelry?"

"Can I help?" asked the maid in a broad country accent.

"My brooch. Have you seen it anywhere?"

"The one Master Marlowe gave you?" A smile darted across the maid's lips.

Audrey's face tightened.

"Yes... the very same."

The maid plucked away some lint from Audrey's shoulder. She stopped in thought.

"Come to think on it, I haven't seen it for days."

"You didn't take it for polishing, did you? Please tell me you haven't. Don't you remember, I expressly told you not to–"

"On my honor, good mistress, I haven't done anything with it! I haven't, I swear!"

"Forgive me, I didn't mean to accuse you," said Audrey pensively. She sat up straighter. "When was... when was the last time you saw it?"

"Well, now, not since the break in." The maid put a hand to her mouth. "Oh, my lady, you don't think the thieves had it, do you?"

A chilling recognition iced its way down Audrey's spine. She didn't answer. She simply looked at herself in the mirror.

Once she had dressed in a cloak to safeguard her gown from dirt, Audrey thanked her maid and left the bedchamber. With soundless steps, she descended the stairs and drifted silently over the hall tiles. Her soft, white leather shoes were punched with tiny holes to appear as lace – they barely tapped the floor as she whisked toward Thomas's study.

At the study door, she glanced casually up and down the corridor, checking for servants. Her hand clasped the doorknob. On the verge of turning it, she froze: voices from the other side hummed through the wood. Her chest rose and fell rapidly. She found swallowing difficult. Without another thought, she tilted her head and pressed her ear against the wood to listen.

Just as she began to hear, Frizer turned the corner ahead. He strolled directly toward her.

Audrey immediately walked onwards from the door. Using every degree of self-control she possessed, she achieved an appearance of calm and minced towards him, her chin tipped up, her eyes set hard in front. As they crossed paths, Frizer grinned at her maliciously.

"Good day, my lady," he said.

She passed him by as if he didn't exist.

Frizer sauntered to the study door. He glanced back over his shoulder and entered the study.

Once he was gone, Audrey fanned her face. She tried to draw the deepest breaths she could within the tightness of her bodice. She turned left and searched for a door that led outside.

Afternoon sunlight warmed the manor grounds. Hot leaves teemed in the borders. Seeds grew shiny and full till bursting. Swallows chirruped and swooped up under the eaves of the manor and the slick back of a grass snake twisted over the lawn. As Audrey nipped down the back of the house toward the secret door, her dress and cloak dragged heavy around her legs. Her toes driving into the gravel, in short, little, steps, she moved along faster and aimed straight for the laurel bush.

Once inside the secret door, she enclosed herself in the dark of the passage. Cool air braced her skin. She traced her way up the staircase carefully, as quietly as possible, hardly daring to breathe, and came to stand at the hidden study entrance. This time, with no one to disturb her, she leant close and listened.

Inside the study, the paneled walls reverberated with the speech of Thomas and Whitgift. They lounged at the chairs around Thomas's desk, their voices oddly raised and clear. Frizer lurked beside the window and waited for his master to conclude business. Both Whitgift and Thomas turned in their chairs and purposely projected their conversation toward the secret study door.

"I trust you've found him now?" said Whitgift.

"Yes," Thomas replied.

"And where was the fellow?"

"Baines didn't return to his normal lodgings. Nevertheless, my men tracked him to Hogg Lane in Shoreditch." Thomas's voice lost some of its clarity, as he were troubled by something. "He has a room there at an inn."

"Can we trust he'll write charges against Marlowe?"

"He'll do it."

"May I ask what makes you so sure?"

"He'll do it..." Thomas repeated distractedly. "...with a little persuasion."

Eyes fixed on the secret door, Whitgift leant close to Thomas and whispered in his ear.

"You're truly sure that she's there?"

Thomas pressed his lips tight, and nodded in reply. After a moment, he peered down at the object in his hand. Over and over, using his thumb and forefinger, he flipped Kit's ouroboros brooch in the center of his palm. His sweat glistened on the golden band.

SCENE FIVE

Nonsuch Palace.

Nonsuch stood six miles out of London in the Surrey countryside. Designed by Henry VIII as a celebration of the Tudor dynasty, its opulence rivaled the magnificent Chateau de Chambord
in France.

The rear face of the palace stretched long and straight, broken by glass-paneled doors lustrous with the early evening
greens, purples, and reds of the garden. Studded between the
doors, tiles painted with scenes of jousting knights decorated the
walls. At either end, the walls suddenly leapt up and scaled the
heights of tall octagonal towers, each topped with statuettes of
knights bearing flags. A lion at the very tip flew the royal crest.
In the center of the palace, the tallest tower of all loomed over an
inner courtyard – the reception area for guests now arriving at the
banquet.

Once Audrey had helped to dress the Queen, she left the royal bedchamber, met with Thomas, and strutted off to the inner
courtyard to partake of the night's festivities. Warmed by a full
day of sun, the evening air kissed the skin as guests left the seclu-
sion of the palace corridors and slowly filed outside to the courtyard. Skirts ballooned and swords rattled on hips. Guests strayed
and chatted through the pillars of a colonnade. Some women carried rose stalks in their gloved hands – remnants from earlier
strolls around the gardens. On the walls of the courtyard, life-like
statues of gilt and alabaster seemed to leap out towards you. The
lowering sun tinged the statues' surface with pink and shadows
brought depth to their pale eyes, curvature to their flat cheeks,

and animation to the crevices of their fingers and toes. Drunken guests had even been known to greet the statues before realizing their mistake and biting their tongue.

To the left of the courtyard, liveried servants stood beside tablecloths fluttering in the breeze. Atop the cloths, bouquets in silver vases interspersed the appetizers. Guests perused the selection of sweet tarts, glazed cakes, and bowls of trembling custard decorated with sprinkles in the image of the royal crest. Meanwhile, musicians strummed their lutes and stopped the holes of their pipes, tainting the air with mellow tunes.

As the earth twisted farther into night, and the crescent moon replaced the sun, parked carriages clogged the palace driveway. Moth wings battered around candles and the courtyard grew busy. Musicians struck a higher tempo. Singers serenaded the guests, their verses mingling with excited whispers in the darkness of the columns. Trays of goblets floated among the voices – through forgotten meetings, careless invitations, laughter, gossip, and drawling conversation about racehorses, falcons, planned estates, and shipments from the colonies. Audrey and Thomas blended in with the rest, almost indistinguishable from the people around them. Everyone anticipated the appearance of Elizabeth. No one knew, however, that a pair of uninvited guests would also join the banquet that night...

At the southern end of the palace, Kit and Will pressed close to an outer wall sheltered under the leaves and boughs of an oak forest. On the other side of the wall lay the palace gardens. Lights glowed from the distant inner courtyard.

As stealthily as possible, they crept along the sides of the giant stone wall. Their feet crackled on dead leaves. Each of them wore a dark hooded cloak – so long that it covered their hands and swallowed their faces in its depth. The wall beside them reached twenty foot high. Kit stopped and gazed up to the very top, craning his neck back to see. Grit fell into his eyes. He blinked.

Will handed him a grappling hook attached to a lengthy coil of rope. Kit tried to judge the distance to the top. With his right hand, he drew out a span of rope and dangled the hook in the air.

He whirled it around in a large circle so fast the rope blurred and they could only hear it move *zzzer, zzzer, zzzer* through the air.

He released the rope and swung the hook up.

Silence.

They watched it climb the lofty height of the wall, skim the air above, and loop down over the other side. The hook dropped quick. Its iron teeth chinked into stone. Will moved closer as Kit gripped the rope in both hands and hesitantly pulled it downwards. On the other side, the hook dragged and scraped its points against the wall. The rope drew taut. Kit tugged it hard but it caught on a stone lip at the very top of the wall and didn't give way.

"Ready?" Kit asked.

"I hope so," Will replied.

"You can still go back, if you want to."

"I'm doing well. Really, I'm fine."

Kit nodded, then hiked up his cloak so it wouldn't catch, and laid a foot against the wall. He clasped the rope tight in his fists and flexed his shoulder muscles. He pulled downwards, tested the rope again, raised himself off the ground, and took a step up the wall. The rope creaked as the fibers stretched under his weight. In seconds, he nimbly scaled the wall.

At the top, he crouched low, scoured the grounds. There must have been guards, but he saw none, and turned back and waved for Will to follow. With a deep breath, Kit dropped over the side and landed quietly in the grass of the palace gardens.

Will watched as Kit disappeared over the side. He closed his eyes and tried to quell the sense of foreboding prickling under his skin. He wiped his greasy hands on his cloak. He stepped closer to the wall and grabbed the rope and pulled. With less skill, he followed Kit up the wall. Eventually, chest panting, hands aching, he clambered awkwardly to the very top.

The gardens of Nonsuch opened proudly before him: reflecting pools smooth and burnished to a solid black; plinths and statues lurking in the shadows; privet hedges clipped in squares and spirals; a fountain gushing with falling droplets, some glinting in the moonlight, sharp and pale as the finest cut diamonds. Beyond,

174

the towers of the palace mounted to the sky in several great tiers, up and up to their slender flagpoles. Almost involuntarily, Will paused and gawked at the sight.

"Such grandeur, such glory..." he gasped.

On the ground below Kit waited impatiently.

"We've no time for soliloquies now, Will," he whispered up.

"Hmm?"

"I said no soliloquies."

"Oh... sorry..." Will quickly regained his focus, peered down and lost his grip. With a tiny yelp, he fell off the wall and walloped down into the palace gardens.

Minutes later, Kit and Will stood together on the inside of the palace wall. Hawthorn trees and rhododendrons hid them from view. After waiting, listening for the movement of any nearby guards, they both removed their cloaks. Underneath, they wore the red and gold royal livery of palace servants: tunics embroidered with the royal arms; buttons with imprints of the crown; sleeves with lace frills; flat caps with a single feather; and thick hose over their legs ending in shiny black shoes. Each of them sported a fake pointed beard to mask their features. Meticulously, they checked over their disguises for tears or stains incurred in the climb.

"Hat's off to Henslowe," said Kit. "He's cheap, but he doesn't skimp on costumes."

"I know! These are some of the best I've ever seen – almost better than the real livery."

"Maybe..."

Will arranged his cap and touched his face.

"Is my beard on right?"

"Yes."

"I'm not sure that the hose fits me. I guess I can make it work, though."

Kit watched as Will continued fiddling with his clothes. He sighed and turned away. Heavy lines furrowed across his brow. The next moment, his eyes fell, and he hung his head, suddenly melancholy.

"Bloody disguises..." he muttered faintly.

"What? You can't really mean that." Will dismissed the comment with a wave of his hand. "You can't hate masks. You're in the theater, for goodness sake!"

"But they don't end with the playhouse."

"They don't?"

"Life is just one mask on another. Clothes cover the body. The body covers the soul."

"Well, speak for yourself – I love disguises." Will began a pompous walk and held out his hand affectedly. "Tonight, I will be Percival the serving man."

Kit frowned at him.

"Percy, you wouldn't love disguises if you'd worn as many as I have for the government."

"No..." Will ceased prancing. "No... maybe not..."

Kit paused at Will's comment. Then he peeked over the rhododendron, watched for guards, and gestured that all was clear.

Crouched low, they both crept out through the trees and made a burst toward the palace.

In single file, Kit leading the way, they stooped level with the rose bushes and bolted between the rows, hurdled flower beds, vaulted a bush, and darted onwards past reflecting pools. They reached the servant outhouses and pressed flat against the wall of a granary.

They gasped for breath. Didn't talk. From a wash-house came the squeaky aroma of soap. Over by the mews and the long block of stables, a horse gave a full-throated whinny. Kit pointed to an area up ahead where servants bustled around a group of buildings.

Torches lit a path snaking between the outhouses and the palace kitchens around the corner. Men with lists in their hands shouted orders and strained to make themselves heeded in the passing chaos of servants. Hands were full. Cheeks flamed with stress. No one had any time. Tense words sounded from the open windows of a bakehouse, and bodies coursed in and out the door-frames.

Gingerly, Kit and Will trod out from the granary, their heads down and serious. They threw themselves into the rush and merged-in seamlessly amongst the hubbub.

"Hey-ho!" someone shouted out. "Yes – you! I'm talking to you!"

Neither of them looked up. They hunched their shoulders and kept moving. Past four men heaving a cask of ale, they hustled down the path, turned the corner, and nipped silently into the steaming kitchens.

SCENE SIX

Nonsuch Palace. Kitchens.

When Kit and Will entered the kitchens their eyes gaped at the furious industry. Great hearths made cavernous hells out of two of the walls. Cauldrons spat and bubbled with soup and sauces. A spit whined under the weight of an entire deer – the skin licked golden-brown by the tongues of flames below. Bread ovens roared with fires and rising loaves. Tables pounded as hammers battered slabs of meat.

Kit panned his gaze across the cooks. To one side lay a network of dented tables surrounded by women in rolled sleeves. The women placed cranberries in rings around the edge of silver plates. Another table held a set of trays – each one stacked with glass goblets filled to the brim. A steady line of serving men frequented the table: they streamed in through one kitchen door, scooped up a tray, and then rotated out through another door in the direction of the inner courtyard.

Upon seeing this, Kit and Will sidled through the sweaty cooks and waited to collect a tray. As they waited, they carefully observed how the serving men swept up the trays with strong hands and waltzed toward the door with fluid steps while keeping their eyes half on the tray and half on potential obstacles in their path. Serving men were among the most highly trained of all the palace servants.

After collecting their trays, they both kept in line with the rest of the serving men and left the kitchen for the coolness of the marble corridors. As they proceeded along, Kit and Will copied the exact posture of the serving men: they straightened their backs, cradled the tray in one hand only, and spread their fingers wide apart, balancing the tray on their fingertips. Within minutes, they arrived at the entrance to the inner courtyard.

Will stopped as soon as he saw the Queen. Surrounded by a large, fawning crowd, Elizabeth stood positioned as near as possible to the light of the candelabras. Even so, tiny shadows still found every line on her face. Despite all the pearls glistening in her hair, the redness of her locks seemed faded, and her white dress joined seamlessly with the paleness of her hands and neck.

"She's older than she looks in her portrait," said Will disappointedly.

Meanwhile, though Kit scanned the crowd for Essex, even he stood dazzled by the display of wealth on show that night. Before him mingled the greatest collection of ambassadors, knights, gentry, barons, countesses, viscounts, dukes and duchesses he had ever seen. Lace ruffs foamed around throats. Diamond bracelets flashed on wrists. Pomanders drugged the air with incense. Gloved hand shook with gloved hand, and painted lips gave painted smiles. The women stood tall, their eyebrows plucked into arches, their hair dyed in various tones of blonde or covered by immaculate wigs. Narrow bodices and capacious gowns contoured their figures dramatically. Beside them, the men chatted in confident voices. They wore fine, trimmed beards upon their chins, and teardrop earrings dangled from their left earlobes. Over their well-fed limbs their skin pulled smooth, conditioned by regular baths in asses' milk. Huge feather plumes waved from their hats and tiny capes swished on their shoulders as they turned to greet friend after friend.

Kit tapped Will on the shoulder and they began to search through the crowd for the Earl of Essex. They dodged gowns, brushed past cloaks, carefully picked their feet around the toes of nobility, and slowed to let groups surge past them. Jeweled hands reached out and plucked goblets from their trays. A moth fluttered before Kit's face and nearly made him sneeze. Once, he spotted Audrey and Thomas speaking idly with another couple. His gaze lingered on Audrey's angular shape, her dark eyes. Light fell in hazel streaks upon her hair. She laced her fingers together

179

and cradled her hands at her waist. She didn't seem to notice him in his disguise and Kit continued searching the crowd but found no sign of Essex anywhere. Soon, Will's tray was nearly empty. He tilted his head near Kit to whisper.

"Found him yet?" Will asked.

Kit struggled to see over the hats in front of him.

"No," he replied lowly. "But I haven't checked everywhere."

"Perhaps there's a chance he didn't come tonight?"

"He wouldn't miss it."

"You're fully sure about that?"

"No." Kit peered harder around the courtyard, examining the guests. Suddenly, his face brightened. He nodded in the direction of a man stood at the center – definitely Lord Essex.

Essex wore possibly the gaudiest doublet in the entire courtyard. Red, gold, and green checks colored his chest and gold slashing adorned his sleeves. A thick, dense ruff around his neck almost rose up to the back of his head, like a bird raising its crest, but no hat covered his exquisitely preened hair. A gold-hilted sword slouched from his hip and a pendant holding the Queen's miniature hung around his shoulders from a black ribbon. At twenty-seven years old, Essex was a man at the peak of physical health who posed and spoke as if he were a king. Indeed, since he descended from Henry IV, he often deemed himself the Queen's equal. That night, he stood with one hand on his hip and the other waving a goblet of wine in the air as he led conversation with group of ladies and noblemen. His laugh was effusive and seemed to ripple out from his chest, encircling those around him. Shoulders held back, head tilted up, he poured witticisms and eloquence from a mouth that never shut, and his eyes jumped from face to face, drinking in the attention of his listeners.

"Hide me a moment," Kit whispered.

"Where?"

"The colonnade."

Quickly, Kit and Will hustled to the side of the courtyard and cut into the shadows. Will stood in front to block Kit from view. Kit reached into his pouch and retrieved the small green bottle of truth potion. He removed the stopper and let two drops fall gently into the mouth of one of the goblets. Afterwards, he returned the bottle to his pouch and cleared off all other goblets from his tray, save for the newly tainted drink. He glanced at the goblet then looked at Will.

"Wish me luck," he said nervously.

Almost as worried as Kit, Will gave him a small pat on the shoulder. With the tray and single tainted goblet, Kit nipped out of the colonnade and headed straight for Essex.

About halfway across the courtyard Kit suddenly noticed that Essex already had a drink. In reaction, he drew a deep draught of air. The tray in his hand slipped a little. His beard itched around his chin. He knew what he had to do and his face soon hardened with determination.

Without breaking stride, he paced up beside Essex, purposefully extended an elbow, and bumped into him hard. Essex's wine spilt everywhere...

SCENE SEVEN

Nonsuch Palace. Inner Courtyard.

In the collision, Essex's goblet dumped its entire contents over his chest. He stopped in mid-sentence. Froze in shock. He whirled around and stared Kit in the eye. Women gasped and everyone seemed to take a step backwards. The musicians kept on playing but no one listened anymore. Will's eyes widened in horror.

Essex stood there soaking with wine and rage, his anger building. Kit lowered his head submissively. Essex flushed so bright even his hands acquired color.

"Look at me!" Essex bellowed. He raised his stained sleeves and shook his dripping hands. "Look!"

"My lord, a thousand apologies, I–"

"I'm soaked through you goatish, pribbling, ill-bred, fen-sucked, clay-brained simpleton!"

"A thousand apologies," Kit repeated meekly.

"This doublet is worth more than your reeking apologies! Fie! I've seen farm yard animals that would make better servants!"

Kit lifted the tainted drink from his tray and humbly offered it to Essex.

"If it pleases your lordship, I could clean off the wine before it settles?" Heart pumping, Kit lowered his head and anxiously awaited the reply.

Essex snatched the goblet and scowled darkly.

"Indeed you will, sirrah!" he snapped. "Indeed you will!" With as much dignity as he could muster, Essex stalked through the courtyard toward the palace doors, muttering all the way. He barreled off into the corridor. Kit tailed him closely and followed him in the direction of the kitchen.

Impatient and blustering, Essex waited while Kit nipped into the kitchen to grab a bowl of water and a cloth. Less than a minute later, he returned to Essex and began mopping the wine from the doublet. With the sodden cloth, he bent low and scrubbed clean the largest stain on Essex's chest. Meanwhile, Essex glowered and sipped at the tainted goblet in his hand.

"Careful, you oaf," said Essex caustically. "Have you no delicacy at all?"

Kit gritted his teeth and continued scrubbing. The hot sounds of the kitchen echoed out into the corridor accompanied by the aroma of cooked meats. He waited for the potion to take effect but it seemed to take forever and several minutes later nothing had happened. Essex grew ever more impatient to return to the inner courtyard and though Kit tried to prolong things he couldn't delay much further. Essex's doublet was nearly clean.

However, just as Kit began to despair, just as he began to curse Lazell under his breath, something extremely odd occurred: Essex's demeanor changed. His anger seemed to dispel. His posture loosened. His eyes ceased to glare and began to twinkle with mirth. As Kit continued cleaning the doublet, Essex peered down his nose.

"Cleaning the Earl of Essex's doublet is quite an honor for you, no?"

Kit remained silent. Essex took a sip of wine and continued:

"Yes, I'll wager it's your greatest wish to be me. Go on, admit it. Don't be shy, sirrah. Tell everything. It's your greatest wish to be me, isn't it?"

Kit glanced up. Essex's lips crinkled at the corners of his mouth as if he were trying not to smile. Kit regarded him with interest.

"But if I were you, my lord," he replied, "who would you be?"

"I would be..." Essex paused and thought about it. "I would be... I would be.... a king." He started giggling.

"What?"

"A king."

"Of course, my lord.

"And a king of England, too." Essex giggled louder. The absurd noise carried down the corridor. "By God, if I were a king I'd put that red-haired strumpet in her place!" He started thrusting his hips rudely. "She needs a royal rogering!"

Kit frowned in surprise, partly amused, partly frightened by Essex's behavior. Swiftly, he put the bowl down, stood up straight and beckoned Essex down the corridor.

Still laughing, Essex followed him and thrust his hips again and again. Once they were far away from the kitchen and all passing servants, Kit waved his hands and tried to quiet Essex down a little.

"Soft, my lord," he said soothingly.

Essex never stopped giggling. In partial disbelief, Kit watched the effects of the truth potion completely take hold: Essex hung his arms loose like a child, his eyes widened, his pupils dilated, and all his movements seemed oddly spontaneous and uncoordinated. Kit drew close and spoke in a slow, hushed voice.

"Hark a moment. I must ask you something important... I need to know about the posters in London. Are you behind Thomas Walsingham's union with Whitgift?"

"The only thing I want to get behind is that Queen!" Essex said through his giggles.

"But aren't you trying to unseat Burghley from power?"

Essex put a finger to his lips.

"*Shhh!*" He clasped Kit's shoulder and pulled him closer, as if imparting some secret. "Burghley's naughty, but Whitgift's on the rise, if you know what I mean." He grabbed the sword on his hip and tilted it up rudely. "What *is* that man's problem? He looks like he sat on his own cross! Damn fool thinks he can even start his own spy circle – make Burghley and I redundant. I'll make *him* bloody redundant!"

Kit stood back and rubbed his brow. His face tense with thought, he mumbled to himself.

"Of course.... Whitgift isn't joined with another lord. He and Thomas are working separately from anyone else... they're forging their very own intelligence network." He closed his fists in glee. "Then all I have to do is prove that they alone posted the libels! My god, I've already got part of the evidence!"

Essex gave a rowdy laugh and glanced at his reflection in his goblet.

"God, I really *am* good-looking..."

Kit frowned and shifted back to his side. He gave Essex a gentle pat on the back, helped him to stand up straight, and gestured toward the inner courtyard.

"You've been very helpful, my lord," he said as if talking to a small child. "Now let's get you back in there."

Essex's face lit up.

"Back in there! Whoa! *Back, in, there!*" He thrust his hips again and giggled as they walked off toward the courtyard...

Later in the evening, trumpets blared with shimmering notes to announce the serving of dinner. Hand in hand, sedate ladies and noblemen drifted away from the inner courtyard and steadily wandered a short distance through the palace to the banquet hall. As they approached, the stately music of minstrels breezed toward them.

The banquet hall's main entrance stood at the eastern end, shaded by a minstrel gallery overhead. The contrast between the darkness of the entry and the subsequent brightness of the hall only added to the splendor that it made on one's first impression. The room was long with generous width and the ceiling soared sixty foot high. A series of oak arches curved along the center of the ceiling. Rich carvings decorated the arches with grooves, layers, and rounded edges – all finished with burnished gold. At the sides of the room, eight gothic windows ran high down the walls, and below each window an arras tapestry depicted scenes from the life of Abraham.

Relaxed and ready to eat, the guests swanned into the room almost to the tempo of the music. They approached a group of long tables set in horseshoe formation: two tables extended down the length of the room, and a single table at the far end straddled the room's width. A paved dais raised the end table slightly above the others, and a throne-like chair sat in the middle for Elizabeth. During the day, an oriel window – larger than any other in the room – shed copious light over the dais and upon the Queen, but now that all the windows were darkened by nightfall, extra candelabras provided the light necessary to focus everyone's attention on the monarch.

Gradually, all the guests arrived and stood behind the exactly spaced chairs. They watched as Elizabeth paraded into the hall, took her seat at the end table, and said the evening's grace. Chair-legs then rubbed and squealed across flagstones as the guests sat down. A host of serving men entered the hall with heavy platters of fruits, nuts, and cheeses in their hands. The banquet had begun.

Beside every plate, napkins folded in the shape of lilies were undone and spread over laps as the ladies and noblemen devoured their appetizers. Serving men continued to circulate around the tables, bringing dish after dish. Meanwhile, as knives clinked on silver plates and prattling voices lifted above the thrum and whistle of the minstrels in the gallery, Kit and Will entered the hall along with the serving men. Kit bore a silver cup of walnuts in his hands and Will carried a bowl of sliced oranges. With Kit in front, they both marched in stately pace down the table, ever nearer to the Queen. Will leant forward and whispered in Kit's ear.

"I knew Lazell was lying about the side-effects. Still, things aren't at their worst – at least you got what you wanted from Essex."

"Yes," Kit replied.

"But tell me, if it's not Essex not behind the conspiracy, then who is it?"

"I'll explain it all later."

"When?"

Kit didn't answer – his eyes fixed on Audrey and Thomas at the end of the table near Elizabeth. Will shook his head, then bent down and set the oranges between two ladies buttering their bread roles. Kit marched onwards down the table and paused behind Audrey. She held a plum in her fingers and was just about to raise it to her lips. On her other side, Thomas leaned away and chatted to a man with a long beard. Pointedly, Kit stooped and placed his cup on the table near her plate. As he did so, he turned his head towards her, caught her eyes, and winked.

She averted her gaze defensively and immediately, as if by instinct. The next moment, however, she gave him a second look and regarded him with intrigue. The plum nearly fell out of her hand. Her jaw dropped.

Scared that she might accidentally give him away, Kit stood up straight and quickly paced around the other side of the table. Her eyes trailed him.

Discreetly, she raised her finger, pointed at him, then herself, and flicked her eyes toward the door. He understood and nodded back at her.

Kit left the hall and strode away to the kitchens. Once inside, he searched for Will. The hearths now burnt hotter than ever, but most of the cooks bustled around the preparation tables, hectically constructing the main courses. Hands darted over the plates, pouring sauces, arranging garnishes. Beside a table of appetizers, Kit found Will waiting to collect more plates. He grabbed Will's arm and took him aside.

"Audrey Walsingham needs to speak with me," he said urgently.

"She does?" Will replied. He raised his eyebrows suspiciously. "Why is that?"

Kit lowered his voice.

"There's no time to explain."

"No, there never is..."

"I just need a distraction. She needs to escape the hall without notice."

They stood quietly while the cooks shot back and forth over the room, yelling at each other. Will stared pensively into mid air. Behind him, the bubbles in a vat of soup popped loudly. He suddenly flinched.

"The truth potion!" he whispered.

Kit looked at him hopefully, drew the green bottle out of his pouch, and handed it over.

"What thoughts have you?" he asked.

Will smiled mischievously and turned around to face the soup cauldrons. The soup was yellow and creamy. It smelt of leek.

He checked over his shoulder, assured himself that all the cooks were busy, then removed the stopper from the bottle and emptied every last drop of potion into the cauldron. The green liquid swirled around in the soup and slowly dissipated.

"Laughter," said Will quietly. "The greatest distraction of all."

SCENE EIGHT

Banquet Hall.

The soup was served.

As before, the serving men, including Kit and Will, filed into the room with silent, ghostly steps. Each carried a single bowl of soup and watched that the little soup-waves didn't splash over the edge as they reached down and set the bowls in front of the ladies and noblemen. Kit made sure he was the one to serve Audrey. She saw him approach and sat up straight. Underneath the table, her hands twisted the napkin anxiously, worried that Thomas might see.

Kit brushed close as he served her the soup.

"Don't drink, my lady," he whispered.

She heard him but gave no reaction. Kit and Will swept around the table and headed for the door. As they left, soup spoons slid into bowls and the nobles tasted it eagerly.

After the soup came the main courses of the banquet. White tablecloths now became a canvas for all the shapes and colors of the food Elizabeth bestowed upon her guests. Bowls of lush green salad washed against wheat loaves in openwork baskets. Steam climbed from plates of rosy venison. Knives cut chunks from yellow mounds of cheese. Pink salmon tails poked over the sides of dishes. Platters bedded with moss circled the room, each laden with slices of pineapple, melon, red grapes, and purple dates. Orange candle-flames gleamed over silver dish covers. Jeweled goblets cast their shadows on the table. Cloves floated in the wine. Beads of moisture collected on the sides of glass cups filled with crushed ice. Jugs, pitchers, and candlesticks obscured the faces of people seated opposite, and eyes peeked over bouquets of roses to see across the room. The centerpiece of the meal was an entire swan served in its own plumage. Everyone clapped when four serving men carried it into the room and set it down on its own little table in the middle. The swan rested on a blue base, as if it were still swimming in a river. A cook came from the kitchen, ceremonially sharpened his knife, and set to work at carving the creature. Serving men then collected the choicest cuts and went around with trays, offered them to the guests, and with a pair of tongs flipped the slices adeptly onto the center of plates.

Once the ladies and noblemen dug deeply into their main courses, the serving men had orders to stand at the edges of the room and wait upon the guests. With backs almost against the wall, Kit and Will stood side by side and surveyed the table. Audrey refused to look at them.

So far, the potion hadn't taken effect. Kit noted the soup bowls had been taken away long ago. He fidgeted. He voiced his concerns to Will, but Will smiled patiently and told him to wait. Kit watched over the table again: nothing out of the ordinary. Everyone merely chatted pleasantly or asked the serving men for more claret or dipped their bread into gravy and listened civilly to their neighbor. The banquet had proceeded with success. Then things gradually began to change...

At the far end of one table, a man garbed in a military sash sat forward and leant his elbow on the tablecloth. With an entirely serious demeanor, his voice grew loud enough to hear above the people nearby.

"...and if it's not meetings with my staff," said the military man in a deep voice, "then it's sessions with the council, or filing report after report." He desperately scanned the faces of the people seated opposite. "I never get time to myself anymore."

Sat next to him, his shrewish wife held a napkin to her lips in embarrassment. She put the napkin down to the table.

"Dear," she said sweetly, "that's not very interesting. Nobody wants to hear you moan."

He turned to her with a bitter grin.

"You know something..."

"What, dear?"

"I think I hate you."

She flushed with embarrassment and picked the napkin back up. The ladies and noblemen seated near them tried to hide their smirks.

In the middle of the table, smiles broke across faces with greater frequency. Conversation steadily grew louder. Kit took a step forward and listened to a plump woman talking gravely with her friend – a lady in a blue dress.

"...no," said the plump woman miserably. "I haven't seen my son in months. But that doesn't stop his gambling, of course." She grabbed a leaf of romaine lettuce and cut it into strips. "At this rate we'll be destitute come July."

Her friend sniggered in reaction.

The plump woman stopped slicing the lettuce and looked at her askance. Her friend shut her eyes, tried to fight it, but her lips cracked into a smile. She sniggered again.

"Forgive me, Sarah," said her friend. "I don't know what's wrong with me tonight."

Over the other side of the table, the staid features of the guests were more at ease. Giggles everywhere now ruptured the polite conversation. In one particularly vocal section, a young wife nattered to an older man seated next to her.

"...oh, not at all," said the wife, batting the air with her hand. "Actually, John's a lousy lover."

The older man raised his eyebrows in surprise. People around them grew quiet and waited to see how the nearby husband would respond. With dilated eyes, the husband looked at the older man and nodded.

"Yes, she's quite right, I am!" he said merrily.

All three of them erupted into a fit of laughter. Everyone seemed to raise their voices in response. Men sat back in chairs and slowed their eating. Women sipped at their wine and waved their hands ardently as they spoke. Like a tiny earthquake, laughter rumbled over the sedate tranquility of the tables and fractured the surface formalities with great rifts of giggles, smirks, and hysterics. Their eyes wide and shocked at their own success, Kit and Will turned to each other and exchanged a guilty look.

For minutes on end, Kit and Will observed the scene, utterly mesmerized. Will smiled a little. In contrast, Kit looked pallid and uncomfortable. He seemed cut by everything he heard. Will glanced at the Queen and noticed that she too wasn't laughing. Instead, she had furrowed her brow at the hysterics and stopped eating.

"What's wrong with Elizabeth?" Will asked.

"Her food's prepared separately," said Kit with a miserable expression. He wiped the sheen of grease from his forehead and tried to loosen his collar. His eyes returned to the tables. "They're all so wretched," he complained. "I had no idea their lives could be this way."

Will spotted Audrey rise from her seat and slink towards the door. He nudged Kit. Once Audrey was gone, Kit paced along the tables and followed her out of the room. With all the wine, laughter, music, chaos, and cavorting no one noticed them leave.

SCENE NINE

Outside Banquet Hall.

Kit found Audrey waiting around the nearest corner. She stood in the recess of the corridor, her hands knotted, her feet shifting. A look of nervous intensity tempered her face. Her cheeks seemed devoid of their usual shapeliness. Her alert eyes kept watch over the serving men that passed to and from the hall. As Kit approached and opened his mouth to speak, she stopped him with a gesture of her hand.

"Follow me," she said under her breath. She turned and beckoned him with her forefinger.

In silence, she led Kit from one wing of the palace to another through a confusing network of halls, lobbies, and corridors, until they reached a broad flight of stairs. While hitching up her gown, she climbed the stairs and kept her pace just in front of him. He followed close behind and tried to ignore the memories flashing back through his head. At every ruffle of her gown he heard her voice in the tailor shop, the sound of her breathing as they stood snagged together by the brooch. At every footfall on the stairs he wandered back into the secret passageway at Scadbury, rediscovered the arousals of her figure, the temptations he fought against as they searched through the study.

Before long, Kit and Audrey approached two giant oak doors flanked by a pair of guards. Both guards were tall, with barrel chests and wide hands. Each held a pike. Without hesitation, Audrey smiled casually as if she knew them.

"The Queen requests her favorite cushion," she yawned.

One of the guards nodded.

"Certainly, my good gentlewoman," he replied. He reached down to his ring of keys and unlocked the door.

Audrey pushed the door open and stepped inside. Kit followed her and passed between the guards without making eye contact.

The room they entered was a bedchamber, but it was not like any Kit had ever known before. A fresco depicting the classical scene of Leda and the Swan spread across the lofty ceiling and from the center of the fresco dropped a long chain weighted at the end by a silver chandelier. Cataracts of light poured down from the chandelier, tripping onto wine-colored rugs covering the floor; the light rippled outwards to the edges of the room, streaming over velvet-covered chairs and gilt stools and marble pillars by the fireplace and flowing drapes at the windows. In the corners, light pooled around screens decorated with flower prints. A gilded dressing table sparkled in a bay window. Beside the table, a large golden dressing mirror stood on the floor with rounded feet. The center of the mirror's glass reflected a crimson blaze from the rosewood bed across the room. Finally, atop the subdued wood panels that covered every wall, tiny currents of light glinted on the varnish of gold-framed pictures. Some pictures were large and rectangle, others were small ovals. If any doubt remained about whose bedchamber this was, one had only to note the subject of the pictures: all were portraits of Elizabeth.

Once Kit had stepped inside, Audrey shut the door behind them. She sashayed into the middle of the room. He peered around nervously and gaped at the portraits.

"You must be out of your wits!" he gasped.

"Careful, don't shout, you must keep your voice low in here," she warned in a tender manner.

"This is the Queen's bedchamber!"

"Yes. Do you like it?"

"We're not safe."

"Oh, no, it's the safest place, the safest chamber, in the entire palace. Only a few have license to enter."

He wandered past the Queen's dressing mirror. On either side of the carved frame, two cherubs held lighted candles. He glanced uneasily at his reflection, then turned and focused his attention towards Audrey.

"What is it you need to tell me?"

"You know, I saw you earlier in the courtyard, but I wasn't sure. You did so well to get in here."

"My thanks."

"Of course, getting out maybe harder. I'm afraid I can't help you with that."

"I'll find a way."

"I'm sure you will." She smiled at him. "Your garb is so convincing. It's such a wonderful disguise."

"What did you want to tell me?"

Her face grew slightly taut.

"Whitgift met with Thomas again in the study. I went in the passageway – listened as best I could. They're set to have Baines make a series of direct charges against you tomorrow."

He raised his eyebrows. For a few moments, he stood quietly and didn't respond. She stepped closer and laid a tentative hand on his shoulder.

"This affair is so galling. I can't imagine what it's doing to you."

"You have Baines's address?"

She pulled out a note from her sleeve and gave it to him.

He unfolded it and his hands shook a little. He read the words:

"Room Six, Hogg Inn – Shoreditch."

With a sigh, he read the note again, paused, and stuffed it inside his pouch. His eyes glazed over pensively.

She gave an anxious sigh and fiddled with a ring on one of her fingers.

"What will you do?"

"I'll have to meet him first," he replied uncertainly. "Convince him against it, somehow."

She tilted her head down, discouraged by the tone in his voice. He clenched his jaw and turned to leave.

Her heart fluttered in alarm. She looked up and frowned. Her dress swished over the rug as she quick-stepped in front of him.

195

"Where are you going?" she said quietly. "You're not leaving, are you?"

He bridled at the question.

"It's too dangerous to stay, my lady."

She gave him a searching look.

"But everywhere's dangerous. It's dangerous to live in poverty and it's dangerous to live in wealth." She raised a hand and gestured dismissively to the room around them. "We're more than all this, Christopher. More than wealth, and titles, and the Queen; more than clothes, gestures, and words."

A tiny silence passed between them. Kit gulped.

"Do you believe in nothing then?"

"I believe in you." She stepped closer to him, eyes bright with emotion, and slowly reached out and took his hand in her soft fingers. "Why can't you do the same?"

He stared at her deeply. The flaw in her iris glowed blue. Loose strands of hair around her head caught the light and softened her image. Down beside the corner of her mouth, the outlines of two freckles showed through her make-up and for the first time he noticed a faint cleft in her chin. She turned her head away from the chandelier, so that her face lay divided in half by darkness and light. She had never looked more beautiful. She stood there, holding his hand, and waited patiently for him to act. He hesitated...

She shook her head sadly and rotated her shoulders to turn away from him. Tears had already collected in her eyes.

Suddenly, he lurched forward.

Grabbed her by the arm.

Pulled her close.

Kissed her.

He kissed her the way a drowning man kisses the air. His blood rioted and coursed through his veins, his heart pumped strong inside his chest, his legs felt oddly weak and unstable. He clung to her and kissed her with all his energy. The force of his embrace surprised her at first, but her arms gradually reached up to hold him. Just as she gripped him tighter, he stopped kissing, pulled back and regarded her. With trembling hands, he pinched the hair of his fake beard and tore it from his flesh. His cheeks seared with pain but he didn't care. Gently, he drew her close. Their arms entwined and their lips met and they kissed with rising passion.

Together they staggered across the room, bumped into a stool, and made it over to the bed. Her lips pressed full, warm, and firm against his own; her cheek rubbed his, smooth and gentle; and her sweet breath caressed his face. He breathed in through his nose. Her hair smelt of vanilla powder. They kissed madly and let their fingers stir over the curves of their chests, the flats of their backs, the inclines of their waists, and the undulations of their hips while breathing ever faster, panting, almost gasping for air, as their lips played, hands explored, and fingertips discovered.

He stroked his hands down over her chest, across her bosom, and pawed at the strings of her bodice. His fingers tugged at them lightly, harder, then frantically – he ripped them undone.

She arched her back and quivered with the emotions surging through her. Her fingers slipped from around his back, traced up to his chest, and fumbled with the buttons of his doublet. One by one, achingly slow, she unhitched the buttons and peeled the cloth from his body.

They sunk onto the bed, breast touching breast, thigh rubbing thigh. His lips traveled down, kissing her lips, her cheek, her chin, her nape. Her thighs loosened. Their legs converged. She clutched the sheets and gasped with anticipation...

Scene Ten

Banquet Hall.

Will couldn't help but grin. Far from lulling, the hilarity of the banquet only seemed to climb to an ever higher pitch. The entire hall rang with howls and shrieks of laughter. The noise rendered the music from the minstrel gallery barely audible but no one had told the minstrels to stop. Lutes kept thrumming their husky notes, lyres twittered softly, flutes burbled, and deep drumbeats pealed out from the gallery – all lost immediately in the cacophony of laughs.

Nothing could stop the merriment. Meats were left half-eaten on plates. Goblets tipped over and stained the tablecloth. Frank revelations and miserable utterances mixed everywhere with bellies shaking, tears of mirth, palms slapping on backs, fists rattling the tabletops, chairs tilting back on their legs, and hands waving in the air.

Upon the dais, a deathly quiet smothered the royal table. Elizabeth sat on her throne-like chair and surveyed the scene with annoyance. Slowly, she chopped a strip of venison with her knife, paused, and let the knife hover over the plate. She clenched her teeth and straightened her posture and held the breath in her lungs.

To Will's horror, she suddenly twisted in her chair toward him. She looked him straight in the eye. He felt as if he could crumple in half. She raised her hand and beckoned him to approach. He prayed that she was pointing at a serving man behind him. She wasn't. When he glanced over his shoulder he found there was no one near.

On quick heels, he marched down the hall and came to stand by the most eminent monarch in the entire world. At her side, he squinted at the light issued from the candelabra's surrounding her, and bent his head close to hear her through the noise.

"What is the source of their amusement?" she said bluntly.

He hesitated and scratched the back of his neck.

"Forgive me, your highness," he replied with a wavering voice. "I really can't say."

"Is it that you can't say, or that you won't say?"

"Um..."

She rolled her eyes at him.

"Enough with you!"

To his relief, she soon sent him away and he scuttled back to stand by the wall. Afterwards, he felt both silly and strangely proud of himself – as if he'd survived an encounter with some terrific and deadly force of nature.

Elizabeth leant forward to the very edge of her chair. With pursed lips, she addressed the table to her right where the military man sat laughing.

"Is it me?" she said loudly. "You laugh at me, do you not?"

The military man shook his head vigorously but continued chuckling. Elizabeth's eyes sparked with anger. She directed her gaze to the man's shrewish wife.

"Then who?" said Elizabeth.

The shrew quelled her laughter slightly and made numerous attempts to answer, yet every time she opened her mouth and tried to reply, she collapsed into uncontrollable giggles.

Elizabeth put her knife down on the plate. Despite the thick layer of white upon her cheeks, somehow she looked red and flustered. In a combative manner, she tipped her head down a little, and the light exaggerated her wide, domed forehead. The lines under her eyes and around the sides of her mouth grew deeper. She raised her voice to address the entire hall.

"Cease laughing," she said forcibly. "I command it."

Nothing happened.

She simmered with anger and rapped her fingers on the table. Her nails made a ticking noise.

199

"I command that you stop laughing this moment."

Still nothing happened. As far as the ladies and noblemen were concerned, the Queen had ceased to exist.

Elizabeth pushed her plate away. Shot to her feet. Slammed her fists on the table. She bellowed at the top of her voice.

"Stop laughing or I'll make you stop!"

This time, everyone stopped. Even the minstrels. All smiles vanished. All voices ceased. A dry, withering silence fell upon the room. Elizabeth narrowed her eyes and glowered, studying the faces of her guests for signs of defiance.

Along the length of the tables, sweat now beaded upon brows, suppressed laughter trembled in chests, twitched on cheeks, and wrinkled on lips. With eyes charged and glinting with mirth, the ladies and noblemen stole flashing glances at one another or desperately fixed their gaze onto the tabletop. For a moment, there was complete and utter silence.

Then someone at the back sniggered.

Someone else sniggered, too.

Suddenly, in one great, unstoppable wave, the laughter returned and rolled down the tables twice as strong as before. *Ha! Ha! Ha!* It surged up into the rafters. Men and women laughed so hard they almost fell out of their chairs.

Confused and threatened, Elizabeth gave a mighty huff. She tossed her napkin at her plate, spun away from the table, and raged toward a small door at the side of the room. The candelabras on the dais flickered with the sudden movement and some blew out. With surprising force for such delicate arms, Elizabeth flung the door back on its hinges and burst out into the corridor. Her ears still ringing, she stormed away as fast as her legs could carry her. Laughter seemed to chase her down the corridor.

SCENE ELEVEN

Queen's Bedchamber.

Half-clothed, Audrey and Kit sat on the Queen's bed and languorously began to dress themselves. Their shadows overlapped on the rug below. Kit closed his shirt around his chest, buttoned it, and tucked a lock of damp hair behind his ear. A warm contentment lulled within his limbs. For the first time without a quill in his hand, he felt within reach of something truly powerful and profound. With her love, there seemed nothing he couldn't accomplish. Anything was possible.

Next to him, Audrey reached down over her skirt, pinched a silk stocking between her thumb and forefinger and inched it up her leg. Hats, pins, shoes, a bodice, and a doublet lay scattered over the rug around the bed. Kit tipped his head back and watched tiers of flames dance among the clouded glass of the chandelier above. Occasionally, Audrey's gown ruffled or one of her buttons snapped into place. He stopped dressing and remained still and a strange phrase entered his mind. He remembered it from his visit to the Earl of Derby.

"What nourishes me destroys me," he mumbled slowly to himself.

"I'm sorry?" Audrey answered.

"Oh... nothing... I was just thinking of something that I heard once."

"How mysterious. You *are* mysterious, aren't you?"

He smiled and leant over the bed to watch her retie her dress. She bent her head down to fiddle with the strings and her eyelashes made shadows on the tops of her cheeks. Her strong, ele-

gant neck rose from the depth of her circular ruff. She sat with a
straight back and crossed legs. Below, a tiny foot covered by a
white stocking stuck out from the hem of her dress. The silk gave
a glossy sheen as she wiggled her toes. His eyes wandered up to
observe her hands – her slender fingers and fine white nails. She
noticed his gaze and smiled. He reached over, took her palm inside his own and lifted the back of her hand to his lips. He recited
a line of poetry:

"...hands so pure, so innocent, nay such,
As might have made heaven stoop to have a touch."
She looked at him lovingly.
"Is it from you new play?"

He nodded. Across the room, his pouch lay near the fireplace. He got up, fetched the pouch, and from it drew a wad of
parchment. After straightening the pages, he sat back down on
the bed and gave them to her. He'd rewritten all the ones lost in
Portsmouth. She received them with a look of reverence, as if
they were a sacred text.

"Hero and Leander," she read aloud, leafing slowly through
the pages.

"Yes," said Kit. "But it's a poem now, not a play."

"Oh, I see, yes, it's a poem."

"You don't mind?"

"Well, yes I do, in fact. I'm afraid you'll have to change it
all."

"What?"

She giggled.

"Of course I don't mind. How could I? Your writing is wonderful in each and every form."

"But is every form wonderful?"

"I... I don't know... I suppose life has too much form, too
much ceremony, about it sometimes. Yet surely everyone feels
like that?"

"I wish life had no form at all. No surface. Just the depth beneath."

She extended her little finger and tapped the play with the
very tip.

"May I ask, Christopher, why did you change it into a poem?"

"I was tired of the stage." He rose to his feet and paced around the room while fastening his doublet. "I didn't think it had relevance anymore."

"Do you still think so now?"

He didn't answer. She halted on one of the pages and studied it closely.

"I remember this, I think – it's a myth." She looked at him for confirmation. "Its origin is from Greek mythology, is it not?"

"That's correct."

"Two lovers divided by the Hellespont – the sea of Hell."

"Leander promises to swim it for Hero."

"Yes, yes, I remember now. He promises to swim it every evening to be with his love. Yet it's a tragedy, no? Doesn't he drown at the end?"

"Maybe I'll change that."

"Oh..."

"I haven't got there yet." He paused by one of the windows and glanced out into the night. "It's only a quarter done."

Above, a mass of cloud wrapped around the sky and only the faintest dusting of moonlight illuminated the windowsill. Kit gazed out and a blur of motion came from the palace below and caught his eye. He peered across a darkened courtyard and looked through a line of windows and into another wing of the palace: a figure in a large dress strode past the windows and a small group of ladies followed at a distance behind her. As the figure moved closer, Kit identified the face. He frowned and turned quickly to Audrey.

"The Queen's left the hall already!" he said with rising panic. "God's blood! She's coming this way!"

Audrey jerked her head and looked at him doubtfully.

"Not this early," she replied.

"Look for yourself."

"It's never this early – the banquet will go on for hours yet. They always do, believe me."

Urgently, Kit beckoned her to the window. She hesitated a moment, as if thinking, then jumped to her feet and rushed over to stand beside him. When she peeped out and looked through the windows of the next wing, her face grew mortally serious. She turned back to him and rapidly started threading the strings of her bodice.

"Quick! Help tie me!"

Away from the bedchamber, across the dark courtyard, through the windows of the next wing, Elizabeth surged down the corridor trailing a wake of handmaids. Her dress billowed out behind her. Her sharp heels clicked on the marble floor. Heat started to rise under her dense sleeves and tight bodice, fanning the flames of her anger. She marched onwards. A double necklace of pearls bounced against her chest, her earrings jogged and swung like pendulums from her earlobes, and a jeweled chain slipped from side to side around her waist.

She sped around a corner and headed for a wide staircase that led to the royal bedchambers. Her gloves squeezed into her wrists like manacles and she tore them off, threw them to the floor, and left them behind. The handmaids exchanged a dark look between themselves and one stooped to collect the gloves. They hustled after the Queen as she mounted the stairs, muttering under her breath with every stride...

Meanwhile, inside the Queen's bedchamber Kit stood with Audrey and tried to lace the strings through the narrow loops of her bodice. Even before he'd finished, she had already fixed her hair, checked her makeup, and slipped her feet into shoes. His fingers trembled as he clutched the strings and struggled to find the right holes. Eventually, as best he could, he managed to tie the strings into a tight web.

They tidied the room and prepared to leave. Kit straightened a chair. Audrey smoothed the quilt covers on the bed. Just before they left, Kit flinched and reminded Audrey about the pillow. She grabbed one from a stool and then led him out through the oak doors.

Outside, lest he appear suspicious to the guards, Kit fought the urge to scan the corridor for the Queen. Audrey held the pillow out in front of her and puffed it to make sure the guards would see. She paced off down the corridor with Kit at her side. For fear of meeting Elizabeth, they walked in the opposite direction from the stairs.

As Kit strode along, he felt a strange queasiness in his stomach. Compulsively, he touched the full pouch swinging from his hip to assure himself he didn't leave the pages of 'Hero and Leander' behind. He reached up to check his beard was stuck on properly. He halted. His eyes widened and he rubbed his chin: it was bare.

"My beard!" he gasped.

Audrey looked over her shoulder and drew close to him.

"I'll make sure the Queen doesn't find it," she said. "You can't go back for it. You simply can't."

A commotion sounded at the other end of the corridor. They turned their heads. In a fearful rage, Elizabeth whisked around the corner and barreled straight for her bedchamber. Audrey pointed the way to Kit and gave him some quick directions on how to return to the banquet hall.

"Farewell," she whispered to him. She started back towards the royal bedchamber.

"Farewell," he replied.

He turned away down the corridor. Without looking back, she hurried along and met up with the handmaid's chasing after Elizabeth.

Scene Twelve

Palace Corridors.

Kit made no pretensions of calm as he wound his way through the maze of corridors: he wanted out. After passing through a dim gallery of paintings and sculptures, he veered outside, cut through an archway and a colonnade, and took a quicker route back to the banquet hall. Once he had reached the hall, he dipped inside to collect Will, reemerged into the corridor, and headed for the kitchens. Minutes later, they both nipped outside to the rear grounds of the palace.

Now that the banquet had come to a premature end, servants and cooks gathered outside around the outhouses to gossip. No one relished the thought of tackling the dirty dishes, goblets, and trays waiting for them inside. Through rings of smoke and swigs of ale, the serving men relayed the unusual events of the banquet to anyone who would listen.

On the edge of one group, Frizer loitered and tried unsuccessfully to engage people in conversation. Slightly bored, he stared off into the gardens, then panned his gaze around the outhouses. His eyes stopped at the kitchens and watched two figures exit the palace. One figure stood taller than the other. The smallest wore a beard and Frizer didn't recognize him, but the other figure was beardless and seemed familiar. He squinted closer. It was definitely Marlowe.

Frizer's face lit up. Without a moment to waste, he jogged off into the palace and ran in the direction of the banquet hall.

Inside the hall, the nobles had regained their staunch composure and most had begun to leave. Although some still remained at the table, sipping at the ends of wine or pecking at meat from bones, most lords and ladies now filtered out of the room. The effects of the truth potion had relinquished and left them all with tired faces, sore stomachs, and bruised ribs.

At one side, Thomas stood talking to a small group of noblemen. During the feast, he had laughed as hard as anyone, but unlike other people the potion had left him with a feeling of release. Frustrations had momentarily ebbed away. The muscles along his back were loose from fear. His heart and lungs felt pleasantly unrestricted by jealously. He cracked his knuckles and nodded his head gently while listening to an old bearded man espouse theories about what had occurred that night. Many people claimed to have forgotten everything said at the table. Thomas agreed, but didn't really believe them.

Frizer jumped into the room and approached him. Thomas took leave of the old man and strolled a few paces away so that no one in the group could listen.

Frizer leant close and whispered his news. Thomas waited a few seconds, struggling to understand him. He arched his eyebrows.

"Are you sure?" he said, unable to contain his surprise.

"Indeed I am, sir," Frizer replied, clearly pleased with himself. "Marlowe left with another man just this minute. It was probably Shakespeare."

Thomas gave him a doubtful look. Frizer blushed, adding to the redness of his cheeks.

"Let your lady's absence vouch for it, sir."

Thomas balked at the idea.

"You mean... he... and she..." He couldn't finish the sentence. Thoughts and images of the coupling suddenly tortured his mind. His body tightened and his face grew stern. He pressed his lips together severely.

At that moment, Audrey appeared at the hall's entrance. Her svelte, angular figure filled half the door frame. She quickly sighted Thomas and Frizer and padded over to them. She held her hands at her waist, kept her head low, and avoided looking Thomas in the eye.

"Her majesty wishes me to stay late again," she said uneasily.

Thomas narrowed his eyes.

"Is that so?"

"The palace will have a carriage take me home later."

He peered down and noticed her bodice was tied wrongly.
Some of the strings missed their holes or lay tangled upon the
others. He gave a bitter smile and stroked his nails along his forelock.

"As you will," he replied, sounding each syllable precisely.

For a moment, she studied him carefully, even suspiciously,
then circled on her heel and swiftly left the room.

Once she had gone, Thomas beckoned Frizer close.

"I'll wait no longer," said Thomas in a low voice. "It's time
our favorite playwright made an exit."

"Yes, sir."

"And I know exactly where it can be done..."

ACT IV

SCENE ONE

Norton Folgate. Kit's Lodgings.

Kit woke from a deep, dreamless sleep and rolled over in bed.

Outside, the morning sun lifted over great meadows and crooked lanes. The half-light of dawn steeped everything in a softly vibrating radiance as if all colors, shapes, and textures were newly revealed after the moon had masked the world in darkness. Trees bared their branches. Pebbles exposed their base yellows and grays. Fields unfurled into vast tracts of land spiked with slender blades of grass. The once draughtless air now stirred with tails of wind, the shadows of fleeting starlings, the soft-murmuring of insects.

After Kit had dressed, he left his room and stepped out onto the road. Norton Folgate was a sparsely populated liberty less than a mile from London. Essentially, it was a road leading from the ward of Bishopsgate in London, to the high street of Shoreditch located a short distance to the north. Homes and shops had clustered around the road, but they were so few in number that the settlement felt as free and open as a country hamlet.

His head clouded by worries, Kit strolled up the road toward Shoreditch. He had no idea how to convince Baines against making incriminating charges. It seemed hopeless. Even so, he had to try something – there was nothing else to do. Hogg lane lurked a short distance ahead but he avoided it for now and continued onwards to meet Will at his room in Shoreditch.

Will lodged at a widow's cottage just off the high street. Kit padded inside the cottage, tramped across the hall, found Will's door and knocked. He waited for over half a minute before it finally opened.

Will shuffled to the doorframe, looking utterly disheveled. He still wore the serving man's livery from last night. He squinted up at Kit.

"Pray tell me it's not that hour already?"

"Afraid so," Kit replied half-frowning, half-smiling. "I think you look how I feel this morning, Will."

"Then you must feel like a cowpat – because that's probably what I look like."

"Didn't you sleep?"

"I can sleep later. I had more important issues to contend with."

"Like what?"

"I needed time to write. The last few days exhausted me more than I thought possible... I hoped seeing the palace and the Queen might give me some level of inspiration."

"And did it?"

Will blinked dismally. He didn't answer. While rubbing the tiredness from his eyes, he beckoned Kit into his room.

From their recent travels, Kit had often seen Will in the morning, but he had never appeared as sallow or sickly as he did now. The last few days had aged him dramatically. His limbs seemed thinner. Bags hung under his eyes. A certain vigor had waned from his movements. In comparison, Kit bristled with energy as he strode into Will's room.

Weary and half asleep, Will changed into a fresh shirt and breeches while Kit spoke about how they would confront Baines today. They shared halves of a biscuit – the only food Will had to offer – and finally set out to find Baines.

They both knew Hogg Lane. It bisected the main thoroughfare between Norton Folgate and Shoreditch and led out to Butcher's Close, a large piggery just beyond the houses. Due to the piggery, the area reeked with warm, lagging fumes of manure piles; and smooth, pink-backed pigs frequently clogged the entire street as farmers moved the grunting herds. The lane consisted of a dirt road squeezed between a solid line of beam and plaster buildings, each packed unnecessarily close together, as if crouching in the other's shadow.

Morning sun lifted higher in the sky and rapidly heated the earth. With careful steps, Kit and Will chanced their way down the muddy lane. They sidestepped litter and skirted ditches with floating debris and apple cores. Dust and noise thickened the air as the street slowly gained activity.

Further down the lane, travelers stopped in coaches to browse the shops. The outside world had grown so brilliant with sun that the light began to invade the dim interiors of the shops. Strange outlines of objects sat on the shelves through the gloom and merchants stood in doorways leaning against the doorframe. Also along the lane, peddlers with shiny satchels touted fake holy relics plundered from Jerusalem. Sun reddened the faces of vagabonds dozing on the ground next to pots of change and some were honest enough to state they wanted cash to buy ale or the company of a loose woman. Indeed, such women were close at hand, for the painted faces of young girls waited in the shade of many open doorways.

Kit and Will neared the end of the street. Kit slowed his gait and his body stiffened. Will took a handkerchief from his sleeve and wiped his flustered brow.

"Are you sure this is the right place?" Will moaned.

"Unfortunately," Kit replied.

"If you can, explain something to me. How did Audrey even come by Baines's address?"

"Well... she found it."

"Where?"

"Thomas's study."

"But how's Thomas connected with all of this, anyway? Didn't you say that nothing happened at Scadbury?"

Almost automatically, Kit avoided giving an answer. Guilt screwed into his conscience but he couldn't tell Will the whole truth just yet. It was better to explain things later. Not now. He gestured toward an inn at the bottom of the lane.

"Here we are," he said nervously.

Hogg Inn identified itself from the surrounding buildings with a simple, crudely painted sign of a boar's head – the lip snarling, the teeth sharp. When contrasted with the building itself, however, the sign looked relatively attractive. Black thatch, as course as a boar's back, covered the inn's roof and flattened down over the corners of the upper windows, giving the building a countenance of drowsiness. Several windows held smashed panes masked with brown wrapping paper.

Inside, the inn was in the midst of repairs. Piles of abandoned bricks lay jumbled in a corner with broken slats of wood, an empty cask, and sloppy pots of paint. A cat lay curled up asleep on the stairs. As soon as Kit and Will stepped inside, they turned and noticed an old man sat at a desk. They waited for him to speak, but he only regarded them with disinterest and looked away.

Kit checked the note in his hand and attempted to find Baines's room.

"Should be number six," he muttered.

They tramped upstairs, hopped over the sleeping cat, and wandered down a row of shut doors. The entire inn lay quiet against the sultry street noise outside: no staff loitered in the halls, no guests opened or shut their doors, and no sounds of shuffling came from within the rooms. Despite this, some rooms were clearly occupied. Outside one door, a pair of boots stood with their heels together, their hobnails shining. Next door, a pin stuck a bill of payment to the door frame.

They searched further along and soon came to the correct room. Before Kit knocked, he bent his head closer to the door to listen for movement inside. He ground his teeth together. The note felt damp in his hand. He tossed it on the floor with the other litter. He rapped twice on the door and took a pace backwards.

No answer. They stood and waited for an entire minute. Will yawned anxiously. Kit tapped his foot. He reached forward and tried the door handle. Locked. A moment passed and they looked at each other.

214

His patience finally ended, Kit stood back – launched his heel into the middle of the door. The boom echoed through the building, but door number six still held fast to its frame.

He kicked again. Something cracked a little. Will joined him and they both lashed the door with their best kicks.

Sloomph! Blam! Sloomph! Blam!

Two more kicks and the door ripped away from its frame – snapped back into the wall behind.

Eyes darting left and right for danger, Kit pulled his dagger and prowled forward and passed inside. His face gradually dropped. The sight before him turned his skin pale: the room was empty. Hopelessly empty. Empty not just of an occupant, but empty of any furniture whatsoever, save for a single chair by the window.

Dismayed, he lifted his gaze to the rafters. As his mind wandered, he stared pensively into the spines of the thatch roof: a dense weave of thick wheat straw. He frowned deeply. Compressed, troubled lines crinkled into his brow. He rambled almost to himself:

"They must have set her up to give me a false address... waste my time... she couldn't... she couldn't have known..."

Will peered around. Through the tiredness of his body, the dirt, the aches and pains, an unforgiving anger slowly arose to the surface. He stomped into the room. Sunlight from the window caught brightly in his eyes.

"I'll have no more lies," he said bluntly.

Kit tilted his head around. With dismay, he noted the change in Will's demeanor. His posture deflated.

"Lies?" he answered feebly.

"It's Thomas who's helping Whitgift, isn't it?"

Kit sighed. He turned to Will and gave him a look heavily laced with guilt.

"Yes... yes, it is."

Will tossed his hands into the air.

"In faith! You've known about this since Portsmouth, haven't you? I should have expected as much!"

215

Kit paced quickly over to the window and didn't respond. He could feel Will's eyes scorch him with anger. He couldn't breathe. The room seemed airless. He knew exactly what Will would say next.

"Tell me," said Will, stalking towards him, "am I some minor character in a play that you can simply use and discard as you like? Am I?"

Kit gulped.

"I pray you, Will, don't put me on the rack about this. I wanted to tell you earlier... but... you haven't lived the life I have. Trust isn't a word for spies. It's an invitation to the grave."

"You speak as if you're dead already." Will turned to go. "From now on you can do what you like, but you'll have to do it without me. I'll have no more of this."

Kit's mouth dropped open.

"Don't leave. I'll change. I promise... I promise I'll tell you everything."

"It's too late."

"I beseech you. Give me another chance."

Will ignored him. He paced across the floorboards and reached the door. Kit turned desperate. He searched for something, anything to make Will stop. His purse banged against his leg.

"I'll get you another patron," Kit blurted. "Thomas is out, but I'll find you someone else when this is over."

Will halted. He spun around instantly, eyes hot with rage.

"To hell with your monies!" he said disgustedly. "Every second I spend with you stunts my writing!"

"I'm sorry for that."

"No, you're not. You're not sorry about anything. All you know is a world limited with violence, secrecy, injustice, and pain. It's corrupted you, and it's corrupting me the longer I stay around it."

Kit smarted at the words.

"And what did you think life was?"

"More than this."

"Like what, exactly?"

"A lot more than this."

"Did you think it could all be fairy dust and summer days? Sorry, Will, sometimes it's filled with poison and bitter winters, too."

"You always did go over the top – especially in your writing."

"Really?"

"Yes, really."

"Well, at least my plots aren't over-complicated!"

"See if this is too complex for you: you're a sniveling, soulless government mongrel with a shilling instead of a heart!"

Kit clenched his fists.

"Oh, get yourself back to Stratford! Go till the fields! London doesn't need another hammy actor who thinks he can write!"

Will shook his head. Without another word, he turned away and shot through the door.

Kit let his hands drop helplessly. He hated everything he'd just said. He barely even recognized the words as his own – they'd lashed out too easily, almost prepared in advance. Immediately, before it was too late, he felt he should run after Will, plead with him, and explain how much he'd valued his company in recent days. He goaded himself into action, quick-stepped across the room, thought of something to say, imagined how it would sound, rushed over to the doorframe, leant out, opened his mouth... he said nothing.

Will's feet trammeled down the stairs. Seconds later, the inn's front door slammed shut.

Kit closed his eyes. A poisonous self-loathing clouded his blood. He turned back into the room. He trembled with frustration. He grabbed the chair and hurled it across the room. It slammed into a wall and fell dead to the floor.

Scene Two

Hogg Lane.

Kit stepped out onto the lane and the sun's heat pierced his back and shoulders. Will wasn't in sight. He turned right and ventured up the road towards Norton Folgate.

As he walked, hot winds blew hot odors from the piggery down the lane. The stench seemed particularly long and rancid today. In an ever darkening mood, he ambled along, eyes downcast, arms heavy at his sides. He walked by ditches permeated with sunlight, but filth still festered on the surface.

Around the middle of the street, Kit passed near a vagabond sitting on the ground. He wore a flat brimmed hat pulled low over one eye, but the other eye watched Kit furtively. Across his chest, a long woolen cloak concealed the left half of his body. The cloak was too thick for such a warm day. Though his brown and black clothes displayed tears and patches something was wrong about him: he was too clean. He bore traces of dirt, yet he seemed to *wear* his dirt rather than live in it. His chest took shallow breaths and his eye kept blinking.

Kit moved closer and peered down at the man's leg – something seemed hidden under it. He looked away and kept his head down as he paced by the man quickly. His heart thumped and boomed in his chest. He tried to keep the man's image in the corner of his eye. He primed his ears for the slightest noise.

Suddenly, just as Kit strode past, the man burst into action. Feet scraped the ground as he sprang up.

Kit drew his dagger. Whirled around to face the man.

"Unfold yourself, sir!" he growled.

The man already had a sword and dagger unsheathed. The hat and cloak were now gone, revealing a hard, youthful face, short cropped hair, and wiry, lanky limbs. The assured way he gripped his sword and dagger showed he knew how to fight. Kit had seen such men before. He was an assassin.

The assassin wasted no time – lunged at Kit, drove a sword at his chest. Kit jerked his dagger up and parried the blow. Their blades clashed together. Sparks spat out from sharp edges. The assassin's moves were fast, precise. The sword jabbed at Kit's gut. The dagger swung at Kit's neck, arms, hands. Steel flashed white in the sun, blurred through the air as it cut toward him.

The spectacle drew attention of everyone in the street. Tramps ceased begging. Merchants left doorways. Travelers stopped in their coaches and whores ran out from brothels, screaming with alarm and excitement. Within moments, a crowd encircled the fight, keeping just out of range. Bawdy mouths shouted:

"Get him!"

"Go on!"

"That's it, lad, that's it!"

Sweat glistened over Kit's face as he struggled. Salt stung his eyes and his crackled lips. He nearly dropped his dagger from the moisture in his hand.

Suddenly, the assassin darted forward and slashed at his waist. The sword tip severed the fabric of Kit's doublet. Ripped into his flesh.

"Fie!" Kit cried out in pain. He pressed his free hand on his side to stem the bleeding.

The assassin grew bolder and made a lightning series of thrusts, pushing Kit backwards, breaking the circle of onlookers, driving him hard into the wall of a house.

Their arms tangled. Torrid breath blasted into their faces. The assassin's dagger missed Kit and chinked into brick. They grappled, tried to wrestle against each other's arms, and the assassin forced Kit's hand towards a rusty wall brazier laden with burning coals. The heat from the coals prickled Kit's skin, seared the back of his hand, drew the skin hot and tight. His arm gave way and his hand plunged deep into the coals. He dropped his dagger as heat tore into his skin, his bones.

"Is that it?" Kit yelled. "Is that your best?"

Kit gave a head-butt, fracturing the assassin's nose in several places. Blood streamed down and over the assassin's lips and he stood there momentarily dazed. Kit glared at him mockingly.

"Red suits you very well – would you like some more?"

Before the assassin could react, Kit tugged at the wall brazier. Yanked it from the screws in the wall. Dashed the glowing coals into the assassin's face.

For the first time, the assassin staggered backwards, weakened, frantically brushing the red hot ash and cinders singeing his eyes and cheeks.

"I imagine that's quite painful," Kit said dryly. "Let's call it a day, shall we?"

While the assassin recovered, Kit retrieved his dagger from the ground and tried to escape. His side throbbed and slowed his movements and the crowd didn't part quick enough to let him out.

"Go to!" he bellowed at them. "Move, damn you! Move!"

Just in time, he turned his head: the assassin pounced toward him again. By now, the man was tired and his aim was ragged. He lashed at Kit with all his strength, unconcerned with over-reaching or exposing himself. The crowd heckled louder, sensing the end was near for one of the men. Kit parried the thrusts, but side-stepped and his foot gave way on the muddy edge of a ditch. He slipped and splashed into the stinking water. The assassin loomed overhead and struck downwards. Kit rolled out of the thrust. The sword sliced by his shoulder and sunk heavily into the mud beneath the water.

While the assassin was stuck helpless, Kit acted fast.

Jumped to his feet.

Thrashed his dagger deep into the assassin's heart.

The wound was instantly crushing. The assassin's face twisted in agony and strength flooded away from him. He dropped dead into the ditch.

Kit gaped at the dead body floating face-down in the water. Two men rushed over to the ditch and checked the assassin for signs of life. Kit turned away as the crowd screamed and shouted and tried to grab him and hinder his escape. He elbowed them aside, winced, and touched his wound. Blood coated his hand and dripped from his fingertips. Sickened and dizzy from shock, he lurched onwards a few more paces. His eyelids twitched. The world swam in laps around his head, the earth becoming the sky and the dirt and the clouds. The ground rushed up viciously to meet his head. He blacked out and collapsed...

Scene Three

Canterbury Cathedral.

In the nave, sublime choral music scaled the height of the rafters. Choir boys stood in the choir stalls and each held a small hymnbook in his hands. Though the choir remained perfectly still, their mouths spouted Latin syllables and their eyes roved, sometimes watching the arms of the earnest choir master waving at their side.

Back from the stalls, along the central aisle, Whitgift observed the choir from a distance. Candlelight threw a glassy sheen over his hair. A melancholy expression resided between the strong lines on his face. He held his powerful hands together, drawn in to his chest, his rings just touching his beard. The music soothed his ears and he stood and listened for some time.

Suddenly, the tiny *slip-slap* of shoe soles flopped up behind him. He turned to find a fat-cheeked choir boy rushing by, late for choral practice. As he passed, the boy's hymnbook slipped from his fingers and splashed to the floor. Mortified, the boy skidded to a halt. His lower lip quivered.

Amused at the boy's reaction, Whitgift bent down, picked the book up, and handed it back. The boy looked up at him with awe.

"Pray pardon," the boy squeaked. "I didn't mean to, your worship. Honest."

Whitgift nodded warmly.

"Be more careful in the future."

"Yes, Archbishop."

"You're forgiven, my son. Go and join the others." The boy smiled, clutched the book tighter, and scampered off to join the choir.

Meanwhile, at the cathedral entrance, Thomas stepped inside and straightened his back. He had spent a long, anxious hour traveling by coach from Chislehurst. He ignored the choir music and paced down the aisle. When he reached Whitgift, he gave a small cough to announce his presence.

Whitgift didn't turn to greet him – just kept his eyes on the choir in the distance. He sighed wearily.

"I'd like to know something..."

"Yes," Thomas replied.

"Why is it God would give a man the urge for fatherhood, yet allot him a position in life that bars such fulfillment?"

Thomas gave an awkward smile, unsure how he should respond.

"I don't know, your worship."

"No, I don't expect you do. Very few people in this life truly understand what it is to doubt... how dangerous it can be..."

For a minute they stood motionless in the aisle. Strains of music echoed between them. Whitgift's face turned grave and his shoulders flexed under the folds of his cassock. Thomas pressed his lips together flat. Finally, Whitgift pushed a hand through the air toward him.

"You're a very lucky man, I believe," Whitgift stated flatly.

"Why so?"

"You're lucky that Marlowe isn't dead."

Thomas drew a short breath. He averted his eyes.

"They're holding him for manslaughter in Marshalsea," he replied.

"And how badly was he wounded by your idiot assassin?"

"I'm not sure."

"Then you must find out."

"Yes." Thomas swallowed awkwardly. "I *do* know that a doctor saw to him."

Whitgift turned and gave him a sharp, cutting glance.

"Disobey me again and I'll grind you under my heel like a grape." He started off towards the side of the cathedral, taking long strides.

Thomas hurried to keep up with him.

"I'm deeply sorry, your worship."

"Your apologies are the last thing I want to hear. We've come too far for half-measures."

"Yes."

"The posters have helped incite the very riots and heresy I need to stop. Marlowe's death will atone for all that, but it must be public – not a cheap back-alley stabbing. Do you understand me?"

"I understand."

"Glad to hear it. I hope for your sake that you won't disappoint me again."

Thomas bowed his head submissively.

"I have Baines," he muttered.

"And where is this elusive man?"

"The sacristy."

Whitgift studied him a moment, then nodded and they strode under pillars towards a side door.

In the sacristy, white tiles made diamonds over the floor. Sacred vessels glistened inside glass cabinets. Hung from pegs in one corner, a range of holy gowns brushed their silk and velvet hems against the floor. In the middle of the room, by a large cross upon the wall, Baines sat on a chair leaning his elbows miserably on the top of a short table. He stared ahead blankly as Whitgift and Thomas hovered around him. So far, he had been less than cooperative.

"...don't be absurd," Thomas said precisely. "Why would you protect him?"

"I'm not," Baines grunted.

"He lost you your job, didn't he? That wasn't my fault. It was Burghley's decision."

Baines didn't answer. Thomas changed his tone and bent his head closer in a friendly manner.

"When Whitgift and I rise to expand our spy network, you won't be forgotten. Have faith in that."

Baines twisted in his chair and leered.

"Faith?"

Thomas stood up correctly.

"That's your department, I believe," he said looking to Whitgift.

Immediately, Whitgift approached and laid a hand on Baines square shoulder. His hand weighed heavy, and Baines shifted, slightly uneasy.

"You'll be justly rewarded for your service, my son," said Whitgift in a paternal voice.

"How?"

"Aside from everlasting glory in heaven – what think you of a priesthood and rectory?"

No response. Whitgift and Thomas traded looks. After a brief silence, Thomas leant forward, frustrated.

"So?" he demanded. "What will it be?"

Baines stared blankly at him.

"What?"

"Did you hear what was said?"

"Yes," said Baines with a look of defiance. "But I want to be an archbishop."

Whitgift pivoted away from the table and snorted derisively.

"For the love of Christendom!"

Thomas pressed his lips together.

"No, I'm afraid that's not possible."

"I won't take less."

"No, there are lots of bishops in England, Baines, but there are only *two* archbishops." He waved two fingers before Baines's nose. "And neither of them will ever be you."

Baines didn't move. He switched his eyes around the room as if only half-understanding.

"Only two archbishops?"

"Anyway," said Thomas curtly, "that's all – take the priesthood or forget it."

For a moment, no one in the room spoke. Whitgift's shoes tapped on the floor and the breeze from his strides ruffled the gowns on pegs in the corner. Baines contorted his face into a grimace. He looked up meekly at Thomas hanging over him. Thomas narrowed his eyes. Baines hesitated and gave a small nod of acceptance.

Scene Four

Marshalsea Prison.

Kit drifted in and out of consciousness. A blurry face asked him his name... his body moved with the sway of a cart... pain issued from his side... metal clanged in his right ear... rotting waste... flagstones beneath him... shafts of light from a window... a flat ceiling... echoes...

When he fully awakened, he found himself lying inside a large cell shared with ten other prisoners. A man with a matted beard sat nearby. Kit shifted upright, asked the man a few questions, and quickly learned the place of his incarceration: Marshalsea Prison.

Marshalsea stood on the edge of Southwark, far back from the Thames. At three hundred prisoners, Marshalsea was the most important prison in the land after the Tower. Opened in 1370, the prison had originally served the Knights Marshall of the Royal Household, but during Elizabeth's reign it had grown to contain an impressive collection of political prisoners. Debtors and petty thieves languished in cells next to wayward clerics, priests refusing to take the oath of allegiance, Catholic conspirators, treasonous plotters, atheists, rabble-rousers, poets, and all others destined for the noose or chopping block. As such, the prison had garnered a reputation for cruelty and shrieks were often heard leaching from the walls of the dungeon. Richard Topcliffe, the most sadistic torturer in England, was rumored to make his home at Marshalsea.

The prison itself consisted of thick-hewn slabs of stone piled three stories high, arranged in a quadrangle with a small recreational yard in the center. At every corner of the yard, black, flat-topped watchtowers rose above the ground, each mounted by a bored, but dutiful guard.

Inside the prison, narrow stone tunnels ran long and deep, itched by the faint-buzzing of flies. Moisture slicked the low ceilings and dripped onto the floor of cold, reeking cells full of men sickening from the damp.

In Kit's cell, some men paced, while others leant on the wall or lay quietly on beds of sawdust. On the front wall, flat bars stretched from the floor to the ceiling – the iron smoothed at the middle by centuries of gripping hands. A waste bucket sat in the far corner and the suffocating pong of excrement filled the cell at all times. Urine made the walls sticky. On the opposite wall to the bars, two windows with hefty grills brought sunlight and street noises to the prisoner's ears.

Kit spent two days recovering before he could move with ease. When he checked his wound he discovered it had been cleaned and dressed. An elderly prisoner told Kit a doctor had treated him soon after he had entered the cell. Carefully, Kit pulled his legs under him, grabbed the wall and raised himself from the numbing ground.

"Marry, that hurt!" he groaned to himself.

While stepping over outstretched feet, he walked slowly around the cell. His side twinged but the pain was bearable. Slyly, he reached inside his shirt and checked Cholmeley's note was still tucked underneath his belt.

A bell suddenly clapped the air. All the men jumped up and stood to the front of the cell. Guards passed down the corridor outside and made a head count. The bells then rang again, signaling the count was correct, and the men stepped back. This ritual occurred up to eight times a day, mainly providing the guards with something to do. After a few hours, the continued violence of the bells raked the eardrums and became a subtle torture to the men.

At midday, the pit of Kit's stomach boiled with acid. He hadn't eaten in days and he lacked the money to buy anything from the guards. Except for beatings and insults, prisoners were given nothing for free: they were charged for every gulp of water, every mouthful of bread.

The day wore on. The long hours grew longer as Kit languished. Forlornly, he watched the slow-creeping of window light across the sawdust and his fingers plucked idly at the buttons on his doublet.

He stopped and tilted his head to the side in thought. Over at the bars, a prisoner spoke with a gruffly-voiced prison guard and tried to barter away his shoes. The guard took the prisoner's shoes, tried them on his feet, but didn't like the fit and eventually shook his head. As he prepared to move away, Kit swiftly unbuttoned his doublet and padded over to the bars.

"Stay," he called. He waved the doublet to get the guard's attention. "Good sir, stay a moment, will you?"

The guard halted and raised his eyebrows.

"What?" replied the guard. "It better not be shoes."

"It isn't. I have—"

"I'm not interested if shoes is all you got."

"No. I have a doublet."

The guard took a step back toward the cell and peered closer. Kit ran his finger down the doublet's velvet lining.

"This is fine cloth," he declared. "The sleeves have silk slashing. I'll trade it for a few leafs of parchment and a quill."

The guard considered the offer.

"That's all you want, is it?"

Kit nodded. The guard reached out and thumbed the collar of the doublet. Finally, he looked Kit in the eye.

"Right you are, then." He pulled the doublet through the bars and cradled it in his hands as he sauntered off towards the end of the corridor.

A nauseating feeling churned inside Kit as he watched the guard leave with the most valuable thing he owned. Someone at the back of the cell muttered Kit would never get his request. With a clear view of the corridor, Kit slumped down in the sawdust, resting his head on the bars.

Hours passed. More hours passed. Light from the window slid further across the sawdust, flared with color, then grew faint and disappeared. The cell darkened and moonlight filtered through the window, dissolving the sawdust into simple white hues. Some of the men fell asleep.

Just as Kit closed his eyes, feet shuffled down the corridor and a hand thrust a pot of slopping ink, a quill, and four sheets of parchment under his nose.

He flinched awake. Took them eagerly. Shuffled to the back of the cell.

Sat against the wall, he positioned himself under the moonlit window. The quill rolled freely in his hand. He laid the paper on his lap and touched it greedily as if it were gold. The window bars above made silhouettes against the moonlight and threw cold, flat shadows across the parchment below. After a deep breath, he ceremoniously blackened the quill nib with ink and started writing...

SCENE FIVE

Canterbury Cathedral.

The same moonlight that shaded Kit's cell also lay broken upon the windowpanes of Canterbury Cathedral. That night, busy figures moved back and forth by the sacristy window.

Inside the sacristy, Thomas, Whitgift, and Baines spent hours drafting a note that Baines would sign to incriminate Kit. Gradually, after much debate, they compiled a long list of Marlowe's 'atheist opinions' against Christianity: some of the opinions were merely standard attacks made by many heretics, though other opinions were tailored to better reflect Kit's cocksure and strident nature. For example, Kit's connection to the morally disreputable lifestyle of the theater made it easy to portray him as a lewd, drug-addicted sodomite, but Baines also referenced Kit's plans to counterfeit coins of the realm. They saved the most masterful and damning stroke for last: that Kit actively spread atheism across the country and persuaded men to follow his ideas. The government feared nothing more. Once the note had been drafted correctly, Whitgift made initial plans for Baines's priesthood and then sent him back to London. Afterwards, Whitgift left the cathedral with Thomas to stroll in the night air.

To the north of the building stood the hushed pillars and brooding arches of the Great Cloister. In darkness, Whitgift and Thomas swept along the sculpted colonnade and passed beneath a ceiling fanned with lace-like ribs and colorful bosses now hidden in the night. Hitherto, they had chatted politely, for the success with Baines had greatly buoyed their spirits. Soon, however, their conversation turned to serious matters and they lowered their voices. Whitgift dreamed of how to increase his power in the government to even greater heights. After he had destroyed atheism, he would seek to annihilate all traces of Catholicism and Puritanism throughout the country. He would need unprecedented authority. Censorship, torture, and execution would not cut deep enough into the problem. He needed the mandate to enact emergency laws, to seize property, to take control of government in the worst affected areas of the country. Meanwhile, Thomas listened critically to Whitgift's plans and identified flaws and speculated on ways to overcome them. Regarding Kit, they recounted the evidence they had amassed against him thus far – the Cholmeley remembrances, the Baines note – to decide if they could try him successfully. Whitgift seemed doubtful. His fingers played with folds of his cassock as he pondered.

"Thomas, it strikes me that there is still some evidence we need to gather."

"Nonsense," said Thomas reassuringly. "We have enough already."

"I believe it pays to have greater patience in this matter."

"But–"

"No, if I'm to go before the Privy Council or the Court of the Star Chamber I'll need more."

Thomas didn't reply. He wanted to argue but suppressed the feeling as best he could manage. His face gradually acquired its studied blankness. Meanwhile, Whitgift tapped his fingers on his lips.

"We have the posters and the charges connected with Cholmeley and Baines, but we lack testimony from anyone close to Marlowe."

"Such as?"

"A friend, perhaps, or a lover."

"Yes..." said Thomas, warming to the idea. "Yes, that would be impressive."

Whitgift stared out through the pillars onto the grass.

"Gather up some of his fellow poets and torture them if necessary."

232

"Won't I need court authorization?"

"I'll see to that. You'll get permission even if I must visit the Queen and secure it myself."

"Very well."

"Just get me something incriminating by the morrow." He looked Thomas straight in the eye to make his point clear. Even now, he still retained an odd warmth in his tone and manner – a paternal generosity that seemed to contrast with the content of his speech. Voiced by Whitgift, anything, even torture, could sound like a blessing.

Thomas bowed his head. He understood the seriousness of Whitgift's command. Without further delay, he bade the Archbishop farewell and strode away into the moonlight.

SCENE SIX

Prison Wagon.

Horses pulled a covered prison wagon through the quiet morning streets of Southwark towards Marshalsea Prison. Two Officers of the Star Chamber sat in the driver seat – men dressed in ordinary hats, hose, and tunics, identified as constables only by long, yellow wooden staffs.

The wagon soon stopped at a station before the Marshalsea front gate. On the other side, bolts slid undone and a winch turned. *Thlack – Thlack – Thlack.* The doors parted to let the wagon draw into the yard. Afterwards, the driver pulled the cart to a standstill outside the official prison entrance. The officers at the rear of the wagon jumped down. As their feet hit the ground, dirt clouded around their shiny black boots. One of the officers unlocked the wagon door.

On watchtowers above, the sentries observed the proceedings carefully.

The wagon door squealed back on its hinges and the other officer clutched his staff, ready to use it as a club. He reached inside and yanked Will Shakespeare out of the wagon.

Will stepped down into the yard sluggishly, as if all his joints were stiff.

"Come, let's move along!" shouted the officer, his voice unnecessarily loud. "Hurry up!"

Droplets of blood lay spattered on Will's linen shirt collar. Clumps of dry blood clung to his hair. His upper lip was fat. With hands tied behind his back, he shuffled awkwardly along the yard. He tripped – slammed his chest into the dirt.

"Can't you walk straight?" yelled an officer.

Will spat the dust out of his mouth.

The officers hooked him under the arms, lifted up his thin body, set him on his feet again, and thrust him toward the entrance. All three of them disappeared inside the building.

Scene Seven

Marshalsea Prison. Kit's Cell.

Kit spent most of the morning planning what to write next in *'Hero and Leander'*. Throughout the rest of the day, however, he wrote nothing, for the prison contained too many interruptions, too many bells and counts, too many stinks from the waste bucket. With only four sheets of paper, he literally couldn't afford to waste words or make a mistake: he possessed nothing else of value he could sell for more parchment.

At night, when the prison quieted and moonlight covered the cell through the grill, he resumed his place under the window and prepared to write. On his lap, two sheets of parchment were already filled with words crammed tightly onto the page – the results of last night's work. Breathing slowly, he read back through his words and slipped his mind inside his poem.

So far, Hero and Leander had met on a feast night and fallen in love. Leander had expressed his love readily, but Hero had denied him, scared of the amorous feelings he excited in her, until she accidentally let word of her true feelings slip through her speech. With her true emotions now revealed, Leander arranged to meet Hero again the following night.

Next evening, Leander stole away to Hero's tower, but their night together remained stifled at a kiss. Hero still feared to lose her virginity. Hence, when morning came, the lovers parted sadly and Leander returned home disappointed. But nothing could quell Leander's passion. Almost mad with longing, pining for a second night with Hero, he wandered back to the banks of the Hellespont, stopped, and gazed over the sea to Hero's faraway tower...

Once Kit had reread the previous night's work, he huddled up and peered around the cell. Again the bars cast shadows over the parchment. For the longest time, his eyes lingered on the bands of light and dark, then he leant forward and returned to Leander at the Hellespont:

'"O Hero, Hero!" thus he cried full oft;
And then he got him to a rock aloft,
Where having spied her tower, long stared he on't,
And prayed the narrow toiling Hellespont
To part in twain, that he might come and go;
But still the rising billows answered, "No."
With that he stripped him to the ivory skin
And, crying "Love, I come," leaped lively in.
Whereat the sapphire visaged god grew proud,
And made his capering Triton sound aloud,
Imagining that Ganymede, displeased,
Had left the heavens; therefore on him he seized.
Leander strived; the waves about him wound,
And pulled him to the bottom, where the ground
Was strewed with pearl, and in low coral groves
Sweet singing mermaids sported with their loves
On heaps of heavy gold, and took great pleasure
To spurn in careless sort the shipwrack treasure...'

Kit paused and glanced over the words. For a few precious minutes, the ceiling above him had opened to the stars of a clean, Grecian sky; the sawdust at his feet had dissolved into ocean; and the snores of his fellow prisoners had deepened and broadened into the crashing of mighty waves about his head.

Just as he prepared to escape back into his poem, he cocked his head at a faint, terrifying noise. Disturbed, his fingertips pressed white around the quill. His skin froze. He shuddered. Ever so slightly at first, but steadily rising, a long scream sounded from somewhere below in the depths of the prison...

Scene Eight

Marshalsea Prison. Dungeons.

Beneath Kit's cell, sunk far into the earth, lay the dungeons of Marshalsea. Here the scream sliced its way through the air again and again, only this time nearer and more shrill.

The dungeons were windowless. Dank. Water streamed down the pillars forming patches of mold. Candles burnt dirty yellow flames against the stone. Down the left side, two doors led into torture chambers used for 'scraping the conscience'. On the right stood a set of narrow, iron doors for cells holding those waiting to be tortured.

Behind one of the doors, Will sat alone on the flat gray floor. The cell lacked sawdust and felt wet. With arms outstretched he could easily place his palms flush against the walls. The only light came from the candlelight snaking under the doorframe from the corridor outside. For the first hours, Will occupied himself by exploring his hands over the bumps and grooves of the cell walls: in several places his fingers discovered scratches, and once he found the letters *'F-A-T-H-E-R'* carved into the stone. He searched for more words, more attempts at creation, but found none. He sat back and shivered against the wall. He kept his sight on the door. Always on the door. With every cold scream echoing outside, he flinched till his frayed nerves made him drowsy.

He twitched awake, all senses alert. Footsteps marched along stopped abruptly outside his door. A key scraped at the lock, clicked, and the door squealed back on its rusty hinges. Two guards held a man in between them and shoved him inside. Will squinted at the man's face and recognized him: Tom Kyd, a fellow playwright at The Rose.

Tom looked as gangly as ever, but his fair locks now seemed pale, even faded. His blues eyes were limpid. He breathed weakly.

The door slammed shut. They both jumped. Will remained on the floor, but Tom stood, paced, turned, and stopped nervously on the spot.

"Tom! I didn't expect to see you," said Will, forcing a dry smile. "Do you come here often?"

Tom ignored the joke and wiped his hand across his brow.

"I won't tell them a thing, I swear," he replied, his voice wavering. "Not a thing. I swear I won't. Not a thing. I'm a playwright not a snitch."

"Of course..."

"I don't care if they have Topcliffe or not. All his tricks. He won't do it."

"Who is... who is Topcliffe?"

"What? Richard Topcliffe. You must have heard about him. What he does."

"I don't think so."

"Then I'll save you from knowing now. Best you don't know."

"I see..."

Tom gave a strange, nervous laugh.

"Let's just say, he's a man whose business is also his pleasure."

"I don't suppose his business would be friendly interrogations, would it?"

Tom sniffed in through his nose and didn't reply. Will shivered again. He rubbed the tops of his arms to keep warm.

"How was it that they caught you, anyway?" he asked gently.

"No one warned me," Tom shot back. "I went to my room after a rehearsal and Officers of the Star Chamber were there, waiting. Swarming over everything. Papers all over the floor."

"What did you do?"

"What could I do about it? I just stood there. Then one of them pulled out some villainous document. Atheist writings, or something. It was in with my books."

"I'm sorry..."

"I tried to explain I'd never seen it before, never even set eyes on it. I told them it was probably Kit's. But they didn't care, did they?"

"Kit's? Oh, but I doubt—"

"Yes, yes, we shared a room one summer. He always had that kind of stuff lying around the place. Pamphlets and such. It was bound to end up mixing with mine."

"I doubt it was really his document, Tom. It's likely that they planted it instead, as they did with me and countless others."

"It was his, not mine. Kit should be the one here. Not me."

"You're wearing a hole in the floor. Why don't you sit down and rest a while?"

"Don't need to rest," he hissed and continued to pace, his feet rasping on the floor. Eventually, he turned to Will. "I heard they can break your spine on the rack. You ever hear that?"

Will nodded.

"Yes, I did hear something like that once..."

A grim silence followed. The scream pierced the dungeons again. They both turned and looked to the door anxiously. The scream sounded tense and high. Strangely, for all its volume, it never lapsed into a yell or formed any words. It just released a torrent of pain; absolute, excruciating pain. Gradually, the pitch rose higher and higher and higher, like a string pulled taut and ready to snap.

240

Scene Nine

Nonsuch Palace. Music Room.

Audrey plucked the strings of a harp and filled the music room of Nonsuch Palace with high, graceful, soothing tones. Over by the fireplace, Elizabeth sat at a table and played cards with three gentlewomen. Located near the royal bedchamber, the music room was the Queen's favorite area of the palace. When young, Elizabeth would go there before bed in her nightgown, without any makeup, and listen to her gentlewomen gossip; but now she never appeared anywhere without pigment and full dress. At the table she looked hot sitting by the fire and fanned herself with her pink, ostrich feather fan.

Elizabeth, Audrey and the gentlewomen occupied only a small corner of the room – the rest of the room stretched away from them, vast and oversized. The ceiling lifted two and a half stories high into coffers and acorn pendants. Fine, hand-rubbed oak panels skirted the long walls.

Apart from Audrey's harp, no other voices or instruments sounded that night. In the darkness of the room, hushed trumpets, flutes, recorders, and drums lay still in the noiselessness. Dreaming gitterns hid their sickle-shaped pegboxes in the shadows. Bagpipes with deflated leather bags slouched atop the painted case of a virginal. Sackbuts gleamed and reflected the ivory curve of a cornetto reposing beside the wall.

Audrey finished playing a composition and sat back on the stool. She cooled the tips of her fingers on her tongue. Just as she started another song, a rattling noise sounded across the room.

Everyone turned to face the door. The handle swiveled and Whit-gift swiftly intruded.

He paced across the room, his feet heavy on the rug, and stopped at the fireplace to bow before Elizabeth. She closed her eyes briefly, as if unhappy.

"Ladies..." she said with a huff.

Immediately, the gentlewomen arose and exited the room. Audrey took longer to gather her dress from around the harp and when she finally got to her feet Elizabeth pointed at her.

"Not you, my dear. Your playing soothes my temper."

Audrey gave a quick, gracious curtsy.

"Yes, your highness." She planted herself back on the seat cushion and the length of her dress spread out on floor. Her fingertips alighted the strings once again, but she now played the harp softer so she could hear everything spoken. She kept her gaze firmly on Whitgift.

Over by the hearth, the red and yellows of the fire danced upon Elizabeth's gown. In front of her, Whitgift stood tall and loomed over the table with an efficient, dutiful look on his face. Once all the other gentlewomen had finally left the room, he filled his lungs.

"Your majesty—"

"Where are the results from your investigation?" Elizabeth snapped. She kept her eyes down, studying her cards.

Whitgift bristled.

"The results, your grace?"

"Yes."

"With respect, I've already arrested and convicted a number of the realm's most notorious atheists and—"

"What about the author of the libels posted in London? That was your main purpose, was it not."

"I come on that very matter tonight." He stepped closer to the table and peered down at her. His fingers fiddled nervously with the sides of his cassock. "I near the conviction of the poet Christopher Marlowe, and request license to torture his associates into speaking truth on his heresy."

The news hit Audrey like a thunderbolt. She missed a note on the harp.

Elizabeth hesitated at the request. Broodingly, she flicked her nail against the cards in her hand. Whitgift's brow knitted into a deep frown.

"I don't need to remind you that it was you yourself who set this investigation underway," he said slightly reproachfully. "Surely you won't protect him now? I already have much proof concerning his heresy."

"Take care with your tone, Archbishop."

"I pray forgiveness. But I'm only doing all I can to bring this investigation to its proper fulfillment. Surely that is best for both yourself and the people?"

"Very well." She put the cards down and gave him a long, steady look. "You have my permission."

"Most wise, your grace."

"But don't stray too far afield in this."

"No."

"Consider me gravely serious on this point. Marlowe himself is not to be touched... yet."

"I will do only the least that is necessary and nothing more; you have my word on it."

She raised her eyebrows. He bowed quickly and headed for the door before she could change her mind.

As soon as he left, Audrey jumped up, swished her dress from around the harp, and rushed over to Elizabeth. Hands clasped together, she sunk to her knees.

"Your majesty," she pleaded urgently, "Perchance you haven't heard yet, but Christopher Marlowe waits helpless in jail!" Tears swelled in her eyes. She tried to control her breathing and did her best to speak with greater calm. "How may he clear his name? He only has a few hours. I beseech you, I plead you, grant him pardon for manslaughter."

Elizabeth refused to look up from the table. Slowly, she collected the cards and made the lines of the pack nice and straight. Audrey waited patiently but received no answer. Exasperated, she raised her voice.

243

"I beg you, please, you must help him!"

Elizabeth lunged to her feet sharply.

"I *must* do nothing at all. By God! Am I to be lectured by gentlewomen as well?"

Audrey lowered her head. Her hands dropped to her sides submissively.

"No, of course not, I crave forgiveness, your majesty."

"What is the root of your interest in this, anyway? I find your interest in Marlowe most troubling. Indeed, it hints at immorality. I trust you've done nothing to concern me? My moral standing is beyond question – the same must be said of all who surround me."

Audrey nodded. Her conscience wormed into the core of her heart and left it riddled with guilt. She knew it was wrong to behave so indiscreetly, to prize the life of her lover beyond the value of her marriage. No argument could convince her otherwise.

Elizabeth scowled at her.

"Then why is it you wander into the mire that a common playwright has made for himself?"

"Because he isn't a common playwright," Audrey replied meekly. "I was merely thinking of you, your majesty, and your enjoyment of his work. Marlowe's voice lifts clear from the chirping of other poets. If he dies you deprive yourself of everything, his plays, all his future work. My fear is this: at the end of a long week rife with the discord of ministers, diplomats, treaties, and tantrums, would you rather be entertained by the twittering of a sparrow or the song of a lark?"

Elizabeth tipped her head to the side, glumly. She turned away and wandered off into the darkness of the room. While gathering her composure, she lingered by a long arched window and drew back the drape. She uttered a sigh.

"Your attempt to manipulate me is very charming, my dear," she said across the room, "but not entirely without truth. I *do* loathe to loose Marlowe. His plays afford a precious escape I rarely find elsewhere."

Audrey raised her head in hope.

"Then you'll grant him a pardon?"

244

Elizabeth remained motionless by the window. After a long pause she finally replied.

"I will trade his pardon for your promise that there is nothing immoral in your relationship with that playwright."

'There is not, your grace."

"So be it," Elizabeth said tersely. "Have your request, too. Fetch me the parchment."

Audrey stood up.

"I offer my undying gratitude, your majesty," she said with solemnity. She curtsied, whirled on the spot, hiked her dress up over her feet, and hurried for the door.

Elizabeth watched her leave. With a sadness masked by the dark, she continued to peer out of the window.

SCENE TEN

Kit's Cell.

During the few days Kit spent in Marshalsea, no one had officially stated the charge against him, nor had he been arraigned in court. No man, however, worried about staying in the prison too long. Even at night the guards removed prisoners or added more men to the cells. Prisons were not the official form of punishment for crimes – they were merely holding places for people expecting their day in court or those waiting to receive the court's punishment. Such punishment was invariably physical in nature, ranging from a short time in the stocks, to execution. In between the two extremes rested a variety of humiliations and mutilations. For drunkards, there was the 'drunkard's cloak': constables cut holes in a an empty ale barrel for the head, hands, and feet, then forced a drunkard to don the 'outfit' and wander around town while people threw jeers, rotten vegetables, and stones at him. Debtors could have their ears cut off. Poisoners were boiled in lead. Gossiping women were forced to wear a headpiece which cut their tongue if they tried to speak. For manslaughter, constables would trap Kit in a cage with rapists and horse thieves, and hang it up in town until he slowly starved. Just before his death, however, they would take him down and rend his body in quarters till he died of the pain.

Later that evening, while editing *'Hero and Leander'* Kit paused and looked elsewhere to rest his eyes from the page. Many prisoners were repeat offenders. Anxiety abounded in them and in order to assuage their rising fear, parish priests made frequent rounds, counseling those condemned to die or due to suffer

terrible injuries. Priestly black robes were a common sight at
Marshalsea and when a man dressed in such cloth walked up to
the cell Kit didn't pay much attention. To his surprise, however,
the figure came to stand opposite him and stared through the bars.
Gradually, Kit's lifted his eyes to the figure.

Through the bars, Baines's meaty face stared back. With his
all stubble, stiff shoulders, and packs of muscle, he seemed absurd in his priestly garments. His movements oozed with a profane crudity. He wore the robes tentatively, as if a strong wind
could tear them from his limbs, and he lacked any knowledge of
postures or expressions normally associated with holiness.

Interested, Kit shuffled up to the bars.

"I see you've found God," he said sarcastically, "or at least
the church."

Baines gazed back at him with menace. Kit's eyes twinkled.
"Oh, I understand..."

"What?" Baines grunted.

"You've come to gloat, haven't you? How nice." He pushed
his face close to the bars and raised his eyebrows mockingly.
"But where's your witty line? You must have a witty line or it
doesn't work. If I were you I'd say 'those bars look good on you,
Kit.'"

Baines didn't move or respond. He didn't even blink. A large
smile drew across Kit's lips.

"No good? Well, you could go with something more threatening. Try this: 'rats are your sole audience now, poet.'" His
smile broadened. "Come, Baines, you can do it. Say it with me:
'Rats are your sole audience now, poet.'" He collapsed into giggles and wiped the tears in his eyes.

Baines grew severe with spite. He picked up the cross around
his neck and glanced at his reflection in the gold. He licked his
lips.

"Will Shakespeare," he said, savoring every word.

Kit stopped laughing.

"What?"

"I said: Will Shakespeare."

"Yes. What about him?"

"I've come to torture him."

"You're a liar!"

"No. Shakespeare's in the dungeons here. I've come to torture him. Goodbye." He grinned at Kit, turned away from the cell, and sauntered off.

Kit stood fixed to the spot, utterly speechless. It took a few seconds for the news to sink in. Still reeling, he pressed close to the bars and beat his hands against the iron. He called after Baines desperately.

"You're a fool! Whitgift and Thomas won't keep you long! It'll be the shortest priesthood ever!"

Baines stopped walking and glanced back.

"No. I got a written guarantee, I have. I might be an idiot... but I'm not stupid." With a smug expression, he waited for Kit's response, but none came. He strolled away whistling to himself and left the corridor.

Back in the cell, Kit rested against the bars, his body half-deflated, his head consumed in thought. He muttered into the depths of the cell.

"A guarantee..."

SCENE ELEVEN

Dungeons.

At midnight, prison guards removed Tom Kyd from Will's cell.

Afterwards, Will paced around, unable to settle. He listened keenly but heard no screams or any cries for mercy – just the sound of his feet scuffing the wet floor. His toes felt frozen. He stamped them for warmth. The noise broke the silence and comforted him. Soon, he began mumbling to himself, then speaking in audible, distracted sentences. First he prepared a noble declaration he would deliver to Topcliffe about how no amount of torture would induce him to betray Kit. Then he worried about Topcliffe himself. About the tortures he had planned. Will remembered all the different types of torture he'd heard about in the past: he laughed at silly ones, like the idea torturers might cover naked prisoners in honey and let bees sting them to death. He doubted others, like the idea a prisoner might be dunked in ice water till his heart slowly froze. His face turned grim as he recounted more realistic tortures, like suffocation, beatings, and the amputation saw. Some people said a torturer might grate arrow tips through a prisoner's fingers. Will put his hands together and prayed no harm would befall his eyes or hands. He needed them to act. To write.

In the dark, time seemed useless against the enduring and endless walls of the cell – hours shrank to the span of minutes – minutes shriveled to the length of seconds – seconds expanded to the length of hours and hours and hours. Will stared at the light around the door. As he steadily approached the threshold of delirium, the cell door seemed to drift open before him and light flooded into the cell. Two guards then crowded the doorframe with Tom suspended between them.

Tom's body now hung limp: his head drooped, his eyes didn't move, his feet dragged as the guards lugged him forward and tossed him into the cell. He landed in a weak, twisted heap on the floor. One of the guards gestured at Will.

"We'll have you next," said the guard.

Will stepped back dizzily but they didn't come for him. Instead, they left him for now, stepped out of the cell, and slammed the door shut again.

When the guard's footsteps had faded away, Will dropped to his knees and crawled over to Tom. His hair felt clammy to the touch. He took long, difficult breaths, as if he'd been running.

"It's over," said Will softly. "It's over now."

Tom gasped for air. He didn't reply.

Scene Twelve

Palace Carriage.

Once she had the Queen's signature on Kit's pardon, Audrey left Nonsuch Palace for Marshalsea. She took a palace carriage harnessed with four horses and raced through the night and into the Surrey countryside. The whole time, Audrey perched on the edge of the seat inside the cab. She picked at the edges of a scroll in her hand. The wax seal still felt slightly warm. She peeked out between the curtains and checked the progress, hoping for the distant glow of Southwark.

Outside, the crescent moon hovered large and near over the horizon, its shape old and white like arsenic powder. Below it, poplars writhed their spindly trunks and wafer-thin branches against the sky. Bunches and spreads of tiny leaves receded from the moonlight, sick and withered, like a thousand poisoned tongues.

The carriage drew into Marshalsea Prison. Audrey lowered a gossamer veil over her face. Without waiting for the footman she marched off toward the prison entrance.

Inside, her heels rapped on the floor up to the front desk. She came face to face with a warden. His bald, wrinkled head regarded her with amusement. Audrey waved the scroll at him.

"I come bearing a royal pardon for the release of Christopher Marlowe."

The warden squinted at her and gestured to the scroll. She showed him the royal seal, broke it, and unfurled the scroll before him. However, she refused to let him touch it until Kit had actually been released. While the warden took his time inspecting the pardon, Audrey's eyes wandered nervously about the room. Directly behind the desk, rows of large iron keys hung from nails on a board. Next to the board lay a rack of pikes and swords. In the corner stood a locked musket cabinet. Facing her, on the opposite side of the room, two guards lounged on stools. They looked back at her candidly and whispered.

Finally satisfied with the pardon's authenticity, the warden unclamped a thick ledger from the desk where a hefty bar pinched it to the wood. He flapped the cover open, turned the yellowed pages, and ran his finger down lines of names. She put a hand on her hip.

"Please, will you hurry, sir," she commanded.

In reaction the warden smiled, but only seemed to slow his pace.

"Marley, was it?" he asked her.

"No."

"Merlin?"

"No."

"You sure he's here?" The warden turned his head and swapped a look of mirth with the guards lounging on the stools.

Audrey took a deep breath and waited as patiently as she could. At last, the warden stabbed the page with his finger.

"Marlowe... Christopher..." He grabbed a key from the board behind and chucked it across the room to one of the guards. "Number five-and-twenty."

The eldest of the guards – a man with small eyes and short legs – twiddled the key in his finger as he approached the front gate. From a separate key ring at his waist, he unlocked the gate and led Audrey away deep into the corridors. As she tailed him, eyed him warily, waves of rank air came from the cells and wrenched her stomach. She fingered her pomander and lifted its cinnamon scents to her nose.

In cell number five-and-twenty, Kit lay awake in a shaft of moonlight. His wounded side was healing slowly, but tonight it throbbed more than usual. Just as he was about to turn over and rest on his back, footsteps echoed toward his cell. He tilted his head up to see.

Audrey arrived with the guard. She peered through the bars, saw Kit under the window and pointed. Without enthusiasm, the guard stuck the key in the lock, swung the door open and beckoned Kit out.

The quick turn of events was overwhelming. Kit hesitated briefly in shock, but soon forced himself to act: almost without time to breathe, he jumped to his feet, scraped together the pages of his poem, put them in his pouch, and strode fast out of the cell.

Once he was in the corridor, he gave Audrey a look of inexpressible gratitude. With every cold minute of separation he'd longed see her again, to hear her voice: memories of their time together had barely sustained him until now. In such surroundings, against the dirty, hopeless faces, the broken skin, mangled limbs, tangled hair, and soiled clothes, she cast a delicate and sculpted shadow. She appeared otherworldly. Under the veil, her blue eyes twinkled at him, warm and sad. She pulled off her glove and reached up to touch his cheek in the cup of her hand. They stared at each other silently. She turned and surrendered Kit's pardon to the guard. He took it and wandered off down the corridor. Kit and Audrey followed after the guard, speaking together in low voices.

"My lady, I fear you risk too much to help me."

"Yes, I probably do. Shall I tell them to put you back?"

Kit smiled but his face soon became somber again.

"What of your reputation? My fate may be set by now – you and I both know that. But I can't bear to think I've caused you reputation to suffer in any–"

"Oh tush, Christopher! I'm the Queen's gentlewoman, not some plain courtier, and I can get away with more than others. Besides, the Queen still favors you a little, everyone knows that. Most people will think I'm acting under her secret orders."

"Perhaps."

"Anyway, how fare's your injury? Is it severe? I trust the doctor I sent you has dressed it well?"

"Yes, it heals gradually. I think a few days of rest have helped to mend it." He caught a waft of vanilla scent from her hair. It distracted him for a moment. He crouched slightly,

253

checked the guard wasn't watching, and lowered his voice to a whisper. "Baines visited me."

"You mean he came here? He visited you here – at your cell?"

"Not long ago."

"On what business did–"

"He accidentally gave me a clue on how to prove the conspiracy."

"What?"

"He mentioned a guarantee. Thomas must have one too, in order to protect himself."

"I don't quite follow you..."

"Thomas was a spy, you see. He knows about betrayal. There's no chance he'd make a union with Whitgift unless he has a safeguard."

"A safeguard? Do you mean something, some evidence, that can incriminate Whitgift?"

Kit nodded.

"A document that links Whitgift directly to the libels. But he wouldn't keep it in the study. It'd have to be somewhere safe. A place where no one else goes."

Audrey slowed a little. She bit the inside of her cheek, as if thinking deeply.

"He has a locked box in his bedchamber, I think," she said, clenching her fists. "Yes, I'm sure of it. I saw it once..."

Kit turned to her cautiously.

"Don't search for it. You can't search for it, my lady."

"Yes, I could find it easily, you know I could."

"No. You've taken enough risks."

She rolled her eyes, annoyed.

"Well, then, you'll have to hurry. You've only a short span before they torture–"

"Fie and fie again!" His body suddenly grew rigid with stress. He ran a hand through his hair uneasily. "I can't believe I forgot!"

"What's that?"

"Will!"

She turned to him. Her voice filled with sorrow.

"Christopher... You can't help him now..."

"Yes. I can't leave him here." He rubbed his brow, desperately trying to think. Finally, he touched her on the shoulder. "I'll venture back to Scadbury later. I can't leave him..."

They stopped at the gate and waited while the guard unlocked it.

Scene Thirteen

Dungeons. Will's Cell.

Will sat on the floor and cradled Tom's head. Tom had lain completely motionless for the last half an hour. He was still terribly weak. Neither of them spoke, save to inhale and exhale. Will couldn't relax, but a strange sense of passivity fell upon him and he laid his head back against the wall and closed his eyes.

The door flung open. Light burst into the cell. Will's eyes could barely open against the brightness, but he saw the silhouettes of two guards beyond the doorframe. The guards dived inside. Grabbed Will by the arms. Fished him out of the cell.

Will didn't try to fight as they dragged him across the corridor. It was useless to resist. He felt a low anger start to ferment in his stomach. The human body was so weak, so limited – it broke so easily.

The torture chamber itself didn't look how he expected: there were no blood-spattered walls, dripping blades, cluttered devices, or skulls stacked in the corner. Instead, the chamber appeared spare and clinical. Above, two bright iron chandeliers bathed the walls in ample light, obliterating most shadows; the flagstone floor shone clean, as if it had just been scrubbed; and empty shackles gleamed on the wall, all of them arranged in neat rows. The mixture of expensive beeswax candles, soapsuds, and polish made the room redolent of a palace or cathedral. The majority of the room was dominated by the single object stood in the center: the rack.

The rack was table-shaped, mainly consisting of a bed of planks with a large cylindrical winch fixed at either end. Dense chains coiled around each winch, trailed down over the planks, and ended in irons for the hands and feet. Attached to the far side of the bed lay a great wheel, like those found on ships, and this was used for tightening or loosening the chains. Regular hand-holds ran around the edge of the wheel – each painted with a white number counting from one to ten.

Will stared at it, eyes wide and moistening. His mouth tasted foul. Efficiently, the guards shoved him forward to the rack, forced him down, and pressed his back flat onto the bed of planks. Irons clapped shut around his ankles and wrists. His legs and arms were pulled straight. Afterwards, the guards nodded to a man on a stool nearby and left the room.

At first, Will was so distracted he didn't even notice the little man sat beside the rack. In his mid-forties, the man was fresh-faced and plump. He puffed cheerfully at his pipe and the smoke wreathed delicately around his hair. He dressed in smart, laced shoes, a green tunic, and a tight leather apron. Once the guards had left, he remained seated but leant over the rack and placed a hand on his knee, like a man relaxing at a tavern. He introduced himself politely as Richard Topcliffe. With a purposefully calm air, he arose and drifted around the corners of the rack checking the chains and adjusting the irons.

"There..." he said tugging the iron on Will's right hand. "Not too tight, I hope? Don't want to cut off the old circulation. I mean there's no point in adding to the pain, is there? That's my motto."

Will lay there petrified and kept his eyes on Topcliffe. When he was finished with the irons, Topcliffe plonked himself back down onto the stool and waved the pipe beneath Will's nose.

"Pipe?" he offered pleasantly.

Will didn't answer. Topcliffe nodded and took a long drag of tobacco.

"Not one for words, ay?" He coughed and gestured his pipe disdainfully around the room. "Of course, I don't blame you. It's a horrid place this. But we do what we must. A job's a job."

Will looked aslant at him and frowned. Topcliffe smiled
back – a large, beaming smile as if he'd known Will all his life.
He leant forward.

"That old bible-basher stepped out for a break... Don't worry,
though, we'll wait for him."

Will couldn't find the strength to answer. He just stared up at
the chandelier. A strained silence drew between the two men.
Topcliffe squirmed on his stool and glanced nervously about the
room.

"Do you think we'll have rain this week?" he said feebly. "I
haven't been out in the garden for ages..."

Will turned his head away and closed his eyes.

Scene Fourteen

Prison Corridor.

Silent and tense with foreboding, Kit and Audrey followed the guard along corridors of cells towards the front office. At the end of every corridor, they encountered an iron gate and stopped while the guard unlocked it. Kit noted the guard used the same key each time: one with symmetrical jagged teeth, third down on the right of the key ring.

As they continued onwards, Kit made sure he walked near the key ring at all times. His eyes scoured his surroundings: they passed other guards, strange doors, and flights of stairs leading to floors above, but he saw no way down to the dungeons.

Finally, they passed a wide flight of stairs and approached the main entrance gate. Audrey wrung her hands anxiously. On the other side of the gate, prison wardens, guards, and off-duty sentries sipped drinks and chatted around the front desk. Kit moved closer to the guard and waited for him to unlock the gate. This time, the guard fumbled at the keys and struggled to find the right one. Kit glanced at Audrey. He turned his head and peered through the gloom behind them. He took a double look – at the far end of the corridor a stocky man in priestly robes ambled away from him. The figure was unmistakable: Baines.

Eventually, the guard unlocked the gate and propped it open for Kit and Audrey to pass through. With edgy steps, Audrey swished her dress into the room beyond, but Kit was slow to follow. His shoulders drew tight. He flexed his hands. Slowly, while feigning indifference, he moved forward to follow in Audrey's path. About half way through the gate, just as he passed the guard, he leapt into action.

Snatched the guard's key ring.

Ripped it from his raggedy belt. Grabbed the guard and rammed him through the gate. Wholly astonished, the guard reeled across the room and tumbled in a heap by the desk.

Everyone in the room jumped up. Before they could act, Kit clanged the gate shut, plucked the correct key from the ring, stabbed it into the lock, heard it click, and secured the gate quickly. He peeped over the heads of guards rushing toward him. Audrey stood a few yards beyond.

"Go!" he yelled. "Get you out of here!"

Startled, she looked at him briefly, then swiveled and hurried for the door. No one stopped her. Instead, every man on the other side dashed for the gate and clanked the iron bars noisily. Oaths colored the dank prison air. A host of keys fought to penetrate and reopen the lock.

Kit, meanwhile, raced off down the corridor after Baines. Hands closed into fists, arms trembling, blood flushing in his face, he clenched the keys and sprinted far away. It was too dark to see easily. He nearly tripped. Ahead, Baines had now disappeared from view.

At the nearest corner, Kit dithered whether to go right or left: either way the corridors were empty. Far behind him, iron crashed into stone as the gate reopened.

He cut left and flew down a corridor of narrow walls. His heart pulsed loudly in his ears. His feet pounded. His legs pumped. His chest throbbed with energy. He veered left again around the next corner and found Baines just steps away.

Baines saw him coming, turned, and raised his hands in readiness for the impact. Too late.

Kit launched forward.

Tackled Baines and bowled him over. Baines's robes flapped around him as they both thudded to the floor and skidded into the wall.

Baines spun over first and pressed his knee into Kit's chest. Winded, Kit reached up, threw him to the side, and sprung to his feet.

Before he could kick Baines in the head, Baines recovered and unleashed a chain of punches at Kit's head and stomach. Kit staggered away, desperately searching for some advantage. His eyes widened as he spied the gold cross hanging from a long, thick chain around Baines's neck.

The next time Baines swung at him, he ducked, grabbed out, wrapped his fingers around the chain. As hard as he could, he yanked down on the cross, pulled Baines to the left, and smacked his forehead into the wall. His legs buckled and he slumped down, knocked-out cold.

Without wasting time, Kit stalked over to Baines's motionless body and gripped his ankles. A faded wooden door stood a few paces down the corridor. Kit dragged the body up to it and tried the handle.

A storage room. Cracked pails, rags, and tangled mops lay strewn about inside. Vinegary fumes hung in the air. For a moment, he paused and listened: distant yells echoed throughout the prison but no footfalls came in his direction. He hauled Baines's body into the room, stepped inside, and shut the door behind him.

SCENE FIFTEEN

Torture Chamber.

Will remained outstretched on the rack and waited for the torture to commence.

At his side, Topcliffe hadn't moved from the stool – indeed, the most Topcliffe had done was reload his pipe with tobacco. He jabbered on relentlessly and filled Will's head with quips and tales and opinions on the government. He recounted his favorite cock-fight of all time, but Will could barely concentrate.

As the time passed, Topcliffe began to fidget on the stool, growing steadily bored. His voice swirled around Will's head.

"...and we have a good jest down here sometimes, we do. We're like a big family. For instance, last week the lads started playing around. Before I knew it they'd strapped me up where you are now, just for fun! They put the irons on me and everything. Hurt like hell, it did!" His chest shuddered as he chuckled to himself.

Will fidgeted and rattled the irons. Topcliffe slowly lurched into a sigh.

"Oh, we can't wait forever." He put his hands on his knees and raised himself to his feet. "It's not fair to you."

Will blinked.

"No," he croaked, his voice weak with fear. "I don't mind."

"I'm sorry, lad, what did you say?"

"I don't mind waiting."

"You sure?"

"Really. I don't mind."

"Ah, that's nice of you to say, that is, but I know you can't want to be here any longer than necessary." He laid his pipe neatly on the stool, then stretched his legs and wandered over to the rack's wheel. Before he touched it he rubbed his pudgy hands together to warm them. "Baines is meant to write down your confession, but I'll remember it well enough."

Will's face paled with fear. His stomach convulsed and he yanked frantically at the irons. The chains slapped against the winches. Topcliffe grabbed handle 'number one' gently and turned it to take up the slack of the chains. He stopped and bent his head near Will.

"Oh, by the way, if you can, try not to scream too much. My ear's a little sore recently."

The chains straightened and stretched Will taut. He gritted his teeth and waited for the pain. He waited... and waited... nothing happened...

Seconds later, the wheel squealed and turned again. The chains pulled harder. Too hard. Irons gnawed into his hands and bit into his feet. He twisted frantically as pain surged through his limbs.

SCENE SIXTEEN

Storage Room.

While Baines was still unconscious, Kit stripped him of the priestly robes. He needed a disguise. He pulled the robes over his own head and grimaced at the acrid fumes of Baines's body odor. The robe, made of thin velvet, fitted him well on the arms but fell short in length – the hem dropped only to his shinbones. Next, he looped Baines's gold chain over his shoulders and the cross swung down to touch the top of his stomach. Lastly, he found a solid, leather-bound bible tucked within Baines's belt and took it to add to his disguise. While he changed, he observed Baines carefully for signs of consciousness. He would soon awaken. Kit hurried, finished dressing, then reached around to the back of his robe and flicked the hood up to obscure his face.

He dragged Baines's body near to a freestanding shelf, found a rag, and stuffed it in his mouth. With some knotted rope left in the bottom of a pail, he tied Baines's wrists, coiled the rope around the shelf, and made sure he couldn't escape.

Now ready to leave, Kit checked that the hood drooped low over his face. His breath turned shallow. Nervously, he touched the cross to stop it from swinging and he gripped the bible harder in his sweaty palms. He pried the door ajar and looked out through the crack. No one around.

Stealthily, he swept out of the room, closed the door, and quick-stepped away.

His heart seized with panic. Two guards rounded a corner and jogged toward him. It was just like Calais – only their swords were already drawn. He nearly broke his stride as they moved closer and closer. Their faces appeared out of the murk. He watched them slow down suspiciously as they passed him. Thankfully, they chose not to stop and continued and dashed off down the corridor.

Kit now searched harder than ever for the dungeon entrance. He hunted through the network of prison corridors, endless corners, dimmed windows, and gates. Minute after minute elapsed and he found nothing.

His face lightened. In the middle of one corridor the wall suddenly broke for a downward staircase. The stairs extended straight and steep. He planted his feet carefully as he started down the steps.

Eventually, at the bottom of the stairs, he came to an arch and discovered a plank door – the entrance to the dungeons. He tried the handle. It wouldn't turn. He drew the key ring out of his sleeve and went through them, hurriedly twisting each one in the lock. None worked. He picked through the keys again and found one he had missed. Frantically, he stuck it in the door and heard it make a full revolution. Something clunked on the other side. He pressed the door's stiff handle down, tore the door open, and strode forward into the dungeon...

In the torture chamber, Topcliffe's fingers clasped handle 'number six' and turned the wheel over gently, stretching Will further. Will lay drenched in sweat. Licks of hair clung to his brow. His eyes stung with salt. At first he had screamed – yelled till his throat was sore enough to bleed – but now he was stretched beyond any great noise. He clenched his teeth, and panted, and struggled to breathe. His chest bulged as he fought to inhale. The chains pulled him still tighter. He moaned under the unnatural stress it placed on his joints. His muscles felt ready to snap; his hips tingled, ready to pop; cold, deep shooting pains struck up his leg from his right ankle, as if it were broken; and the blood trickled strangely down his arms. The chains had pulled him so taut his back no longer rested on the bed of planks but hovered half an inch in the air. He moaned again and gasped to inhale. Topcliffe put his palm on handle 'number seven' and averted his eyes as he began to turn the wheel.

The door behind opened and Kit entered carrying Baines's bible. Topcliffe gave a casual glance over his shoulder, mistook him for Baines, and continued turning the wheel.

"Where have you been?" asked Topcliffe. "We started without you, bible-basher."

Kit didn't reply. With swift feet, he flashed across the room, rose tall behind Topcliffe, and slammed the bible down on his head. Topcliffe swooned under the impact.

"He bashed me..." muttered Topcliffe, his eyes swimming. "He bashed me... With the..." He fell to the floor unconscious.

Kit hastened over to the irons on Will's hands and released him. At first, Will didn't recognize the figure in black robes helping him. When he sat upright, air poured into his lungs, the draught cooler and more bracing than a December wind. He rubbed his sore wrists distractedly. His face looked gaunt with exhaustion and shock. Gradually an expression of great relief bloomed onto his face and his eyes truly connected with Kit's.

For support, Kit put an arm around Will's slight frame and helped him to shuffle to the door. Will's ankle felt too weak to put much weight upon and he moved slowly but they soon made it outside to the main corridor. With as much speed as they could manage, they hurried past the dungeon cells. Will's head hung low and he concentrated only on moving his feet. His strength seemed to return with every minute. Kit, meanwhile, glanced around and frowned at the cell doors. The keys up his sleeve jingled as he walked.

Before they left the dungeon, he stopped and leant Will against the wall, then hustled back along the cells and unlocked every door. Will watched as twenty startled prisoners emerged. All shifted around silently and kept their eyes on Kit.

Kit dashed back up to Will. Just as he turned to address the prisoners, Will tugged on his sleeve.

"Did you find Tom Kyd?"

"Who?" Kit replied.

"Tom Kyd... He shared the cell with me."

"No. I'm sorry. They must have taken him somewhere else."

Will looked down and turned his head away.

Some of the prisoners peered into the torture chamber and gawked at Topcliffe's body lying on the floor. Mumbles filled the corridor. Kit raised his hands and gathered their attention.

"Mark this!" he called to them, keeping his voice as low as possible. "If you want to escape, we'll need more numbers!"

Some prisoners nodded in response. Others merely watched and listened. He glanced at the key ring in his hand, then rushed into the torture chamber, found a set of keys on Topcliffe, and handed them to a young, able-bodied prisoner nearby. Afterwards, he strode up to the main door of the dungeon and turned to the prisoners once again.

"Free the men on the floors above. I'll cause a distraction at the front gate."

"What if they catch us?" someone whispered.

Kit shook his head.

"No. We can do this. Prisons can only hold prisoners, not people. All of you have your own names, don't you? Your own thoughts and feelings. Loved ones whom you want to see again. You're not prisoners. You're men and you can take this prison down." He curled his hand into a fist. "Now let's do it! Let's take it down!"

Eagerness glinted in the eyes of the men watching him. Kit put his arm around Will and helped him toward the exit. The men crept behind, growing ever more excited. All of them stole out of the dungeon.

Kit approached the front gate. His priestly robes billowed about his legs. The hood reached around his face, still hiding his features. At his side, Will staggered one pace in front, limping on his right foot. He kept his hands behind his back at all times as if they were tied. Kit escorted him like a prisoner in custody. Way behind them both, twenty shadows flitted along and opened all the cells as they passed. Men arose quickly from their slumbers and woke their neighbors. Feet shuffled over the sawdust. Whispers drifted out through the bars as the men escaped. Occasionally, the men sneaked up to a guard and quickly overwhelmed him, taking his set of keys. The further they progressed through the prison, the more guards they overpowered, the more cells they opened, the more men they set free.

Kit escorted Will up to the main gate in the prison. He pressed close to the bars and peered through. On the other side, the guards and the warden gave him a shifty look. When Kit spoke to them he altered his voice, mimicking Baines's stentorian, blank patter of speech.

"Christopher Marlowe's out. This prisoner's not safe here, no longer. I got orders to take him away."

The bald-headed warden at the front desk rose from his chair and padded up to the gate. His eyes scanned over Kit, then Will. Cautiously, he opened the gate and let them through. Kit watched the guards' movements carefully from under his hood. Will tucked his hands tight behind his back and tried to keep them from view. Meanwhile, in the background, unseen by the warden, over fifty men swept noiselessly down the corridor. The youth with the keys led the way. They turned the corner and rushed up the wide staircase to the floor above.

The warden shut the gate immediately once Kit had stepped through. While ushering Will in front, Kit didn't stop as he passed the other guards. By now, the musket cabinet was unlocked and emptied. Pikes and swords once on the rack now rested in the palms of the men around them. Kit headed straight for the exit. Almost at the door, he halted as a voice called out from behind.

"Forsooth!" said the warden, confused. "Where are you going, mate? I need to see papers first."

Kit turned back and saw the warden's bald head looking at him from the desk. Everyone in the room seemed to turn and watch Kit's reaction. After a few seconds, the warden opened the ledger and leafed through it to find the right page. Kit hesitated. He shifted his weight uneasily and tried to still his trembling hands.

The warden raised his wrinkled head with annoyance.

"Come on, then. Haven't got all night."

Kit didn't respond.

A guard on his left suddenly took an interest in Will's hands and stepped in front of Kit and crouched to see under his hood. The guard flinched.

"You're not..." He spun around to the others in alarm. "Hey! He's not Baines!"

The guards immediately shot to their feet. They loomed toward Kit and Will. Pike shafts cut off any escape to the yard. Will stumbled closer to Kit as the guards moved in, but Kit remained where he stood. Musket barrels, steel blades, and pike tips floated through the air and wavered before them. Will glanced at Kit with uncertainty.

At that moment, a racket sounded upstairs: first came the slam and crash of a gate, then the roar of men's voices as if the ground had split open. An eruption of feet blasted down the steps bolstered by cries, whistles, and lengthened yells reverberating off the stone walls. The warden and all the guards and sentries in the room traded looks of fear. Everyone turned to face the gate. From around the corner surged a black mass of faces and shoulders. Hundreds of men gushed forward and thrashed against the locked gate.

In response, the guards opened fire. Musket barrels flared and spat powder. Bullets bit into the chests and stomachs of the men at the gate, yet no one fell. Pikes lowered, guards charged at the mass of arms and hands reaching through. Steel rived through flesh, but the fingers of the men grasped the shafts and blades and yanked them through the gate, disarming the guards.

The guards turned back to the warden in panic.

"Do something!" the warden yelled.

On the other side, hands gripped the bars and viciously shook the gate. At first, it appeared strong, but soon the gate's hinges wiggled in the wall and the frame juddered back and forth, back and forth, working lose. Iron scraped on stone. The men roared louder. In a burst of sublime anger, the gate collapsed under their force.

Men rushed into the room – an unstoppable, colossal drive forward. The guards retreated fast, banging shoulders with Kit and Will. Everyone was pushed outside and into the prison yard.

269

SCENE SEVENTEEN

Prison Yard.

Two huge and deep and durable wooden doors loomed before the rioters and their escape into the streets of Southwark.

Guards tumbled over each other as the rioters propelled them out of the prison office and tackled them to the ground. On the watchtowers, the silhouettes of sentries stood to attention. They raised horns to the air and blasted notes of alarm. The yard rumbled with freed men and yet still more coursed out from the prison office. A few of the boldest guards tried to resist and push back, but the men fought savagely, stripped them of weapons, and knocked them away. Some rioters took offense at the alarm horns and descended upon a nearby watchtower. One man climbed up the scaffolding and swung from the freestanding struts. Other men bashed against its legs. The tower lurched and shifted and toppled to the ground, smashing into a wall, launching splinters and planks everywhere. Most of the men, however, headed straight for the wooden doors that lay between themselves and freedom.

Across the doors rested a vast iron bar that could only be raised by two barrel-shaped winches. Already, some of the guards had disabled the winches, rendering them useless. Undeterred, the rioters pushed forward and tried to lift the bar through sheer force. They reached up, hands stretching, fingers straining, but the bar rested too high above and most couldn't touch it. Soon riflemen and archers marched in squads along the ramparts. Weapons loaded, they stopped over the doors and took aim.

The men below ducked. Fanned out.

A hail of shot and arrows tore down into the dirt. Sliced chunks out of the winches. Hammered into backs and arms. Everywhere men fell to the ground, some wounded, some dead, but the rioters regrouped and raged at the doors blindly. This time they pummeled the wood with heels, knees, fists, shoulders, anything. The tallest still tried to shift the bars. Others clawed at the hinges or pressed their backs hard into the wood. Nothing made the doors budge.

Kit stood to the side protecting Will from passing guards. Terrified, he looked at the ramparts over the entrance doors: archers and riflemen had finished nocking their arrows and reloading their muskets for another attack. *Zzzumpt! Zzzumpt!* Arrows strafed into the rioters. Rifles cracked with bursts of gunpowder. Shot rained into bodies – arms – faces – hands. Nearly a third of the men dropped to the ground or staggered away clutching wounds. Gunners in the cannon ports worked on turning the cannons away from the outside and aiming them down into the yard below. Once the cannons were finally positioned and the fuses had been lit the men would have no hope of breaking free.

Pity struck into Kit's limbs with every shot fired. The prisoners weren't all innocent, or all guilty, but there was something horrific in how easily the guards killed them. Life required so much vigilance to maintain, tolerance to endure, and labor to succeed and yet it could still be robbed by a shard of metal. It was obscene.

From the body of a guard lying prostrate in the dirt, Kit fetched a sword and handed it to Will.

"Take this and don't move."

"Where are you going?" asked Will.

"I have an idea."

"Kit... be careful..."

"Just don't move till I come back."

Will nodded anxiously and lifted the sword, feeling the weight. He prayed he wouldn't have to hit anyone. Kit rushed off into the yard. His wound gave a twinge and he put his hand on top of the bandage for support. As he approached the wooden doors he barked at the top of his voice.

271

"Hark! Gentlemen!"

Some of men turned to face him. He waved a hand in the direction of the prison office.

"Use the iron gate! We can use it as a battering ram! Use the gate! Come on!"

Few heard him clearly, but a band of ten men soon followed as he raced away from the yard and back into the prison. Will watched them disappear.

Twenty seconds elapsed... Forty seconds...

Will waited, his eyes keenly trained on the prison office, but Kit didn't return. Gunners swiveled the cannons fully into place. Riflemen and archers reloaded for a third wave of attack. The men below still battered the doors, but their energy dwindled, and every strike became more futile than the last. Will turned his head away, unable to watch the impending slaughter.

A movement came from the front office. Will perked up. Suddenly, Kit and ten men staggered out, sweating and grinding their teeth, hauling the iron gate on its side between them. Suspended on their shoulders, the gate's enormous mass crushed down on them, bent their backs, the weight so heavy their legs could hardly stand straight.

With Kit in the lead, they hurried toward the two giant entrance doors. The other men in the yard responded instantly and did all they could to help. Fired with a new hope, they surrounded the gate, grabbed a hold, and charged with it toward the doors, using it to ram the wood. With their faces sweating and their hands heaving, the men combined their might and swung the iron to and fro, impelling it forward, rocking it backward, pitching forward, swaying backward, momentum rolling, rising, pulling, driving, swifter, faster, rapid, quick. In unison they chanted and thrust the gate toward the doors.

"One... Two... *Three!*"

The gate pounded into the wood. The doors shuddered with the impact but didn't break. The men swung again.

"One... Two... *Three!*"

The gate struck the doors harder. In the center, the wood started to fracture. The men swung again.

272

"One... Two... *Three!*"

The iron prongs of the gate punched through the planks of the doors. They could see the road beyond. The men swung again.

"One... Two... *Three!*"

The gate hurtled forward. Ruptured the doors. Punctured cleanly through, whipping the doors back, almost tearing them asunder from their hinges.

Cheers fluttered into the air like streamers. The men powered forward out of the prison and leapt over shards and twisted planks. Cannons boomed behind them. Shot and arrows blistered the ground, but all to no avail. Kit and Will quickly joined the men pouring out from the prison and dashed away into the darkened cobbled streets.

SCENE EIGHTEEN

Southwark.

Kit and Will ran for the shadows. The rioters around them dispersed into single runners or groups of two and three. Some fled out into the fields and leapt over hedgerows or splashed into ditches and did their best to hide. Some sprinted down to riverbanks and hurried toward the lanterns of wherries at Bankside. And a few, like Kit and Will, threaded their way into the crooked alleys of Southwark.

Almost immediately, guards from the prison followed in pursuit of the men. Horses' hooves thundered through streets. Hounds barked down by the riverbanks. Torches bobbed through the nearby fields as posses scoured the earth for footprints, thrashed hedges with clubs, stuck ditches with pikes, and craned their heads back to see into the upper limbs of trees. Some of the most wounded prisoners were captured quickly, but too many men had spread out in too many directions for the guards to retrieve them all.

When they were both sure they hadn't been followed, and that other men from the prison were far away, Kit and Will stopped in a back alley to gather their strength. Their faces were red. Their limbs shook from the exertion. Kit watched his breath cloud into the night air.

"God," he muttered, "I hope Audrey made it away unscathed."

"I'm sure she did," Will replied. "They wouldn't dare endanger the Queen's gentlewoman."

"No… they wouldn't…"

Will appeared fatigued yet also slightly enlivened by the burst of energy. He rubbed his sore joints and glanced up at Kit.

"My thanks," he said gratefully. "I thought I'd never see you ever again."

"Well, we're not out of danger yet," Kit replied.

"Even so, that was truly one of the most courageous acts I've ever witnessed."

Kit shrugged. He smiled back at Will.

"How are you?"

"A little taller than before, I think."

They both gave a small chuckle. The next moment, however, a strange silence followed and their faces soon grew serious. The longer Will looked at Kit the more he remembered his earlier offenses. The lies. The hesitant, reluctant answers. The self-indulgent excuses linked to Kit's life in the government. Then the whole scene at Hogg Inn replayed through his head and he realized their last meeting had ended in argument. An acidic sense of bitterness soon dissolved his feelings of gratitude about the rescue. After all, if wasn't for Kit, he wouldn't have been taken to Marshalsea in the first place.

Kit stood upright. His eyes wandered about restlessly. He understood the reasons for Will's silence.

"What I said earlier..." he began awkwardly, but his throat constricted with too many emotions and he couldn't finish.

Will nodded.

"But it doesn't change anything, Kit."

"Can't we–"

"I don't think I can involve myself in this any longer."

"Oh."

"I wish you the greatest fortune and I hope you prove the conspiracy..."

"But?"

"...I don't have the strength to help anymore."

"You're stronger than I am."

"And what does that matter? As you've said in the past, some things in this world can't be overcome." Will sighed indignantly and tried to stand on his lame foot. "Anyway, you can handle this on your own. You don't need anyone or anything."

"Don't say that."

"It's true. You're Christopher Marlowe, remember?"

Kit hesitated and looked down despondently.

"Yes..." he replied with reluctance. "Yes... I'm Christopher Marlowe."

Will paused, his head lost in a cloud of exhaustion, anger, confusion, and doubt. He bade Kit farewell and turned and stumbled off into the darkness of the alleyway. He didn't look back.

Disheartened, Kit watched him go till his figure blended away into the darkness. His gaze fell to the floor. A sharp ache issued from his wound and he touched the bandage at his side. He tried to ignore the flies droning about his head.

SCENE NINETEEN

Scadbury Manor. Kitchen.

Moonlight fell through the mullioned windows and stained white squares upon the floor. At a kitchen table, Audrey sat alone and pecked at a meal she had prepared for herself. Departure from Marshalsea Prison hadn't been easy once Kit set the alarm. At first, the guards tried to interrogate her and the warden had even suggested detention. They all quickly changed their minds, however, when she fully explained her role at court and began describing how the Queen would react to news that a Gentlewomen of the Privy Chamber was being held in a prison with escaped convicts. After that, the guards clamored to be the first to assist her to her carriage and escort her safely from the prison grounds.

She glanced down at her plate. Hunks of cheese lay near the rim next to a crust of bread. She tried to eat but found it hard to swallow. With a swig of brandy she eventually finished it and collected her candelabra and left the room.

After climbing the stairs and creeping down the corridor toward her bedchamber, she paused anxiously and her eyes switched over to Thomas's room on the opposite side. No light came from beneath his doorframe to signal that he might still be awake. Relieved, she lowered the candelabra, opened the door to her own bedchamber and entered.

With a tiny yawn, she took two steps and shone the candelabra around the walls. Her stomach grumbled. Traces of brandy tasted sugary on her lips. Tonight, with all her worries over Kit, she wouldn't sleep. Nevertheless, there were several hours left before dawn and she started the mechanical ritual of undressing herself. One by one, she took the pins off her hat and carefully laid them on a chest by the wall. She remembered the door was still open. She padded across the room, extended a slow, tired hand to shut it, but something attracted her eye and her fingers never reached the handle.

Something bright had sparkled in the dark. She'd seen it from the corner of her eye. Curiously, she lifted the candelabra and threw the light towards her dressing table.

She took a sharp breath. Her stomach pulled tight. Her eyes strained ahead in disbelief.

On top of the dressing table, laid neatly in the center, was Kit's brooch.

For a moment, the discovery knocked her clear of her senses. Her legs weakened and her thoughts disintegrated into dizziness. She did her best to gather herself. Slowly, barely breathing, she crept toward the table, staring at the golden band. Perhaps the maid had found it? No. She knew better than that. It was a message and she knew the sender. As she reached out toward the brooch, she felt the powerful bite of immorality gnaw down upon her, sinking its teeth into her conscience. No matter how many times she'd convinced herself against such feelings, they wouldn't go from her mind. They wouldn't release her.

Out in the corridor the floorboards squeaked. Squeaked again. Someone's footsteps.

She jumped with alarm. The hairs on her arms rose straight and her cheeks blushed. She took her hand away from the brooch. Hesitantly, she turned her head, peered over her shoulder, and squinted through the half-darkness.

Thomas appeared in the doorway.

With his shoulders bent, lips pressed tight, eyes open and unblinking, Thomas looked incredibly grave. He stood with his head tipped slightly forward so that his forelock was sharply set against his skin. Deliberately taking his time, he stepped into the chamber.

In silence, he stared at her as if brooding on something painful. No sound came from anywhere in the house. They each breathed noiselessly – almost without disturbing the air. His appearance had caught her off guard but she resolved not to show it. Instead of her usually submissive manner, she returned his gaze frankly and was the first to break the silence.

"So, Thomas, what did you expect?"

"Love and obedience," he answered dryly.

"Is that *really* what you wanted? You expect that after everything that's happened, or not happened, over the last year?"

"Those were your vows, I believe."

"Vows! Oh, how noble of you to remember. For a while, I thought you'd forgotten our marriage – forgotten it completely."

"Be careful, Audrey."

"Well, I made no vow to strangle my feelings. If my marriage is cold I must find warmth elsewhere."

"In Hell, perhaps?"

Wearily, she set the candelabra down and took a seat at her dressing table.

"I've tried..." she moaned. "I've tried with all my heart..."

"And you think I haven't?"

"No... perhaps... sometimes..."

"You're the one most at blame for this failed union of ours."

"Yes, I'm sure you're right."

He wandered past the bed and ran a finger across the sheets.

"Is it my fault you don't evoke the passions within me that you should?"

"You don't have any passions."

"No. The fault is yours. No man could love a whore like you."

"And yet they do," she said defiantly. "What is it that repulses you more, I wonder? That I should lie with another man, or that another man should lie with me... rather than yourself."

He lurched near her with a murderous look.

"Be very careful, Audrey."

She gripped the arms of her chair, frightened but unrepentant.

"You've been unfaithful too – if not with your body, then with your mind."

279

"Don't speak another word!"

"I've seen how you look at Christopher!"

He lunged and grabbed her by the neck, shaking with anger.

"You strumpet, I'll cut your tongue out!"

She struggled to hide her fear. They watched each other tensely, neither daring to make the next move. She fought to breathe against the fingers pressing into her throat.

"You know, this is the first time, in months, that you've touched me."

He hesitated, then slowly withdrew his grip and began to calm down. All the tension in his limbs seemed to abandon him.

A short silence followed. Audrey rubbed her neck and looked away toward the window. Thomas hung his head.

"We can't continue this way," he said quietly. "There'll be no place at court for either of us."

She didn't reply and kept her eyes on the window. His heel ground on the floorboards as he turned, paced away from her, and prowled around the room.

"We broke the playwright Tom Kyd a few hours ago. Everything is now in place."

"Punish me, if you must, but leave Christopher and everyone else alone."

"No. This is bigger than just you. And things have gone too far to stop now. Come the morrow, Christopher will be caught." He flexed his jaw. "Because of you, I expect he'll come here. I have the guards prepared and ready."

"Why are you doing this?"

He ignored the question and narrowed his eyes.

"He'll be taken to the Privy Council. He hasn't a chance... unless I help him."

"Oh, I understand, you want something from me."

"Yes."

"What? What in Christendom do you want?"

He smiled bitterly.

"I'll let Christopher flee the country one condition: that you break off the affair. If you agree never to see him again, I'll let him live."

"How reasonable of you," she said mockingly. "Do you think me some idle-headed simpleton?" She raised her arm sharply and thrust a finger at the door. "You're a liar Thomas, a pathetic liar, and I won't play your games. Leave me. I have no more words for you."

"I won't make this offer again."

"Leave, Thomas. Now."

He bridled at her tone. For a moment, he glared and shook his head. He strolled off toward the door and drew a key from the pocket on his sleeve.

"Then he goes to the council," said Thomas, crisply sounding each syllable.

She responded with a huff and turned her back and faced the dressing table. She stared at him in the mirror. He glanced over her shoulder and saw the glint of Kit's broach.

"And by the way," he sneered, "don't even think of warning your dear poet…"

Before she could react, he left the room and slammed the door shut. A key grated in the lock and the bolt clicked over, making her prisoner of her own room.

She heard his feet stamp away along the corridor, then trample all the way down the stairs. Once he was gone, she held a shaking hand to her mouth, overcome with emotion.

Scene Twenty

Southwark.

Kit escaped the town early since there was a good chance someone in the area might recognize him. In the bare twilight hours before dawn, he stole through the streets to Bankside, made it over to The Rose, and convinced a stable groom to loan him one of Henslowe's horses. Afterwards, as fast as possible, he rode out into the countryside of Kent and traveled towards Scadbury Manor. To his relief, no one seemed to follow him.

Above, in the twilight sky, the moon turned a shade of grayish blue and assumed the tone of frozen skin. Clouds stretched down to the horizon, each one long and thin, like scars made by a whip.

Finally, after a long ride, Kit galloped his horse up to the forest skirting Scadbury manor and hastily jumped down from the saddle. Behind a thicket of blackberries, he tied his horse to a tree and made sure it was out of view from the nearby road. With long strides he then moved off into the forest.

As he hiked, a light wind brushed through the tops of oak trees. Leaves chattered. Ancient boughs twisted and squeaked. Moths fluttered in the shade. A snake's tail slithered through clumps of leaves. For three quarters of an hour, he hiked onwards till he reached the edge of the manor grounds.

The back lawns to the rear wall of the house seemed an unbearably vast distance to run – at least four hundred yards. Crouched low, he observed the sides of the house for patrolling watchmen. He took a few deep draughts of air, held it in his lungs, and felt it push against the walls of his chest, charging his blood. He tilted forward onto the balls of his feet and crouched lower, his muscles tense and ready.

He burst out into the open. Sprinted past flower beds at the side of the garden. Dew immediately soaked through his leather shoes and kicked up in a spray around his calves. He drove the balls of his feet into the grass, streaking over the lawn. Thighs pushing, back straight, eyes tunneling ahead, he raced toward the back door. Two hundred yards... One hundred-and-fifty... One hundred... He hurdled a border of red stocks. His heel clipped the top blooms. He dashed over the gravel path, shot over to the wall, and pressed himself flat against the cool stones. From there, he tried the handle of the nearby door: it clicked open and he slipped inside the house.

Stealthily, he darted down passages through the manor. Most servants still lay asleep or worked only in the kitchens. Within two minutes, he arrived at the hall and stopped to listen for danger. His eyes checked the shadowed recesses of the area. He stepped forward onto the tiles. His foot squelched, still sodden from the lawn. On his tip-toes, he crept across the tiles, leaving a trail of watery footprints as he headed for the stairs.

About half way across, the pit of his stomach burnt ferociously. The hairs on his neck prickled. Something was wrong. He ignored the feeling and took another step towards the stairs. Then it happened. From somewhere behind him came the sound of Thomas's voice.

"Up early this day, are we?"

Kit froze. Slowly, he twisted his body around.

Unknown to him, across the hall a door had opened silently and Thomas now emerged with two armed guards. Swords drawn, the guards rushed past Thomas and stalked over the tiles. Kit pivoted in the opposite direction. From niches beside the front door, three more guards entered the hall, closing off his exit. He stopped in his tracks and shook his head.

"Well done, Thomas."

"Go quietly," Thomas replied. "Make it easier on all of us. There's no use resisting now."

"What exactly do you hope to gain from this?"

283

Thomas narrowed his eyes. He circled Kit like a hawk watching its quarry.

"I get rid of you."

"Is that all?"

"Yes. Whitgift wants you dead and I'm the man to do it."

"Whitgift's a walking lie. You know that. He'll throw you to the wind when he's finished. You don't honestly believe him, do you?"

"I'm afraid I do."

"Well... then... I don't know what to say. I'm sure you and Whitgift will make a very lovely couple."

"Jest all you like, Christopher. Your death will be the ashes to my phoenix. There'll be nothing to endanger my advancement once you're gone."

"Glad I could help. I'll do anything for a friend."

"Ah, but you're not my only helper." He paused and studied Kit's face. "Audrey played her part, too."

"What?"

"Yes, I think of all my spies, she's the very best."

Kit raised his eyebrows and gave a doubtful look.

Thomas smiled deliciously.

"Don't believe me? Hear it for yourself."

Thomas beckoned Kit up the stairs and led him to the door of Audrey's bedchamber. He unlocked it and tapped sprightly on the wood.

"Audrey! We have a guest!"

Kit stood motionless and waited. His toes felt cold in his sopping wet shoes. Everything was happening too fast. Nearby, guards kept their swords extended towards him, their faces solemn and pale.

Thomas remained at the door and kept his sight on the handle. After her initial refusal, it was a gamble whether she would really lie as he wanted. Nevertheless, it was a calculated risk: he felt sure she would try anything when she saw the dire extent of Kit's situation.

Within moments, the handle turned, the door opened hesitantly, and Audrey appeared in the frame. She hadn't changed from the night before and her body made a crisp 'A' shape in her dress. She held her hands together as she stepped into the light.

"What do you want with–" She stopped dead, shocked at the sight of Kit encircled by guards and swords.

Thomas stared up at her coldly.

"Tell Christopher that you were always working for me," he commanded.

She didn't react. Gradually, she looked at Thomas... then the guards... then worked her eyes back to Kit. She breathed deeply. Her face tightened.

"Tell him," Thomas repeated.

She took the bait. Without a trace of emotion, she sashayed forward into the corridor and looked Kit straight in the eye.

"You must have suspected it?" she said candidly. "Couldn't you tell? Didn't you know I wasn't really in love with you?"

Kit threw his head back and snorted derisively.

"Wonderful! This is quite a play you've arranged, Thomas."

Audrey stepped closer to him.

"Oh, don't worry, this isn't one of your long-winded dramas."

"I think I know acting when I see it, my lady."

"Do you? Do you, indeed?"

"Yes."

"But didn't you wonder why we visited the tailor alone? Or how I knew about the secret passageway? Or how I gained Baines's address so easily?"

Her manner unnerved him. Bravely, he clapped his hands at her.

"Bravo! You're almost convincing."

Audrey glanced over at Thomas. She turned desperate and approached Kit viciously.

"My acting was good even that night at the palace, wasn't it? By god, I couldn't bear having to touch you again after that." She pushed her face close to his. "Thomas arranged the assassination... but I begged him for it."

The words pierced into Kit like a barb in the heart, striking at all his doubts and insecurities. He swallowed with difficulty and

285

ran a hand through his hair. He looked at her searchingly, tried to find some sign that it wasn't true, but her face was harder than he'd ever seen it. In the faint light, her skin acquired the luster of white marble. Red veins cracked through her eyes. Her gaze never broke away. She stood completely still with arms at her waist and her posture erect and her head slightly to one side – as still and beautiful and dead as a Grecian statue.

Thomas strolled around him in a circle. He grinned bitterly.

"Dipped your quill in the wrong ink pot this time, I'm afraid."

Kit didn't reply. Thomas gestured to the guards.

"Get him to Westminster."

All the pent-up energy within the guards now released itself. They fell upon Kit and grabbed him roughly, thrusting his arms behind him, gripping the collar and the front of his shirt. He didn't fight as they lugged him down the stairs and dragged him toward the front door. Audrey and Thomas followed behind and stopped in the hall. Kit's eyes stayed on Audrey the whole time.

Horrified, Audrey turned and scowled at Thomas.

"What are you doing? You promised!"

Thomas didn't reply. He watched as the guards opened the door and hauled Kit out of the house. For the first time, he looked troubled, even remorseful. He stared after Kit, hoping, praying for some sense of gratification at his victory. Instead, his heart sank. The idea of hurting Kit seemed far better in theory than in practice. He spoke quietly under his breath, almost to himself.

"There's no other way…"

Audrey began to shake with rage. Tears glistened in her eyes. She flew at Thomas and lashed out, slapping at his face, shoulders, chest. He stepped aside and threw her to the tiles. She landed hard and collapsed to her knees. Her dress ballooned around her in swathes of fabric. She sat there, back bent, sobbing with rage.

"You can't love anyone!" she cried disdainfully. "Not me! Not Christopher! Not yourself!"

Thomas's face suddenly weakened. Cut by Audrey's words, he glared down at her, pivoted swiftly on his heel, and paced off.

She continued to sob. Her sobs filled the shining, polished corners of the hall and echoed up into the beams overhead.

Outside, guards shoved Kit toward a prison cart now waiting on the gravel drive. In the east, the first rays of sun cut through the horizon and clouds lashed the sky with red. Strong winds roused the leaves of the forest. Lawns shimmered gray with dew. Swallows sliced their wings past the walls of the house, and insects scraped their spindly legs over flower petals in the garden. Kit's stomach ached and filled him with the urge to vomit. His eyelids drooped. His mouth gaped. The crunch of feet over the gravel sounded incredibly loud and hurt his ears.

As he approached the prison cart, he craned his head away from the drive and gave a dispirited glance to the sky. The last thing he saw before the guards loaded him into the cart was the faded moon dissolving into a sky of endless blue.

ACT V

SCENE ONE

Westminster Palace. Star Chamber.

Kit found himself in a courtroom staring up at a blue ceiling painted with stars. Recent events had passed around him in a blur. He stood and waited in the room while two guards behind watched his every movement.

The strange ceiling belonged to a notorious courtroom known as the Star Chamber. The court originated hundreds of years ago from the proceedings of the King's Royal Council – an administrative body entirely separate from the common-law courts. Over the following centuries the council slowly became its own judicial entity, and sixty years ago it changed into a 'pure' court, operating without the direct presence of the monarch. Compared to the common-law courts, the Court of the Star Chamber was designed to dispense with sensitive cases in a swift, flexible manner. Court sessions occurred in secret without rules concerning evidence or the burden of proof. There were no indictments or rights of appeal. No juries. No witnesses. Evidence was presented in writing only. Although the Star Chamber was secret, rumors of its existence had filtered into the general population, and accounts of its speed and severity had long made its name a byword for injustice.

The Star Chamber itself was quite small: stripped of any ornamentation, four white walls bounded the room and dark oak panels ran underfoot. Kit lingered at the far end and two large tables made a 'T' shape before him. The longest table stretched down the length of the room with places to seat ten people. At the opposite end, a smaller table lay crosswise, covered in red cloth

trimmed with gold, like the covering of an altar. The only interesting feature of the room was the ceiling. High above, black
beams made squares over the ceiling, and dark blue panels sunk
between them, each painted with a single gold-gray star in the
center. Looking up, it gave one the impression of seeing the night
sky through a grid of bars. That morning, inside the windowless,
sealed room, the effect was surreal: a new world created by an
unknown god.

Kit waited for over half an hour in the courtroom while minor officials with straight mouths and downcast eyes busied
themselves with preparations. One of the officials approached Kit
and issued instructions on how he should deport himself. Once
the official had finished lecturing, he left Kit to stand alone at the
tables. As if some mysterious signal had suddenly been given,
everyone else in the room turned away and left noiselessly. Only
the guards remained and stood behind Kit at the door.

Moments of quiet passed through the chamber. The air
touched Kit's skin with a strange deadness. He felt his heart grow
small and tight with anxiety. His lungs shook as he tried to
breathe. Before him, the light from a wall candle made streaks
over the glossy wood panels of the floor.

For some time, he remained standing in a half-crooked position, brooding intensely. It was insanely difficult to think of a defense. The evidence would be too damning. He couldn't do it any
more. Why not wait quietly? After all, the gallows were inevitable – he'd known that since he first spied the poster.

He stood and waited. The tall doors at the back drifted open
and the members of the Court of the Star Chamber proceeded into the room...

In total, thirteen officials filed into the chamber and stood at
their places at the tables. Two common-law judges entered first,
dressed all in red gowns. Next, six Lords of Her Majesty's Most
Honorable Privy Council stepped into the room. Their gold-
tasseled shoes led the way. Black cloaks swept along the floorboards behind. After the counselors, the cassocks and flat caps of
the Bishop of London and the Archbishop of York paraded into
the chamber. The Bishop wore only a fur scarf around his neck,

but the Archbishop displayed a respectable chain of gold. They stood behind their chairs at the last places at the long table.

Finally, the three most important members of the court entered the room. Lord Essex strutted inside first. The youthfulness of his face set him in stark contrast to everyone else in the chamber. He carried himself proudly as he approached the short table at the end.

After Essex, Whitgift marched across the floor. His hands swung through the air. Strong limbs shifted beneath the black and white fabric of his cassock. The dim light added to the brown of his skin and turned harsh against the deep creases of his cheeks. He looked sharp. Fully alert. His heels pounded as he strode over to his chair at the short table. His eyes never looked at Kit. Instead, he regarded some papers in his hands.

Last of all, Lord Burghley entered the chamber – his graceful, long body leaning heavily on his cane as it tapped the floorboards with every step. He sat down at the head table between Essex and Whitgift. Afterwards, everyone else sat down, too.

Kit shifted uncomfortably on his feet. He felt oddly exposed. From his position, his sun-strained eyes looked down the long table directly into the face of Burghley.

With a shaking hand, Burghley lifted a gavel and rapped it formally. He sat erect in his chair.

"I hereby call into session her majesty's Court of The Star Chamber," he said in his croaky voice. He peered across the room at Kit.

Kit's body drew tense. He corrected his posture and raised his chin. He stared over the heads of the court.

Burghley set the gavel down.

"Christopher Marlowe, playwright to The Rose, appears today to explain himself on the charge of atheism. The charge is lodged by direct petition of his holiness, John Whitgift, Archbishop of Canterbury." He raised his wispy eyebrows. "Does the defendant hold himself innocent or guilty of this crime?"

"Innocent," Kit replied. He shuddered at the feeble sound of his voice inside the room.

"The defendant realizes this court has the power not only to impose fines and severe physical punishment, but may also recommend his public execution to the Queen?"

Kit gulped. He nodded once. Burghley paused, as if reluctant, and then turned in his chair toward Whitgift.

"Proceed at will, Archbishop."

Whitgift had been scanning through the pages in his hands. Now he slowly raised his head, puffed out his chest, plucked a scroll from the table, and pushed himself up from his chair to begin the inquisition.

He made a short opening statement. With a tone of utmost gravity, he declared the ungodly content of Kit's plays. He mentioned the blight of posters around London bearing Kit's words and Kit's signature. He reminded the court of the dangerous, increasing popularity of theatres. And he affirmed the need to set an example for other playwrights and players that atheism would not be tolerated.

All the while, Kit stood rigidly on the spot and listened. He ground his teeth. Once or twice he nearly blurted out words of defense, but he held his tongue and remained silent.

Whitgift stepped away from the head table. With a grim expression, he paraded around the floor brandishing a scroll.

"These charges were recently leveled at Richard Cholmeley and show him to be an unprincipled rogue... Yet who is to blame for Cholmeley's corruption?" He paused. His eyes swung over the faces at the table. He pivoted toward Kit and stabbed his finger through the air. "This wanton poet! Cholmeley credits Marlowe for his atheism. Indeed, he states Marlowe has also tried to convert others, including members of the government, with his atheist lectures."

At the head table, Burghley sat forward to hear every word. Next to him, Essex slouched and sighed, seemingly bored with the ordeal.

Whitgift unfurled the scroll and set it before Burghley on the red cloth. Burghley skimmed through it with incredible speed, as if he knew the contents already. Afterwards, he showed it to Essex, and then passed the scroll down to the long table. The others regarded it with dour faces.

While they studied the scroll, Whitgift stalked toward Kit. He seemed energized by the effect the scroll had on his audience.

"You are an associate of this Cholmeley, no?"

Kit shrugged.

"What can I say, your lordships?" he replied, shaking his head. "I don't know how to respond to such charges."

"It's odd that you should have trouble voicing your opinion now, is it not? Your plays never seem to lack for words – no, nor the libels you've posted around London."

"I must have a moment to think."

"No. I will repeat the question once more: you are an associate of Richard Cholmeley, are you not?"

"I have never met him. I have never consorted with a man named Cholmeley."

"Don't deny it. You are both scoundrels and you are both in league to spread atheism around this country."

"This is ridiculous!"

"That is not an answer!"

"Anyone could create these charges against me."

"Then it shouldn't be hard to create a defense against them, should it?"

Kit opened his mouth to reply, but stopped – suddenly speechless. Emotionally devastated by recent hours, Whitgift's pounding tone only crushed him further with every syllable uttered. He could hardly think his own thoughts. He felt Cholmeley's note inside his shirt, tucked under his belt, but it seemed pointless to use it now without a supporting argument. It was simply too hard to keep fighting. With every minute, surrender and passivity seemed easier, more inviting, more seductive. His eyes floated up to the blue ceiling and he tried to think of a response.

At the head table, Essex sat upright. He raised his voice grandly.

"Yes," said Essex. "Why should we believe the defendant's story?"

295

The faces at the long table turned toward Kit with interest.

Kit continued to stare at the ceiling, consumed with thought. Finally, he hung his head.

"My lords," he pleaded, "I have had no time to prepare a defense."

"You mean you've had no time to concoct a story to mask your atheism," Whitgift responded quickly.

"If I was given a mere hour or two... some time in order to think..."

An expression of triumph sprang onto Whitgift's face. He turned toward the long table. His lips peeled into a smile.

"The court will agree that an innocent man needs no time to think. In fact, an innocent man need not think or prepare anything at all. Innocence is not the stuff of plans."

After a moment, Burghley looked searchingly at Kit and shifted in his seat. He issued a small huff, unable to hide his dismay.

"Continue, Archbishop..."

Whitgift swiftly fetched two more documents, held one in each hand, and marched over to the other side of the room. He looked searchingly into the eye of every court member.

"These are the very documents of Marlowe's damnation." He raised his left hand theatrically. "Mark this! Direct, detailed accusations made by Richard Baines."

The faces at the long table darkened. Eyebrows lowered. Fingers tapped decisively. Quills scratched notes onto parchment.

Whitgift surveyed the document himself.

"Hearken to just one charge! Marlowe has said the New Testament is so poorly written that he himself could have done better! Can you doubt such bombast and blasphemy from the author of '*Doctor Faustus*'?"

Two counselors peered over to see as Whitgift set the document down on the table between them. He raised his right hand and waved the other document in the air.

"And should any doubts remain, cast your eyes upon the words of Thomas Kyd – Marlowe's fellow playwright at The

Rose. Not until he was tortured would this man admit to Marlowe's monstrous opinions."

"Such as?" Essex called across the room.

"Let's see..." Whitgift glanced at the document. "...that Christ did love St. John with an extraordinary love."

A few of the privy counselors squirmed in their chairs, trying not to smirk. They traded fleeting looks of mirth between themselves.

Incredulous, Whitgift halted on the spot, scandalized at their reaction. A scowl cut across his face. In a burst of anger, he slammed the document down onto the table.

"Do not forget the libels and riots linked to this man!" he cried.

The sudden noise shocked the air. It left a tense silence in its wake. Everyone sat back and stared at him with surprise.

"Atheism ravages both God and nation," he continued. He strode back and forth alongside the table. "Like children, the people look to us to show them right from wrong. They depend upon us for their protection. I ask you: shall we succumb to the violent pox of atheism or shall we purge it forever from this land?"

At the table, heads turned and followed his path. The Archbishop of York and the Bishop of London gave stern looks to the rest of the court members.

Whitgift stopped at the head table.

"My lords, there is only one true choice. You must act now." He stood up tall and straight and perfectly defined like a stained glass figure. "You must find the defendant guilty of posting the libels, guilty of spreading atheism, guilty of attacking the foundations of Christianity, and guilty of destroying the harmony and stability of our blessed Kingdom."

Everyone seemed affected by his stirring speech. His passion infected every counselor, every judge, and both members of the clergy. Murmurs of agreement rippled across the long table.

Lord Burghley cleared his throat and the noise in the room immediately quelled. He looked desperately at Kit.

"You have no words of defense?" he asked. "You have no way to protect yourself from the wrath of this court?

Kit rubbed his brow. He hesitated and peered up to the ceiling and then closed his eyes. Everyone awaited his answer. Finally, he clenched his fists.

"No, your lordship. Not without more time."

Burghley immediately shook his head.

"Then we shall deliberate. This session is hereby closed and the court will retire to consider its verdict." He snatched the gavel and rapped it. "Guards, remove the defendant from the–"

Before he could finish, everyone's head swiveled toward the courtroom door. Footsteps of someone running close echoed down the corridor outside. The slapping of feet came nearer, nearer still, almost at the door.

A scuffle sounded: the noise of arms twisting and grappling against the doorframe. Kit straightened his posture, alert.

Suddenly, the door flung open.

Will Shakespeare burst into the room, tussling with a palace guard.

SCENE TWO

Star Chamber.

Will rushed inside carrying an envelope. Below the starred ceiling, shocked faces stared back at him from the tables. Some court members leapt to their feet in alarm. Whitgift raised his hands, outraged by the intrusion.

"I won't brook this!" he growled. "You see that Marlowe has planned a subversion of the court! Condemn him this minute!"

Will's hair flapped in his eyes as he grappled with the guard in front of him. He panted deeply. A look of urgency mingled with the redness of his cheeks. His right foot still pained him, but he flew towards Kit with terrific force.

Eyes large, Kit pressed forward to help him.

"Will!"

"I'm not too late, am I?" Will yelled back. "I trust there's still time?"

Before Kit could answer, the guards next to him reacted, jumped in front and blocked him. The guard on his right lunged forward and checked Will in the chest with the shaft of his pike.

"Stand fast, sir!" yelled the guard.

"Out of my way!"

"Stand fast! I won't warn ya again."

Will pushed back against the pike shaft but couldn't get beyond. He stood on his tiptoes to see Kit.

"I have something for you..." He skimmed the envelope across the floor to Kit's feet. "...from Audrey."

The name seemed to sting the air around Kit's head. Rapidly, he bent down to pick up the envelope but the guard in front of him pinioned his arms and twisted them behind his back. Kit groaned in agony. He slammed his shoulder backwards into the guard's chest, freed his hands, and shoved the guard away.

Kit stooped, reached out, and snatched the envelope from the floor. He tore it open at one end and tipped the package up: the ouroboros brooch fell out onto his hand along with a document.

"What is this?" he asked.

The guard recovered his strength and lurched forward to take it. Kit grabbed the collar of the guard's cuirass, wrenched it up, and held him back with one arm.

The guard by Will jerked his pike forward and rammed it into Will's chest. He put his full weight behind the shaft and drove Will back from the courtroom. Will struggled but could only slow his departure. He peered over the shoulder of the guard and his hopeful, caring face stood out in the gloom.

"Audrey found me and gave me it," he called back to Kit. "You can make them listen! Create the argument they need to hear!"

Kit listened thoughtfully to every word. The next second, Will's guard finally succeeded and pushed him around the corner and out of sight. The echoes of their struggle resounded off the stone walls as they moved away.

Kit looked at the document and turned it over. He nodded his head with satisfaction: the original draft of the libel with Whitgift's signature on the back. His gaze shifted and lingered on the brooch and he rubbed it with his finger. The smooth of his thumb passed over the scales of the snake, its mouth, its circular body. The guard beside him relented, exhausted from the struggle. Slowly, Kit's face brightened.

"Then she *was* acting..." he mumbled to himself. "Thomas didn't have her for a spy."

Silence pervaded the courtroom once again. The candlelight made quiet streaks on the varnish of the wooden floor. Kit looked up at the faces of the old men around the tables.

"My lords, I beg your forgiveness of my friend's disturbance. He meant no disrespect – he wished only to help me with this document."

Essex sat back down in his chair and rubbed his stomach as if feeling hungry.

"Yes, and I'm sure master Shakespeare's enthusiasm is very admirable," Essex replied sarcastically, "but he has not improved the court's feeling toward you. This has gone on long enough for my taste. It's time for dinner already."

"Perhaps the court will change its opinion by this document? Might I show it to you?"

A vein in Whitgift's jaw swelled, but he refrained from speaking until Burghley had made a decision.

At the head of the long table, Burghley watched every member of the court and listened to every comment. He peered down at a scrap of parchment on which he had scribbled a list of the advantages and disadvantages of punishing Kit. The column of advantages was longer. His face held an expression of sad reluctance.

"I'm not sure how it can change the court's decision at this stage... but your request is sustained. You may present the document."

Whitgift's eyes flashed.

"Your lordship!" he cried. "The defendant was already granted the chance to plead his case and he declined to do so. Is not the time for argument now over?" His fingers twitched at the folds of his cassock but he tried to appear confident.

Kit ignored him and strode down the table towards Burghley. His fingers gripped the signed libel.

"The Archbishop's case was certainly interesting, but I do have one problem with it. How does it connect with my background?"

"Explain..." said Burghley, growing intrigued.

"I was a loyal servant to her majesty, was I not?"

"You were employed in my service for over two years, and you served under Sir Francis Walsingham for a much longer period." Burghley addressed the long table with a louder voice. "Aside from the recent counterfeiting, I am willing to endorse the fact that there have been few ill marks against the defendant's character."

"Exactly." Kit's eyes narrowed. "So why would I suddenly decide to post libels everywhere? And why would I do it without any forethought? During my service as a spy, I've learnt many strategies to evade capture. If I wanted to incite open rebellion I would've at least made a few plans first, wouldn't I?" He turned to Whitgift with a mischievous expression. "So far, I haven't seen any plans connected with me. Have you seen any plans, Archbishop?"

Whitgift dithered.

"Well..." he replied.

"None at all?"

"This is beside the point and you're wasting the court's valuable time."

"Correct me if I'm wrong, but didn't you imply earlier that a guilty man makes plans? I think you did. In fact, I'll repeat your very words. You said–"

"I know what I said!" He turned to the court exasperated. "But that clearly doesn't apply in this context. The charges against Marlowe demonstrate–"

"Your charges prove nothing. This document, however, proves you planned and manufactured this case against me." Kit waved the libel in the air.

Eyes followed him as he moved. At the end of the table, he stopped in front of Burghley and Essex. They took the document from him, interested. Whitgift gaped in horror as they read it closely, turned it over, and regarded his signature with a frown. They looked askance at Whitgift and passed the document down the long table.

His face luminous, Whitgift stomped over and snatched the document from the hands of a privy counselor. He took a peek at his signature and laughed derisively.

"Mere forgery! This is nothing for a man who counterfeits on the side!"

Several court members nodded their heads in agreement. Everyone looked back to Kit for his reaction.

Kit wiped the sweat from his brow. He reached inside his shirt and produced another document – the agreement between

Thomas and Cholmeley that he had stolen from Thomas's study. Quickly, with trembling hands, he unfolded it, and gave it to Burghley.

"I didn't believe in using this before. I had no way to support it."

"Explain yourself," Burghley commanded.

"It's from the study of Thomas Walsingham. It shows him in league with Cholmeley. They never tried to catch him. The charges against him were dreamt-up to incriminate me. They did it. Whitgift and Walsingham have conspired all along."

Whitgift stamped his foot.

"No more of these lies! I insist you remove him! Remove him from this court!"

Burghley's expression turned grave. He passed the document to Essex and let his eyes rest upon Kit.

"And what of the charges against you?"

Kit paused at the question. He stood tall and straightened his back. He couldn't find a quick answer.

"How can I prove I'm not an atheist?" he muttered.

He stood there motionless with the entire court's attention focused solely upon him. Some counselors became restless. Whitgift rolled his eyes. Kit felt the cold touch of metal from the brooch in his hand. His body grew rigid and he flinched slightly as if suddenly struck by an idea.

Essex tapped his fingers on the top of the table.

"Quick about it, sirrah!" he snapped. "You've exhausted this court's patience enough already."

Kit took a breath.

"Look to my plays," he said confidently. "I am my words. Christopher Marlowe has written himself." He paced beside the table and filled his lungs. "I ask you, does the Queen disapprove of my work?"

A few heads shook. Kit continued with a louder voice.

"Well, does she?" he asked again insistently.

"No," someone mumbled.

"Does she or does she not, gentlemen?"

"No," a few more of the counselors answered.

303

"She does not. Thus, since the Queen is chosen by God to rule, how could she possibly embrace something negative to God? She cannot, my lords, and so I cannot be an atheist."

Whitgift raised his hand automatically. His lips parted in order to reply but nothing issued from his mouth. He stood speechless.

With a secret look of mirth, Burghley surveyed the room: everyone appeared deep in thought. Some had their heads down in contemplation. A few conferred quietly with their neighbor. At the head of the table, Essex put his hand to his chin, played with his beard, and gradually nodded his head.

Kit smiled. A sudden sense of relief hit him in a wave and washed his energy away. His shoulders sunk. His fists turned to open hands. He felt like dropping to his knees, collapsing to the floor, but he resisted and remained standing. He blinked to stop tears from rising to his eyes. Slowly, he drew a long draught of air and sighed with elation. He smiled to himself and looked up at the ceiling unafraid.

SCENE THREE

Outside Westminster Palace.

After the court had released him, Kit strolled out of Westminster Palace as a free man and met up with Will on the palace steps outside. Despite the fatigue of the last few days wearing on the bodies of both men, nothing could diminish their joy at the court's outcome. Kit was innocent on all charges.

Eyes slightly moist, he peered down at Will and smiled.

"What are you doing here, anyway?

"Oh, did I bother you earlier?" Will replied. "Sorry, I didn't mean to interrupt. I beg your pardon... or should I say I *begged* your pardon?"

"Shouldn't you be writing?"

Will shrugged nonchalantly.

"No, I thought I'd procrastinate a bit and go to court. Save a friend. The usual."

They smiled at each other knowingly. Kit gave a joyous laugh and slapped Will on the back, half-winding him. Spirits high, they soon caught a wherry across the Thames and traveled over to Bankside to celebrate at The Rose.

As soon as Kit entered the theater, he was received like a long lost son. Stagehands, writers, even the actors that once had chided him, now collected around him in glee to hug him, punch him on the arm, and shake his hand. Henslowe was the happiest of all to have his star playwright back again. In moments, one of the stagehands found a keg and rolled it out into the yard. Someone else fetched a set of mugs and Henslowe made a toast.

"Now, now, you lot can all be quiet a moment. I'd like to say a few words."

Taller than everyone else, Ned Alleyn raised his voice in response.

"Only a few, Henslowe? That'll be a first!"

"You shut it over there, too," said Henslowe with mock offense. "This is serious. I want to be serious a moment… I like to think of The Admiral's Men as more than just a play company. We're like family to one another. Maybe we're a family of scoundrels, but we're a family all the same. Ned's married to my stepdaughter, after all. And there's one man whose plays, whose many successes, keep us together and make it all possible." He turned to Kit. "To Christopher Marlowe: the muses' darling."

"The muses' darling," everyone repeated in admiration as they clunked their mugs together. Afterwards, all eyes were trained on Kit.

He smiled and his cheeks flushed a shade of red.

"Alright…" he said regaining his composure. "Now if Henslowe hasn't made everyone too queasy, we have a keg over here that needs a good draining!"

Everyone broke into a boisterous cheer and quickly set about refilling their mugs.

For the next hour, ale flowed over brims, tipped over lips, and sloshed onto the sawdust of the yard. Will and many others huddled loudly around the keg to refill their tankards. Kit felt so giddy he had to lean on the edge of the stage. He found a prop dagger lying by his hand and picked it up. Playfully, he pushed on the dagger's dulled blade and watched as it retracted inside the hilt. It was set on a spring so it didn't move in too rapidly. His fingers brushed against a coating of sticky tar around the hilt edge. He stabbed the blade onto the stage and let it go. The dagger remained firm and upright, as if wedged deep into the wood.

"Tar makes it stay in place…" Kit mumbled. "…clever."

He took the dagger in his hand and regarded it with intrigue.

When the last dregs of ale had finally gone, and everyone reluctantly resumed their work, Will and Kit's thoughts turned to food. Henslowe kindly agreed to pay for them to eat at the fancy

'Golden Hinde Restaurant' in Deptford. Originally, he planned to join them, but then cited some previous appointment at court in Greenwich Palace. However, since Greenwich lay in the same direction as Deptford, Henslowe offered Kit and Will a ride in his carriage.

As Henslowe's carriage trundled out of London and into the countryside, a light mist crept along the river. In the afternoon sky, white and gray clouds mixed with blue as sea fog moved in across the land, high at first, but threatening to descend.

Inside the comfort of the carriage, Will told Henslowe all that had occurred at Marshalsea Prison. Henslowe grew particularly concerned when he learnt about Tom Kyd's torture: apart from Will, no one else had seen Tom since a squad of Star Chamber officers broke into his room, ransacked his belongings, and took him into custody. Henslowe hoped he wasn't dead and Will tried to reassure him. Meanwhile, throughout the journey to Deptford, Kit sat on the cushion opposite and remained strangely quiet, only half-listening to the conversation.

Three miles southeast of London, spread long upon the southern banks of the Thames, Deptford was a small but valuable port town known for its shipyards and naval dock. Since the port was one of the last stopping points before the taxes at the Legal Quays in London, it was also notorious for smugglers and thieves, and the taverns conducted a flourishing black market trade. Here one could buy cheap Chinese silk, Indian peppers, or Persian scarves that had 'fallen off' the backs of ships returning from voyages.

When Henslowe's carriage finally reached the very edge of the Deptford docks, he handed Kit a small purse of coins and ordered the driver to stop. Kit and Will bade Henslowe farewell, stepped outside, and wandered off towards the restaurant.

Situated on board the famous galleon once captained by Sir Francis Drake, the Golden Hinde Restaurant was one of the most unique establishments in the entire Kingdom. Over ten years ago, Drake had returned to Deptford in the ship after circumnavigating the globe. Many people still remembered how the crowds roared and cheered as he docked his galleon in port. The Queen herself

307

even waited for Drake to arrive and she knighted him right then and there on the deck. Since that time, the ship had been retired from service and had now become a popular attraction and upper-class restaurant.

Via a thin boarding plank with ropes, Kit and Will stepped onto the top deck of galleon. Over their heads, three brown masts struck toward the sky, surrounded by a thicket of lines. Hooked lanterns hung from rigging directly over the tables.

Everywhere was busy. Between the tables, graceful waiters glided by with armfuls of balanced trays, their legs adapted to the random shifts and tilts of the ship. Eventually, Kit spotted a free table up on the quarterdeck and they both climbed the steep stairs and took a seat.

They browsed the menu and ordered duck breast with a juniper berry glaze and two tankards of ale known as 'Dog Bolter' flavored with lupin. At first, Kit chatted to Will pleasantly about Anne and the children; but when Will started to mention the future, Kit's face slowly changed. The food came shortly and Will raised his tankard in a toast.

"What shall we drink to?" he said cheerfully.

"To Henslowe."

"Why?"

"He bought the food."

"Don't be so tedious! We can't make such a toast on a day like today. No, we should toast to your victory over Whitgift and all his machinations. How about that? To victory."

"Yes..." Kit muttered. "Victory."

Will tipped his tankard up and gulped the ale down heartily. A little streak of honey-brown liquid ran away from the corner of his mouth.

In contrast, Kit only sipped from his tankard before placing it back down on the table. He picked his knife up carefully and started eating his duck.

Will wiped his chin and looked at him with curiosity.

"What? Pray tell me which manner of thoughts bothers you now?"

"Oh. Nothing."

"Any normal man would be overjoyed at such an outcome as today. They cleared you of all charges, did they not? You should be glad."

"I *am* glad."

"You are?"

"Yes."

"Well, you have a strange countenance to show for it. I've seen hooked fish with happier faces than yours!"

Kit didn't answer. He cut a chunk of flesh from his duck breast. At nearby tables, chatting voices filled the air with jovial conversation. Hemp ropes creaked. Floorboards squealed.

Will chewed his meat slowly and watched Kit. He leant forward.

"What say you we join forces for a new play?" he suggested. "A work authored from both our quills?"

"Interesting. But I'm not sure that—"

"Don't worry, it was just an idle fancy." Will peered down at his food. "I shouldn't have mentioned anything about it. I simply thought it was worth a little consideration, that's all."

Kit smiled sadly at him.

"No," he said. "What I mean is that I'm finished with the stage."

"Finished?"

"Yes."

"You can't be finished."

"Well, I am."

Will almost choked in surprise.

"You don't really mean that, do you? I can't think why you'd even say such a thing. You can't mean it – you're the best writer in all Christendom."

"Theatre will survive without me."

"No, it won't."

"It'll have to, I'm afraid. And I no longer work for the government either. That life is dead to me now." The boat swayed slightly in the tide and Kit grabbed his plate to stop it from sliding.

309

"What life will you have, then?" asked Will, struggling to understand.

"No life at all, if some have their way."

"But... but this is ludicrous... who's to stop you?"

"Whitgift."

"Don't talk pig-swill! Burghley's launched an inquiry into Whitgift and all his dealings."

Kit shook his head. He turned away and ran his eyes over the pegs on the side of the ship, the loops of rope, the complex knots. Over at the bow, ropes lashed two anchors to the hull of the ship.

"Will, there won't be an inquiry," he said bitterly. "There won't be an inquiry at all. Whitgift's the Archbishop."

"Yes, but Burghley has power too, doesn't he? He might be a little old but he's still the Lord High Treasurer."

"That doesn't matter. The inquiry's just a threat – a sign of the Queen's displeasure."

"What makes you so sure?"

"England can't risk such a scandal. Not now. Not ever."

Will paused, refusing to believe it. Slowly, little by little, the realization sunk in and his face dropped into a look of misery. His whole body seemed to drown in his chair.

After they had finished dinner, they continued their sullen conversation while wandering down by the docks. Night closed in around them. Sea fog descended and pushed through the ships in patches of white. Masts blurred. Outlines faded. Above, the moon dazzled the air in diffused, luminous rings, and seemed close and large. Will fastened the buttons of his coat. Kit shivered in his shirt.

"...no, I can't," said Kit with dismay. "As long as Whitgift lives, he won't let me alone. I'll always be the same Christopher Marlowe."

Will kept his eyes on the ground. His face grew heavy with despair. He nodded but didn't reply.

Kit glanced over, sighed, and patted him gently on the shoulder. He forced a tone of hopefulness into his voice.

"Anyway, just think of your future..."

"What?" said Will flatly.

"My plays will be off the stage."

"So?"

"It'll be easier for your comedy to bloom."

"There is no comedy."

"But I thought you said you were—"

"How can I write anymore? What can I say to such a world?"

Kit stopped walking. He frowned in surprise at Will's seriousness and looked at him searchingly. He tried hard to answer, but couldn't find the words.

"Without hope," continued Will, "without transcendence, there's no place for humor. We overcome nothing... so what do we have to laugh about?"

Kit opened his mouth to speak, but craned his head around, distracted by the patter of feet nearby. Through the mist and shadows of the harbor, a man dressed in the livery of a royal messenger sped over to them.

"Christopher Marlowe?" asked the messenger, flicking his eyes between them.

For a moment, Kit hesitated then stood up straighter and nodded. The messenger presented him with a note.

"From Lord Burghley, sir."

Kit peered down at the note and recognized the seal on the back as Burghley's. He opened it and read it fast. His eyes glazed over thoughtfully. He looked back at the messenger.

"Tell him... tell him I agree," said Kit.

The messenger bowed curtly and spun on his heel and rushed away into the darkness. Once he had gone, Will looked at Kit and waited for him to explain. Kit shuffled his feet, his face still pensive and tense.

"I'm to meet Burghley on the morrow's eve," he said.

"Where?"

"Here in Deptford."

"Why would he meet you in Deptford rather than Westminster?"

Kit didn't answer. They continued walking again and Will looked up at him fretfully.

311

"Maybe you shouldn't go to this?"

With effort, Kit strained his lips into a weak smile.

"No, it's alright. I've been there before. It's just a meeting house. I'll take a few precautions, anyway." He stared away into the watery masts of the harbor.

Will tried to sound optimistic.

"Perhaps this means there *is* be an inquiry into Whitgift after all?"

"Perhaps," said Kit raising his eyebrows, unconvinced. "Will, I want you to do something for me… I need you to promise me something…."

"What?"

"Three days from now, I need you to go to St. Nicholas's churchyard. It's just a short walk from here near the Deptford town green. I want you to find the north tower and scout around the gravestones for a note."

"A note? But why? What's happening?"

"I don't know myself yet. It's just a safety measure. Promise me you'll do as I say."

"But I don't–"

"Promise me it, Will. Please…."

Will expelled a short sigh.

"Yes. I'll do as you wish."

By now, half the docks had disappeared in the mist. Kit blinked and continued to gaze into the white.

Scene Four

Deptford. High Street.

Kit took his leave of Will and wandered away from the docks and up to the high street. Eventually, he made his way over to the town green and found a large tavern opposite St Nicholas's Church. Before he entered, he checked the purse Henslowe had given him and counted the number of coins left over from supper. It was probably enough. Sailors and women caroused around the tavern's entrance. He brushed past them and stepped through the door.

Kit wasn't interested in drinking. Instead, he scanned the stools, benches, and tables of the room for smugglers and thieves. He didn't have to look far: as soon as he entered, a man with a large hoop earring and a bald head tugged on his arm.

"How 'bout a Persian carpet, ay?" said the man, his voice gruff and jovial. "A case of rum? Perfume for the ladies? I got better prices than London, mate."

Kit took him to one side and whispered in his ear.

"A bag of gunpowder?"

The man's eyes widened a little, but he nodded his head.

"I can getcha that... yeah, I can get it. When d'you need it?"

"Tonight."

He paused and rubbed his shiny forehead, as if considering it.

"You got a deal, mate."

"Good."

"Why don't we step into my office?"

Kit agreed and the man led him toward the back of the tavern.

At one of the corner tables, they sat down and negotiated the price through the rambunctious noise of the tables nearby. As they haggled, the man lounged on his stool and loaded tobacco into a pipe. Minutes later, they reached an agreement and shook hands. Just as the man went to light his pipe, an idea suddenly struck Kit and with the last of his money he bought both the man's pipe and pouch of tobacco...

The gunpowder exchange took place at midnight. Kit lingered in the alley behind the tavern, his hand on the hilt of his dagger, ready to draw at any time. As arranged, the man from the tavern soon appeared with a ten pound bag of gunpowder. Kit felt the weight of the canvas bag. He undid the drawstring to smell the contents: the poisonous scent of saltpeter, charcoal, and sulfur wafted past his nostrils. Satisfied, he handed over his purse. They traded without a word and swiftly departed in opposite directions.

With a determined, sober look on his face, Kit strode through the town to find the meeting house. While he walked, he held the bag tucked under his right arm. He quickened his pace, turned a few corners, nipped down another alley, and cut into a street near the outskirts of town. He finally passed in front of the meeting house.

Officially, the house was registered in the name of the widow Eleanor Bull – a close relation of both Lord Burghley and Blanche Parry, the Queen's chief Gentlewoman of the Privy Chamber. In reality, however, no one lived at the home: instead, it occasionally functioned as a safe house for government agents in danger or as a place for meetings too sensitive for the inside of a palace. The existence of the house was kept highly secret: even in Burghley's circle of spies, only a few people were aware of its location. Unfortunately, as Kit well knew, one of those people was Thomas Walsingham.

Set back from the road, a brick path bent through the garden up to the front door. The lawns either side were closely sheared. Though the brick house raised two and a half stories high, it seemed to huddle within its own garden. To one side, a great laburnum tree drooped its yellow flowers out of the darkness and covered half the front wall.

Kit scoured the windows of the house: all were dark and shut. He glanced up and down the street to check no one had seen him, then swept across the lawn and dashed down the side of the house to the back garden.

At the rear, he bent his head close to a dirty window and peeped inside a room: dust-filled and empty. Through the murk appeared a dining table, some chairs, and a fireplace on the far wall. He stood back, lifted his eyes to a chimney stack, and searched for the best way to climb up.

To free his hands, he clamped his teeth onto the canvas bag. The weight pulled on his neck. With a foot on the windowsill, he reached up, grabbed onto the hood mould above, and raised himself off the grass.

Using the bars of a trellis heavy with clematis, he pulled himself up, higher and higher, leaving the ground behind, finding footholds wherever he could. Soon the trellis creaked and began to tease away from the wall. When he reached an upper-floor window, he transferred some of his weight to the sill and slapped a hand onto the edge of the roof. Much to his relief, he quickly climbed off the trellis and heaved his body up onto the rooftop.

Low and creeping, without stopping for a breath, he moved over the rooftop toward the chimney stack. He took the bag from his aching mouth and wedged it back under his arm. Nervously watching his steps, he crawled up to the chimney stack and peered down the flue. Darkness. His cold fingers fumbled at the drawstring of the bag. He undid it, tipped the bag on its side, and poured the contents gently over the edge...

Black powder rushed out of the bag.

Whooshed down the chimney.

Hit the dining chamber.

Whoolumph! It landed heavy in fireplace below and spread out thick, coating the logs and charcoal. Some of the powder even drifted a few feet out of the hearth and dappled the dining chamber's dusty oak floorboards.

Kit peered down after the powder, then swiftly drew his head back and blinked. Trails of gunpowder jumped back up the chimney and plumed into the air around his head. He coughed and swore under his breath. With as much stealth as possible, he moved back over the slimy tiles, inched his way over to the edge of the roof, and clambered down.

SCENE FIVE

Deptford. St Nicholas' Churchyard.

Cycles of thin mist rolled through the still morning streets.
Awake and shivering, Kit had spent most of the night curled up
by the churchyard wall.

At the entrance to the graveyard stood two posts with a stone
carving of a skull at the top. Behind the posts, enveloping the
church on all sides, the graveyard was full of tablets and headstones – some stubby, some tall, some carved with angels, and
some blank and nameless. The eastern sky strengthened with ev-
er-growing intensities of color and sunlight flooded around the
yard, washing gold against the bases of the stones. By contrast,
the western moon still hovered above the horizon, its shape large
and hazy and old.

Kit raised his head from the ground and sat up with a groan.
He rubbed his eyes. They felt dry and ached when he shifted
them from side to side. Hunger scraped in his stomach and thirst
constricted his throat. Hands wavering in the cold, he felt down at
the pouch on his belt and pulled out the pipe he had bought and
the tobacco. After regarding them closely he put them away
again. From his pouch he then withdrew a pencil and a thick wad
of parchment: his poem *'Hero and Leander'*. Some of the pages
were bent, but he straightened them and set them on his lap. He
turned to the back page and found it was still blank – the only one
he hadn't used at Marshalsea Prison.

For some time, he sat there reading the poem from the very
start, but his mind wandered and he had to reread the words. He
turned to the blank page and prepared to write. The pencil-tip
trembled as he lowered it nearer the surface. He shook his head,

his lips twisted into a bitter smile, and he looked away. Hunger, thirst, coldness, anxiety, and frustration sunk their hooks into him and tore away at his energy, his sanity.

His face hardened with resolution. He lowered his eyes, fixed his mind on the poem, and started writing.

As if there had been no break between the poem's last sentence and the words he now scribbled onto the parchment, Kit continued his verse urgently, finally completing Leander's quest to spend a second night with Hero. Thus far, Leander had swam the Hellespont, risked the waves, survived the amorous clutches of the sea god Neptune, and eventually reached the sands below Hero's tower. Naked and dripping wet, Leander now entered Hero's bedchamber and strived to embrace her.

For the morning after their night of passion, Kit wrote the following words:

> '*And them, like Mars and Erycine, display*
> *Both in each other's arms chained as they lay.*
> *Again, she knew not how to frame her look,*
> *Or speak to him, who in a moment took*
> *That which so long so charily she kept,*
> *And fain by stealth away she would have crept,*
> *And to some corner secretly have gone,*
> *Leaving Leander in the bed alone.*
> *But as her naked feet were whipping out,*
> *He on the sudden clinged her so about,*
> *That, mermaid-like, unto the floor she slid.*
> *One half appeared, the other half was hid.*
> *Thus near the bed she blushing stood upright,*
> *And from her countenance behold ye might*
> *A kind of twilight break, which through the hair,*
> *As from an orient cloud, glimpsed here and there,*
> *And round about the chamber this false morn*
> *Brought forth the day before the day was born.*
> *So Hero's ruddy cheek Hero betrayed,*
> *And her all naked to his sight displayed...*'

Kit's pencil slowed. He glanced up at the graveyard. The headstones now stood in greater sunlight. With a look of utter calm and peacefulness he wrote the words: *'The End'* abruptly under the lines of the poem. For a moment, he studied those last words then crossed them out and closed his eyes.

When he raised his eyelids again he had to squint in order to see around him. Sunlight. Full, ripening sunlight. Though the mist was still dense, the sun had risen and breached the horizon and the churchyard. He sat still and stared upwards. Something strange happened. The sun and moon resided in different quarters of the sky, yet to his eyes they seemed equally splendid orbs. They were indistinguishable. The light and the mask of light were not divided or opposed at all: they were the same ultimate existence. For the briefest of moments he felt oddly satisfied, joyful, even ecstatic. He saw the world and he loved it.

Something glimmered on his chest. He looked down and his ouroboros brooch caught his eye. He sat up straighter with excitement as if enamored with an idea.

"What nourishes me..." he said slowly to himself. "What nourishes me... destroys me..."

The sun rose higher above the horizon. A smile bloomed upon his face: the answer to his problem was clear and inviting and had been within his reach all along. It should have been obvious for a playwright, but he didn't see it until now. He continued to gaze at the brooch and run his finger around its circular form. Almost chanting to himself he repeated the words again and again:

"What nourishes me destroys me..."

SCENE SIX

Deptford.

Kit waited nervously for the evening. With no money, and no where else to go, he could do nothing else but wait.

To help pass the time, he meandered over to the riverbanks near the wherries of watermen and sat down to rest his legs. Seagulls above scored the air with sharp, laughing cries. He removed the pipe and the little bag of tobacco from his pouch and studied them both. The pipe was made of clay and had a long shank carved with a lion near the bowl. He filled it with tobacco, then left the banks and found a wall brazier along a side street. He tore a poster in half, rolled it, and lighted it on the hot coals of the brazier. Afterwards, he held the flame just above the pipe bowl and made the surface gently smolder. With hesitation, he took a drag of tobacco, let the smoke circle around his mouth, brush against his palette, and fizzle on his tongue. He took another drag and watched the tobacco glow brighter.

While still hidden in the side street, he knelt and flattened the other half of the poster on knee, pulled out a pencil and wrote the following note:

> 'Dear Will,
> I have a tragedy for you: if you are reading this note then you already know I am dead.
> I have been murdered.
> The meeting house was known to Thomas, and thus also to Archbishop Whitgift. Undoubtedly, they will have prepared a story to mask their crime but do not believe it: I was not killed in an

accident, or in a brawl, or by someone acting in self-defense. I was murdered with premeditation by Thomas Walsingham, Archbishop John Whitgift, and any number of their associates (probably including Richard Baines).

Give this note to Lord Burghley without delay and there may yet be a chance for justice.

Take care, my friend. I would have cherished seeing your comedy on the stage, but that is not to be anymore...

Yours truly,
Christopher Marlowe
May 30th, 1593, Deptford.'

Once he was finished, he flitted through the alleyways and ventured back to the graveyard. Ten paces from the north tower, he discovered the crevice of a crumbling gravestone, folded the note, and wedged it inside the stone. He hoped Will would never have to find it.

Seven o'clock in the evening. With a solemn face, his shoulders low, Kit finally strolled back through town to the meeting house and stopped at the garden gate.

He paused. From a house across the street, two children ran out of the door and skipped away over the cobblestones, squealing with laughter as they chased each other. Kit watched them go. He took a drag on his pipe and smoke drifted out between his lips. He turned and his eyes scoured the front of the meeting house for any sign of change. It looked the same as the night before – only the garden now had touches of color. In the dim light, the laburnum hung with boughs of pendulous and poisonous golden chains of flowers.

Kit walked through the garden with a stiff gait, clenching his fists all the way. At the door, he let his hand hover above the handle. He puffed on the pipe and the smoke lingered in his mouth and he smiled, trying to relax himself. He lowered his hand and cranked the door handle around and entered the house...

SCENE SEVEN

Meeting House.

As soon as he stepped into the hallway, he flinched, caught a glimpse – a blur – of blonde hair out of the corner of his eye.

From the shadows, Poley leapt at him from the side. Swung a club at his head.

"Now!" cried Poley.

Kit ducked. The club whirred overhead. Cracked into the door frame. Splinters ripped away from the edge.

The next second, he whirled around in panic. Heavy footsteps rushed up behind him. Baines charged him into hard and rammed him over.

As he fell, Kit snatched onto Baines's cassock and dragged him down too. Their bodies pounded onto the floorboards.

Baines squirmed on top of Kit, ran a knee into his chest, and pressed down with all his bulk and muscle. Kit struggled, but Baines pinned his arms on the lower step of the staircase.

"Hurry!" Baines yelled. "Search him!"

Poley fumbled on the floor for his glasses, then shuffled across to Kit and patted his stumpy fingers up and down Kit's legs, waist, and chest.

Finally, Poley stood up straight.

"Just this." He took Kit's dagger from his scabbard and passed it to Baines.

Baines yanked Kit up to his feet. With the other hand, he poked the dagger tip into Kit's side. Kit filled his lungs with air. His teeth champed on the pipe bit. Somehow in the tumble he'd managed to keep the pipe in his mouth.

For a moment, no one in the hall moved. Kit twisted his neck and glanced at Baines.

"Baines," he said wryly, "tell me something: you *do* realize you're ugly, don't you?" He puffed a mouthful of smoke into Baines's eyes, making him blink. "I just thought I should mention it."

Baines grunted and shoved Kit haltingly through the door of the dining chamber.

The dining chamber was mid-sized with a dark floor and white plaster walls. A circular iron chandelier hung in the center of the room and reflected its flames on the surface of a dining table below. At the back, a herringbone brickwork mantelpiece hooded the fireplace. A hefty layer of black powder coated the hearth's cold logs, but no one seemed to notice. Just as Kit had anticipated, three familiar figures waited for him inside: Frizer, Thomas, and Whitgift.

He panned his gaze across the men. Frizer looked back with white, startled eyes. In his right hand, a flintlock pistol pointed dead at Kit's stomach.

Toward the middle of the room, Whitgift stood squarely beside the table. He looked stiff. Defined. Formidable. His eyes glinted like pieces of glass. He faced Kit and never once looked away.

Finally, near the back of the room, Thomas lingered about and stared out through a windowpane into the darkening rear garden. He leaned against the wall and seemed oddly withdrawn and crumpled. His mouth was bunched up tight like a coin purse.

Kit smiled at them all coldly.

"Nice to see you again, gentlemen." He nodded to the back of the room. "Thomas, you look well."

Thomas paled and didn't answer. Kit detected a slight sense of compassion in his posture – it reminded him of that night in the guest chamber. A quick silence breezed into the room.

Whitgift paced toward Kit, his face grim.

"We all know why we're here," he said sternly. "I can't make a public example of you anymore, but you'll not live to write another god-forsaken play. You'll not live to harm the people a second longer." His eyes lifted over Kit's shoulder to the face of Baines. "Strap him to a chair... and remember it must look like an accident."

Baines pushed Kit toward the table. Kit dug his heels in. He resisted with all his strength.

"No! Listen! Listen to me! Stay a minute! There's a way for us all to be content. I have created a plan that—"

"Yes, I'm sure you have, my son," Whitgift interrupted with a strange fatherly tone. "But we've all seen enough of your creations. Though I despair at taking another life, it's easier and safer for everyone just to kill you."

The men immediately reacted. Their eyes quickly trained on Kit, ready for trouble, ready for anything. Poley raised his club. Frizer cocked his pistol. Baines pressed the dagger harder into Kit's ribs and jostled him toward a chair. At the back of the room, Thomas turned away, unable to watch the next events.

Kit's face darkened as the men closed in around him. With his free hand, he reached up for his pipe and pulled it from out of his mouth.

"So be it," he muttered through clenched teeth. In one sharp, rapid movement, he drew his hand back, whipped the pipe forward, and lobbed it across the room like a knife.

Watched by everyone, the pipe spun through the air toward the fireplace. The tobacco in the pipe bowl glowed bright as the air rushed through its coarse fibers. Kit closed his eyes and crouched as the pipe made one last turn, dropped, and plummeted into the black powder.

Baalooom!

The fireplace erupted.

Bursts of white, red, black dazzled their eyes.

A percussion wave shocked the air. Clapped on their ears. *Frooosh!* Gusts of ash and soot billowed out, swirled off the walls, and eclipsed the room instantly. Splinters, coal, chunks of wood, and shards of stone rocketed past heads, cut flesh, scorched hands, shot into the table, strafed the ceiling, hurtled against the walls. Kit's head buzzed. Heat singed his cheeks, his hair, his nose. His ears rang, his eyes stung, and he blinked to see.

Smoke tasted bitter in his mouth. *Blick – Blick – Blick.* Debris showered around him. He stood up tall and tried to peer through the smothering blackness. He was the only one still standing.

Thomas had been nearest the explosion – the blast had pounded on his back and flipped him over. Whitgift lay on the floor, knocked flat on his face. Over by the wall, Frizer crawled on his hands and knees, struggling to see. Poley knelt beside a bench, a gash on his brow leaking blood over his glasses. Kit turned. Behind him, Baines crouched over and shook his head. Traces of soot made rings around his eyes.

The explosion was brighter and louder than it was powerful, and through the layers of smoke came glimpses of a room still intact: the windows still held most of their glass panes; the table still stood in the middle; and the fireplace still retained most of its bricks. Even so, the shock gave Kit the edge he needed.

While Baines was still bent over, Kit lunged, punched downwards and gave him a hefty slug in the face, pitching him to the floor. Kit pivoted and dashed through the smoke for Poley, kicked high in the center of Poley's back and sent him crashing into a cabinet.

While gasping for air, trying not to choke, Kit planned his next move. His stomach pinched tight with anxiety. For a moment, smoke blew before his eyes and he couldn't see anything around him.

A figure stumbled to the right. To the left. It turned, caught sight of him, and pounced. The smoke separated a little and revealed Baines with the dagger in his hand.

Baines stabbed – cut at him again and again and again. Kit wove, ducked, side-stepped, and tried to hit back. The smoke wafted between them so thickly that the knife became invisible.

Meanwhile, away from the scuffle, Frizer regained consciousness, climbed to his feet and careened about with his pistol, searching for Kit. He followed the noises of the fight, saw two murky figures through the smoke, and raised the pistol barrel.

"Baines!" yelled Frizer. He waved his hand. "Stand back! Stand back, I say!"

Baines ignored him and continued to swing at Kit with the dagger. Suddenly, Poley dived out of the smoke and flailed the club at Kit wildly. It smashed him on the shoulder, nearly broke the bone. He flew backwards and slammed into the window.

In the slight beams of moonlight from the window, Frizer recognized Kit's outline and aimed the pistol at his chest.

"I have him!" Frizer cried.

Just in time, Kit saw the danger and jerked to the right. With lightening fast hands, he grabbed Baines and swung him in front.

The trigger clicked.

The pistol flashed and cracked.

An unseen bullet tore through the smoke, ripped through Baines's arm, and pierced a hole in a window. The wound startled Baines and he clutched his arm and swore in agony.

Kit wasted no time: he kneed Baines in the stomach, stripped him of the dagger, and tossed him into Poley. Their bodies collided heavily and tumbled to the floor.

Footsteps pounded through the smoke. Kit turned his head. A figure dashed for the door, trying to escape.

Whitgift.

In order to cut him off, Kit ran forward, jumped up, slid over the table, and caught Whitgift's shoulder, spinning him around.

Whitgift backed away, ferocious and undefeated. Suddenly, he hurtled down the side of the table. Grabbed a chair with both hands. He took several hulking breaths and built his strength for an attack. Kit planted his feet. He waited. Eyes and ears alert, blood surging, body aching, he waited for the charge. His knuckles whitened around the dagger hilt.

Whitgift gave an ear-breaking roar. With the chair legs speared outwards, he rolled forward onto his toes, broke into a sprint, and charged across the room. Kit waited and waited, stood in place till Whitgift was nearly upon him, then jumped out of the way.

He moved too soon. Whitgift reacted to the mistake. Changed direction. Drove the chair legs into his chest and stomach. Swept him up, almost lifted him off his feet, and carried him backwards. Kit held his breath, waited for his the impact into the wall, but it didn't come. Instead, Whitgift launched him into a shut window.

Kissssssh!

They crashed straight through the window frame and plunged outwards and into the night...

In the garden, Kit landed first, slamming back-down into the moist soil. Below his feet, Whitgift clattered to the ground, still gripping the chair. The men inside the meeting house crammed forward to the window. Arcs of glass in the window frame made a circle around their stunned faces.

For a second, Kit lay still on the lawn. His body was so battered and gashed from the broken glass he felt a gradual tiredness seduce his limbs. The cool smell of earth filled his nostrils. Leaves of grass whispered against the edge of his ears. Blood leached onto his shirt and tasted coppery in his mouth.

Close by, heavy feet padded on the grass and thumped over to his body. He tipped his head up. The dagger was still in his hand and he raised it urgently. Whitgift's muscular bulk shambled overhead with bare hands outstretched.

He dropped down on top of Kit. Rammed his hands at Kit's throat to strangle him. Kit struck up with the dagger, but Whitgift grabbed his arm, took hold of his wrist and forced it to turn so that the dagger pointed down at his chest. To Kit's absolute horror, Whitgift leaned on his arm with all his weight and strength. He tried to resist but Whitgift's force was overpowering.

Slowly, inch by inch, the dagger tip moved down, closer and closer, to the center of his breast.

"Don't fight it, my son!" Whitgift hissed.

"I'm not your son!" Kit groaned back. "You're no one's father. You're not a father in the flesh – just the cloth!"

Whitgift glared, astonished by the words.

Through the back door, Thomas and the men rushed outside the house to watch as the final action unfolded.

With his free hand, Kit tried to push up against Whitgift, but it had no effect. He slugged Whitgift in the face. Nothing changed. He hit again. Nothing changed.

The knife blade descended further and hovered just above the fabric of his shirt.

In a burst of vital energy, Kit tensed his muscles to the full, thrust upwards, and pushed with every ounce of strength. It didn't work. His limbs were no longer plaint to his wishes.

He groaned. The knife made contact with his chest. His body shuddered as the blade plunged down sharply. Whitgift increased the pressure.

The blade slid in half-way to the hilt. Kit fought desperately, but his strength faded fast. Tears formed in his eyes.

The blade slid in further. Whitgift's face shook with exertion, his veins bulged, and his sweat dripped off his forehead onto Kit's cheek.

The blade sunk in to the very hilt. Kit clenched his jaw so hard his teeth almost cracked. His eyes glazed over. Breathing turned difficult. Unnecessary. Gently, the muscles in his neck relaxed, followed by his arms, his legs, his stomach. His whole body weakened and fell limp. He relented and eased into it gratefully. He laid his head back onto the soft grass and breath hardly filled his lungs and his chest slowed its rhythm and gently, in, small, gasps, he stopped breathing completely.

Whitgift waited to make sure. He still held the pressure on the knife, but Kit didn't move again...

Afterwards, he rolled off the corpse and flopped onto his back, exhausted. Not until now did he register all his wounds or feel the toll the struggle had taken on his own body. He felt his age keenly. His muscles were strained. His energy had been frayed away. For a whole minute, he breathed hard, his lungs rising and falling like bellows. Eventually, he sat up and raised himself to his feet.

Thomas and the men stood with their mouths agape as they looked upon Kit's fallen body. His cut, mangled corpse lay sprawled on the grass. Moonlight paled the crown of his head and the tops of his shoulders. His eyes remained open, but they hung saggy and dull in their lids. His lips were flat, no longer able to taste the air. Dark blood drenched his shirt and made the fabric cling to his ribs. The dagger protruded firm and still and upright from his motionless chest.

Whitgift tried to compose himself but failed. Almost with embarrassment, he wiped his bloodied hands on the waist of his cassock and approached Thomas warily.

"I trust you can still fashion it as an accident?" he asked meekly.

Thomas's intelligent eyes looked back without blinking. He seemed hunched and cold. In the moonlight, his forelock pointed down harshly. He didn't reply. Whitgift shifted uncomfortably on the spot.

"If the men clean the house we could still claim that it his death was accidental. I truly believe the original plan is still the best under the present–"

"We'll attend to it, Archbishop," said Thomas in a precise tone. "You should go now. The explosion may have alerted someone. It would be ill for anyone to see you here."

"My deepest thanks to you, my son."

"Just go."

"I guarantee your reward will be tenfold higher than–"

Thomas pointed abruptly into the night.

"Go!"

Whitgift stiffened his back. While favoring a wounded back, he peered over at the faces of Baines, Frizer, and Poley. Without wasting another second, he paced away through the garden. They watched as his cumbersome figure disappeared around the side of the house.

Thomas swiveled towards the men. He felt the urgent need to be alone.

"Frizer, Poley – you two start cleaning the dining chamber. By the time you're finished I don't want to see any traces of a struggle in that room, understood?" Without letting them reply he waved a finger towards Baines. "And you, search upstairs for bed sheets to wrap his body in." He clapped his hands together aggressively. "Now, gentlemen! Why are you still here? Go to! Go to, this moment!"

Nervous at his tone, the men jerked into action and quick-stepped back toward the house. Poley sighed and Baines muttered something under his breath to Frizer. They brushed shoulders as they stepped through the back door and vanished from sight.

Thomas pressed his lips together thinly. He held the air tight in his lungs. For a while, he kept very still, afraid of betraying the emotions carefully locked within his breast. Tears crowded into his eyes, but he didn't move until they dried away. Eventually, with hesitant, solemn steps, he approached Kit's body.

Moonlight gave Kit's skin a luminous, ghostly quality. Grass twitched about his arms. Wind blew in his hair and made him look alive. Thomas stooped down to his side and leant over him sadly. He breathed heavily and spoke in a painful, barely audible whisper.

"You idiot… you bloody idiot, Christopher… why did you come here? I never wanted this. You brought it on yourself. You must have suspected the message. You must have known this would happen to you."

Slowly, his hand trembling, he reached out to touch the dagger protruding from Kit's chest.

Just as he did so, just as his fingers neared the dagger hilt, something strange happened and he jumped back...

Kit's head turned toward him. His eyelids fluttered and blinked rapidly. He groaned and uttered a small cough.

"Good god!" Thomas gasped. He flinched and almost fell over backwards.

Almost unaware of Thomas, Kit moaned again and gave a rasping cough. His eyes were blurred and stinging from being held open so long. With a tremulous hand, he reached up to his chest, grabbed the dagger hilt, and pulled the blade smoothly away from his body. The dulled blade extended to its full length again, no longer retracted inside the hilt. He winced and wiped his hand over the supposedly wounded area. Sticky tar smeared itself across his fingers.

"Christ!" he said through clenched teeth. "It's only a prop dagger. I didn't know it could hurt that much!"

Thomas watched, utterly amazed, as Kit eased himself on to his side, pulled his legs underneath him, and slowly arose to stand fully upright. His shirt was yellowed from sweat, brown with dirt, and steeped in dark blood. Blemishes marked his face. Blood-clots matted his hair. He looked an utter wreck of a man. But it didn't matter. He was alive.

Eventually, Thomas expelled a quivering breath and raised his eyebrows. Kit looked back at him candidly. Thomas worked up enough resolve to speak.

"But how?" he asked, raising his hands into the air.

Kit paused. His lips curled into a faint smile.

"What?" he replied playfully. "Haven't you been to the theater?" He stepped closer and smiled widely. "I've written countless death scenes in my life... Now I've acted one, too."

Thomas gave him a blank stare, unsure how to react and Kit's face gradually returned to seriousness.

A wary silence opened between them. The sound of Baines's voice echoed from inside the meeting house. Thomas cocked his head toward the dining chamber and took a half-step backwards. Kit watched him suspiciously.

"Don't call them, Thomas."

"And why shouldn't I?"

"Because you can't succeed. On the morrow, if I don't leave here alive, someone will receive a note naming you and your men as my murderers. The note will go directly to the government."

Thomas shook his head cynically.

"Maybe I'll take that chance."

"No you won't... we both know you don't really want to kill me..."

"Nonsense."

Kit gulped.

"Thomas... I'm truly sorry for everything that's happened... whether you believe me or not, I did value your friendship. It was never my intention to hurt you."

"It's too late for all this," Thomas said brusquely, his resolve beginning to weaken. "What is it you expect from me now?"

Kit gazed up at him hopefully.

331

"Look, there's a way out of this for us both. No one has to die, least of all me. I have a plan that can make us both satisfied."

Thomas rubbed his chin.

"I don't know. Even if I want to, I'm not sure I can just let you walk out of here with your life."

"I agree," said Kit, nodding his head. "Christopher Marlowe cannot leave this house alive...

"What?"

"...but I don't have to die."

"What in all Christendom are you talking about?"

With a twinkle in his eye, Kit leaned forward and said his next words slowly.

"Christopher Marlowe has to die, *but not me.*"

Thomas raised his eyebrows, intrigued.

SCENE EIGHT

Meeting House. Side Garden.

Kit and Thomas moved into the shadows of the lawn. Nearby inside the house, mops squelched on wood as Frizer and Poley cleaned the dining chamber. Bumps and scrapes sounded from upstairs where Baines rummaged through chests for some bed sheets. Once out of view from the dining chamber windows, Kit huddled with Thomas and rushed to tell his plan as fast as he could. They kept their voices low as they discussed it. It was bold, daring, ingenious – and yet not entirely foreign to their experience in spy circles. Such a plan was uncommon, but Thomas had known previous attempts to be successful. They agreed upon its benefits. They also understood that no one beyond the confines of the house could ever know what they were about to do.

Once the story had been set, and the arrangements fully made, little more remained to be said. Thomas crept back into the meeting house, instantly reappeared with a hooded cloak, and passed it to Kit. While nursing the cuts and grazes all over his body, Kit slipped inside the cloak and flipped the hood up – it was deep and curled around his face, hiding his features.

Carefully, listening for the men inside the house, Thomas led Kit back toward the front garden. For a moment, neither man spoke.

"You're sure you can convince the others?" Kit asked.

"Of course," Thomas whispered with a curt nod. "They're only here under orders. I can't work for Burghley now but I can still approach Essex's network. If those men want a future, they'll do as I say. Besides, they're all so poor it only takes a little money for them agree to anything."

"Even Baines?"

"Especially Baines. That's all he wanted from you at Portsmouth, wasn't it?"

"Yes."

"Anyway, Baines may hate you, but he fears me."

"As he should."

The back door of the house squealed open and the scratch of someone's footstep sounded on the garden dirt. Thomas's eyes bulged in alarm. With swift hands, he delved into a pouch on his belt, retrieved a note, and shoved it at Kit.

"What is it?" Kit asked urgently.

"Meet this operative in the Netherlands. He'll get you safely across the continent to Italy."

"My thanks."

"I'll arrange everything else. Just get yourself across the channel tonight and never return here."

Kit scanned the name on the note then put it away. Thomas stared Kit directly in the eye.

"Never return," he said drawing his lips tight. "Never."

Kit nodded seriously.

Thomas hurried back toward the rear lawn before anyone discovered the missing body. The underlid of his left eye had begun a nervous twitch, but he hoped it was unnoticeable. He felt he would die if a single tear carved down his cheek. He didn't experience any happiness at saving Kit nor did he receive any liberation from his own terrible emotions and desires. By now, however, he didn't expect to feel any sense of relief. He knew nothing would end his suffering. Life held only suffering. Before turning the corner, he glanced after Kit for a second. It was enough. He walked away around the corner. He never saw Kit again...

As sprightly as he could manage, Kit whisked back through the sleeping streets of Deptford and approached the churchyard. He retrieved the note addressed to Will from the crumbling gravestone and tore it into pieces. Thoughts of Will flitted through his mind, but he couldn't stop. Every minute was crucial. His mind focused and aware, he stole away through the headstones, crossed the town green like a shadow, and vanished in the direction of the docks.

Kit's eyelids wilted as he searched along the moored vessels in the harbor. Sea-salt made the air drowsy and rich. His cloak weighed upon his sore limbs aggravating his cuts and his movements were beginning to slow and lose coordination. He couldn't stop yet. He needed a boat small enough to steal without notice, small enough to manage on his own. The docks were at their quietest now: the nearby taverns had shut, and most of the town's fishermen were tucked up in their beds. Some fishermen, however, chose to sleep on their boats at the moorage in order to start early the next day. Kit struggled to keep his senses active, his breathing silent, and his steps as mute as possible. At the end of the last walkway he discovered a tiny white skiff that looked suitable. It was small but sturdy enough for the English Channel. The skiff's cedar planks curved in a firm, lapstrake fashion around oak frame ribs. A canvas sail lay furled on the single mast.

The skiff swayed as he crept down into it. His foot knocked against three fish hooks nestled under a plank seat at the stern. With heavy, unresponsive hands he crouched down and set to work at feeling his way around the vessel in the dim light. He tried to find the oars.

For a while, as he readied the skiff to leave, he was so distracted and tired that he didn't notice a figure approach him on the docks.

Tall heels rapped on wood nearby. Above him, a woman's dress swished to a halt.

He flinched defensively and looked up at her. She held her hands neatly together at her narrow waist, her thumbs just touching the cascades of silk around her hips. He couldn't see her face, but he knew it was Audrey.

In reaction, he jerked upright. His wounded shoulder flared with pain and he clutched it with his hand. Unsteady in the rocking boat, he stood up.

"Audrey! I never expected to-" He clenched his teeth as another burst of pain traveled through his body. Carefully, he lifted his leg, planted his foot on the walkway, and took hold of Audrey's hand as he stepped out of the skiff.

"I followed Thomas to the house," she replied. "I hid in a nearby alleyway, kept watch, and I waited and waited, and when I saw you step up to the front door I didn't know what to do. I wanted to cry out, to warn you, but I thought... Oh forgive me, Christopher, I didn't know what to do, I should have warned you."

Her voice was rising and he put a finger to his lips, telling her to be quiet. He moved closer and spoke in a deliberately soothing voice.

"You should have done no such thing. These few days, you've helped me more than I could have imagined. I knew what I was doing."

Their eyes met and Audrey grew more peaceful. They stood silently in each other's presence. He kept her hand within his own. Her supple fingers touched lightly on his grazed palm. When she turned her head, the light cast brighter across her face. Her sapphire-blue eyes glistened with the build-up of tears. Her lips parted just enough to expose the clean, straight edges of her lower teeth. She forced a tiny smile onto her face.

"How do you fare? You look quite well, all things considered."

"Yes," Kit replied dryly. "I feel good, too." He pulled up the side of his cloak and showed her the gashes and bruises around his chest.

Her face dropped. She gasped at the sight of it.

"Oh, God... Oh, dear God..." She slowly extended her hand but her fingers stopped short and didn't dare to touch the skin.

He lowered his cloak and recovered the wounds.

"My chest feels a little tight to breathe. But everything's stopped bleeding now."

"You're certain?"

"I'll be fine."

She glimpsed over shoulder at the skiff lightly bobbing in the water.

"But *where* will you be fine? What scheme makes you leave me?"

His face turned deadly serious. Reluctantly, he lowered his head to hers and whispered the details of his plan into her ear. She gasped at the start, but listened steadily until he had completely finished.

She stood there frozen save for the rise and fall of her breast. She looked him in the eye.

"Is there anything I can do," she offered, half in shock. "Anything you need?"

"Not for me. But perhaps you might find the owner of this bark and pay him some small amount? I have no choice but to steal it."

She shrugged.

"What else? I'll give you all I have, you know that, I'll give you anything."

He felt a pouch on his belt bang against his thigh. He reached down.

"Actually, I have something of my own to give you."

She looked down. From his pouch he produced a batch of papers with the title *'Hero and Leander'* and gave them to her. She held the pages in her hands, but peered up at him mournfully.

"I can't bear for us to part like this. Does it really have to be this way?"

He nodded. After a moment, he pointed to the poem.

"The last of *'Hero and Leander'*," he said brusquely.

"Oh, I see, you've finally written it all."

"No. The ending is unfinished."

She took a shuddering breath and scanned through the pages. "Unfinished? Why?"

"Because love is unfinished..." He stepped closer and put his hands upon her hips.

Tears pooled in her eyes and spilled over, tracing lines down her cheeks. She turned to the last page and read the words aloud.

"And now she wished this night were never done,

337

And sighed to think upon th' approaching sun;
For much it grieved her that the bright daylight
Should know the pleasure of this blessed night..."

With a shaking hand, she closed the page and raised her head to him sadly.

He closed his fingers tighter around her waist.

"Farewell, my lady."

She opened her mouth, but tears choked her words and she could not answer. Her fingers reached up, combed tenderly through his hair, then she gently wrapped her arms around his neck and drew his head down towards her own. Bodies pressed close, they embraced and shared a final lingering kiss.

SCENE NINE

St Nicholas' Churchyard.

Two days later, on the morning of June 1st, Will travelled back to Deptford.

News of the killing spread fast. Will had heard about it while he browsed the book stalls around St Paul's Cathedral in London. At first, he'd wanted to throw up. A slow-fermenting anger festered inside him until it almost made him ill. It thrashed around inside his gut. It rent his mind to pieces. Kit was dead: it was impossible to believe. The concept loomed above him and raised the world into a monstrosity – a place too hard, too crushing to be endured.

Nevertheless, once the severity of Will's initial reaction had quelled, he regained some mastery over his thoughts and recalled his final conversation with his friend. Kit's last words haunted him. He remembered the mysterious promise Kit forced him to make. What was the purpose of the note? What had Kit known but been too afraid to tell him? Will could think of little else...

In the graveyard, mist now buried the slanting headstones to their very tops. Carved angels made silhouettes against the white. Will stepped through the entrance gates and nervously eyed the stonework skulls atop the posts. His fingers gripped the cuffs of his doublet to stop the cold air from drifting up his sleeves. A seagull's distant laugh echoed through the graveyard. His head swiveling for danger, his ears alert to the smallest noise, he moved nearer the north tower. Overhead, the corners of the tower looked awkward and limited against the vast round sky. More of the graveyard stretched out before him. Just as he began to search the gravestones for Kit's note, he stopped dead.

Ten yards in front, an open grave yawned in the earth: Kit's burial was due today. Mounds of freshly-dug soil lay at the corners and small traces of dirt tumbled down the pile and dropped into the grave's mouth. However, the sight that troubled Will lurked just beyond the grave – a figure dressed in a red cloak and hood. The figure stood with its back to him. He couldn't see the face.

His heart drummed faster, faster, faster. Pounded through his thoughts. He kept still. Kept very still. His sweaty hands shrunk up his sleeves. His lips wrinkled into a crooked, anxious smile.

Drafts of mist passed in front of him and the figure's outline blurred and sharpened in the vapor. It was a statue – then a phantom – a statue – then a phantom.

He tried to swallow, but his Adam's apple felt like a cannonball. With effort, he slowed his breathing and calmed himself. He stepped forward bravely to address the figure.

"Do I–" he choked a little, his mouth dry. "Do I look upon the ghost of Christopher Marlowe?"

The figure turned around with an almost surreal composure. Will craned his neck and peered up into the hood.

The face belonged to Audrey.

Vexed and wary, he backed away, ready for anything. He studied her closely, his eyes shining and full of mistrust.

"There isn't a note anymore, Will, so you needn't look," Audrey said serenely. "It was Christopher's last wish that I should tell you in person about what has happened."

"I'm afraid I know it already, Lady Walsingham." Will replied. "He died tragically at the meeting house."

"No."

Will tilted his head, curious.

"There's more?"

"A lot more. You see, I was the last person to speak with him."

"You spoke to him before the meeting house?"

"Afterwards."

"But... how could you? He was dead afterwards."

"Yes and afterwards he was alive, too."

Will paused and tried to think it though. His brow crinkled deeply and he hung his head in contemplation. His next words were ponderous.

"You mean… then it isn't true what they say? He didn't die in a brawl about money? He didn't die in a fight over the reckoning of a bill?"

"No."

"Then how *did* he die?"

"He didn't."

"I don't understand."

"He faked his death."

Will felt the words strike down upon him physically, like a building breaking apart and falling about his head.

"What? You… you can't be serious." He looked at her closer and squinted. "You *are*, aren't you? You're serious about this."

She gave a knowing smile.

"Deadly."

With a tranquil and patient tone, she proceeded to explain Kit's plan in all its glorious detail. She started by describing the story Kit had created to cover his death. Thomas's men would tell the authorities the following account: At ten o'clock before noon on May thirtieth, Kit met with three friends at a dining house in Deptford. One of those friends was Frizer. The meeting was held to celebrate Kit's acquittal on charges of atheism. After dining, he and his friends spent several quiet hours strolling in the back garden. At six o'clock in the evening they finally returned to the house for supper. While supper passed without conflict, as the evening drew to a close a disagreement soon erupted between Frizer and Kit over the reckoning of the bill for the entire day's food. Kit became incensed at having to pay a share. Everyone knew his temper, his sudden rages. Without warning, he uttered malicious words, drew Frizer's dagger, and attacked Frizer from behind. The other men leapt to Frizer's aid. In the ensuing struggle Kit received an accidental blow from Frizer's knife just above the right eye. He died instantly from the wound.

Kit and Thomas had both agreed it was best for Frizer to take the blame for the death: despite his weasely features, his red

341

cheeks sometimes gave him an oddly innocent demeanor. Frizer had also appeared in court many times before as a plaintiff and won several cases. This experience would make him an effective, convincing person to take the stand at the coroner's hearing. Finally, and most importantly, Frizer was hitherto unknown to the authorities – unlike Poley and Baines. Of course, all the men would be exceedingly careful to tell the story in a way that emphasized Frizer's actions as self-defense. To fortify this, Frizer would stay with the body instead of fleeing like a murderer, and Baines and Poley would provide testimony as supporting witnesses. Thomas could have Frizer pardoned and out of jail within a week. It was also agreed that neither Thomas nor Whitgift would be mentioned in any testimony, so as not to complicate matters. Instead, Poley and Baines would serve as the sole witnesses to the death.

His face puzzled, Will plucked the edge of his shirt collar idly.

"Hmm… the story is fitting enough… although if it were mine I might tweak it here and there. But what about the body? There was a body, no? I heard talk that a man's body wrapped in sheets was taken from the house and loaded into a coroner's wagon."

Audrey closed her eyes and nodded.

"Yes, it was, you're quite correct."

"Then how? Stories might be in easy supply but bodies are not."

"Actually, the reverse has more truth, I'm afraid. Perhaps grief makes you forget the place and age we live in?" She opened her eyes and looked straight at him. "Have you not heard of John Penry?"

He shrugged his shoulders uncertainly.

"I vaguely know the name. He's a preacher, isn't he?"

"He *was* a preacher. He was executed on June 29th."

"Oh…"

Audrey continued and explained how John Penry had been executed only the day before Kit went to the meeting house. At five o'clock in the afternoon, Penry had been hanged by Whitgift for writing radical Puritanical tracts. The site of his death was at St. Thomas-a-Watering, a small town less than three miles from Deptford and easily within riding distance for Baines and Poley to fetch the body. Penry was just one year older than Kit and possessed roughly the same build and the same dark features. He had been hanged so suddenly that even his family had not visited him or identified his corpse: hence, there was still time to make the body 'disappear' before anyone grew very suspicious.

"Yes, I suppose so…" Will said, his mouth falling slightly agape. "I see how that could work. Yet doesn't all of this depend ultimately on the Coroner? He would have to accept the story and the identity of the body without asking too many questions; otherwise, the whole thing would never work."

Audrey nodded, completely unfazed. Will raised his eyebrows at her.

"You have an answer for that, too, don't you?" he said.

She gave a faint smile and told him how Elizabeth happened to be in residence at Greenwich Palace during the time of Kit's murder. This meant that Deptford officially fell 'within the verge' – less than twelve miles from the presence of the Queen. Hence, by the laws of the realm, all crimes fell under the Queen's direct authority and William Danby, the Coroner to the Queen's Household, would oversee the coroner's report and inquest. Danby had worked sympathetically with the nation's espionage networks in the past: he was certainly accustomed to the 'negligent questions', 'accidental overlooks', and 'lapses in judgment' sometimes required when reaching a verdict. Under a little persuasion from Thomas, Danby could be relied upon to record the coroner's report without trouble. Once the inquest was over, gravediggers from St Nicholas's church would throw Kit's body into a large, unmarked grave filled with diseased bodies: a plague pit. The truth would be buried there, too…

By now, the morning sun streamed brightly through St Nicholas's churchyard and bathed the north tower in lustrous gold. Mist swirled around the open grave and dusted the feet of Will and Audrey.

They stood closer now and Will's face no longer seemed cynical. His eyes glittered as he looked around wondrously, still trying to take it all in.

Audrey gave him a smile but her look was tainted by unspeakable sadness. Part of her wanted to celebrate with Will, to laugh, to rejoice, but she couldn't escape the thoughts gathering inside her head like a storm. How could she return to Thomas after all this? How could she withstand the grinding routine of the palace? How could she stomach the bitter, long, unending years that still lay ahead? She didn't have any answers. There were no real answers. Even so, she knew she'd find a way to bear it all: she'd always found a way, as had her mother, as had her grandmother – it was as necessary as breathing. To save herself from such immediate heartbreak, she fixed her gaze on Will and tried to concentrate solely on his reaction to the news.

Will took a pace toward the grave and strolled along its edge and looked away thoughtfully.

"I can't believe it's possible..." he murmured. "To overcome it all... to author such a miracle..." In an awe-struck manner, he crossed his arms and continued to think it over. Slowly, he smiled and a buoyant, gentle laugh shook within his chest. The noise sounded odd against the solemnity of the graveyard. He didn't care. He glanced over at Audrey and she gazed back at him tenderly. He laughed again. Tears brimmed in his eyes. He laughed louder and louder and louder.

Scene Ten

Westminster. Whitehall Palace.

Whitgift strode through the corridors and tried not to attract attention. Mild summer air fermented around him. It tasted sour and dust-riddled.

He felt old beyond his years. Over the passing weeks, the bruises on his jaw had faded into unsightly blemishes that lingered on his skin. His hands now dangled limp by his side. At times, the light from the windows caught the edges of his beard and withered it from gray to sterile white. His posture, once so full and straight and potent, now seemed flaccid and wasted. He feared he would never recover.

Before long, he approached a great open doorway: the entrance to court. From inside, murmurs of conversation wafted out into the corridor. A constant flow of people coursed in and out of the doorway. Ministers carried books in their hands. Self-important ambassadors dragged their ermine pelts across the floor. Lords swaggered gaily, swords rolling at their hips, one arm tucked under the velvet shoulder capes as they strutted inside the room.

Whitgift twiddled his fingers nervously. His body grew tense. He paused and regarded the door. Two guards with pikes flanked the entrance. Hesitantly, he pushed forward. He almost made it through...

Just as he drew abreast with the doorframe, the guards lowered their pikes in front of his path. The shafts crossed together, clanged rudely, and barred his way.

He blinked with shock and gave them both a foul look as if they had committed a grave offense.

"What *do* you think you are doing?" he said disdainfully.

"Orders, your worship," said the guard on the right.

"Whose orders? I'll have you both flogged for such bare-faced contempt. Do neither of you know who I am?"

"Yes, Archbishop. Her majesty still doesn't wish to see you."

"You're mistaken, sir, very much mistaken. I have it on good authority that her anger has relented and that I am welcome to return. Now let me through."

"Afraid we can't, your worship."

"And how do you know she doesn't want to see me?"

"She told us."

Whitgift's lips parted.

"She told you, did she? I highly doubt that you understood her well." For a moment, he paused and considered it. He knew it was likely the truth. Without hope of his own spy network, he needed the Queen's favor more than ever, but over the last weeks she had consistently refused to see him or read his petitions. His powers had been curtailed more than he feared possible. He blamed the atheist ministers that surrounded her, poisoning her mind with doubts against him. Even so, he refused to be turned away so easy. "Are you entirely sure of her meaning?"

"Well, she said: "Let the archbishop through and I'll have your heads."" The guards exchanged a transitory look of mirth. "Sounds fairly certain if you ask me."

Whitgift stood up straight and defiant. He shook with a sudden flare of anger.

"I don't believe you!" With both his fists, he knocked the pikes out of his path. The guards hesitated. Before they could act, he barged past through them and into the court.

The court was broad, with arched recesses along the walls, and carved stone pillars that splayed up into a lofty ceiling. At Whitgift's intrusion, the ministers, ambassadors, and lords halted their conversation. Blank faces turned toward him. Over their heads, at the back of the room, Elizabeth stood on the lowest step of a marble dais. The gilt edges of her throne arose behind her.

346

Her pale forehead and red hair shone harshly in the light from two giant candelabras by her side. Chains of pearls dangled from her neck and hung down to her waist. She put her hand on her hip. Her lips pressed flat into a slit of red. Her black eyes fixed coldly on Whitgift.

He didn't take another step. His cheeks flushed and his mouth gaped. He knew the meaning of that look. As she continued to glare his body slowly crumpled inside his cassock.

Two hands reached out behind him and seized his shoulders. The guards pulled him back out of the room. At first, he didn't resist. Yet as they dragged him through the door frame, he suddenly tensed his muscles, and raised his hand desperately.

"I don't understand!" he cried. "My Queen... My Queen..."

Elizabeth didn't respond. She turned away and resumed speaking with her courtiers as if Whitgift had ceased to exist. General conversation returned to the room.

Whitgift's face darkened. His limbs fell passive and the guards hauled him around the corner and out of view.

Scene Eleven

Bankside.

 $\mathbb{F}$ our months later, once the outbreaks of plague in London had diminished, the Master of Revels finally reopened the theaters...

Over in the town of Bankside, cool September winds swept through the streets and ushered in the end of summer. For such an early afternoon, however, the streets were strangely empty. Everyone was at The Rose.

Above the circular theater, a little flag emblazoned with a red rose flew on a pole and snapped in the wind, announcing the afternoon's performance. Below, more than two thousand people loitered outside the dirt entrance of the theater and waited for the show. Excited voices babbled against the theater's black oak timbers and lime plaster walls. Hands gripped flyers with *'As You Like It'* printed in black ornate letters. Amid the throng, families huddled in groups, and mothers held tightly onto their children. Three young men stood on their toes and yelled out to a friend. A fiddler busked near the theater door and filled the air with reedy, spirited notes. Tramps begged for change. Hawkers patrolled the mob with trays of apples and figs and walnuts, pastry tarts, and gingerbread cakes. Flower girls sold bushels of lavender from their baskets. To one side, a boyish preacher stood on a crate and earnestly delivered a sermon to anyone who would listen.

Far back from the crowd, tall carriages waited in a line. The carriages had shiny doors and carved gilt edges. Out of the windows, ladies peered towards the theater impatiently, their faces veiled to protect their reputations. At long last, a bell's ring echoed from the theater and the gates opened and the crowd closed in around the entrance.

At the entrance gate, four of Henslowe's men held wooden collection boxes. Pennies chinked in the boxes as the punters surged inside to the yard. On the way, they passed a gauntlet of refreshment stalls and stands flogging toy daggers, puppets, or duck feather cushions – a penny for each one. Peasants, servants, and yeoman hurried quickly into the yard. Sawdust scuffed around their heels as they jostled to get nearest the stage. In contrast, money-lenders, merchants, and wealthier artisans tramped up the stairs to sit in the tiers. At the entry to each tier, one of Henslowe's men rattled a box and more pennies chinked inside it. For the cost of two pennies, a punter could sit in the second tier, and for three pennies a punter could go to the third tier. Of course, the noblemen and veiled ladies requested to sit apart from the mob. They entered the theater via a back door and ushers escorted them onto the stage itself where they took seats at the back or to the side.

Half an hour elapsed before the play started. During that time, the groundlings – punters who stood in the yard – brushed shoulders and bore the full sun on their backs. The sun heated the rims of their hats and reddened their cheeks and noses. Up in the tiers, people without cushions shifted their buttocks and tried to sit comfortably on the hard benches. People seated to the left of the theater felt draughts of river wind descend through the open roof and chill their limbs. At the very top, the wives of merchants pointed their bejeweled fingers at the stage and tried to guess which ladies and noblemen were in attendance.

The stage itself was set in a pastoral scene: painted cloths hung on the walls of the tiring house and provided a forest background of oak leaves and hawthorn branches. Overheard, musicians scraped and tooted instruments in the gallery.

A trumpet suddenly blared. All mouths clapped shut. People sat nearer the edge of their benches. Groundlings squished forward a little more. From the middle door of the tiring house, the characters of Orlando and Adam appeared from the shadows and paced into view. Their heels boomed on the oak stage. Thousands of eyes blinked at them and waited.

Orlando cleared his throat and spoke first:

"As I remember, Adam, it was upon this fashion bequeathed me by will but poor a thousand crowns, and, as thou say'st, charged my brother, on his blessing, to breed me well; and there begins my sadness..."

The speech continued and the first scene of the first act commenced before the audience.

Throughout the performance, odd voices drifted in from the road outside the theater. Cart wheels trundled past. A dove's wings fluttered at the edge of the roof. Nothing, however, seemed to distract the audience and they soon warmed to the story. At moments of seriousness, their faces grew appropriately solemn and pensive; and when the actors tossed out jokes and cavorted across the stage, the theater came alive with laughter.

Backstage, Will peered out behind one of the curtains in the tiring house and closely studied the reactions of the crowd. He tapped his finger on his lip, stressed. He cringed at the delivery of certain lines, and let out sighs of relief when a scene finished without mistake. Around him, actors flurried about, tearing off costumes and slipping into new ones. They moaned about the reek of garlic and the stink of beer on the breath of the groundlings. Nearby, stagehands lined up chairs, fountains, trees ready to push onto the stage in between scenes. Henslowe stayed in the box office and made sure all the collection boxes were stored safely; then he strode around and whispered orders, checked costumes, and tried to allay the nerves of the actors due to appear next onstage.

In Act II, Scene 7, Will watched anxiously as Jaques spouted the following words:

"All the world's a stage,
And all the men and women merely players;
They have their exits and their entrances;
And one man in his time plays many parts..."

As Will gazed out into the theater, his eyes lifted into the tiers, then fell upon the rapt faces of the groundlings. He frowned. He pushed closer to get a better peek through the curtain.

At the back of the yard stood an intriguing man: he wore a dark tunic and a dark, broad-rimmed hat; a real and dense beard covered his chin; long black hair rested on the tops of his shoulders; and a pipe protruded from his lips, sending a thin tail of smoke up into the stands. He didn't look familiar; in fact, he bore only a slight, vague resemblance to Kit. And yet...

Will didn't turn away. He couldn't take his eyes off the dark man. For an entire act of the play he watched the man while ignoring all else on stage. He watched for some revealing sign, some reaction that might betray the man's true identity. Nothing. The man simply stood there and smoked.

Eventually, Henslowe spotted Will and his face broadened into a smile. He put his hands on his paunchy stomach and bounded up beside the curtain. With a peek over Will's arm, he gazed out into the theater and gave Will a playful nudge.

"It's a winner this one," he whispered. "Always knew comedy would come back in fashion."

Will turned and put a finger to his mouth.

"Shhh!"

Confused, Henslowe stuck out his lower lip.

"What's wrong now, ay? What have I got to '*shhh!*' about?"

Will turned and peered through the curtains again. Past the players, among the heads of the groundlings at the back of the yard, the dark man had moved slightly – he now leant against one of the posts supporting the tiers above. Coils of smoke still circled away from the pipe bowl. Will pointed at him.

"Do you see that man over there?" he asked.

"Which man? There's more than one, you know."

"The one dressed in a dark hat and dark doublet. He's smoking a pipe."

"Sorry... can't say I do..."

"You're not looking properly. Over *there* – at the back."

Henslowe strained harder to see out into the theatre. He shook his head.

"Nope. You're mad, you are. What's so important about this man, anyhow? You don't owe him some money?"

"No."

"If you do, you'll have to wait for all the boxes to be properly counted. Could take a few hours – even days. I doubt there'll be any profits this soon. Not for a while yet, indeed."

"No, I just thought there was something... something interesting about him, that's all."

As Act III, Scene 3 unfolded in the theater, Will narrowed his eyes with interest, still transfixed by the dark man. On stage, Touchstone, the court jester wore patches of red, black, orange, blue, and brown. A three-pronged hat with bells at each end jangled from his head. He strode over the boards in spiky shoes and wheeled his eyes around the audience:

"When a man's verses cannot be understood, nor a man's good wit seconded with the forward child understanding..."

Will mouthed the next words as they were spoken on stage.

"...it strikes a man more dead than a great reckoning in a little room..."

At the back of the groundlings, the dark man suddenly flinched at the words – it was obviously a reference to the meeting house at Deptford. He stood up straight. He peered around the theater. His eyes searched the windows of the tiring house and he gazed hard at the doors. At last, he caught sight of Will at the curtain. For one brief, fleeting moment, their eyes connected.

Will's mouth dropped open. His heart accelerated. His breathing almost ceased. He struggled to believe it.

Without pausing to think, he spun around and dashed past Henslowe. He flew toward the side exit of the tiring house. Henslowe pinched his tuffs of hair and frowned.

"Wait! Come back, Will!" he said, trying to keep his voice low.

"One moment!" Will called back.

"Where are you going?"

"I'll return anon, don't worry!"

"But... you can't leave now!"

352

Will didn't stop. He batted the comment away with his hand, dived out through the door, jumped down two steps, and landed onto the sawdust of the yard. Slowly, he shifted through the closely packed bodies, the garlic-laden breath, and worked his way toward the back of the theater.

The dark man saw him coming. Jerked into motion. Cut left and shuffled through the crowd in the opposite direction.

Will quickened his pace, bumped into shoulders, tripped on someone's feet and grabbed a woman's arm to stop from falling. Oaths colored the air. He didn't stop. He locked his eyes on the dark man's hat bobbing up and down as he darted away in front.

At the edge of the yard, the dark man halted and looked toward the main exit. Too many bodies were packed between himself and the gate for an easy escape. Instead, he twisted right and veered toward the stage. As if he knew his way around, he nipped close to the stage, sidled down its length, and found a space between a beam and the edge of the tiring house. He squashed through the space and entered a back passageway.

Will traced the same path, gaining on the man with every stride. He swiftly approached the gap. With his stomach sucked in, he forced his body through the gap, but tripped on the other side and stumbled headfirst into the blackness of the passageway.

Sounds from the tiring house now echoed close. The passageway seemed empty. Gloom pressed around him. The walls confined his body. He squinted to see and picked his next steps hesitantly as he crept forward. When he rounded a corner he stopped abruptly at the sight ahead.

The dark man now waited beside a rear door that led outside the theater. His body made a half-turn in Will's direction. The two men stood and faced each other. Neither one of them moved. Neither one spoke a word. The dark man opened the door and intense sunlight flooded into the passageway and cast his figure into a silhouette. Will took a step closer but raised his forearm and shielded his eyes from the radiance. The man stepped into the doorway and lingered as Will tried to see him. Slowly, Will's eyes adjusted to the light and he almost began to distinguish the man's features.

Suddenly, from the theater yard came a wave of raucous laughter. Will cocked his head. Henslowe's voice echoed from the tiring house and distracted him. He turned to away to look.

"Will!" called Henslowe's voice. "Where are you? Will! Come back!"

The door squealed and banged shut against its frame. Will craned his head back to see. Too late.

The man had disappeared through the door. For a second, Will dithered and leant forward to follow, but he didn't move. A tiny smile played upon his lips. He understood that Kit had returned not just to say goodbye or to see the play or to the bestow the work with his blessing: he had returned to give proof that he'd created a new life. Even so, Will understood their lives had now diverged forever. They would never meet again.

"Good-bye, Kit," he muttered into the darkness.

Strangely satisfied and jubilant, he turned around and headed back toward the tiring house.

Out on the stage, the actors cavorted around and continued their fevered antics. The crowd erupted into laughter once again. Their laughter was strong and unrestrained now. It drowned out the wicked tongues of propriety and class. It escaped the stamping boots of the law and the state. It removed the mask of God and joined everyone in its sound. The noise soared above the heads of the groundlings, circled up through the stands, spiraled out through the open roof, and lifted into the open blue sky.

Today, the sun was ripe and hot and ready for life.

Exeunt.

AUTHOR'S NOTE

The majority of information known about Marlowe and his life is gleaned from the official documents of Elizabeth's totalitarian government – hardly a paragon of truth. Nevertheless, the reader may be interested to know how much of this story correlates with conventional historical 'fact'.

Characters

Christopher Marlowe was indeed the most famous playwright of his era: the style and content of his plays were revolutionary and made 'The Admiral's Men' the most popular theatrical company in England. He was also connected to the spy world, though his exact duties are unknown. His patron, and the three men that he met with at Deptford on May 30th, were all involved in espionage to varying degrees. Marlowe also had friends at the highest levels of government: for example, in 1597 when Cambridge University tried to ban his master's degree because of lengthy absences from residence, the Privy Council itself interceded on Marlowe's behalf and stated that his absences were due to *"matters touching the benefit of his country"*. This action by the Privy Council, the nation's supreme legal authority after the Queen, is unprecedented and leads many scholars to speculate that Marlowe was recruited for espionage work while still a student.

William Shakespeare was born the same year as Marlowe (1564) but lacked higher education and took longer to develop his talent. He certainly knew Marlowe. In 1589, 'The Admiral's Men' merged with another theatre company called 'Lord Strange's Men', who employed the young Shakespeare as a writer and reviser of plays. Thus, Marlowe would have come into contact with Shakespeare on a daily basis, and there is some evidence to suggest that Marlowe collaborated with him on parts of the *'Henry VI'* trilogy as well as *'Titus Andronicus'*. Shakespeare makes open reference to Marlowe in numerous places throughout *'As You Like it'*.

John Whitgift was Archbishop of Canterbury from 1583 until his death in 1604. He led a vigorous campaign against religious heresy in England, particularly against Puritanism. Throughout his time as Archbishop, Whitgift always held the special favor of Elizabeth and even attended her on her deathbed. He punished non-conforming ministers, executed numerous heretics, and publically burnt unorthodox texts. His exact views on Marlowe are unknown, but there are many indicators that he disapproved of the playwright. For example, in 1587 he was Vice-Chancellor of Cambridge University and undoubtedly played a role in trying to ban Marlowe's master's degree. He was a member of the Privy Council throughout the investigation into Marlowe's involvement with the libels. And in 1599 he publically burnt Marlowe's translation of Ovid's *'Elegies'*.

Thomas Walsingham was Marlowe's patron and was also highly connected to the intelligence network, due to his cousin Sir Francis Walsingham (the Queen's chief advisor and spymaster). However, there is no evidence to suggest he was a homosexual.

Audrey Walsingham was Thomas's wife, though it is uncertain when they married. Her maiden name was Shelton – an old and distinguished family, indirectly connected to Anne Boleyn, the Queen's mother. She eventually rose to become one of Elizabeth's Gentlewomen of the Privy Chamber and there were rumors that she later became the mistress of Sir Robert Cecil (Lord Burghley's son).

Events

The episode with the guards in Calais is imagined, but one of the most common duties for an Elizabethan spy was the transport of important documents between nations. This was danger-ous work and often required the use of disguises. For example, a Spanish courier traveling through Scotland in the 1500's posed as a dentist and carried secret letters in a hidden compartment in his bag. Spies were also known to conceal messages by having them sewn into the buttons of their coats.

The posting of the libel occurred around midnight on May 5th, 1593 at a Dutch church on Broad Street in London. It was one of many libels posted around London since April 15th. It didn't quote Marlowe's work and was not signed with his name – in-stead, it threatened violence against foreigners and made frequent reference to Marlowe's plays, such as *'The Jew of Malta'* and *'The Massacre of Paris'* and was signed with the moniker "Tam-burlaine", Marlowe's most famous character. In reaction, the Privy Council resolved to find and punish the author for inciting rebellion. Days later, on May 10th, a proclamation was read at Guildhall offering 100 shillings for any information about the author. On May 11th, the Privy Council granted permission for the use of torture on persons suspected of posting the libels.

The Earl of Derby's poisoning is a suspected result of his connection with Catholic radicals. His cousin, Richard Hesketh, was a Catholic traitor who tried convincing Derby to seize the throne from Elizabeth. Derby refused to comply and subsequent-ly revealed the plot, which lead to the execution of several con-spirators. Derby died at a mysteriously young age (34 yrs old) and many scholars think he was slow-poisoned in retaliation for revealing the conspiracy against the Queen.

Marlowe's arrest for counterfeiting took place in the Dutch town of Flushing (rather than Portsmouth) in January, 1592. Under charges made by Richard Baines, Marlowe was ar-rested and deported back to England to face Lord Burghley. Strangely, he was never prosecuted for the crime.

Marlowe's swordfight in Hogg Lane, Shoreditch occurred in September, 1589. The aggressor was William Bradley (not an assassin) and Marlowe didn't fight alone: he quickly withdrew from the fray after Thomas Watson, a fellow writer, came to his aid. Bradley died on the scene from wounds inflicted. Both Watson and Marlowe were arrested and sent to Newgate Prison (rather than Marshalsea), although both were later released after the coroner accepted Watson's claim of self-defense.

Shakespeare's torture is invented, but it reflects the terrible fate suffered by Thomas Kyd, another talented and popular playwright at The Rose theatre. As part of the investigation into the libels, Kyd's rooms were searched and documents *"denying the deity of Jesus Christ"* were found. Thereafter, Kyd was arrested and imprisoned on charges of atheism. Under pain of torture, he named Marlowe as the owner of the heretical documents (they had shared rooms in the summer of 1591) and denounced Marlowe as an atheist. Kyd never recovered from the harm inflicted by his torture and died soon after at 36yrs old.

The trial at the Court of the Star Chamber in Westminster Palace is imagined, although the Star Chamber was a very real and notorious court. Instead, Marlowe appeared on trial for atheism on May 20th, 1593 at Nonsuch Palace in Surrey. Two days earlier, after the incriminations voiced by Thomas Kyd, Marlowe had been arrested at Scadbury Manor (the home of Thomas Walsingham) and was subsequently escorted to court to stand before the Privy Council. Top Privy Counselors at the time were the Earl of Essex, Archbishop Whitgift, and Lord Burghley and it is likely that Marlowe faced at least some of these figures at the trial. The 'remembrances' against Richard Cholmeley and the 'Baines note' were real documents that incriminated Marlowe, although they were not presented at the hearing. After the trial, Marlowe was released on an arrangement similar to bail – he had to make daily attendances upon the council for the indefinite future.

Marlowe's death at Deptford occurred on May 30th, 1593, at a meeting house belonging to the widow Eleanor Bull. Present at the scene of the death were Ingram Frizer (Walsingham's secretary), Robert Poley (a senior spy) and Nicholas Skeres (a thief and sometime spy who is replaced with Baines in the novel). The coroner's report records his killing as self-defense: he drew Frizer's dagger, attacked Frizer from behind, and in the ensuing struggle received a fatal blow from the dagger just above his right eye. He was buried at St. Nicholas's Churchyard in Deptford on June 1st in an unmarked grave. Much suspicion has surrounded his death ever since...

Further Research

I consulted a wide-range of sources too numerous to mention here, but for readers interested in learning more about Christopher Marlowe there are a few selected works that I recommend.

Books:
Nicholls, Charles. The Reckoning: The Murder of Christopher Marlowe. Illinois: University of Chicago Press, 1995.
Kuriyama, Constance Brown. Christopher Marlowe: A Renaissance Life. Ithaca, New York: Cornell University Press, 2002.
The above works of nonfiction both provide scholarly, balanced, and comprehensive accounts of Marlowe's life. They also examine the documents and circumstances surrounding his death in great detail.

Documentaries:
Much Ado About Something. Dir. Mike Rubbo. The Helpful Eye and Chili Films, 2001.
Very few documentaries about Marlowe currently exist. However, the film cited above involves an excellent, insightful discussion of Marlowe's death (and also ventures into the Shakespeare-Marlowe authorship debate).

Websites:
www.gutenberg.org
For readers wishing to enjoy Marlowe's works, I suggested downloading the free public domain texts at Project Gutenberg. This site contains a complete collection of his plays and poetry, including the poem *'Hero and Leander'*.

www.marlowe-society.org

The official site of the Marlowe Society based in the U.K. The society promotes Marlowe's work and provides education about his life. They present extensive biographical information for free on the web, but also offer newsletters, research journals, events, and meetings to their members.

www.mgscarsbrook.com
Readers may also consult my own website for a biography, timeline, descriptions of Marlowe's known associates, and transcripts of all the key Marlowe-related documents.

Ultimately, wherever the reader goes to learn more about Marlowe I emphasize the importance of critical thinking in all matters. If Marlowe's plays can offer us any wisdom it is this: the individual's own thoughts and feelings are of paramount value in the world. As Marlowe himself once wrote: *"There is no sin but ignorance."*

M. G. Scarsbrook
Southern California, 2010

READ AN EXCERPT
OF
M. G. SCARSBROOK'S
LATEST NOVEL

POISON IN THE BLOOD
The Memoirs of Lucrezia Borgia

1497, Renaissance Rome

As the daughter of Pope Alexander VI, Lucrezia Borgia is a young noblewoman immersed in all the glamour of the Vatican Palace. Yet after a brutal killing shocks the city, Lucrezia learns that a dark truth lies beneath the surface of the Papal Court: in their ruthless quest for power, her father and brother are willing to poison their enemies.

Her family are murderers.

After discovering that her new husband is next to die, Lucrezia struggles to help him escape from Rome before the assassins strike. Against a barrage of political intrigues, papal spies, and diabolical tricks, Lucrezia uses all her wits to defy her family and save her husband from assassination. But as tragedy looms ever closer, and her plans gradually fail, she finds herself confronting an enemy far more sinister than she ever imagined…

I

The Roman Carnival
February 1497

One hour before a man was killed, his body run through with a sword, the city of Rome gave no warning of the violence yet to come. Excited people bustled in the twilight streets, their faces hidden behind painted masks, their tunics or bodices now swapped for brilliant costumes of white, red, or gold fabric.

I wandered through the crowds to enjoy the final minutes of the celebration. Around me, candlelight gleamed in every quarter of the city, shining among the shadows, burning away the darkness. Tonight was a time of merriment and mayhem, a festival that upturned the world and made anything possible.

"Without a light!" a voice shouted nearby. "Without a light!"

Such chanting filled the air as my brother Cesare and I weaved along the Via del Corso. The cobblestone avenue was now engulfed in the most riotous event of all, the Night of Candles. All hands carried a glowing candle, and everyone played at extinguishing all other flames while guarding their own light. Whenever revelers snuffed a flame, they chanted *"without a light, without a light!"* in celebration of their victory. I watched and marveled at the intensity of their games: the year was already marred by plagues, famines, and bloodshed, and yet the people could still banish their worries in the joy of the Carnival. I envied them deeply.

Cesare kept pace at my side and raised his torch high above any grasping hands. Firelight glistened off his silver, unicorn-mask. His shoulders lay broadly under a silver satin doublet. In contrast, I wore the plain clothes of a peasant girl – a brown leather bodice and green circle skirt. My mask was small, concealing my eyes and cheeks, but it kept snagging in the waves of my golden waist-length hair.

"Doesn't it feel strange to be here without a papal escort?" I said to Cesare, as we strolled through the crowds. "It's a shame we can't normally walk the streets in safety without a disguise. I like being in Rome without being noticed or stared at, don't you?"

"I don't care," he replied in his deep, monotone voice. He looked down at my bodice and skirt. "Tell me your costume again?"

"I'm a peasant girl. I wanted to be an ordinary person, for a change."

"Why?"

Before I could answer, a firecracker boomed overhead and distracted us. I stopped and held my hands protectively around the candle I carried. Suddenly, a carriage laden with youths, confetti paper, and sugar plums jostled past, nearly running us beneath its wheels. My brother grabbed my arm and yanked me to the side of the road.

"Villains!" Cesare shouted at the carriage, as it disappeared back into the mob. "They should be hung – all of them!"

The roar of his voice cut through the chants and conversations nearby and a few people turned their heads to look at us.

"Don't worry, I'm fine," I said, rubbing my arm where his fingers had pressed my skin. "But you can't blame them. Nobody knows who we are, remember. They can't be expected to treat us as the son and daughter of the pope. What would be the use of disguises, otherwise?"

"They're still scoundrels," he replied, allowing his temper to ease.

2

I looked toward the south of the city and thought of a plan.

"Why don't we return home now?" I said. "We've seen enough of the night's festivities. Carnival's almost over, anyway."

"There's no need to rush back to Città del Vaticano," he replied.

"Yes, but I thought we might take the longer route to our quarters. We might even pass through the southern roads and piazze?" A tiny sense of guilt tingled in my bones. I felt certain he would know exactly where I wanted to go, and precisely whom I hoped to see.

Instead, he gave only a shrug. "If you insist."

We moved away, still gaping at all the sparkling costumes, the wild dancing, and the cunning tricks. Nearby, two women dressed in white feathers huddled past us. Remnants of red, green, and blue confetti speckled their hair. A jester wearing crimson breeches danced in front, pelted them with eggs, and knocked out both their flames. Behind him, youths leapt from the street onto passing carriages to snuff the lanterns. Oranges and sugar plums buzzed overhead and bombilated the walls of homes, shops, and palazzi, infusing the air with tangs of citrus. Above all the mayhem, ladies leaned over balconies and poured honey down onto candles below.

Careful to avoid Sant'Angelo, the rione controlled by our enemies, we left the Via del Corso and wandered down quieter streets. The lights around us were gradually doused and the city became darker and less chaotic. As we ambled along, five-story homes and palazzi loomed overhead. Aromas of cooked artichoke, rich meats, garlic and mint, wafted out from open arched windows.

Cesare and I soon passed by the piazza of Campo de' Fiori, a small marketplace surrounded by ale-houses and inns, many of them catering to pilgrims who came to visit the tomb of St. Peter. From the distant doorways, laughter spilled into the piazza, and a group of drunkards amused themselves with silly antics. One man sat on a barrel while the others tried to roll him across the marketplace.

3

Suddenly, a woman passed behind the window of an inn. Her blonde hair flashed in the lantern light, but she vanished again almost as quickly as she'd appeared. My heart fluttered and I stopped. Her name was Vannozza dei Cattanei. Our mother.

I nudged Cesare. "Over by the window. Didn't you see her?"

"No," he replied flatly. "But we shouldn't stop here."

I stood still. "She has three inns there now, or so I've heard. She owns *'The Cow'*, *'The Lion'*, and *'The Eagle'*. We could cross the piazza and take a closer view?"

He peered into the gloom of the buildings. "Father wouldn't approve. You know that."

"Aren't you even a little interested to look at her now?"

He turned to me quizzically. "Why? What is she to us? How many times have you spoken with her recently?"

"Not once in ten years. Not since my seventh birthday."

"Exactly. She was just our father's mistress, nothing more. Why should that make her important?"

"Cesare! How can you speak so coldly? She did more than simply give birth to us – she also raised us for years in her house in the Ponte. Father would've married her, but he was a cardinal. If he hadn't climbed so high in the Curia, he wouldn't have ended his affair with her."

"Is that what you think?"

"And he wouldn't have taken us away, either. I wonder what life would've been like if we'd stayed in her care, and not gone to live at his palazzo instead?"

"It would've been a life without ambition. Why should I desire that?" He shook his head. "We don't know her anymore, Lucrezia. When was the last time you even had a letter from her?"

"She stopped writing after father was elected Pope."

"So you haven't heard from her in at least five years. Tell me, then, what kind of a mother is she?"

My cheeks flushed and I couldn't answer.

He walked off a few paces and urged me to follow. His voice became softer: "There's no reason to stay here. Let's go."

I desperately searched for a way to prolong our visit. Even though my father hated the idea of us seeing Vannozza again, I yearned to walk just a few steps more into the piazza. I stared at Cesare, then let my eyes wander around the nearby street, hoping for something to spike his interest and delay our return to the palazzo.

"The Teatro di Pompeo is less than a hundred yards down that road, isn't it?" I said innocently. "That's where Emperor Julius Caesar was murdered. I don't mind staying here for a minute, if you want to go and look at the site."

He narrowed his eyes and considered it, his attitude slowly warming to the notion. From childhood, he'd always been fascinated with the dramatic life and death of his ancient namesake. My suggestion was irresistible.

"I don't know," he replied. "It's not safe for you to be alone."

"But you'll be able to see me the whole time, the Teatro is so close to Campo de' Fiori. As long as I stay at the edge of the piazza, I'll never be out of your sight." I wiped a tear from the corner of my eye. "Please, Cesare, allow me a moment longer. I promise not to move."

He wavered before giving a reluctant nod, unwilling to upset me again. "Five minutes and no more." He strode off from the piazza and called back: "And shout for me if any one approaches you, understood?"

I agreed and watched him saunter away down the road, his broad shape slowly merging with the other revelers.

As soon as he'd gone, I turned back to the piazza and stared opposite at the blazing windows of the inn. Vannozza was just a short, tantalizing distance away from me. I hadn't been so close to her in years, and it was unbearable not to see her now. Without moving, I judged the length of the marketplace and realized that I could make it across to the inn and back in only a few minutes. Cesare would be so distracted that he'd never be the wiser.

I stepped forward, then paused remorsefully. My father had pleaded with me never to meet with Vannozza again, for he always feared that she might turn my heart against him in some manner. A good daughter would not defy her father over this matter now, I knew that. After all, for the last decade, I had lived

5

solely in his care, enjoying a life of great privilege. He didn't deserve such ingratitude from me in return.

And yet, what if I only looked at her from a distance? Was that really so awful? I didn't have to speak with my mother, I could just peek through the window or the doorway. My father would never have to learn of my disobedience.

Before taking another step, I pondered the dangers of leaving my brother's sight. We had many enemies in the city, including the powerful houses of the Colonna and Orsini. I knew that it was safer to stay here and not wander off; that it was easier to return to the palazzo and not see Vannozza for another year. But I couldn't do it. Not tonight. I glanced around at the other people in their fantastical masks. The Carnival celebrated risks and rule-breaking, not safety and obedience. If not now, when would I ever find the strength to see her again?

At last, I summoned my courage, trained my sights on my mother's inn, and hurried into the piazza. My feet tapped over the cobblestones, exhilarated and quick. My heart drummed in my ears. I wondered if she would still appear as beautiful as I remembered, still as graceful and gentle. What if she caught me peeking through the doors at her? Would she recognize my face? Had I changed so much since childhood? I longed to know the answers, but I never had the chance to find out...

Halfway across the piazza, I passed by a group of drunken men. One of them danced up to me with a menacing leer. He wore a mask with a long curved nose, like a scythe.

"What's that, my dear?" he said, gazing at the candle I sheltered in my hands.

I didn't reply and quickened my stride towards the inn. Unhappily, he kept pace with me, dancing around in circles, making me dizzy. His hand lashed out and snuffed my candle.

"Without a light!" he chuckled. "Without a light!"

I gave a thin-lipped smile and hoped he might leave me. Instead, he leaned closer, his breath sour with fumes of ale.

"Now, now, don't be upset," he said with a teasing, drunken slur. "You can have my flame, if you like." He lowered his candle near his crotch and thrust his hips rudely. "I got another wick. It's in me breeches. Want to see?"

"No, I think I'd vomit," I replied coldly, trying to step around him. "Please leave me, good signore. I don't wish for trouble."

"I'm no trouble, my dear. All the harlots like me. I can pay, you know, I can pay."

In horror, I realized that my disguise had confused him: from my plain skirt and tight bodice, he thought I was one of Rome's many courtesans. Before I could explain, he lunged forward, slung his arm around my waist, and dragged me toward a nearby alleyway. I tried to scream. His hand closed over my mouth. I waved frantically at the other drunkards in the marketplace for help, but they only laughed and cheered the man onwards.

He thrust me into the alley and shadows enveloped us both, hiding us from the piazza. I tried to wiggle under his arms and yelled:

"Cesare! Cesare! Help!"

The man gripped me tight. His sweaty hands roamed over my bosom. A swarm of kisses landed on my neck and cheeks. He pressed against my thighs and his fingers clawed at my skirt, trying to lift it up.

"Off me, you lout!" I pushed back with all my strength, and tried to batter him with my fists. Sobs rose into my throat. "Stop it. Please, you don't understand. I'm not a wench. This is just a disguise. It's Carnival. Now stop! I beg you! The pope will know of this!"

He continued to grope me, but his mouth contorted into a snarl. "Who cares for the pope, ay? Bloody Borgias!" He pressed his kisses harder into my face. "I'm much nicer, my dear. You'll like me. You can't like them. They're nothing but murderers. The whole lot!"

"They don't murder! How can you say that!"

He opened his mouth to answer, but was interrupted by a distant noise. The Ave Maria bells chimed out across the darkness from the tower of Basilica di San Pietro. It was twelve o'clock and the sound marked the end of Carnival and the onset of Lent.

The man stood still and listened, as if the bells struck some cord of reverence within him. His grasp on my hips weakened slightly and I hoped his change in mood might work in my favor. I tried frightening him into releasing me and took off my mask, revealing my face.

"Do you recognize me, signore?" I said. "I am Lucrezia Borgia, daughter of Pope Alexander VI. Perhaps my costume has deceived you, but Carnival is now over. You shall free me this moment or it won't be forgotten."

I waited for his response, praying that he might bow down humbly and beg forgiveness. Instead, far from being submissive, he responded by stripping off his own mask. I scanned his pudgy cheeks, his dilated eyes, his thick nose and didn't recognize him.

"Free you?" he slurred in reply, grinning. "Why would I do that, my dear? I'm a guard in the House of Orsini."

My heart sunk at the name. In revealing my face, I had made the worst of all mistakes – the Orsini were the greatest enemy of my family.

"See that tower?" He pointed across to the nearby rooftops. The prow of a watchtower peeked over the rooflines. "We're not far from Sant'Angelo, the rione of the Orsini. This may be your city, my dear, but that's our district." With a chuckle, he yanked my arm and tried to drag me off toward the watchtower.

I ran my heel down his shin and stamped on his foot. He yelped and clutched at his leg instinctively, releasing my hands.

I span around, dashed out of the alley, and ran back across Campo de' Fiori.

His drunkenness didn't slow his pursuit. Within seconds, he caught up with me, grabbed my arm, twisted it back, and pinned me against the wall. On the next street, a few people gawked at the sight of our struggle.

"Let's take you to Palazzo Orsini," he said loudly into my ear. "I'm sure the pontiff will pay handsomely for your safe return."

I struggled and screamed: "Cesare! Cesare!"

The guard lifted his fist to hit me.

Luckily, my brother had been searching the area since I first entered the piazza. At the sound of my voice, he sprinted around the corner and into the marketplace. Without the slightest hesitation, he tore off his mask, whipped his sword from it's sheath, and stalked directly toward us. The onlookers parted the way.

The Orsini guard swore, threw me aside, stepped back, and drew his sword fast. He struck out and made a poor thrust at Cesare. My brother sidestepped it easily, slashed down at the guard's blade, and broke it in two. The severed piece tinkled onto the ground. The guard held up his fractured sword feebly and Cesare hovered over him, unsure whether to run him through.

I recovered my breath and hurried to my brother's side. "No, don't do it," I pleaded. "He's not worth it, Cesare. He's just a drunkard. He doesn't know what he's doing."

Cesare glared. "It's too late. He insulted you. I can't let it pass."

The guard panicked and fumbled at his belt to draw his dagger. Cesare reacted instantly, raised his sword, and sliced downward.

It was done before I could shut my eyes.

A stream of blood coursed over the cobblestones and shone blackly against the light. Just a few feet away, the guard lay flat on the road, his body slashed, quivering, and lifeless. I'd seen executions before, but never so dreadfully close. The crowd ran off in shock.

By now, the sleepy watchman on the Orsini tower was awake. A horn blasted the alarm.

Cesare returned to my side and searched the nearby street for a quick escape. Panting heavily, he shouted: "Follow me!"

He grabbed the reins of a passing horse, knocked off the rider, and jumped up into the saddle.

"Hurry!" he yelled, hoisting me onto the horse behind him.

My arms encircled his torso and I held on tightly as he whipped the reins, kicked his heels, and spurred us into a gallop.

With frightening speed, we rode from one neighborhood to another, swerving around corners, desperately evading any sign of the Orsini. After galloping to the edge of Rome and crossing the Tiber river, we raced back to the protective walls of Città del Vaticano.

At long last, we returned to the safety of our home.

II

A Dangerous Decision

W ithin the grounds of Palazzo Apostolico, Cesare drew our horse to a halt at the stable house. We dismounted, our feet thudding onto the straw-matted ground, and I felt a sudden sense of relief weigh upon my limbs. A groom hurried towards us, offered a formal greeting, and led the horse away into a stall. As he did so, I spied something interesting at the far end of the stables: my brother Juan, accompanied by his personal valet.

I hadn't seen Juan all evening, for he'd chosen to spend the Carnival with his friends, rather than Cesare or me. He was now dressed in the silk costume and white turban of a Persian gentleman. Unlike us, he and his valet were not returning home. Instead, they waited for their horses to be saddled and intended to go into the city. I dashed up to them immediately.

"Juan, you can't go out tonight! Something terrible has happened!" I stopped and caught my breath. "There was a fight at Campo de' Fiori. An Orsini guard attacked me. Cesare killed him with a sword!"

Juan arched his eyebrows, unimpressed. "Is that right?" he replied in his sharp, nasal tone. "Well, it's no major loss to the world. The Orsini deserve it. Thanks for the news, I'll make sure to keep my wits about me."

I tried not to feel hurt that he showed no concern over my welfare. Although he was several years older than me, I still felt the need to protect him. With growing frustration, I grabbed his arm: "You don't understand. The Orsini will take revenge. Why put yourself at risk? Carnival's already over–" "It's not over! I haven't finished celebrating yet, for heaven's sake! There's a whorehouse in the ghetto that I've never been to before." He pulled his arm away and gestured for the groom to bring his horse out to the yard. "My friends are waiting across the river. I'll have a valet with me, anyhow."

Cesare swaggered up to us. "Don't be such an idiot. She's right. It's too dangerous to go out – any fool can see that."

"And who are you to question me?" Juan replied, his angular face turning pink. "Did you forget your place in this family? I don't take orders from people like you."

Cesare stared back, eyes glittering. He towered over Juan.

"Get out of my way," Juan said. "I'm leaving."

Cesare didn't move. Juan waited, then stepped closer, his cheeks burning a deeper shade of red: "Out of my way. I won't tell you again. By god, I'll have you whipped!"

Before the argument could escalate, I jumped between them: "Let him go, Cesare. There's been enough fighting tonight already. We can't force him to stay."

Cesare paused, sneered at him, and slowly moved aside. In response, Juan narrowed his eyes triumphantly and strode into the yard.

"Will you at least return before dawn?" I called out.

There was no reply. I stood at the stable house entrance and watched as Juan and the valet rode through the palazzo gates and charged away to meet their friends...

Cesare and I soon returned within the Vaticano and sat together in the Sala dei Misteri. This hall was part of the larger Appartamento Borgia, the private living space of my father, my two brothers, and me. With a damp cloth, I tended to a small wound scored on Cesare's left forearm, the only damage he sustained from the fight. He didn't wince as I ran the cloth over his cut. Now without his mask, his face displayed a thin auburn moustache and beard. Many women considered him the most hand-some man in Rome, and more than one artist had modeled a vi-sion of Jesus on his looks. Nevertheless, I always felt there was something vaguely dangerous in his face and body that prevented him from appearing Holy.

"There," I said, wiping away the last of the blood. "No real harm done. You'll live a few years more."

"Not many," he replied seriously.

"What? Why do you always say such things? You're only twenty-two years old."

"I won't see my thirtieth year. I know it."

"Nonsense! You don't know anything. I've never seen any-one as strong as you. You'll outlive us all."

He seemed not to hear my answer. His gaze remained pen-sive and he shifted awkwardly in his seat. "The Orsini guard... he didn't... did he?"

My eyes dropped to the floor with embarrassment. I shook my head. He took a breath and relaxed again.

"Cesare, I'm grateful for what you did tonight. And I know it was unavoidable. Only, I wish you hadn't killed–"

He stood up and pulled his shirt down over his wounded arm. I peered towards the window and immediately changed the subject.

"Juan will be safe tonight, won't he?"

He paced around the edge of the room. "Who cares?"

"You're not still angry about what he said in the stables? He doesn't mean to treat you so badly, you know."

"He's a spoiled fool. He has no talents or interests, except in the whores of Rome."

"That's not true. Why would father give him a dukedom, then? Or the control of the papal army? I'm sure that Juan has a few redeeming features. He must deserve at least *some* of his titles."

"And what about me? Do I deserve to be nothing in this world? A mere cardinal?"

"I didn't say that, but father knows what's best for the fami-ly. Perhaps he'll give you more responsibilities one day?"

Poison In The Blood

Cesare glanced above at the semi-circular vaults, each one adorned with murals painted by the artist Pinturicchio. One of the scenes depicted the Resurrection and it showed our father kneeling at Christ's tomb. At last, he replied firmly:

"Impossible. Father has chosen to honor Juan, and he can't change that now. We'd look weak to our enemies." He sighed loudly. "Juan will always have power, as long as he lives."

I frowned at his unsettling tone. "The city isn't too dangerous tonight, I hope? We've already lost our mother. The family is small enough already, no?"

I waited for him to agree, but instead he laughed grimly. My hands fidgeted in my lap.

"Your mood's peculiar this evening. What's so amusing now?"

"Not you, sister." His eyes again swept across the murals in the room. With a quieter voice, he said: "It's just... there are things about this family you don't know... things you should never know."

I waited for him to continue, yet he said no more.

"What things?" I said, with growing concern. "Cesare, what things?"

He refused to answer. I stood up urgently, ready to press him further on the topic. Before I could speak, an unwelcome noise interrupted us.

Footsteps pattered down the corridor outside and echoed into the hall. Within a few moments, a small herd of giggling courtesans filled the doorframe. They turned and parted the way. Behind them, his pace slow and steady, appeared the most powerful man in the world: my father, Pope Alexander VI.

III

The Troublesome Night

As he drifted into the hall, a robe of crimson brocade covered my father's body in vast, shapeless folds, obscuring the lines of his rotund belly. A white night cap concealed his bald crown. Despite his age, Alexander still carried his weight firmly, and his mind had never been sharper or more adroit. Indeed, he was now over sixty years of age, the time when Aristotle says men are at their wisest.

He raised his hand deliberately to his courtesans and they retreated from the room. Approaching Cesare and me, he said in a rich melodious tone: "My dear children, why do you speak with raised voices at this late hour? You know how such noise disagrees with my nerves."

"Forgive us, father," I replied. In my tiredness, I forgot to address him formally, the etiquette he required even from his own children. "I mean *'your Holiness'*."

He glided over to a chair, settling himself onto the plush velvet seat. "I didn't expect to find you home so early from the Carnival. Tell me, where is Juan this evening?"

I crept up to his chair. "Out in Rome. But the city isn't safe for him. There was a skirmish and Cesare's hurt. It happened as we passed by Campo de' Fiori…" I stopped and wished I'd not spoken the last few words.

"Campo de' Fiori?" said Alexander, his face darkening. "And why, of all the splendid places in our city, were you at that specific piazza tonight?"

"I didn't talk to her. You have nothing to fear. I promised you I would never do that, and I haven't."

He tilted his head doubtfully and regarded me with an unblinking stare. Above all else, his eyes were his most impressive feature – dark, magnificent, and hypnotic.

"She didn't speak with Vannozza," Cesare grumbled from the corner. "She was only trying to tell you there was a fight. I killed an Orsini."

"A disturbance with our rivals?" said Alexander, his voice fluttering.

I put my hand on his shoulder. "Yes, and Juan's still out there, your Sanctity. I warned him to stay home, but he wouldn't listen."

Alexander leaned on the gilded arms of the chair. He twisted his head toward Cesare and studied him closely. I felt he looked at my brother with the slightest hint of fear. His fleshy chin wobbled and he seemed a little older. For the briefest of moments, some source of hostility seemed to pass between them. Cesare's jaw looked so taught it could snap.

"It's late and I'm tired," said Cesare. "Goodnight."

Alexander offered his hand formally. Cesare stepped forward, kissed my father's golden Pescatorio ring, then stalked out of the room.

The hall fell silent and I remained at my father's side. Ever since I'd mentioned the Orsini guard, a terrible question had pestered my thoughts. I didn't want to voice it now, but the issue wouldn't leave me alone.

"Your Holiness," I said. "I want to ask a question, but you must promise not to be angry."

"Very well," he replied, stroking the ends of my hair.

Before I began, my throat felt dry, and I gave a tiny cough.

"Lucrezia!" he said with annoyance. "My nerves, please! Not so loud."

I waited a moment, then spoke quietly. "You see, the Orsini guard that Cesare fought with earlier, he said something unpleasant to me. He said our family was full of murderers. That was a lie, wasn't it?

"It's always correct to defend the honor of our name."

"Yes, I know, but that wasn't entirely my meaning."

"My child, are you asking if the charge is true? If so, I must remind you that we are from Valencia; we are not of Roman or Italian blood; we are outsiders to this state. In consequence, there will always be villains who seek to destroy the name of a foreign pontiff. I warn you, pay no attention to their charges."

"So, the answer is…"

"I've already given the answer."

I held the breath in my lungs. I didn't want to ask again, since it wasn't wise to keep pushing the issue. "But we're not murderers, are we?"

He stopped running his fingers across my hair. "Surely, I didn't hear that question come from my own daughter?" He raised himself from his seat with enormous effort. "I'm an old man, Lucrezia, but I carry a power of singular importance. I am God's Supreme Vicar on earth, ruler over all spheres of Christendom, heir to the spiritual authority of St. Peter, and successor to the temporal command of Emperor Constantine. This burden is enough to break the back of any man, but it soothes me to know that I'm supported by the strength, love, and loyalty of all my family. My spirits would be crushed if this were not true."

I sighed. "I'm a loyal daughter, your Sanctity."

"I hope so," he said slowly, turning away to leave.

As he reached the door, I thought of something to impress him. "I'll wait to make sure Juan gets home safely. I couldn't sleep if I thought someone in our family might be in danger."

He paused, nodded his head without looking at me, then continued out of the hall.

True to my word, I stayed in the Sala dei Misteri for the rest of the night and waited for a sign that Juan had returned from the city unharmed. The hall's arched windows overlooked a small courtyard commonly used to access the Appartamento Borgia. If Juan returned that night, and I managed to stay awake long enough, I should see him pass below the window on his way to his bedchamber. I drew a chair over to the window and settled in for a long wait.

Hour after hour passed, but there was no sign of Juan. He often stayed out late, carousing across the city, escaping the pressure of his daily duties with wine and women. I was sure tonight would be no exception. Time dragged onwards and my eyelids drooped. To keep alert, I resorted to playing at word games, my usual source of amusement whenever I was bored and alone. I sat back and thought of anagrams, discovering that *'sword'* could be reshuffled into *'words'*; that *'listen'* could become *'silent'*; and that *'stifle'* was a transformation of *'itself'*. I yawned and my eyes grew small and tiny beneath my lids and my chin touched my chest. *'Please'* was an anagram of *'asleep'*...

Something screeched in the darkness.

I jolted awake in the chair. A metallic screech sounded again, arising from outside.

At the window, I peered down into the courtyard and expected to find Juan walking across to the Appartamento. Instead, from a cellar door at the base of the Torre Borgia – a tower adjoining our quarters – it was Cesare who stepped out into the courtyard. He carried a small torch and it cast his shadow on the wall. The hinges of the cellar door screeched again as he shut it, turned a key in the lock, and attached the key to a ring on his belt. I tipped my head closer to the glass. He still walked about in full dress. His spurs tinkled on the flagstones as he strode away swiftly and vanished into the darkness. I waited for his return, but he didn't reappear.

Why on earth was he still awake at this hour? There was no reason for him to be fully dressed. And what business did he have in the cellar? I'd seen the door a thousand times: small, plain, and uninteresting. Presumably, it led to a storage chamber below the tower, the type of place that only servants would visit. I knew he was probably going out now. Yet where would he go to, and who

18

would he meet at such a time? He had several favorite courtesans in the city whom he frequented, but somehow I didn't feel convinced. The haste of his movements, the speed of his gait across the courtyard, the strange door and the lateness of the hour, it all held something rather furtive. He didn't move like a man expecting a pleasurable encounter.

I remembered the curious way he spoke to me earlier: *"there are things about this family you don't know... things you should never know."* What was he talking about? What things?

I pondered the matter further and felt that I *did* know at least this much: something troublesome was happening now, and I didn't like it – I didn't like it at all.

IV

The Search Party

Golden hues of daylight filtered into the Sala dei Misteri as a pair of gentle hands shook me awake. I'd spent the entire night curled up in the chair waiting for Juan. The elderly shape of Panthasilea, my chief handmaid, now stooped over me. She had small brown eyes, gaunt cheeks, and grey hair in a tight bun. Like all of the palazzo servants, she was a Catalan, for my father trusted only his fellow countrymen rather than any Italians.

"It's daylight, madonna," she said, with her gravelly voice. "Time to rise."

I groaned and stretched my arms, trying to regain the feeling in my hands. "Panthasilea, could you please fetch me something to eat? Maybe some cheese, a slice of Pecorino Romano?"

"Certainly, madonna." Her mouth drew small. "I must remind you, though, it's Lent. Today is Ash Wednesday, and before you do anything we must put you in a black dress. You can't wear this costume any longer."

I glimpsed out of the window. "What time did my brother return last night?"

"Cesare?"

"No, Juan."

"Well, I don't think he's returned yet, madonna."

The news unsettled me. With Panthasilea at my side, I hurried away to my bedchamber to change my clothes. She helped me slip into a new chemise of white cambric, a black silk underdress, and a raven overdress of thick taffeta that gathered under my bust. Almost before she could finish tying my sleeves, I left her behind and hustled off to Juan's room.

Outside the door, I stopped and listened for any sound inside the bedchamber. I turned the door handle quietly, so I wouldn't wake him, and peered inside. My face dropped. No one slept in the canopy bed. The sheets lay clean and smooth. I knew immediately what needed to be done and I rushed away to tell my father.

On arriving at my father's suite, I was instructed to remain in the antechamber until Alexander was fully dressed. The hour was still early and my father wouldn't see anyone without his formal attire. My hands worked impatiently on a handkerchief, tying it in knots while I waited. Nearby, some of Alexander's courtesans were already clothed – as much as they ever wore clothes – and they currently engaged themselves in draping their bodies across a window seat. Fiammetta, the prettiest one, combed her long hazelnut hair and batted her eyelashes at me.

"Any news, Lucrezia?" she said in a chirpy tone. "You look weary today, your eyes have grey circles. Didn't you get any sleep?"

"Something worries me this morning, that's all."

"Oh, no! I trust it's nothing to do with the girls or me?" She dipped her head closer and whispered as if telling me a secret. "You're not mad at us, are you – because of what we do? You know that your father never touches us. We just dance for him or sing, sometimes with our clothes on, sometimes not. Of course, when he gets excited–"

"Yes, that's quite enough!" I said, holding up my hand. "Are there any scissors nearby?"

"Why?" she asked with a frown.

"I need to cut off my ears."

Mercifully, before she could reply, the doors of the papal bedchamber creaked back on their hinges. I shot through into the room and left Fiammetta far behind.

Inside the bedchamber, Alexander stood by the fireplace while two papal gentleman tended to his clothes, brushing and flattening the velvet mozzetta cape around his shoulders. A violet stole hung around his shoulders and drooped loosely on his belly.

"Your visit's somewhat earlier than usual, my child," he said evenly.

I marched straight across the room toward him.

"Stop, stop!" He recoiled and gave a little twitch of his head. "What in the name of all goodness is that terrible scratching sound?" He stared down at my feet. "Are you wearing those slippers with the hard soles again, Lucrezia?"

"I don't know."

"Time and time again I tell you they make an appalling scratching noise on these floors. I'll have to get you some new lambskin ones, soft and soundless. In the future, you must wear them any time you may be in my presence."

"Yes," I said, through clenched teeth. "Anyway, I come on a more important issue than my slippers. Juan didn't return home last night and I'm worried. I think we should send out a search party."

"Do you?" he said slowly. "Do you, indeed?" His eyes floated away from mine. "I don't think we need to make such a decision just yet. At this juncture, it'd be poor work to harass the city of Rome with search parties, simply because Juan hasn't slept in his own bed. Indeed, it's likely that your brother is still at some house of ill-repute, as stated when he last spoke to you."

"Still at a brothel? By this hour?"

"Yes, it's possible that he has merely overslept at some poor establishment. He may not be willing to leave it now that daylight would reveal his affairs to the common people."

"But—"

"I'm sure that he'll return as soon as darkness falls." He studied me and saw that I was still doubtful. "However, if he isn't back at the palazzo by dusk, we'll discuss what course of action will be appropriate. In the meantime, promise me that you'll stop panicking and scratching the floors."

I looked into his large, never-closing eyes. More than the content of his speech, I heard the smooth, relaxed and comforting harmonies of his voice. A sense of assurance washed over me and cleansed away most of my fears. Juan's return seemed almost inevitable.

After the morning ceremonies of Ash Wednesday, I spent the next hours quietly reading my lessons in Latin and Greek. By noon, Juan still hadn't returned. The time passed and my confidence dwindled further... one o'clock... two o'clock... still no sign of him anywhere.

With Panthasilea as my companion, I strolled out into the winter gardens of Città del Vaticano. We took a turn down mossy stairways and winding walks that snaked away from the rear of the palazzo. Cypress trees stood in giant columns along damp pathways and bosky terraces. Before returning to the palazzo, I noticed Cesare at the fringe of a distant lawn. He clutched a crossbow in his hand and shot at a practice target fifty yards away. I left Panthasilea and trailed my skirt across the wet grass to join him. I had a few questions to ask.

He heard my approach, but kept his eye on the target for another shot. His finger curled around the trigger. Another arrow struck into the target's center and I patted my hands together.

"Don't applaud," he said, reloading the crossbow. "It wasn't accurate."

I squinted at the target. "Oh, yes, it missed dead-center by an entire hair's breadth."

He raised the bow again. The trigger clicked. The arrow sliced through the air and sunk into the absolute heart of the target. He turned to me proudly.

I refused to clap. "Sorry, but the moment has gone now, I'm not impressed anymore."

He smiled and pulled another arrow from the quiver by his feet. Although he was Cardinal of Valencia, nothing in his appearance suggested the church. All the other cardinals now wore fuchsia satin cassocks for Lent, but he stood arrayed in a brown

23

velvet doublet studded with rubies and pearls – the clothes of a prince.

"How long have you been out here?" I asked, giving a deliberate yawn.

"Since daybreak," he replied. "You look tired."

"Do I? Perhaps it's because I waited all night for Juan to return. You know, he's still not back yet." I moved closer to him. "Was your sleep troubled, too? I thought I saw you in the courtyard last night?"

He didn't answer and steadily reloaded the crossbow. I let the question hang in the air.

"Sorry if I disturbed you," he muttered.

"Oh, no, you didn't. I just saw you and wondered what you were doing, that's all."

"Looking for crossbow targets."

"In the tower cellar? But wasn't it too late for that? Why not send a servant down there at dawn?"

"I didn't want to bother anyone." He turned away and spent a long time focusing his sights on the target.

I wasn't sure if I believed him. Why would he suddenly get up in the middle of the night and search around for a crossbow target? And for what reason would he be fully dressed at such a late hour? Perhaps he slept in his clothes that night? It was possible. One question, though, still nagged at me beyond all others.

"Did you go out anywhere interesting afterwards?" I asked casually.

He frowned. "Why do you say that?"

"No reason, only I thought I heard your spurs jangling. They awoke me."

"I wasn't wearing spurs."

"How strange! I could have sworn that I heard–"

"No, I wasn't wearing them," he said sharply. "Now can I get back to my practice?"

I stood still as he fired another shot at the target. It missed the center by half a foot.

My worries intensified over Juan's absence for the rest of the afternoon. By six o'clock, the sun faded upon the towers, cupo-

24

las, and campaniles of Rome and darkness finally crept into the streets. Inside the palazzo, I intruded upon a meeting between two cardinals and my father, and I informed him that Juan was still missing. He dismissed the officials instantly, so we could speak in private, and he summoned Cesare.

"It's a difficult situation," said Alexander gravely. "On the one hand, I have the citizens of Rome to consider. They will be alarmed when a search party of papal soldiers thunders through their peaceful neighborhoods and sleeping piazze, especially if Juan is soon discovered lazing at the bedpost of some courtesan. And yet, on the other hand, if the alarm is not false and Juan *is* in danger…"

Cesare stood silently, his back straight, his arms crossed so that the fabric of his doublet stretched tight around his muscled shoulders. I stood beside him anxiously.

"It's all my fault," I said. "I provoked the Orsini guard's attention yesterday and caused the fight, and now Juan's in danger because of me. You'll send out a search party, won't you? You must do something."

Alexander stroked his eyebrow with the edge of his plump forefinger. He paced back and forth across the room, planting each step with slow, deliberate care. His pectoral cross swayed, shifting from side to side. He raised his head to Cesare.

"My son," he said resolutely. "I'd like you to take a squad of soldiers from the barracks and lead a search for your brother."

"Me?" replied Cesare.

"Yes, I'd like you to do it. It would be appropriate in light of the circumstances… or am I wrong in thinking that you can take care of such an important matter?"

I watched as yet another strange moment occurred between them, just as it had the night before in the Sala dei Misteri. Cesare drew himself up tall and his eyes gleamed. Alexander waited for his response, his hands trembling slightly at the mysterious tension passing through the room.

I touched Cesare on the shoulder. "Do it for me, brother. I beg you."

He looked at me hesitantly, then span on his heel, and strode toward the door.

"If I must!" he called back hotly.

With a gang of soldiers, Cesare soon rode out of Città del Vaticano and launched into the rioni of Rome. While I awaited the result of their search, I decided to visit the tomb of St. Peter and pray for Juan's safe return.

Amid a forest of columns, Panthasilea and I threaded through the hordes of pilgrims now crammed inside the world's largest church, the Basilica di San Pietro. Woolen cloaks, bony limbs, and tapping canes clustered around us as we moved. In the center of all the marble shrines, we finally jostled over to a space at one of the pews. From my seat, I looked at the gold cross above the grand raised tomb of St. Peter. Focusing my thoughts, I prayed for Juan, quietly reciting the Ave Maria many times over:

"Ave Maria, gratia plena, Dominus tecum. Benedicta tu in mulieribus, et benedictus fructus ventris tui, Iesus. Sancta Maria, Mater Dei, ora pro nobis peccatoribus, nunc et in hora mortis nostrae. Amen."

As Panthasilea and I departed the Basilica, we halted outside at the steps leading down to Piazza San Pietro. I breathed-in the cool night air, the aroma of cooked chestnuts, roasted ceci beans, figs, and shellfish wafting up from the busy stalls of the piazza. Everywhere little kiosks sold cheap rosaries to pilgrims, promising a bargain.

Panthasilea grabbed my arm and pointed across the piazza. "Look, madonna! Your brother has returned already."

My eyes jumped over to the Ponte Sant'Angelo. Beneath the gallows ranged along the bridge, Cesare galloped across swiftly, whipping his horse, spurring it faster. I'd never seen him ride so hastily. Twenty soldiers struggled to keep pace behind him. I had expected to find Juan among their numbers, yet he was still not in sight.

"It can't be good," I said breathlessly. "Dear lord, it can't be good, it can't be good!" With Panthasilea in my wake, I dashed back to the palazzo.

On my arrival, a commotion sounded at the central hall, the Sala Reale. Before I entered the room, cardinals, prelates, and soldiers buzzed around in front of me, blocking my view.

Seconds later, I saw the cause of the turmoil: ten papal gentlemen emerged from the hall carrying my father's unconscious body in their arms. His head flopped onto his chest. His arms hung limp at his sides. He was so heavy they almost had to drag him along the corridor.

"What's happened?" I cried. "Where are you taking him?"

One of the gentlemen carrying Alexander's legs turned to me and answered: "His Holiness has suffered a grave shock, madonna. We're taking him back to the Appartamento."

They struggled as they hauled Alexander down the corridor and disappeared from my sight. Immediately, I plunged into the cavernous depths of the Sala Reale and found Cesare encircled by soldiers. He stood near the papal throne and his face appeared hard and bleak.

"Juan?" I asked. "Tell me you found him?"

He stepped closer to me. "Not yet. But we have a firm idea of where he is now."

"Then... then why haven't you brought him home?"

"We spoke to an eyewitness. This morning, at the banks of the Tiber, the body of a young man was seen dumped into the river."

I repeated his words, trying to absorb their meaning.

Suddenly, the world around me turned to grayness and shadow. My body felt light, as if the limbs were now withered. All voices became no more than empty whispers, susurrations that echoed with nonsense in my ears. I remember only blackness seeping in from the edge of my eyes... my knees buckling... the floor rushing upwards to my head...

V

A Funeral

My brother's corpse was soon located in the Tiber and dragged to the surface, his body hauled onto the river-bank like a piece of refuse.

I didn't stand present at this wretched scene, but the mere thought of it filled me with the deepest pity and sorrow for his fate. Juan had been a man with many faults, but he'd done nothing to deserve such cruel treatment. Although he was sometimes arrogant, lazy, and spiteful, the worst elements of his character had only been nurtured in his late youth, when my father had started bestowing him with excessive privileges. Despite his flaws, I'd known my brother in ways that most people did not. I knew that he was capable of great generosity to his friends, that he possessed an endearing sense of humor, and that he embraced his life with the utmost enthusiasm and pleasure. It haunted me to think about his last minutes before death. How much did he suffer? Did he still breathe as they plunged him into the water? The brutality of it sickened me to the core.

Although I could've stood vigil at his side, mourning his loss for days without count, by the time his body was brought back to the palazzo, his flesh was already decaying from the water's touch.

We had to bury him without delay.

In a cortege led by two hundred torchbearers, gentlemen from the papal household bore Juan's body through streets lined with thousands of onlookers. The procession worked its way from the Vaticano to the nearby Basilica di Santa Maria del Popolo. I watched the funeral bier decorated with black velvet cloth, ribbons, and lilies move along the roads, surrounded by shocked faces and hushed, gossiping voices. Porters had prepared the body so well that no injuries marred his face, and to me, it seemed my brother was not dead but sleeping. Since my father was still too distraught from the death to attend the funeral service, only Cesare and I watched as the body was finally interred at the family's cappella. We laid Juan in a tomb once intended for our mother. He was only twenty-one years old.

While I stood present at the burial, the funeral had occurred so swiftly that I still didn't understand many of the circumstances surrounding his untimely death. Papal officials stated that Juan had probably been murdered, yet I knew very little beyond this fact. Since I'd fainted when I first heard the news, everyone now worried about upsetting me again, and they refused to tell me more than just a few details. This only gave me a greater determination to find out the mysterious circumstances on my own. I was resolved to know about it, one way or the other.

Thus, when I returned home, I had Panthasilea sneak into Rome to fetch a common pamphlet about Juan's death. Cleverly, she smuggled it back to my bedchamber.

Such pamphlets were cheaply sold leafs of parchment, often distributed around Rome after any major event that affected city life. Enterprising pamphleteers copied the herald's official announcement on the subject, garnished it with a little investigative work, or a few statements from witnesses, and then sold it to the public for a trifling sum. The pamphlet on Juan's death read as follows:

TO THE PEOPLE OF ROME,

on this tragic day of February 16th, in the year 1497, we announce that Juan Borgia, Duke of Gandia, and son of Pope Alex-

29

ander VI, has been found dead in the Tiber River, murdered by a person unknown.

The disappearance of Juan Borgia was first discovered on Ash Wednesday: at the hour of seven o'clock, the pontiff's Spanish Guards, led by Don Cesare Borgia, stormed through the city in a desperate effort to find the lost duke. Women and children fled inside their dwellings and locked the doors, frightened for their lives. Members from the Houses of Orsini and Colonna feared a vendetta and took measures to fortify their palazzi against attack.

Soldiers soon found a timber dealer near the Ponte Ripetto who possessed dramatic information concerning the Duke of Gandia. The dealer, Giorgio Schiavi, told papal guards that he had been unloading cargo at the riverbank on the night the duke was last seen alive. After falling asleep in a barge moored at the shoreline, he suddenly awoke to find two men acting suspiciously by the riverbanks. From the cover of his barge, Signor Schiavi watched the men signal a companion. As he told papal officials:

"From the shadows there appeared a rider on a white horse, carrying a body slung across its saddle, the head and arms hanging on one side, the legs to the other. Having reached the point where refuse is normally thrown into the river, the horseman turned his horse nearer the water and the two men on foot took hold of the body by the hands and legs. With all their strength they flung the body into the river. The corpse soon sunk below the waterline, but the dead man's cloak quickly resurfaced and continued to float around. Once the two men noticed it, the horseman threw some stones at the cloak and made it sink. This done, all the men went away from the river by an alley which leads to Ospedale San Giacomo." When questioned why he had not come forward earlier with his report, Giorgio answered that: "...in my day I have seen a hundred such corpses thrown into the river, without anyone troubling to ask such questions."

Reaction followed swiftly from the Vaticano. By next dawn, teams of fishermen and boatmen dragged the Tiber, spurred onwards by a 10 ducat reward offered to anyone who could locate the body of the missing duke. Before noon, a fisherman by the name of Battisto da Taglia recovered a body in his net – the corpse of a young man fully dressed and disfigured by eight stab wounds to his legs and torso. There had been no attempt at robbery, for the corpse was still in possession of a jeweled collar and a purse of 30 ducats.

After the discovery, officials removed the body to Castel Sant'Angelo where members of the Borgia family confirmed the corpse was indeed that of Juan Borgia. Reportedly, Alexander VI was so upset by the news that he shut himself in his rooms and wept bitterly for hours.

An investigation into the Duke of Gandia's death is now underway. To stay informed of the inquiry, seek out future pamphlets sold at the piazze and street corners of our blessed city.

As soon as I'd finished reading the pamphlet, I read it over and over again so many times that I almost memorized the words.

Something about the contents unnerved me. It wasn't just the ghoulishness of reading such details about my brother's death, it was something else. My mind filled with questions and suspicions regarding the people responsible for the crime. Whoever had committed Juan's murder was still free from any punishment, their identity still a mystery to the law. I wondered, could it even be someone inside the palazzo, someone whom I knew and spoke with in my daily life? The thought was absolutely terrifying.

VI

My New Fate

Cesare and I stood together in the Sala delle Arti Liberali, a hall in the Appartamento that my father used as a study. I was clad in black and still felt grief-stricken over Juan's recent death. Alexander had summoned us both without explaining the reason why, and we now waited anxiously for his arrival.

At long last, he shuffled into the room, his face serious. He took off his skull cap and wiped his hand across his smooth bald crown.

"Is it about the murder investigation?" I asked. "I know it's only been a month, but has there been a development yet? The last I heard, there were still no suspects."

"Yes, there has indeed been a development," he replied. "I've summoned you both to announce the investigation is now concluded."

Cesare stood mutely at the back of the room. In contrast, I stepped forward and took a seat nearby at the oak desk. "Tell me," I said, my heart galloping. "Who did it? What criminal has been caught for the murder?"

"Criminal? My dear child, I'm afraid you misunderstand me. When I say the investigation has finished, I mean that it has exhausted all lines of inquiry. The chief constable informs me that he has never before seen a case knotted with so many problems."

"But I don't understand, the investigation can't be over if there's no result. Shouldn't the chief constable search until he finds the person responsible?"

"Unfortunately, the order has already been issued to terminate the inquiry."

"Who gave such an order?"

"I did."

I lunged to my feet, outraged. "You! Why would you of all people do such a cursed thing? You can't cancel the investigation. It's only been a few weeks! Don't you want to find Juan's killer and bring him to justice?"

Alexander settled himself into a chair. He leaned forward on the desk, his fingers making prints on the dusty surface. "My child, I insist that you allow me to explain this matter."

"Explain it?"

"Yes, I believe that more than one person is responsible for your brother's death. In fact, the real culprit may be an entire organization – a family. Only one of Rome's most powerful houses would dare order such an attack on a son of mine, and then have the audacity to hide the assassin and protect his identity. Was it the Orsini? Maybe so, but there are certainly others who also possess powerful motives. It could easily have been the Colonna, the Savelli, or the Cenci, or even some unknown enemy from the rebellious Papal States. Since no family has stepped forward to accept responsibility, I hold all of them accountable for the crime. All of them have killed my son by fostering an atmosphere of defiance to Borgia rule."

I frowned. "What are you saying?"

"I'm saying that it's time for this house to strike back and assert complete control not just of the city, but of all states within papal dominion."

"War?"

"Yes, we will go to war," he said gently. "Yet before any action is possible, we must grow strong again and patiently await the juncture when all our enemies turn placid and peaceful – then we shall strike. Meanwhile, our task will be to forge a greater network of alliances."

I sat down in the chair, knowing exactly what *'network of alliances'* meant.

"You've arranged a marriage for me?" I asked.

In the corner of the room, Cesare scuffed the heel of his boot. Alexander watched him, then turned his lidless eyes to me and smiled.

"So far, Lucrezia, your life has been remarkably easy. Indeed, most women your age are married or installed at a convent by now. When you came of age at fourteen, I already had two offers of marriage for you, but neither proposal was satisfactory, and since that time I have passed over countless other suitors, always delaying for the right alliance. Even so, you knew this day must arrive sooner or later."

"What have you arranged?"

"You'll marry into a household that not only controls the bountiful lands of Spain, but also the magnificent Kingdom of Naples, the largest of all the Italian states."

"The Aragons?"

"Yes, I've negotiated your betrothal into the royal bloodline of the House of Aragon, the most powerful family in the world."

I didn't respond. Alexander stared at me, perplexed and uncertain.

The reaction of most noblewomen to such news would have been a giddy mixture of shock and pleasure. Yet I wasn't struck by the honor of such a powerful match, only by a profound sense of loss. I didn't want to leave Rome, to live in Spain or Naples, or to lose the close company of my father and brother.

"Does my husband have a name?" I said, becoming slightly flustered. "I don't think it's legal to marry an entire household."

"Your future husband will be the honorable Alfonso of Aragon, Duke of Bisceglie. The duke is the natural son of Alfonso II, the late King of Naples." He watched me closely. "Well, my child, feel at liberty to express your gratitude."

I sneezed at the nearby dust.

Alexander fell back in his chair, mortified. "How dare you, Lucrezia! Oh, my nerves, my poor elderly nerves! Such loudness! You've taken a year from my life, I swear it."

"Could I have a description of my future husband?" I said sharply. "Or will it be a surprise for my wedding day?"

He didn't answer and lay slumped in his chair, fanning his face. To my astonishment, Cesare strode over to me and put his hand on my shoulder.

"Don Alfonso is seventeen," he said. "Same age as you."

I twisted towards him. "You knew about it, you knew before I did?"

"Yes."

"And you never mentioned it? What about the investigation? Did you know all about that, as well?"

He ignored the question. "We think he'll be a worthy match. The duke is known to be a handsome man."

"And what about his mind? Is he clever, too? Or is he just a pawn of his family, like me?"

Cesare rolled his eyes and walked back to the window. Finally, Alexander recovered enough strength to speak. He put his skull cap on again:

"Lucrezia, don't be so unkind to your brother. We only desire what is best for you. As I'm sure you know, our family's current power will be gone when I'm deceased. Unlike other titles, the Papacy isn't an honor that a son can inherit. To secure our future now, we must establish sources of power outside of the church. If not, the light of the Borgia dynasty will soon fizzle-out." He put a hand on his barrel chest and looked at me with sorrow. "I'm sure that you don't wish to defy me over the matter of your engagement. I'm sure I have a loyal and dutiful daughter; a daughter who's willing to help empower the House of Borgia. Am I correct in thinking this?"

Despite my protests, it was useless to resist. Marriage makes sense, not love – I'd known that from a young age – and this marriage did seem a wise decision, at least from my family's perspective. I wasn't pleased about it, but I knew the arrangement would proceed regardless of whether I consented to it or not. My father's wish and my family's future would prevail over all other concerns, even my own happiness.

"I'll agree," I said glumly. "I'll support the betrothal. What other choice do I have?"

Without another word, I stepped out of the room, making no attempt to hide my displeasure.

As the door shut behind me, I closed my eyes and fantasized about unleashing a scream down the deserted corridor. More than the shock of the cancelled investigation, more than the surprise of the marriage arrangements, I was hurt by the fact that my father and brother had plotted my fate so readily. They didn't seem to care about abandoning me to an unknown duke, in an unfamiliar court, faraway in Naples. And why did Cesare know so much about it all? Almost overnight, he had leapt from the status of a forgotten son, to my father's innermost confidence.

While I stood by the door, a raised voice sounded from inside the room: Cesare's gruff timbre. I decided to eavesdrop and find out why. Once I felt satisfied that no palazzo chamberlains, squires, or prelates lurked nearby, I bent my head closer to the door and listened to the conversation within.

Cesare's voice seethed with scorn. "Not good enough! It's already been done for Lucrezia."

"There is no need to fret, my son," replied Alexander. He sounded a little scared. "I'll have you married into the House of Aragon, too, but these things require planning and patience."

"Give me a date."

"As I've stated, it will occur at the appropriate moment, in the fullness of time when everything has been properly–"

A heavy object inside the room crashed into the wall and interrupted Alexander. I guessed it was a chair.

"Don't give me your honeyed words, old man!" Cesare bellowed. "I want results, not sermons! I've earned the right to that much, haven't I?"

More nervously than before, my father replied: "I've made my promise to you and I intend to keep it."

"Yes, you will. By my sword, I'll make sure you do."

Alexander coughed. "The first thing that must be done prior to any marriage proposal, is the removal of your cardinalate. As we converse here, you should know that I've already started the process of divestiture with the Sacred College."

"Good." Cesare's footsteps pounded across the hall to the desk. "And after that, you will approach the Spanish Aragons. It's they who hold the real power. Not the minor branch in Naples. I won't take less than Princess Carlotta, is that clear?"

"Are you aware that the Spanish have already set very high plans for their princess?"

"Then they'll have to change their plans, won't they?"

"In that case, may I ask, how will you gain their consent when you lack the slightest rank or noble title?"

"Louis XII."

"The new King of France? I'm afraid your strategy is still rather opaque, my son."

"Louis desperately wants a divorce. He's already applied to you for it. You'll agree, but on the condition that I gain a French duchy in return."

Silence followed. Obviously, the plan surprised my father a great deal. Cesare soon continued:

"We need the French king, anyway. Princess Carlotta lives at his court and he can help to sway her in my favor, especially if I must visit France."

I didn't hear the reply, but since no violent explosion came from inside the hall, I assumed my father had agreed. Alexander spoke again, this time soft and weary, his voice tainted with resentment.

"My son, while I applaud your new ambitions, I hope your eye will always stay fixed upon the good of your family, rather than on your own personal glory?"

"You mean, will I stay obedient?" Cesare's voice turned hard and threatening. "Listen, your Sanctity, I'm not just the first-born son, I'm the only son now. And I'll let nothing hold me down again. Nothing."

"Yes," Alexander replied, almost whispering. "I don't question it."

Poison In The Blood

I stood back from the door, growing more and more concerned. As the only living son, Cesare finally had the means to bend my father to his will. He'd always been misplaced as a cardinal, and now he could leave the church and attain both a noble title and a high-ranking marriage. Only a month ago, this situation would have seemed impossible. Juan's death had certainly opened up a new life for my eldest brother…

Could Cesare have been involved with Juan's murder? God knows, he had the motive: he'd always despised Juan for the way my father unjustly elevated him and showered him with titles, wealth, and power. It seemed that hardly a day had ever passed without Cesare threatening to kill Juan in some painful manner. I always laughed when he said such things. Maybe that was a mistake.

My thoughts returned to the night of the Carnival and the content of the pamphlet. The eyewitness saw Juan's body dumped into the Tiber at five o'clock in the morning – around this time, I saw Cesare below the Torre Borgia acting as if he were about to leave the palazzo. One of the men who dumped Juan's body was a horseman – I heard Cesare's spurs clink through the courtyard. There were also many ways my brother could gain the use of a white horse. But if Cesare was a suspect, why hadn't the city officials discovered this already?

Or *had* they? Was this the true reason why the investigation was so abruptly cancelled? Did Cesare demand that my father end the inquiry when it started pointing to himself?

I hurried away through the Appartamento. Despite my suspicions, it was vile to think such awful thoughts about my brother. No evidence I'd seen could prove his guilt, it was just a series of coincidences, nothing more, and he deserved my support.

Ultimately, the whole matter revolved around the cellar. To ease my doubts, I needed to go to the cellar myself and prove that nothing sinister lay within it. My feet flitted down the stairs of the Appartamento as I ventured off to the courtyard. Although it was daylight, Cesare and Alexander still spoke inside the hall, allowing me the chance to visit the cellar unseen.

Outside, cool river breezes drifted across the yard, and I approached the soaring grey stone column of the Torre Borgia. Tendrils of leafless brown wisteria twined up the tower and climbed to the sky. Directly beneath it lay a tiny cellar door.

I gripped the handle, but it was locked.

After checking over my shoulder, I plucked my personal skeleton key from a pocket in my sleeve and twisted it in the door. The key should have opened every chamber in the palazzo, yet it didn't work here. How strange!

If I didn't have the key for the cellar, then presumably none of the papal staff had one either. In fact, it seemed clear that only one man had the power to undo this particular lock. I shivered in the cold wind. To enter the cellar undetected, I had only one option now: despite the formidable difficulties, the potential for embarrassment, even the possible risks if caught, I must sneak into my brother's bedchamber tonight and pilfer the key during his sleep. I must steal it from Cesare himself.

VII

The Secrets In The Cellar

A tranquil evening gradually settled on the palazzo halls, but I waited deep into the night before attempting my theft of Cesare's keys.

I crept into the corridor outside my bedchamber, checking that none of the palazzo staff were near. Cesare's room lay only a short distance from my own. I arrived at the entrance and delicately pushed the door open.

Immediately, I entered an antechamber separate from Cesare's private bedroom. This chamber was used for meetings with friends, business associates, and envoys. I left the outer-door ajar and slinked through the room carefully, worried that I might trip on something in the darkness. At his bedchamber door, the handle creaked stiffly as I turned it downward.

Within Cesare's bedroom, the air was musty and airless with sleep. I squinted at my brother lying sprawled across his mattress, his body unmoving in a deep noiseless slumber. For a man with such a loud voice, I'd expected him to snore with enough violence that the bedposts would shake. He also rested oddly in his sheets, the quilt pulled up so high I couldn't see his head, only the long lump of his motionless body.

Ignoring the strangeness of it all, I hunted about for the keys. Mirrors of polished metal hung on every wall and reflected the shadows as I moved about in the gloom. The key-ring lay on Cesare's bedside table. I collected it with deft hands, cushioned the metal in my grasp, and hurried from the room before he awoke.

Outside the Appartamento, the moon's shade fell white on the flagstones of the courtyard. I tiptoed up to the cellar door, tried all of Cesare's keys, and finally opened the lock.

As I pressed back the door, the rusty hinges squealed.

I halted and listened for a response: somewhere in the distance, the voices of papal sentries chatted lowly. A horse rattled its halter chain. No sound was close enough for alarm.

To light my way, I plucked a wall torch from its holder in the courtyard, then slipped past the cellar door and closed it gently behind me.

Torch flames spluttered near my cheeks as I descended a short stairway beneath the tower. At the bottom, I found a cavernous room supported by many pillars. Torchlight illuminated a jumble of scrap objects lying among the columns: chairs with broken legs, coils of rope, slats of wood, and casks stacked to the ceiling. Perhaps this was exactly the place someone might search for crossbow targets, after all?

I explored the room and chanced upon a tiny area almost hidden at the far corner. Unlike the rest of the cellar, here the floor was newly swept and free of clutter. Several neat rows of shelves lined the wall, each one holding a series of labeled pots. Below, on the dented surface of a desk, the buckles of leather-bound manuscripts gleamed back at me. A single roll of parchment lay slanted across them.

At first glance, the area seemed harmless enough, yet I decided to inspect things a little closer. I unfurled the parchment and it appeared blank on both sides. Next, I lifted the torch and shone it across the shelves to read the labels on the dusty pots above:

'Foxglove', 'Monkshood', 'Mad Honey', 'Mercury Vapor', 'Destroying Angel Mushroom', 'Cantharidine Power', 'Arsenic'.

41

Poison In The Blood

I recognized the names instantly – they were poisons! The labels listed the fatal dose, the symptoms, and the cure of each venom. The nearest label read:

BELLADONNA
FATAL: 1 leaf
SYMPTOMS: Nausea, Confusion, Suffocation
CURE: Calabar Bean

With shaking hands, I scrutinized the manuscripts at the desk. Two were Greek texts: *'Theriaca'* by Nicander of Colophon; and *'Materia Medica'* by Dioscorides. The third was a more recent work in Latin: *'The Book of Venoms'* by Magister Santes de Ardoynis. They were all guides to the classification, properties, and treatments of poisons.

Inside one of the volumes, I spied a handwritten note on the front leaf. The title read *'Cantarella: A Preparation'* and below it was written the detailed method for combining all the poisons into the recipe for one brilliant white, sweet-tasting powder. The recipe claimed this new compound would have no existing antidote. Regretfully, I knew the handwriting. The smudges and flaws of the style were unmistakable. It was the hand of Cesare.

Although nothing here yet incriminated Cesare in Juan's slaying, I had stumbled onto something equally horrific. Obviously, this corner of the cellar was the secret base for my family's newest and darkest operation. The House of Borgia intended to strike back against its enemies by stooping to the use of poisons.

Now I understood why I'd seen Cesare creeping out from the cellar. He had possessed enough foresight to start preparations on the very night of Juan's disappearance. He knew that the Orsini guard's death would provoke a revenge attack, and he'd already begun preparing the means to respond to it. The rumors would soon be true: if my family hadn't already murdered people in the past, they would do so in the near future.

I wanted to tell someone immediately and prevent any more deaths, yet I knew there was no one I could ask for help. There was no authority in the world, neither spiritual nor legal, higher than my father. If Cesare had somehow convinced him to start on the path of murder, who could stop either of them from following this course? I also couldn't tell anyone about the poisons I'd seen tonight – not one cardinal, not one constable, not one citizen of Rome could know about this or their life might be jeopardized. Everyone I knew was either loyal to my family or within easy reach of being destroyed by it.

The more I deliberated, the more I doubted that I could ever reveal my family's secrets. They were plotting something diabolical, but it was no worse than the tactics used by many rulers of the Italian states. Indeed, poison was a very common weapon to dispatch one's foes without raising suspicion. It was clean, efficient, hard to trace, and the symptoms were easily confused with natural diseases. You could smile with your victim as he sips from a poisoned cup, wish him well as he departs for home, and even comfort his relatives as they mourn at his funeral. No one could tie you to the death. No one would take vengeance on you in response.

Never had I been so ashamed in all my life, not only of Cesare and Alexander, but also of myself. No matter how my brother and father acted, they were my kin, and I couldn't betray them. I wouldn't betray them. They were all I had in the world. If there was poison in the House of Borgia, in my own bloodline, I had to accept that it was also part of myself from now onwards. For better or worse, there was poison in my blood.

"I'll leave this place…" I said into the darkness. "I'll leave it and never come back…"

Before I rushed away, I glanced again at the scroll and unrolled it fully. While the parchment was blank, I wafted it closer and sniffed at the faint fumes of citrus. The discovery was certainly curious, but it offered no further revelations, and I placed it back on the desk.

With nimble feet, I scaled the stairs to the courtyard, locked the door, and scurried off to Cesare's bedchamber to return the key. Inside his room, it was as quiet and stifling as before. I replaced the key-ring on his bedside table and prepared to leave. As

43

a precaution, I peered over to the bed and checked that he was asleep. He still lay motionless and soundless, hidden under the quilt. I frowned at his lumpy shape. He was a little too motionless and soundless...

I approached his bed and listened: no sound of breathing and no movement of sheets. Fearing he was dead, I decided to risk the danger of waking him up. I reached out and poked his shoulder, but my finger felt no resistance.

I tore back the quilt. Nothing lay in the bed except a bundle of sheets and clothes arranged into the shape of a body.

A trick!

He must have heard me when I'd entered the antechamber, and reacted instantly before I reached his bedroom. He'd been hiding in the shadows while I stole his keys! I backed away from the bed, panic-stricken. If Cesare wasn't in his room now, then where on earth was he?

I shot out of the bedchamber, banging the doors behind me as I fled. Suddenly, I had a very good idea of his location. On arriving outside my own room, candlelight glowed under the door-frame and confirmed my suspicions. By creeping about tonight, I had given Cesare the chance to sneak into my very own bed-chamber.

I took a draught of air to calm myself, then shuffled inside. Before me, Cesare reclined on my bed, reading through a bundle of letters beside him. I looked at him warily.

"Good evening, sister," he said, peeking over the top of a let-ter. "I didn't mean to alarm you. Something disturbed me tonight, that's all. I couldn't sleep. I came to speak with you, but you we-ren't here, so I waited."

I snatched the bundle of letters from the bed. "And while you waited, you thought it'd be nice to go through all my private cor-respondence? These letters are from my mother. I didn't want anyone else to look at them."

"I found them by accident." He stood up and gave me the let-ter in his hand. "I didn't think it was wrong to lie here and read them."

"The problem with you, Cesare, is you think that you can lie wherever you want!"

And he *was* lying. The only way he could have accidentally found my letters in their hiding place, was if he'd tripped, fallen under the bed, and stuck his hand beneath the mattress.

"You look cold." He pointed to my blotchy arm. "Did you go out somewhere?"

"What did you want to speak to me about? That's why you're here, remember."

"Yes, I just wanted you to know that many things will change soon. Our world inside the palazzo will change. The world outside will change, too. But whatever occurs, you'll always be safe. I'll never let you come to any harm. Do you believe that?"

I nodded, slightly afraid of him.

"Say it, Lucrezia," he said sincerely.

"Yes," I replied. "You have the face of Jesus – how could I not believe you?"

He watched me closely, unsure what to think. Finally, he said goodnight. Of course, he knew exactly where I'd been this evening and what I'd discovered. He'd only visited to learn my reaction. He wanted to know how I would judge him.

After he'd left my room, I counted all my letters to make sure none were missing. Satisfied, I searched about my bedchamber and found a new hiding place. As I tucked them away behind the panel of one of my clothing chests, I made a silent and solemn promise with myself. I resolved to forget everything I'd seen in the cellar. Cesare was right, there were things about my family that I hadn't known, and that I didn't want to know.

During the rest of the night, I lay under the canopy of my bed, eyes open, my mind agitated with a variety of thoughts. I remembered my father's dramatic revelation earlier in the day: my impending marriage to Alfonso of Aragon, Duke of Bisceglie.

To my surprise, I no longer regarded the match so unfavorably. For the House of Borgia, this union was simply a political alliance that would establish strong ties with the House of Aragon. It would also bestow me with a title, the Duchess of Bisceg-lie. For me, however, the marriage could be so much more. Al-fonso was someone different, someone fresh who could rejuve-nate my life. It didn't hurt matters that he was also young and very handsome. Even so, when we finally met each other, I knew that I might find him boring, indifferent, or loathsome.

But what about the alternative? What if I felt some small tenderness toward him from the start? What if my affection slow-ly grew into something more profound? What if we found love upon a single glance?

What if...

POISON IN THE BLOOD

Soon Available
From Most Bookstores

MATTHEW GRAHAM SCARSBROOK is a prize-winning screenwriter and novelist. He recently adapted *The Marlowe Conspiracy* into a script and won the nationwide Writers On The Storm Screenwriting Contest, placing first out of 1000 entries. He is also the author of *Poison In The Blood: The Memoirs of Lucrezia Borgia*, a mystery / thriller set in renaissance Rome during the reign of the Borgias. Matthew now lives in Southern California and is currently at work on a new detective series.

To learn more, please visit his website at
www.mgscarsbrook.com

Made in the USA
Lexington, KY
03 December 2011